1 MONTH OF
FREE
READING

at

www.ForgottenBooks.com

By purchasing this book you are eligible for one month membership to ForgottenBooks.com, giving you unlimited access to our entire collection of over 1,000,000 titles via our web site and mobile apps.

To claim your free month visit:
www.forgottenbooks.com/free102593

ISBN 978-0-483-80880-5
PIBN 10102593

The
Trail of the Axe

A Story of the Red Sand Valley

BY RIDGEWELL CULLUM

Author of "The Watchers of the Plains,"
"The Sheriff of Dyke Hole," etc.

WITH FRONTISPIECE IN COLORS
BY CLARENCE F. UNDERWOOD

A. L. BURT COMPANY
PUBLISHERS   NEW YORK

CONTENTS

The Trail of the Axe

CHAPTER I

DAVE

DAVE was thirty-two, but looked forty; for, in moulding his great, strong, ugly face, Nature had been less than kind to him. It is probable, from his earliest, Dave had never looked less than ten years older than he really was.

Observing him closely, one had the impression that Nature had set herself the task of equipping him for a tremendous struggle in the battle of life; as though she had determined to make him invincible. Presuming this to have been her purpose, she set to work with a liberal hand. She gave him a big heart, doubtless wishing him to be strong to fight and of a great courage, yet with a wonderful sympathy for the beaten foe. She gave him the thews and sinews of a Hercules, probably arguing that a man must possess a mighty strength with which to carry himself to victory. To give him such physical strength it was necessary to provide a body in keeping. Thus, his shoulders were abnormally wide, his chest was of a mighty girth, his arms were of phenomenal length, and his legs were gnarled and knotted with muscles which could never be satisfactorily disguised by the class of "store" clothes it was his frugal custom to wear.

For his head Nature gave him a fine, keen brain; strong, practical, subtly far-seeing in matters commercial, bluntly honest and temperate, yet withal matching his big heart in kindly sympathy. It was thrilling with a vast energy and capacity for work, but so pronounced was its dominating force, that in the development of his physical features it completely destroyed all delicacy of mould and gentleness of expression. He displayed to the world the hard, rugged face of the fighter, without any softening, unless, perhaps, one paused to look into the depths of his deep-set gray eyes.

Nature undoubtedly fulfilled her purpose. Dave was equipped as few men are equipped, and if it were to be regretted that his architect had forgotten that even a fighting man has his gentler moments, and that there are certain requirements in his construction to suit him to such moments, in all other respects he had been treated lavishly. Summed up briefly, Dave was a tower of physical might, with a face of striking plainness.

It was twelve years since he came to the Red Sand Valley. He was then fresh from the lumber regions of Puget Sound, on the western coast of the United States. He came to Western Canada in search of a country to make his own, with a small capital and a large faith in himself, supported by a courage that did not know the meaning of defeat.

He found the Red Sand Valley nestling in the foot-hills of the Rocky Mountains. He saw the wonders of the magnificent pine woods which covered the mountain slopes in an endless sea of deep, sombre green. And he knew that these wonderful primordial wastes were only waiting for the axe of the woodsman to yield a building lumber second to none in the world.

The valley offered him everything he needed. A river that flowed in full tide all the open season, with possibilities of almost limitless " timber booms " in its backwaters, a delicious setting for a village, with the pick of a dozen adequate sites for the building of lumber mills. He could hope to find nothing better, so he stayed.

His beginning was humble. He started with a horse-power saw-pit, and a few men up in the hills cutting for him. But he had begun his great struggle with fortune, and, in a man such as Nature had made him, it was a struggle that could only end with his life. The battle was tremendous, but he never hesitated, he never flinched.

Small as was his beginning, six years later his present great mills and the village of Malkern had begun to take shape. Then, a year later, the result of his own persistent representation, the Canadian Northwestern Railroad built a branch line to his valley. And so, in seven years, his success was practically assured.

Now he was comfortably prosperous. The village was prosperous. But none knew better than he how much still remained to be achieved before the foundations of his little world were adequate to support the weight of the vast edifice of commercial enterprise, which, with his own two hands, his own keen brain, he hoped to erect.

He was an American business man raised in the commercial faith of his country. He understood the value of " monopoly," and he made for it. Thus, when he could ill spare capital, by dint of heavy borrowings he purchased all the land he required, and the " lumbering " rights of that vast region.

Then it was that he extended operations. He abandoned his first mill and began the building of his larger enterprise further down the valley, at a point where he had decided that the village of Malkern should also begin its growth.

Once the new mill was safely established he sold his old one to a man who had worked with him from the start. The transaction was more in the nature of a gift to an old friend and comrade. The price was nominal, but the agreement was binding that the mill should only be used for the production of small building material, and under no circumstances to be used in the production of rough " baulks." This was to protect his own monopoly in that class of manufacture.

George Truscott, the lumberman with whom he made the transaction, worked the old mills with qualified success for two years. Then he died suddenly of blood-poisoning, supervening upon a badly mutilated arm torn by one of his own saws. The mill automatically became the property of his only son Jim, a youth of eighteen, curly-headed, bright, lovable, but wholly irresponsible for such an up-hill fight as the conduct of the business his father had left him.

The master of the Malkern mills, as might be expected, was a man of simple habits and frugal tastes. In his early struggles he had had neither time nor money with which to indulge himself, and the habit of simple living had grown upon him. He required so very little. He had no luxurious home; a mere cottage of four rooms and a kitchen, over which an aged and doting mother ruled, her establishment consisting of one small maid. His office was a shack of two rooms, bare but useful, containing one chair and one desk, and anything he desired to find a temporary safe resting-place for strewn about the floor, or hung upon nails driven into the walls. It was all he needed, a roof to shade him from the blazing summer sun when he was making up his books, and four walls to shut out the cruel blasts of the Canadian winter.

He was sitting at his desk now, poring over a heap of letters which had just arrived by the Eastern mail. This was the sort of thing he detested. Correspondence entailed a lot of writing, and he hated writing. Figures he could cope with, he had no grudge against them, but composing letters was a task for which he did not feel himself adequately equipped; words did not flow easily from his pen. His education was rather the education of a man who goes through the world with ears and eyes wide open. He had a wide knowledge of men and things, but the inside of books was a realm into which he had not deeply delved.

At last he pushed his letters aside and sat back, his complaining chair protesting loudly at the burden imposed upon it. He drew an impatient sigh, and began to fill his pipe, gazing through the rain-stained window under which his untidy desk stood. He had made up his mind to leave the answering of his letters until later in the day, and the decision brought him some relief.

He reached for the matches. But suddenly he altered his mind and removed his pipe from his mouth. A smile shone in his deep-set eyes at the sight of a dainty, white figure which had just emerged from behind a big stack of milled timber out in the yard and was hurrying toward the office.

He needed no second glance to tell him who the figure belonged to. It was Betty—little Betty Somers, as he loved to call her—who taught the extreme youth of Malkern out of her twenty-two years of erudition and worldly wisdom.

He sprang from his chair and went to the door to meet her, and as he walked his great bulk and vast muscle gave his gait something of the roll of a sailor. He had no lightness, no grace in his movements; just the ponderous slowness of monumental strength.

He stood awaiting her in the doorway, which he almost filled up.

Betty was not short, but he towered above her as she came up, his six feet five inches making nothing of her five feet six.

"This is bully," he cried delightedly, as she stood before him. "I hadn't a notion you were getting around this morning, Betty."

His voice was as unwieldy as his figure; it was husky too, in the manner of powerful voices when their owners attempt to moderate them. The girl laughed frankly up into his face.

"I'm playing truant," she explained. Then her pretty lips twisted wryly, and she pointed at the lintel of the door. "Please sit down there," she commanded. Then she laughed again. "I want to talk to you, and—and I have no desire to dislocate my neck."

He made her feel so absurdly small; she was never comfortable unless he was sitting down.

The man grinned humorously at her imperious tone, and sat down. They were great friends, these two. Betty looked upon him as a very dear, big, ugly brother to whom she could always carry all her little worries and troubles, and ever be sure of a sympathetic adviser. It never occurred to her that Dave could be anything dearer to anybody. He was just Dave—dear old Dave, an appellation which seemed to fit him exactly.

The thought of him as a lover was quite impossible. It never entered her head. Probably the only people in Malkern who ever considered the possibility of Dave as a lover were his own mother, and perhaps Mrs. Tom Chepstow. But then they were wiser than most of the women of the village. Besides, doubtless his mother was prejudiced, and Mrs. Tom, in her capacity as the wife of the Rev. Tom Chepstow, made it her business to study the members of her husband's parish more carefully than the other women did. But to the ordinary observer he certainly did not suggest the lover. He was so strong, so cumbersome, so unromantic. Then his ways were so deliberate, so machine-like. It almost seemed as though he had taken to himself something of the harsh precision of his own mills.

On the other hand, his regard for Betty was a matter of less certainty. Good comradeship was the note he always struck in their intercourse, but oftentimes there would creep into his gray eyes a look which spoke of a warmth of feeling only held under because his good sense warned him of the utter hopelessness of it. He was too painfully aware of the quality of Betty's regard for him to permit himself any false hopes.

Betty's brown eyes took on a smiling look of reproach as she held up a warning finger.

" Dave," she said, with mock severity, " I always have to remind you of our compact. I insist that you sit down when I am talking to you. I refuse to be made to feel—and look—small. Now light your pipe and listen to me."

"Go ahead," he grinned, striking a match. His plain features literally shone with delight at her presence there. Her small oval, sun-tanned face was so bright, so full of animation, so healthy looking. There was such a delightful frankness about her. Her figure, perfectly rounded, was slim and athletic, and her every movement suggested the open air and perfect health.

"Well, it's this way," she began, seating herself on the corner of a pile of timber: "I'm out on the war-path. I want scalps. My pocketbook is empty and needs filling, and when that's done I'll get back to my school children, on whose behalf I am out hunting."

"It's your picnic?" suggested Dave.

"Not mine. The kiddies'. So now, old boy, put up your hands! It's your money or your life." And she sat threatening him with her pocketbook, pointing it at him as though it were a pistol.

Dave removed his pipe.

"Guess you'd best have 'em both," he smiled.

But Betty shook her head with a joyous laugh.

"I only want your money," she said, extending an open hand toward him.

Dave thrust deep into his hip-pocket, and produced a roll of bills.

"It's mostly that way," he murmured, counting them out.

But his words had reached the girl, and her laugh died suddenly.

"Oh, Dave!" she said reproachfully.

And the man's contrition set him blundering.

"Say, Betty, I'm a fool man anyway. Don't take any sort of notice. I didn't mean a thing. Now here's fifty, and you can have any more you need."

He looked straight into her eyes, which at once responded to his anxious smile. But she did not attempt to take the money. She shook her head.

"Too much."

But he pushed the bills into her hand.

"You can't refuse," he said. "You see, it's for the kiddies. It isn't just for you."

When Dave insisted refusal was useless. Betty had long since learned that. Besides, as he said, it was for the "kiddies." She took the money, and he sat and watched her as she folded the bills into her pocketbook. The girl looked up at the sound of a short laugh.

"What's that for?" she demanded, her brown eyes seriously inquiring.

"Oh, just nothing. I was thinking."

The man glanced slowly about him. He looked up at the brilliant summer sun. Then his eyes rested upon the rough exterior of his unpretentious office.

"It meant something," asserted Betty. "I hate people to laugh—in that way."

"I was thinking of this shack of mine. I was just thinking, Betty, what a heap of difference an elegant coat of paint makes to things. You see, they're just the same underneath, but they—kind of look different with paint on 'em, kind of please the eye more."

"Just so," the girl nodded wisely. "And so you laughed—in that way."

Dave's eyes twinkled.

"You're too sharp," he said. Then he abruptly changed the subject.

"Now about this picnic. You're expecting all the grown folk?"

The girl's eyes opened to their fullest extent.

"Of course I do. Don't you always come? It's only once a year." The last was very like a reproach.

The man avoided her eyes. He was looking out across the sea of stacked timber at the great sheds beyond, where the saws were shrieking out their incessant song.

"I was thinking," he began awkwardly, "that I'm not much good at those things. Of course I guess I can hand pie round to the folks; any fellow can do that. But ——"

"But what?" The girl had risen from her seat and was trying to compel his gaze.

"Well, you see, we're busy here—desperately busy. Dawson's always grumbling that we're short-handed ——"

Betty came up close to him, and he suddenly felt a gentle squeeze on his shoulder.

"You don't want to come," she said.

"'Tisn't that—not exactly."

He kept his eyes turned from her.

"You see," he went on, "you'll have such a heap of folk there. They mostly all get around—for you. Then there'll be Jim Truscott, and Jim's worth a dozen of me when it comes to picnics and 'sociables' and such-like."

The girl's hand suddenly dropped from his shoulder, and she turned away. A flush slowly mounted to her sun-tanned cheeks, and she was angry at it. She stood looking out at the mills beyond, but she wasn't thinking of them.

At last she turned back to her friend and her soft eyes searched his.

"If—if you don't come to the picnic to-morrow, I'll never forgive you, Dave—never!"

And she was gone before his slow tongue could frame a further excuse.

CHAPTER II

A PICNIC IN THE RED SAND VALLEY

SUMMER, at the foot of the Canadian Rockies, sets in suddenly. There are no dreary days of damp and cold when the east wind bites through to the bones and chills right down to the marrow. One moment all is black, dead; the lean branches and dead grass of last year make a waste of dreary decay. Watch. See the magic of the change. The black of the trees gives way to a warming brown; the grass, so sad in its depression, suddenly lightens with the palest hue of green. There is at once a warmth of tone which spreads itself over the world, and gladdens the heart and sets the pulses throbbing with renewed life and hope. Animal life stirs; the insect world rouses. At the sun's first smile the whole earth wakens; it yawns and stretches itself; it blinks and rubs its eyes, and presently it smiles back. The smile broadens into a laugh, and lo! it is summer, with all the world clad in festal raiment, gorgeous in its myriads of changing color-harmonies.

It was on such a day in the smiling valley of the Red Sand River that Betty Somers held her school picnic. There were no shadows to mar the festivities she had arranged. The sky was brilliant, cloudless, and early in the season as it was, the earth was already beginning to crack and parch under the fiery sun.

A dozen democrat wagons, bedecked with flags and filled to overflowing with smiling, rosy-faced children, each wagon under the charge of one of the village matrons, set out at eight o'clock in the morning for the camping-ground. Besides these, an hour later, a large number of private buggies conveyed the parents and provender, while the young people of the village rode out on horseback as a sort of escort to the commissariat. It was a gay throng, and there could be little doubt but that the older folk were as delighted at the prospect of the outing as the children themselves.

Dave was there with the rest. Betty's challenge had had its effect. But he came without any of the enthusiasm of the rest of the young people. It was perfectly true that the demands of his mill made the outing inconvenient to him, but that was not the real reason of his reluctance. There was another, a far stronger one. All the years of his manhood had taught him that there was small place for him where the youth of both sexes foregathered. His body was too cumbersome, his tongue was too slow, and his face was too plain. The dalliance of man and maid was not for him, he knew, and did he ever doubt or forget it, his looking-glass, like an evil spirit, was ever ready to remind and convince him.

The picnic ground was some five miles down the valley, in the depths of a wide, forest-grown glen, through which a tiny tributary of the Red Sand River tumbled its way over a series of miniature waterfalls. The place was large and magnificently rock-bound, and looked as though it had originally been chiseled by Nature to accommodate a rushing mountain torrent. It gave one the impression of a long disused waterway which, profiting by its original purpose, had become so wonderfully fertilized that its vegetation had grown out of all proportion to its capacity. It was a veritable jungle of undergrowth and forest, so dense and wide spreading as almost to shut out the dazzling sunlight. It was an ideal pleasure camping-ground, where the children could romp and play every game known to the Western child, and their elders could revel in the old, old game which never palls, and which the practice of centuries can never rob of its youth.

All the morning the children played, while the women were kept busy with the preparations for the midday feast. The men were divided up into two sections, the elders, taking office under the command of Tom Chepstow, organizing the children's games, and the other half, acknowledging the leadership of Mrs. Tom, assisting those engaged in the culinary arrangements.

As might be expected, the latter occupation found most favor with the younger men. There was far more fun in wandering through the tangled undergrowth of the riverside to help a girl fill a kettle, than in racking one's brains for some startlingly unoriginal and long-forgotten game with which to dazzle the mind of Malkern's youth. Then there were the joys of gathering fire-wood, a task which enlisted the services of at least a dozen couples. This was a much favored occupation. There was no time limit, and it involved a long, long ramble. Then, too, it was remarkable that every girl performing the simplest duty, and one in which she never required the least assistance when at home, found it quite impossible to do so here without the strong physical and moral support of the man she most favored.

Thus the morning passed. While the girls and men flirted, and the older women took to themselves a reflected enjoyment of it all, the children shrieked their delight at the simplest game, and baited their elders with all the impudence of childhood. It was a morning of delight to all; a morning when the sluggish blood of the oldest quickened in the sunken veins; a morning when the joy of living was uppermost, and all care was thrust into the background.

It was not until after dinner that Dave saw anything of Betty. As he had anticipated, Jim Truscott never left her side, and his own morning had been spent with Tom Chepstow and the children. Then, at dinner, it had fallen to his lot to assist the matrons in waiting upon the same riotous horde. In consequence, by the time he got his own meal, Betty and the younger section of the helpers had finished theirs and were wandering off into the woods.

After dinner he sought out a secluded spot in

which to smoke and—make the best of things. He felt he had earned a rest. His way took him along the bank of the little tumbling river. It was delightfully restful, cool and shadowed by the overhanging trees that nearly met across it. It was not an easy path, but it was calmly beautiful and remote, and that was all he sought.

Just above one rapid, something larger than the others he had passed, he came to a little log footbridge. It was a delicious spot, and he sat down and filled his pipe. The murmur of the rapids below came up to him pleasantly. All the foliage about him was of that tender green inspired by the humidity of the dank, river atmosphere. Here and there the sun broke through in patches and lit up the scene, and added beauty to the remoter shadows of the woods. It was all so peaceful. Even the distant voices of the children seemed to add to the calm of his retreat.

His pipe was nearly finished, and an insidious languor was stealing over him. He nodded once or twice, almost asleep. Then he started wide awake; a familiar laughing voice sounded just behind him, calling him by name.

"Oh, Dave! So this is where you are! I've been hunting for you till—till my feet are sore."

Before he could move Betty had plumped herself down beside him on the bridge. He was wide enough awake now, and his delight at the girl's presence was so apparent that she promptly and frankly remarked upon it.

"I do believe you're glad I came, and—woke you up," she laughed.

The man leant back luxuriously and propped himself against the post of the hand-rail.

"I am, surely," he said with conviction. "I've been thinking about picnics. It seems to me they're a heap of fun ——"

"So you stole away by yourself to enjoy this one."

Betty's brown eyes glanced slyly at him. There was a half smile in them, and yet they were serious. Dave began to refill his pipe.

"Well, Betty, you see I just thought I'd like a smoke. I've been with the kiddies all morning."

Suddenly the girl sat round facing him.

"Dave, I'm a little beast. I oughtn't to have made you come. I know you don't care for this sort of thing, only—well, you are so kind, and you are so fond of making people happy. And you— you —— Oh, Dave, I—I want to tell you something. That's—that's why I was hunting for you."

She had turned from him, and was gazing out down the stream now. Her face was flushed a deep scarlet. For an instant she had encountered his steady gray eyes and her confusion had been complete. She felt as though he had read right down into her very soul.

Dave put his pipe away. The serious expression of his rugged face was unchanged, but the smile in his eyes had suddenly become more pronounced.

"So that's why you hunted me out?" he said gently. "Well, Betty, you can tell me."

He had seen the blushing face. He had noted the embarrassment and hesitancy, and the final desperate plunge. He knew in his heart what was coming, and the pain of that knowledge was so acute that he could almost have cried out. Yet he sat there waiting, his eyes smiling, his face calmly grave as it always was.

For nearly a minute neither spoke. Then the man's deep voice urged the girl.

"Well?"

Betty rested her face in her hands and propped her elbows on her knees. All her embarrassment had gone now. She was thinking, thinking, and when at last her words came that tone of excitement which she had used just a moment before had quite gone out of her voice.

"It's Jim," she said quietly. "He's asked me to marry him. I've promised—and—and he's gone to speak to uncle."

Dave took out his pipe again and looked into the bowl of it.

"I guessed it was that," he said, after a while. Then he fumbled for his tobacco. "And—are you happy—little Betty?" he asked a moment later.

"Yes—I—I think so."

"You think so?"

Dave was astonished out of himself.

"You only think so?" he went on, his breath coming quickly.

Betty sat quite still and the man watched her, with his pipe and tobacco gripped tightly in his great hand. He was struggling with a mad desire to crush this girl to his heart and defy any one to take her from him. It was a terrible moment. But the wild impulse died down. He took a deep breath and—slowly filled his pipe.

" Tell me," he said, and his tone was very tender.

The girl turned to him. She rested an arm on his bent knee and looked up into his face. There was no longer any hesitation or doubt. She was pale under the warm tanning of her cheeks, but she was very pretty, and, to Dave, wildly seductive as she thus appealed to him.

" Oh, Dave, I must tell you all. You are my only real friend. You, I know, will understand, and can help me. If I went to uncle, good and kind as he is, I feel he would not understand. And auntie, she is so matter-of-fact and practical. But you—you are different from anybody else."

The man nodded.

" I have loved Jim for so long," she went on hurriedly. " Long—long before he ever even noticed me. To me he has always been every-thing a man should and could be. You see, he is so kind and thoughtful, so brave, so masterful, so— so handsome, with just that dash of recklessness which makes him so fascinating to a girl. I have watched him pay attention to other girls, and night after night I have cried myself to sleep about it. Dave, you have never known what it is to love anybody, so all this may seem silly to you, but I only want to show you how much I have always cared for Jim. Well, after a long time he began to take notice of me. I remember it so well," she went on, with a far-away look in her eyes. " It was a year ago, at our Church Social. He spent a lot of time with me there, and gave me a box of candy, and then asked permission to see me home. Dave, from that moment I was in a seventh heaven of happiness. Every day I have felt and hoped that he would ask me to be his wife. I have longed for it, prayed for it, dreaded it, and lived in a dream of happiness. And now he has asked me."

She turned away to the bustling stream. Her eyes had become pathetically sad.

" And ——" Dave prompted her.

" Oh, I don't know." She shook her head a little helplessly. " It all seems different now."

" Different? "

" Yes, that wildly happy feeling has gone."

" You are—unhappy ? "

The man's voice shook as he put his question.

" It isn't that. I'm happy enough, I suppose. Only—only—I think I'm frightened now, or something. All my dreams seem to have tumbled about my ears. I have no longer that wonderful looking forward. Is it because he is mine now, and no one can take him from me? Or is it," her voice dropped to an awed whisper, " that—I—don't ——"

She broke off as though afraid to say all she feared. Dave lit his pipe and smoked slowly and thoughtfully. He had gone through his ordeal listening to her, and now felt that he could face anything without giving his own secret away. He must reassure her. He must remove the doubt in her mind, for, in his quiet, reasoning way, he told himself that all her future happiness was at stake.

"No, it's not that, Betty," he said earnestly. "It's not that you love him less. It's just that for all that year you've thought and thought and hoped about it—till there's nothing more to it," he added lamely. "You see, it's the same with all things. Realization is nothing. It's all in the anticipation. You wait, little girl. When things are fixed, and Parson Tom has said ' right,' you'll— why, you'll just be the happiest little bit of a girl in Malkern. That's sure."

Betty lifted her eyes to his ugly face and looked straight into the kindly eyes. Just for one impulsive moment she reached out and took hold of his knotty hand and squeezed it.

"Dave, you are the dearest man in the world. You are the kindest and best," she cried with unusual emotion. "I wonder ——" and she turned away to hide the tears that had suddenly welled up into her troubled eyes.

But Dave had seen them, and he dared not trust himself to speak. He sat desperately still and sucked at his pipe, emitting great clouds of smoke till the pungent fumes bit his tongue.

Then relief came from an unexpected quarter. There was a sharp crackling of bush just above where they sat and the scrunch of crushing pine cones trodden under foot, and Jim Truscott stepped on to the bridge.

" Ah, here you are at last. My word, but I had a job to find you."

His tone was light and easy, but his usually smiling face was clouded. Betty sprang to her feet.

" What is it, Jim ? " she demanded, searching his face. " Something is wrong. I know it is."

Jim seated himself directly in front of Dave, who now watched him with added interest. He now noticed several things in the boy he did not remember having observed before. The face in repose, or rather without the smile it usually wore, bore signs of weakness about the mouth. The whole of the lower part of it lacked the imprint of keen decision. There was something almost effeminate about the mould of his full lips, something soft and yielding —even vicious. The rest of his face was good, and even intellectual. He was particularly handsome, with crisp curling hair of a light brown that closely matched his large expressive eyes. His tall athletic figure was strangely at variance with the intellectual cast of his face and head. But what Dave most noticed were the distinct lines of dissipation about his eyes. And he wondered how it was he had never seen them before. Perhaps it was that he so rarely saw Jim without his cheery smile. Perhaps, now that Betty had told him what had taken place, his observation was closer, keener.

" What is it, Jim ? " He added his voice to

Betty's inquiry. Jim's face became gloomier. He turned to the girl, who had resumed her seat at Dave's side.

" Have you told him?" he asked, and for a moment his eyes brightened with a shadow of their old smile.

The girl nodded, and Dave answered for her.

" She's told me enough to know you're the luckiest fellow in the Red Sand Valley," he said kindly.

Jim glanced up into the girl's face with all the passion of his youthful heart shining in his handsome eyes.

" Yes, I am, Dave—in that way," he said. Then his smile faded out and was replaced by a brooding frown. " But all the luck hasn't come my way. I've talked to Parson Tom."

" Ah !" Dave's ejaculation was ominous.

Suddenly Jim exploded, half angrily, half pettishly, like a disappointed schoolboy.

" Betty, I've got to go away. Your uncle says so. He asked me all about my mill, what my profits were, and all that. I told him honestly. I know I'm not doing too well. He said I wasn't making enough to keep a nigger servant on. He told me that until I could show him an income of $2,500 a year there was to be no talk of engagement. What is more, he said he couldn't have me philandering about after you until there was a reasonable prospect of that income. We talked and argued, but he was firm. And in the end he advised me, if I were really in earnest and serious, to go right away, take what capital I had, and select a new and rising country to start in. He pointed out that there was not room enough here for two in the lumbering business; that Dave, here, complained of the state of trade, so what chance could I possibly have without a tithe of his resources. Finally, he told me to go and think out a plan, talk it over with you, and then tell him what I had decided upon. So here I am, and —— "

" So am I," added Betty.

" And as I am here as well," put in Dave, " let's talk it over now. Where are you thinking of going ? "

" Seems to me the Yukon is the place. There's a big rush going on. There's great talk of fabulous fortunes there."

" Yes, fabulous," said Dave dryly. " It's a long way. A big fare. You'll find yourself amongst all the scum and blacklegs of this continent. You'll be up against every proposition known to the crook. You'll get tainted. Why not do some ranching? Somewhere. around here, toward Edmonton."

Jim shook his head gloomily.

" I haven't nearly enough capital."

" Maybe I could manage it for you," said Dave thoughtfully. " I mean it as a business proposition," he added hastily.

Jim's face cleared, and his ready smile broke out like sunshine after a summer storm.

" Would you ? " he cried. " Yes, a business

proposition. Business interest. I know the very place," he went on ardently. " Betty, wouldn't that be bully? How would you like to be a rancher's wife?"

But his spirits quickly received a damper. Betty shook her head.

" No, Jim. Not at Dave's expense." Then she turned to the man who had made the offer. " No, no, Dave, old friend. Jim and I know you. This is not business from your point of view. You added that to disguise your kindly intention."

" But ——" Dave began to protest.

But Betty would have none of it.

" This is a debate," she said, with a brightness she did not feel, " and I am speaking. Jim," she turned gently to her lover, " we'll start fair and square with the world. You must do as uncle says. And you can do it. Do it yourself—yourself un-aided. God will help you—surely. You are clever; you have youth, health and strength. I will wait for you all my life, if necessary. You have my promise, and it is yours until you come back to claim me. It may be only a year or two. We must be very, very brave. Whatever plan you de-cide on, if it is the Yukon, or Siberia, or anywhere else, I am content, and I will wait for you."

The girl's words were so gently spoken, yet they rang with an irrevocable decision that astonished her hearers. Dave looked into the pretty, set face. He had known her so long. He had seen her in almost every mood, yet here was a fresh side to her character he had never even suspected, and the thought flashed through his mind, to what heights of ambition might a man not soar with such a woman at his side.

Jim looked at her too. But his was a stare of amazement, and even resentment.

" But why, Betty ? " he argued sharply. " Why throw away a business offer such as this, when it means almost certain success ? Dave offered it himself, and surely you will allow that he is a business man before all things."

" Is he ? " Betty smiled. Then she turned to the man who had made the offer. " Dave, will you do something for me ? "

" Why, yes, Betty—if it's not to go and wash up cups down there," he replied at once, with a grin.

" No, it isn't to wash cups. It's "—she glanced quickly at Jim, who was watching her with anything but a lover-like stare—" it's—to withdraw that offer."

Dave removed his pipe and turned to Jim.

" That ranch business is off," he said.

Then he suddenly sat up and leant toward the younger man.

" Jim, boy, you know I wish you well," he said. " I wish you so well that I understand and appreciate Betty's decision now, though I allow I didn't see it at first. She's right. Parson Tom is right. I was wrong. Get right out into the world and make her a home. Get right out and show her, and the rest of us, the stuff you're made of. You won't

fail if you put your back into it. And when you
come back it'll be a great day for you both. And
see here, boy, so long as you run straight you can ask
me anything in the name of friendship, and I'll not
fail you. Here's my hand on it."

Something of Dave's earnestness rather than the
girl's quiet strength seemed to suddenly catch hold
of and lift the dejected man out of his moodiness.
His face cleared and his sunny smile broke out
again. He gripped the great hand, and enthusiasm
rang in his voice.

" By God, you're right, Dave," he cried. " You're
a good chap. Yes, I'll go. Betty," he turned to
the girl, " I'll go to the Yukon, where there's gold
for the seeking. I'll realize all the money I can. I
won't part with my mill. That will be my fall-back
if I fail. But I won't fail. I'll make money by—
no, I'll make money. And——" Suddenly, at the
height of his enthusiasm, his face fell, and the
buoyant spirit dropped from him.

" Yes, yes," broke in Betty, anxious to see his
mood last.

Jim thought for a moment while the clouds gathered on his face. Then he looked steadily at Dave.

" Dave," he said, and paused. Then he began
again. " Dave—in friendship's name—I'll ask you
something now. Betty here," he swallowed, as
though what he had to say was very difficult. " You
see, I may be away a long time, you can never tell.
Will you—will you take care of her for me ? Will
you be her—her guardian, as you have always been

mine? I know I'm asking a lot, but somehow I can't leave her here, and—I know there's her uncle and aunt. But, I don't know, somehow I'd like to think you had given me your word that she would be all right, that you were looking after her for me. Will you?"

His face and tone were both eager, and full of real feeling. Dave never flinched as he listened to the request, yet every word cut into his heart, lashed him till he wondered how it was Jim could not see and understand. He moistened his lips. He groped in his pocket for his matches and lit one. He let it burn out, watching it until the flame nearly reached his fingers. Then he knocked his pipe out on his boot, and broke it with the force he used. Finally he looked up with a smile, and his eyes encountered Betty's.

She smiled back, and he turned to her lover, who was waiting for his answer.

" Sure I'll look after her—for you," he said slowly.

Jim sprang to his feet.

" I can never thank ——"

But Dave cut him short.

"Don't thank me, boy," he said, preparing to return to the camp. " Just—get out and do." And he left the lovers to return at their leisure.

CHAPTER III

FOUR glowing summers have gone; a fifth is dawning, driving before its radiant splendor the dark shadows and gray monotony of winter's icy pall. Malkern is a busy little town, spreading out its feelers in the way of small houses dotted about amidst the park land of the valley. Every year sees a further and further extension of its boarded sidewalks and grass-edged roadways; every year sees its population steadily increasing; every year sees an advancement in the architecture of its residences, and some detail displaying additional prosperity in its residents.

Behind this steady growth of prosperity sits Dave, large, quiet, but irresistible. His is the guiding hand. The tiller of the Malkern ship is in his grasp, and it travels the laid course without deviation whatsoever. The harbor lies ahead, and, come storm or calm, he drives steadily on for its haven.

Thus far has the man been content. Thus far have his ambitions been satisfied. He has striven, and gained his way inch by inch; but with that striving has grown up in him a desire such as inevitably comes to the strong and capable worker. A steady success creates a desire to achieve a master-stroke, whereby the fruit which hitherto he has been content to pluck singly falls in a mass into his lap. And therein lies the human nature which so often upsets the carefully trained and drilled method of the finest tempered brain.

Dave saw his goal looming. He saw clearly that all that he had worked for, hoped for, could be gained at one stroke. That one stroke meant capturing the great government contract for the lumber required for building the new naval docks. It was a contract involving millions of dollars, and, with all the courage with which his spirit was laden, he meant to attempt the capture. His plans had been silently laid. No detail had been forgotten, no pains spared. Night and day his thoughtful brain had worked upon his scheme, and now had come that time when he must sit back and wait for the great moment. Nor did this great moment depend on him, and therein lay the uncertainty, the gamble so dear to the human heart.

His scheme had been confided to only three people, and these were with him now, sitting on the veranda of the Rev. Tom Chepstow's house. The house stood on a slightly rising ground facing out to the east, whence a perfect view of the wide-spreading valley was obtained. It was a modest enough place, but trim and carefully kept. Parson Tom's stipend was so limited and uncertain that luxury was quite impossible ; a rigid frugality was the ruling in his small household.

It was Saturday. The day's work was over, and

the family were watching the sunset and awaiting the hour for supper. The parson was luxuriating in a pipe in a well-worn deck-chair at one extremity of the deep, wild-cucumber-covered veranda. Dave sat near him; Mary Chepstow, the parson's wife, was crocheting a baby's woolen jacket, stoutly comfortable in a leather armchair; while Betty, a little more mature in figure, a little quieter in manner, but even prettier and more charming to look at than she was on the day of her picnic nearly five years ago, occupied a seat near the open French window, ready to attend at a moment's notice to the preparing of supper.

Betty had been silent for quite a while. She was staring with introspective gaze out in the direction of the railroad depot. The two men had been discussing the best means of raising the funds for the building of a new church, aided by a few impracticable suggestions from Mrs. Chepstow, who had a way of counting her stitches aloud in the midst of her remarks. Suddenly Betty turned to her uncle, whose lean, angular frame was grotesquely hunched up in his deck-chair.

" Will old Mudley bring the mail over if the train does come in this evening ? " she inquired abruptly.

The parson shook his head. His lean, clean-shaven face lit with a quizzical smile as he glanced over at his niece.

" Why should he ? " he replied. " He never does bring mail round. Are you expecting a letter— from him ? "

There was no self-consciousness in the girl's manner as she replied. There was not even warmth.

" Oh, no ; I was wondering if I should get one from Maud Hardwig. She promised to write me how Lily's wedding went off in Regina. It is a nuisance about the strike. But it's only the platelayers, isn't it ; and it only affects the section where they are constructing east of Winnipeg ? "

Her uncle removed his pipe.

" Yes. But it affects indirectly the whole system. You see, they won't put on local mails from Regina. They wait for the eastern mail to come through. By the way, how long is it since you heard from Jim ? "

Betty had turned away and was watching the vanishing point of the railway track, where it entered the valley a couple of miles away. Dave's steady eyes turned upon her. But she didn't answer at once, and her uncle had to call her attention.

" Betty ! "

" Oh, I'm sorry, uncle," she replied at once. " I was dreaming. When did I hear ? Oh, nearly nine months ago."

Mary Chepstow looked up with a start.

" Nine months ? Gracious, child—there, I've done it wrong."

Bending over her work she withdrew her hook and started to unravel the chain she was making.

" Yes," Betty went on coldly. _" Nine months since I had a letter. But I've heard indirectly."

Her uncle sat up.

" You never told me," he said uneasily.

The girl's indifference was not without its effect on him. She never talked ·of Jim Truscott now. And somehow the subject was rarely broached by any of them. Truscott had nominally gone away for two or three years, but they were already in the fifth year since his departure, and there was as yet no word of his returning. Secretly her uncle was rather pleased at her silence on the subject. He augured well from it. He did not think there was to be any heart-breaking over the matter. He had never sanctioned any engagement between them, but he had been prepared to do so if the boy turned up under satisfactory conditions. Now he felt that it was time to take action in the matter. Betty was nearly twenty-seven, and—well, he did not want her to spend her life waiting for a man who showed no sign of returning.

" I didn't see the necessity," she said quietly. " I heard of him through Dave."

The parson swung round on the master of the mills. His keen face was alert with the deepest interest.

" You, Dave? " he exclaimed.

The lumberman stirred uneasily, and Mary Chepstow let her work lie idle in her lap.

" Dawson—my foreman, you know—got a letter from Mansell. You remember Mansell? He acted as Jim's foreman at his mill. A fine sawyer, Mansell——"

" Yes, yes." Parson Tom's interest made him impatient.

" Well, you remember that Mansell went with Jim when he set out for the Yukon. They intended to try their luck together. Partners, of course. Well, Mansell wrote Dawson he was sick to death of worrying things out up there. He said he'd left Jim, but did not state why. He asked him if my mill was going strong, and would there be a job for him if he came back. He said that Jim was making money now. He had joined a man named Broncho Bill, a pretty hard citizen, and in consequence he was doing better. How he was making money he didn't say. But he finished up his remarks about the boy by saying he'd leave him to tell his own story, as he had no desire to put any one away."

Mrs. Chepstow offered no comment, but silently picked up her work and went on with it. Her husband sat back in his chair, stretching his long muscular legs, and folding his hands behind his head. Betty displayed not the least interest in Dave's haltingly told story.

The silence on the veranda was ominous. Chepstow began to refill his pipe, furtively watching his niece's pretty profile as she sat looking down the valley. It was his wife who broke the oppressive silence.

" I can't believe badly—three treble in the adjacent hole "—she muttered, referring to her pattern book, " of him. I always liked him—five chain."

"So do I," put in Dave with emphasis.

Betty glanced quickly into his rugged face.

"You don't believe the insinuations of that letter?" she asked him sharply.

"I don't."

Dave's reply was emphatic. Betty smiled over at him. Then she jumped up from her seat and pointed down the track.

"There's the mail," she cried. Then she came to her aunt's side and laid a hand coaxingly on her shoulder. "Will you see to supper, dear, if I go down for the mail?"

Mrs. Chepstow would not trust herself to speak, she was in the midst of a complicated manipulation of the pattern she was working, so she contented herself with a nod, and Betty was off like the wind. The two men watched her as she sped down the hard red sand trail, and neither spoke until a bend in the road hid her from view.

"She's too good a girl, Dave," Chepstow said with almost militant warmth. "She's not going to be made a fool of by—by ——"

"She won't be made a fool of by any one," Dave broke in with equal warmth. "There's no fear of it, if I'm any judge," he added. "I don't think you realize that girl's spirit, Tom. Here, I'll tell you something I've never told anybody. When Jim went away Betty came to me and asked me to let her study my mills. She wanted to learn all the business of 'em. All the inside of the management of 'em. If I'd have let her she'd have learnt how to run the saws. And do you know why she did it? I'll tell you. Because she thought Jim might come back broke, and he and she together could start up his old mill again, so as to win through. That's Betty. Can you beat it? That girl has made up her mind to a certain line of action, and she'll see it through, no matter what her feelings may be. No word of yours, or mine, will turn her from her purpose. She'll wait for Jim."

" Yes, and waste the best of her life," exclaimed Mrs. Chepstow. " One, two, three—turn."

Dave smiled over at the rotund figure crocheting so assiduously. Although Mary Chepstow was over forty her face still retained its youthful prettiness. The parson laughed. He generally laughed at his wife's views upon anything outside of her small household and the care of the sick villagers. But it was never an unkind laugh. Just a large, tolerant good-nature, a pronounced feature in his character. Parson Tom, like many kindly men, was hasty of temper, even fiery, and being a man of considerable athletic powers, this characteristic had, on more than one occasion, forcibly brought some recalcitrant member of his uncertain-tempered flock to book, and incidentally acquired for him the sobriquet of " the fighting parson."

" I don't know about wasting the best of her life," he said. " Betty has never wasted her life. Look at the school she's got now. And, mark you, she's done it all herself. She has three teachers under her. She has negotiated all the finance of the school herself. She got the government by the coat-tails and dragged national support out of it. Why, she's a wonder. No, no, not waste, Mary. Let her wait if she chooses. We won't interfere. I only hope that when Jim does come back he'll be a decent citizen. If he isn't, I'd bet my last cent Betty will know how to deal with him."

" She'll sure give him up, if he isn't," said Dave with conviction.

Mary looked up, her round blue eyes twinkling.

" Dave knows Betty better than we do, Tom. I'd almost think —— I'm not sure I like this shade of pink," she digressed, examining her wool closely. " Er—what was I saying? Oh, yes—I'd almost think he'd made a special study of her."

A deep flush spread slowly over Dave's ugly face, and he tried to hide it by bending over his pipe and examining the inside of the bowl.

Parson Tom promptly changed the subject. He shook his head and turned away to watch the ruddy extravagance of the sunset in the valley.

" Dave has got far too much to think of in his coming government contract to bother with a girl like Betty. By the way, when do you expect to hear the result of your tender, Dave ? "

" Any time."

The lumberman's embarrassment had vanished at the mention of his contract. His eyes lit, and the whole of his plain features were suddenly illumined. This was his life's purpose. This contract meant everything to him. All that had gone before, all his labor, his early struggles, they were nothing to the store he set by this one great scheme.

"Good. And your chances?" There was the keenest interest in the parson's question.

"Well, I'd say they're good. You see, that find of ours up in the hills opens a possibility we never had before. The new docks require an enormous supply of ninety-foot timber. It's got to be ninety-foot stuff. Well, we've got the timber in that new find. There's a valley of some thousands of acres of forest which will supply it. Tom," he went on eagerly, "we could cut 'em hundred-and-twenty-foot logs from that forest till the cows come home. It's the greatest proposition in lumbering. It's one of the greatest of those great primordial pine forests which are to be found in the Rockies, if one is lucky enough. At present we are the only people in Canada who can give them the stuff they need, and enough of it. Yes, I think I'll get it. I've set the wires pulling all I know. I've cut the price. I've done everything I can, and I think I'll get it. If I do I'll be a millionaire half a dozen times over, and Malkern, and all its people, will rise to an immense, prosperity. I must get it! And having got it, I must push it through successfully."

Mary and her husband were hanging on the lumberman's words, carried away by his enthusiasm. There was that light of battle in his eyes, the firm setting of his heavy under-jaw, which they knew and understood so well. To them he was the personification of resolution. To them his personality was irresistible.

"Of course you'll push it through successfully," Tom nodded.

"Yes, yes. I shall. I must," Dave said, stirring his great body in his chair with a restlessness which spoke of his nervous tension. "But it's this time limit. You see, it's a government contract. They want these naval docks built quickly. The whole scheme is to be rushed through. Since the Imperial Conference has decided that each colony is to build its own share of the navy for imperial defense, in view of the European situation, that building is to be begun at once. They are laying down five ships this year, and, by the end of the year, they are to have docks ready for the laying down of six more. My contract is for the lumber for those docks. You see? My contract must be completed before winter closes down, without fail. I have guaranteed that. Well, as I am the only lumberman in Canada that can supply this heavy lumber, if they do not give it to me they will have to go to the States for it. Yes," he added, with something like a sigh, "I think I shall get it. But—this time limit! If I fail it will break me, and, in the crash, Malkern will go too."

Mary Chepstow sighed with emotion. Her crochet was forgotten.

"You won't fail," she murmured, her eyes glistening. "You can't!"

"Malkern isn't going to tumble about our

ears, old friend," Parson Tom said with quiet assurance.

Dave had fallen back into his lounging attitude and puffed at his pipe.

" No," he said. Then he pointed down the trail in the direction of the depot. " There's Betty coming along in a hurry with Jenkins Mudley."

All eyes turned to look. Betty was almost running beside the tall thin figure of the operator and postmaster of Malkern. They came up with a final rush, the man flourishing a telegram at Dave. Betty was carrying a number of letters.

" I just thought I'd bring this along myself," Mudley grinned. " Everything's been delayed through the strike down east. This, too. Felt I'd hate to let any one else hand it to you, Dave."

Dave snatched at the tinted envelope and tore it open, while Betty, nodding at her uncle and aunt, her eyes dancing with delight, made frantic signs to them. But they took no notice of her, keeping their eyes fixed on the towering form of the master of the mills. Dave was the calmest man present. He read the message over twice, and then deliberately thrust it into his pocket. Then, as he returned to his seat, he said —

" I've got my contract, folks."

" Hurrah! " cried Betty, no longer able to control herself. The operator had previously imparted the fact to her. Then, with a jump, she was on the veranda and flung some letters into her uncle's lap, retaining one for herself that had already been read.

The next moment she had seized both of Dave's great hands, and was wringing them with all her heart and soul shining in her eyes.

" I'm so—so glad, I don't know what I'm doing or saying," she cried, and then collapsed on her uncle's knee.

Dave laughed quietly, but her aunt, her face belying her words, reproved her gently.

" Betty," she said warningly as the girl scrambled to her feet, "don't get excited. I think you'd better go and see to supper. I see you got your letter. How did the wedding go off? "

Betty was leaning against one of the veranda posts.

" Oh, yes," she said indifferently. " I'd forgotten my letter. It's from Jim. He's coming home."

Her aunt suddenly picked up her work. The parson began to open his letters. Dave's eyes, until that moment smiling, suddenly became serious. The girl's news had a strangely damping effect. Dave cleared his throat as though about to speak. But he remained silent.

Then Betty moved across to the door.

" I'll go and get supper," she said quietly, and vanished into the house.

CHAPTER IV

DICK MANSELL'S NEWS

For Dave the next fortnight was fraught with a tremendous pressure of work. But arduous and wearing as it was, to him there was that thrill of conscious striving which is the very essence of life to the ambition-inspired man. His goal loomed dimly upon his horizon, he could see it in shadowy outline, and every step he took now, every effort he put forth, he knew was carrying him on, drawing him nearer and nearer to it. He worked with that steady enthusiasm which never rushes. He was calm and purposeful. To hasten, to diverge from his deliberate course in the heat of excitement, he knew would only weaken his effort. Careful organization, perfect, machine-like, was what he needed, and the work would do itself.

At the mills a large extension of the milling floors and an added number of saws were needed. In its present state the milling floor could hardly accommodate the ninety-foot logs demanded by the contract. This was a structural alteration that must be carried out at express speed, and had been prepared for, so that it was only a matter of executing plans already drawn up. Joel Dawson, the foreman, one of the best lumbermen in the country, was responsible for the alterations. Simon Odd, the master sawyer, had the organizing of the skilled labor staff inside the mill, a work of much responsibility and considerable discrimination.

But with Dave rested the whole responsibility and chief organization. It was necessary to secure labor for both the mill and the camps up in the hills. And for this the district had to be scoured, while two hundred lumber-jacks had to be brought up from the forests of the Ottawa River.

Dave and his lieutenants worked all their daylight hours, and most of the night was spent in harness. They ate to live only, and slept only when their falling eyelids refused to keep open.

Only Dave and his two loyal supporters knew the work of that fortnight; only they understood the anxiety and strain, but their efforts were crowned with success, and at the end of that time the first of the " ninety-footers " floated down the river to the mouth of the great boom that lay directly under the cranes of the milling floor.

It was not until that moment that Dave felt free to look about him, to turn his attention from the grindstone of his labors. It was midday when word passed of the arrival of the first of the timber, and he went at once to verify the matter for himself. It was a sight to do his heart good. The boom, stretching right into the heart of the mills, was a mass of rolling, piling logs, and a small army of men was at work upon them piloting them so as to avoid a " crush." It was perilous, skilful work,

and the master of the mills watched with approval
the splendid efforts of these intrepid lumber-jacks.
He only waited until the rattling chains of the
cranes were lowered and the first log was grappled
and lifted like a match out of the water, and hauled
up to the milling floor. Then, with a sigh as of a
man relieved of a great strain, he turned away and
passed out of his yards.

It was the first day for a fortnight he had gone to
his house for dinner.

His home was a small house of weather-boarding
with a veranda all creeper-grown, as were most of
the houses in the village. It had only one story,
and every window had a window-box full of simple
flowers. It stood in a patch of garden that was
chiefly given up to vegetables, with just a small
lawn of mean-looking turf with a centre bed of
flowers. Along the top-railed fence which enclosed it were, set at regular intervals, a number of
small blue-gum and spruce trees. It was just such
an abode as one might expect Dave to possess:
simple, useful, unpretentious. It was the house of
a man who cared nothing for luxury. Utility was
the key-note of his life. And the little trivial decorations in the way of creepers, flowers, and such
small luxuries were due to the gentle, womanly
thought of his old mother, with whom he lived, and
who permitted no one else to minister to his wants.

She was in the doorway when he came up, a
small thin figure with shriveled face and keen,
questioning eyes. She was clad in black, and wore

a print overall. Her snow-white hair was parted in the middle and smoothed down flat, in the method of a previous generation. She was an alert little figure for all her sixty odd years.

The questioning eyes changed to a look of gladness as the burly figure of her son turned in at the gate. There could be no doubt as to her feelings. Dave was all the world to her. Her admiration for her son amounted almost to idolatry.

"Dinner's ready," she said eagerly. "I thought I'd just see if you were coming. I didn't expect you. Have you time for it, Dave?"

"Sure, ma," he responded, stooping and kissing her upturned face. "The logs are down."

"Dear boy, I'm glad."

It was all she said, but her tone, and the look she gave him, said far more than the mere words.

Dave placed one great arm gently about her narrow shoulders and led her into the house.

"I'm going to take an hour for dinner to-day sure," he said, with unusual gaiety. "Just to celebrate. After this," he went on, "for six months I'm going to do work that'll astonish even you, ma."

"But you won't overdo it, Dave, will you? The money isn't worth it. It isn't really. I've lived a happy life without much of it, boy, and I don't want much now. I only want my boy."

There was a world of gentle solicitude in the old woman's tones. So much that Dave smiled upon her as he took his place at the table.

" You'll have both, ma, just as sure as sure. I'm not only working for the sake of the money. Sounds funny to say that when I'm working to make myself a millionaire. But it's not the money. It's success first. I don't like being beaten, and that's a fact. We Americans hate being beaten. Then there's other things. Think of these people here. They'll do well. Malkern'll be a city to be reckoned with, and a prosperous one. Then the money's useful to do something with. We can help others. You know, ma, how we've talked it all out."

The mother helped her son to food.

" Yes, I know. But your health, boy, you must think of that."

Dave laughed boisterously, an unusual thing with him. But his mood was light. He felt that he wanted to laugh at anything. What did anything matter? By this time a dozen or so of the " ninety-footers " were already in the process of mutilation by his voracious saws.

" Health, ma?" he cried. " Look at me. I don't guess I'm pretty, but I can do the work of any French-Canadian horse in my yards."

The old woman shook her silvery head doubtfully.

" Well, well, you know best," she said, " only I don't want you to get ill."

Dave laughed again. Then happening to glance out of the window he saw the figure of Joe Hardwig, the blacksmith, turning in at the gate.

" Another plate, ma," he said hastily. " There's Hardwig coming along."

His mother summoned her " hired " girl, and by the time Hardwig's knock came at the door a place was set for him. Dave rose from the table.

" Come right in, Joe," he said cheerily. " We're just having grub. Ma's got some bully stew. Sit down and join us."

But Joe Hardwig declined, with many protestations. He was a broad, squat little man, whose trade was in his very manner, in the strength of his face, and in the masses of muscle which his clothes could not conceal.

" The missus is wantin' me," he said. " Thank you kindly all the same. Your servant, mam," he added awkwardly, turning to Dave's mother. Then to the lumberman, " I jest come along to hand you a bit of information I guessed you'd be real glad of. Mansell—Dick Mansell's got back! I've been yarnin' with him. Say, guess you'll likely need him. He's wantin' a job too. He's a bully sawyer."

Dave had suddenly become serious.

" Dick Mansell!" he cried. Then, after a pause, " Has he brought word of Jim Truscott?"

The mother's eyes were on her son, shrewdly speculating. She had seen his sudden gravity. She knew full well that he cared less for Mansell's powers as a sawyer than for Mansell as the companion and sharer of Jim Truscott's exile. Now she waited for the blacksmith's answer.

Joe shifted uneasily. His great honest face looked troubled. He had not come there to spill dirty water. He knew how much Dave wanted skilled hands, and he knew that Dick needed work.

"Why, yes," he said at last. "At least—that is ——"

"Out with it, man," cried Dave, with unusual impatience. "How is Jim, and—how has he done?"

Just for an instant Joe let an appealing glance fall in the old woman's direction, but he got no encouragement from her. She was steadily proceeding with her dinner. Besides, she never interfered with her boy. Whatever he did was always right to her.

"Well?" Dave urged the hesitating man.

"Oh, I guess he's all right. That is—he ain't hard up. Why yes, he was speakin' of him," Joe stumbled on. "He guessed he was comin' along down here later. That is, Jim is—you see ——"

But Dave hated prevarication. He could see that Joe didn't want to tell what he had heard. However he held him to it fast.

"Has Jim been running straight?" he demanded sharply.

"Oh, as to that—I guess so," said Joe awkwardly.

Dave came over to where Joe was still standing, and laid a hand on his shoulder.

"See here, Joe, we all know you; you're a good sportsman, and you don't go around giving folks away—and bully for you. But I'd rather you told

me what Mansell's told you than that he should tell
me.   See ?   It won't be peaching.   I've got to hear
it."

Joe looked straight up into his face, and suddenly
his eyes lit angrily at his own thought. " Yes,
you'd best have it," he exclaimed, all his hesitation
gone ; " that dogone boy's been runnin' a wild racket.
He's laid hold of the booze and he's never done a
straight day's work since he hit the Yukon trail.
He's comin' back to here with a gambler's wad in
his pocketbook, and—and—he's dead crooked.
Leastways, that's how Mansell says.   It's bin
roulette, poker an' faro.   An' he's bin runnin' the
joint.   Mansell says he ain't no sort o' use for him
no ways, and that he cut adrift from the boy directly
he got crooked."

" Oh, he did, did he ? " said Dave, after a thoughtful pause. " I don't seem to remember that Dick
Mansell was any saint.   I'd have thought a crooked
life would have fallen in with his views, but he preferred to turn the lad adrift when he most needed
help.   However, it don't signify.   So the lad's
coming back a drunkard, a gambler and a crook ?
At least Dick Mansell says so.   Does he say why
he's coming back ? "

" Well, he s'poses it's the girl—Miss Betty."

" Ah ! "

Joe shifted uneasily.

" It don't seem right—him a crook," he said, with
some diffidence.

" No."   Then Dave's thoughtful look suddenly

changed to one of business alertness, and his tone became crisp. " See here, Joe, what about that new tackle for the mills ? Those hooks and chains must be ready in a week. Then there's those cant-hooks for the hill camps. The smiths up there are hard at it, so I'm going to look to you for a lot. Then there's another thing. Is your boy Alec fit to join the mills and take his place with the other smiths ? I want another hand."

" Sure, he's a right good lad—an' thankee. I'll send him along right away." The blacksmith was delighted. He always wanted to get his boy taken on at the mill. The work that came his way he could cope with himself ; besides, he had an assistant. He didn't want his boy working under him ; it was not his idea of things. It was far better that he should get out and work under strangers.

" Well, that's settled."

Dave turned to his dinner and Joe Hardwig took his leave, and when mother and son were left to-gether again the old woman lost no time in discuss-ing Dick Mansell and his unpleasant news.

" I never could bear that Mansell," she said, with a severe shake of her head.

" No, ma. But he's a good sawyer—and I need such men."

The old woman looked up quickly.

" I was thinking of Jim Truscott."

" That's how I guessed."

" Well ? What do you think ? "

Dave shook his head.

"I haven't seen Jim yet," he said. "Ma, we ain't Jim's judges."

"No."

"I'm going down to the depot," Dave said after a while. "Guess I've got some messages to send. I'm getting anxious about that strike. They say that neither side will give way. The railway is pretty arbitrary on this point, and the plate-layers are a strong union. I've heard that the brakesmen and engine-drivers are going to join them. If they do, it's going to be bad for us. That is, in a way. Strikes are infectious, and I don't want 'em around here just now. We've got to cut a hundred thousand foot a day steady, and anything delaying us means—well, it's no use thinking what it means. We've got to be at full work night and day until we finish. I'll get going."

He pushed his plate away and rose from the table. He paused while he filled and lit his pipe, then he left the house. Joe Hardwig's news had disturbed him more than he cared to admit, and he did not want to discuss it, even with his mother.

CHAPTER V

JIM TRUSCOTT RETURNS

DAVE was on the outskirts of the village when he fell in with Parson Tom. Tom was on ahead, but he saw the great lumbering figure swinging along the trail behind him, and waited.

" Hello, Dave," he greeted him, as he came up. " It's ages since I've seen you."

The master of the mills laughed good-naturedly.

" Sure," he said, " my loafing days are over. I'll be ground hollow before I'm through. The grindstone's good and going. It's good to be at work, Tom. I mean what you'd call at your great work. When I'm through you shall have the finest church that red pine can build."

" Ah, it's good to hear you talk like that. I take it things are running smoothly. It's not many men who deserve to make millions, but I think you are one of the few."

Dave shook his head.

" You're prejudiced about me, Tom," he replied smiling, " but I want that money. And when I get it we'll carry out all our schemes. You know, the schemes we've talked over and planned and planned. Well, when the time comes, we won't forget 'em ——"

" Like most people do. Hello!" The parson

was looking ahead in the direction of a small crowd standing· outside Harley-Smith's saloon. There was an anxious look in his clear blue eyes, and some comprehension. The crowd was swaying about in unmistakable fashion, and experience told him that a fight was in progress. He had seen so many fights in Malkern. Suddenly he turned to Dave —

" Where are you going ? " he inquired.

" To the depot."

" Good. I'll just cut along over there. That must be stopped."

Dave gazed at the swaying crowd. Several men were running to join it. Then he looked down from his great height at the slim, athletic figure of his friend.

" Do you want any help ? " he inquired casually.

Parson Tom shook his head.

" No," he said, with a smile of perfect confidence. " They're children, all simple children. Big and awkward and unruly, if you like, but all children. I can manage them."

" I believe you can," said Dave. " Well, so long. Don't be too hard on them. Remember they're children."

Tom Chepstow laughed back at him as he hurried away.

" All right. But unruly children need physical correction as well as moral. And if it is necessary I shan't spare them."

He went off at a run, and Dave went on to the

depot. He knew his friend down to his very core. There was no man in the village who was the parson's equal in the noble art of self-defense. And it was part of his creed to meet the rougher members of his flock on their own ground. He knew that this militant churchman would stop that fight, and, if necessary, bodily chastise the offenders. It was this wholesome manliness that had so endeared the " fighting parson " to his people. They loved him for his capacity, and consequently respected him far more than they would have done the holiest preacher that ever breathed. He was a man they understood.

The spiritual care of a small lumbering village is not lightly to be entered upon. A man must be peculiarly fitted for it. In such a place, where human nature is always at its crudest; where muscle, and not intellect, must always be the dominant note; where life is lived without a thought for the future, and the present concern is only the individual fitness to execute a maximum of labor, and so give expression to a savage vanity in the triumph of brute force, the man who would set out to guide his fellows must possess qualities all too rare in the general run of clergy. His theology must be of the simplest, broadest order. He must live the life of his flock, and teach almost wholly by example. His preaching must be lit with a local setting, and his brush must lay on the color of his people's every-day life.

Besides this, he must possess a tremendous

moral and physical courage, particularly the latter, for to the lumber-jack nothing else so appeals. He must feel that he is in the presence of a man who is always his equal, if not his superior, in those things he understands. Tom Chepstow was all this. He was a lumberman himself at heart. He knew every detail of the craft. He had lived that life all his manhood's days.

Then he possessed a rare gift in medicine. He had purposely studied it and taken his degrees, for no one knew better than he the strength this added to his position. He shed his healing powers upon his people, a gift that reaped him a devotion no sanctity and godliness could ever have brought him. Parson Tom was a practical Christian first, and attended only to spiritual welfare when the body had been duly cared for.

Dave went on to the depot, where he despatched his messages. Then he extracted from Jenkins Mudley all the information he possessed upon the matter of the plate-layers' strike, and finally took the river trail back to the mills.

His way took him across the log bridge over the river, and here he paused, leaning upon the rail, and gazed thoughtfully down the woodland avenue which enclosed the turbulent stream.

Somehow he could never cross that bridge without pausing to admire the wonderful beauty of his little friend's surroundings. He always thought of this river as his friend. How much it was his friend only he knew. But for it, and its peculiarities, his work would be impossible. He did not have to do as so many lumbermen have to, depend on the spring freshet to carry his winter cut down to his mill. The melting snows of the mountains kept the river flowing, a veritable torrent, during the whole of the open season, and at such time he possessed in it a never-failing transport line which cost him not one cent.

The hour he had allowed for his dinner was not yet up, and he felt that he could indulge himself a little longer, so he refilled his pipe and smoked while he gazed contemplatively into the depths of the dancing waters below him.

But his day-dreaming was promptly interrupted, and the interruption was the coming of Betty, on her way home to her dinner from the schoolhouse up on the hillside. He had seen her only once since the day that brought him the news of his contract. That was on the following Sunday, when he went, as usual, to Tom Chepstow's for supper.

Just at that moment Betty was the last person he wanted to see. That was his first thought when he heard her step on the bridge. He had forgotten that this was her way home, and that this was her dinner-time. However, there was no sign of his reluctance in his face when he greeted her.

" Why, Betty," he said, as gently as his great voice would let him, " I hadn't thought to see you coming this way." Then he broke off and studied her pretty oval face more closely. " What's wrong?" he inquired presently. "You look—you look kind of tired."

He was quite right. The girl looked pale under her tan, and there was an unusual darkness round her gentle brown eyes. She looked very tired, in spite of the smile of welcome with which she greeted him.

"Oh, I'm all right, Dave," she said at once. But her tone was cheerless, in spite of her best effort.

He shook his great head and knocked his pipe out.

"There's something amiss, child. Guess maybe it's the heat." He turned his eyes up to the blazing sun, as though to reassure himself that the heat was there.

Betty leant beside him on the rail. Her proximity, and the evident sadness of her whole manner, made him realize that he must not stay there. At that moment she looked such a pathetic little figure that he felt he could not long be responsible for what he said. He longed to take her in his arms and comfort her.

He could think of nothing to say for a long time, but at last he broke out with—

"You'd best not go back to the school this afternoon."

But the girl shook her head.

"It's not that," she said. Then she paused. Her eyes were fixed on the rushing water as it flowed beneath the bridge.

He watched her closely, and gradually a conviction began to grow in his mind.

" Dave," she went on at last, " we've always been such good friends, haven't we? You've always been so patient and kind with me when I have bothered you with my little troubles and worries. You never fail to help me out. It seems to me I can never quite do without your help. I—I "— she smiled more like her old self, and with relief the man saw some of the alarming shadows vanishing from her face, " I don't think I want to, either. I've had a long talk with Susan Hardwig this morning."

" Ah!"

The man's growing conviction had received confirmation.

" What did that mean?" Betty asked quickly.

Dave was staring out down the river.

" Just nothing. Only I've had a goodish talk with Joe Hardwig."

" Then I needn't go into the details. I've heard the news that Dick Mansell has brought with him."

It was a long time before either spoke again. For Dave there seemed so little to say. What could he say? Sympathy was out of the question. He had no right to blame Jim yet. Nor did he feel that he could hold out hope to her, for in his heart he believed that the man's news was true.

With Betty, she hardly knew how to express her feelings. She hardly knew what her feelings were. At the time Mrs. Hardwig poured her tale into her ears she had listened quite impersonally. Somehow the story had not appealed to her as concerning herself, and her dominant thought had been pity for the man. It was not until afterward, when she was alone on her way to the school, that the full significance of it came to her; and then it came as a shock. She remembered, all of a sudden, that she was promised to Jim. That when Jim came back she was to marry him. From that moment the matter had never been out of her mind; through all her school hours it was with her, and her attention had been so distracted from her work that she found her small pupils getting out of band.

Yes, she was to marry Jim, and they told her he was a drunkard, a gambler, and a " crook." She had given him her promise; she had sent him away. It was her own doing. Her feelings toward him never came into her thoughts. During the long five years of his absence he had become a sort of habit to her. She had never thought of her real feelings after the first month or two of his going. She was simply waiting for him, and would marry him when he came. It was only now, when she heard this story of him, that her feelings were called upon to assert themselves, and the result was something very like horror at her own position.

She remembered now her disappointment at the first realization of all her hopes, when Jim had asked her to marry him. She had not understood then, but now—now she did. She knew that she had never really loved him. And at the thought of his return she was filled with horror and dread.

She was glad that she had met Dave; she had longed to see him. He was the one person she could always lean on. And in her present trouble she wanted to lean on him.

" Dave," she began at last, in a voice so hopeless that it cut him to the heart, " somehow I believe that story. That is, in the main. Don't think it makes any difference to me. I shall marry him just the same. Only I seem to see him in his real light now. He was always weak, only I didn't see it then. He was not really the man to go out into the world to fight alone. We were wrong. I was wrong. He should have stayed here."

" Yes," Dave nodded.

" He must begin over again," she went on, after a pause. " When he comes here we must help him to a fresh start, and we must blot his past out of our minds altogether. There is time enough. He is young. Now I want you to help me. We must ask him no questions. If he wants to speak he can do so. Now that you are booming at the mills we can help him to reopen his mill, and I know you can, and will, help him by putting work in his way. All this is what I've been thinking out. When he comes, and we are—married," there was the slightest possible hesitation before the word, and Dave's quick ears and quicker senses were swift to hear and interpret it, " I am going to help him with the work. I'll give up my school. I've always had such a contingency in my mind. That's why I got you to teach me your work when he first went

away.   Tell me, Dave, you'll help me in this.   You
see the boy can't help his weakness.   Perhaps we are
stronger than he, and between us we can help him."

The man looked at her a long time in silence, and
all the while his loyal heart was crying out.   His
gray eyes shone with a light she did not compre-
hend.   She saw their fixed smile, and only read in
them the assent he never withheld from her.

" I knew you would," she murmured.

It was her voice that roused him.   And he spoke
just as she turned away in the direction of the
schoolhouse trail, whence proceeded the sound of
a horse galloping.

" Yes, Betty—I'll help you sure," he said in his
deep voice.

" You'll help him, you mean," she corrected,
turning back to him.

But Dave ignored the correction.

" Tell me, Betty," he went on again, this time
with evident diffidence : " you're glad he's coming
back?   You feel happy about—about getting married?   You—love him ? "

The girl stared straight up into the plain face.
Her look was so honest, so full of decision, that her
reply left no more to be said.

" Five years ago I gave him my promise.   That
promise I shall redeem, unless Jim, himself, makes
its fulfilment impossible."

The man nodded.

" You can come to me for anything you need for
him," he said simply.

Betty was about to answer with an outburst of gratitude when, with a rush, a horseman came galloping round the bend of the trail and clattered on to the bridge. At sight of the two figures standing by the rail the horse jibbed, threw himself on to his haunches, and then shied so violently that the rider was unseated and half out of the saddle, clinging desperately to the animal's neck to right himself. And as he hung there struggling, the string of filthy oaths that were hurled at the horse, and any and everybody, was so foul that Betty tried to stop her ears.

Dave sprang at the horse and seized the bridle with one hand, with the other he grabbed the horseman and thrust him up into the saddle. The feat could only have been performed by a man of his herculean strength.

" Cut that language, you gopher!" he roared into the fellow's ears as he lifted him.

" Cut the language!" cried the infuriated man. " What in hell are you standing on a bridge spooning your girl for? This bridge ain't for that sort of truck—it's for traffic, curse you!"

By the time the man had finished speaking he had straightened up in the saddle, and his face was visible to all. Dave jumped back, and Betty gave a little cry. It was Jim Truscott!

Yes, it was Jim Truscott, but so changed that even Betty could scarcely believe the evidence of her eyes. In place of the bright, clever-looking face, the slim figure she had always had in her mind during the long five years of his absence, she now beheld a bloated, bearded man, without one particle of the old refinement which had been one of his most pronounced characteristics. It seemed incredible that five years could have so changed him. Even his voice was almost unrecognizable, so husky had it become. His eyes no longer had their look of frank honesty, they were dull and lustreless, and leered morosely. Her heart sank as she looked at him, and she remembered Dick Mansell's story.

All three stared for a moment without speaking. Then Jim broke into a laugh so harsh that it made the girl shudder.

"Well I'm damned!" he cried. "Of all the welcomes home this beats hell!"

"Jim—oh, Jim!"

The cry of horror and pain was literally wrung from the girl. Nor was it without effect. The man seemed to realize his uncouthness, for he suddenly took off his hat, and his face became serious.

"I beg your pardon, Betty," he said apologetically. "I forgot where I was. I forgot that the Yukon was behind me, and ——"

"That you're talking to the lady you're engaged to be married to," put in Dave sharply.

Dave's words drew the younger man's attention to himself. For a second a malicious flash shone in the bloated eyes. Then he dropped them and held out his hand.

"How do, Dave?" he said coldly.

Dave responded without any enthusiasm. He was chilled, chilled and horrified, and he knew that Mansell's story was no exaggeration. He watched Jim turn again to Betty. He saw the strained look in the girl's eyes, and he waited.

" I'll come along up to the house later," Jim said coolly. " Guess I'll get along to the hotel and get cleaned some. I allow I ain't fit for party calls at a hog pen just about now. So long."

He jabbed his horse's sides with his heels and dashed across the bridge. In a moment he was gone.

It was some time before a word was spoken on the bridge. Dave was waiting, and Betty could find no words. She was frightened. She wanted to cry, and through it all her heart felt like lead in her bosom. But her dominant feeling was fear.

" Well, little Betty," said Dave presently, in that gentle protecting manner he so often assumed toward her, " I must go on to the mills. What are you going to do?"

" I'm going home," she said ; and to the keenly sympathetic ears of the man the note of misery in her voice was all too plain.

CHAPTER VI

IT was nearly five o'clock and the table was set for tea. Betty was standing at the window staring thoughtfully out upon the valley. Ordinarily her contemplation would have been one of delighted interest, for the scene was her favorite view of the valley, where every feature of it, the village, the mill, the river, assumed its most picturesque aspect.

She loved the valley with a deep affection. Unlike most people, who tire of their childhood's surroundings and pant for fresh sights, fresh fields in which to expand their thoughts and feelings, she clung to the valley with all an artist's love for the beautiful, and a strength inspired by the loyal affection of a simple woman. Her delight in her surroundings amounted almost to a passion. To her this valley was a treasured possession. The river was a friend, a fiery, turbulent friend, and often she had declared, when in a whimsical mood, one to whom she could tell her innermost secrets without fear of their being passed on, in confidence, to another, or of having them flung back in her face when spite stirred its tempestuous soul.

She knew her river's shortcomings, she knew its every mood. It was merely a torrent, a strenuous mountain torrent, but to her it possessed a real personality. In the spring flood it was like some small individual bursting with its own importance, with its vanity, with resentment at the restraint of the iron hand of winter, from which it had only just torn itself loose, and stirred to the depths of its frothy soul with an overwhelming desire for self-assertion. Often she had watched the splendid destruction of which it was capable at such a time. She had seen the forest giants go down at the roar of its battle-cry. She had often joined the villagers, standing fearful and dismayed, watching its mounting waters lest their homes should be devoured by the insatiable little monster, and filled with awe at its magnificent bluster.

Then, in the extreme heat of the late summer, when autumn had tinged the valley to a glorious gold and russet, she had just as often seen the reverse side of the picture. No longer could the river draw on the vast supplies of the melting mountain snows, and so it was doomed to fall a prey to the mighty grip of winter, and, as if in anticipation of its end, it would sing its song of sadness as it sobbed quietly over its fallen greatness, sighing dismally amongst the débris which in the days of its power it had so wantonly torn from its banks.

There was a great deal of the girl's character in her love for the river. She possessed an enthusiastic admiration for that strength which fights, fights until the last drop of blood, the last atom of power is expended. Fallen greatness evoked her enthusiasm as keenly as success, only that the enthusiasm was of a different nature. With her it was better to have striven with all one's might and encountered disaster than to have lived fallow, a life of the most perfect rectitude. Her twenty-seven years of life had set her thrilling with a mental and physical virility which was forever urging her, and steadily moulding her whole outlook upon life, even though that outlook carried her no farther than the confines of her beautiful sunlit valley.

Something of this was stirring within her now. She was not thinking of that which her eyes looked upon. She was thinking of the man to whom she had given her promise, her woman's promise, which carries with it all the best a woman has to give. She was no weakling, dreaming regretfully of all that might have been; she had no thought of re-tracting because in her heart she knew she had made a mistake. She was reviewing the man as she had seen him that noon, and considering the story of his doings as she had been told them, quietly making up her mind to her own line of action.

He was presently to come up to her home to have tea with them, and she would be given the opportunity of seeing the man that five years' absence in the wilds had made of him. Once or twice she almost shuddered as the details of their meeting on the bridge obtruded themselves. She tried to shut them out. She understood the rough side of men, for she lived amongst a people in

whom it was difficult enough to trace even a semblance of gentleness. She allowed for the moment
of provocation when the man's horse had shied and
unseated him. She realized the natural inclination
it would inspire to forcibly, even if irresponsibly,
protest. Even the manner of his protest she con-
doned. But his subsequent attitude, his appearance, and his manner toward herself, these were
things which had an ugly tone, and for which she
could find no extenuation.

However, it should all be settled that afternoon.
She unfolded and straightened out a piece of paper
she had been abstractedly crumpling in her hand.
She glanced at the unsteady writing on it, a writing
she hardly recognized as Jim's.

" Will come up to tea this afternoon. Sorry for
this morning.—Jim."

That was the note he had sent her soon after she
had reached home. There was no word of affection
in it. Nothing but a bare statement and an apology
which scarcely warranted the name. To her it
seemed to have been prompted by the man's
realization of an unpleasant and undesired duty to
be performed. The few letters she had received
from him immediately before his return had borne
a similar tone of indifference, and once or twice she
had felt that she ought to write and offer him his
freedom. This, however, she had never done, feeling that by doing so she might be laying herself
open to misinterpretation. No, if their engage-

ment were distasteful to him, it must be Jim who broke it.   Unlike most women, she would rather he threw her over than bear the stigma of having jilted him.   She had thought this all out very carefully.   She had an almost mannish sense of honor, just as she possessed something of a man's courage to carry out her obligations.

She glanced over the tea-table.   There were four places set.   The table was daintily arranged, and though the china was cheap, and there was no display of silver, or any elaborate furnishings, it looked attractive.   The bread and butter was delicate, the assortment of home-made cakes luscious, the preserves the choicest from her aunt's store-cupboard.   Betty had been careful, too, that the little sitting-room, with its simple furniture and unpretentious decorations, should be in the nicest order.   She had looked to everything so that Jim's welcome should be as cordial as kindly hearts could make it.   And now she was awaiting his coming.

The clock on the sideboard chimed five, and a few moments later her uncle came in.

" What about tea, Betty ? " he inquired, glancing with approval at the careful preparations for the meal.

" I think we ought to wait," she replied, with a wistful smile into his keen blue eyes.   " I sent word to Jim for five o'clock—but—well, perhaps something has detained him."

" No doubt," observed the parson dryly.   " I

dare say five minutes added on to five years means
nothing to Jim."

He didn't approve the man's attitude at all.   All
his ideas on the subject of courtship had been outraged at his delay in calling.   He had been in the
village nearly five hours.

The girl rearranged the teacups.

" You mustn't be hard on him," she said quietly.
" He had to get cleaned up and settled at the hotel.
I don't suppose he'd care to come here like—
like ——"

" It doesn't take a man five hours to do all that,"
broke in her uncle, with some warmth.   Then, as
he faced the steady gaze of the girl's brown eyes,
he abruptly changed his tone and smiled at her.
" Yes, of course we'll wait.   We'll give him half an
hour's grace, and then—I'll fetch him."

Betty smiled.   There was a characteristic snap in
the parson's final declaration.   The militant character of the man was always very near the surface.
He was the kindest and best of men, but anything
suggesting lack of straightforwardness in those from
whom he had a right to expect the reverse never
failed to rouse his ire.

For want of something better to do Betty was
carrying out a further rearrangement of the tea-
table, and presently her uncle questioned her
shrewdly.

" You don't seem very elated at Jim's return ? "
he said.

" I am more than pleased," she replied gravely.

Parson Tom took up his stand at the window with his back turned.

" When I was engaged to your aunt," he said, smiling out at the valley, " if I had been away for five years and suddenly returned, she would probably have had about three fits, a scene of shrieking hysteria, and gone to bed for a week.   By all of which I mean she would have been simply crazy with delight.   It must be the difference of temperament, eh ? "   He turned round and stood smiling keenly across at the girl's serious face.

" Yes, uncle, I don't think I am demonstrative."

" Do you want to marry him ? "

The man's eyes were perfectly serious now.

" I am going to marry him—unless——"

" Unless ? "

" Unless he refuses to marry me."

" Do you want to marry him, my dear?   That was my question."

Her uncle had crossed over to her and stood looking down at her with infinite tenderness in his eyes.   She returned his gaze, and slowly a smile replaced her gravity.

" You are very literal, uncle," she said gently. " If you want an absolutely direct reply it is ‘ Yes.’ "

But her uncle was not quite satisfied.

" You—love him ? " he persisted.

But this catechism was too much for Betty.   She was devoted to her uncle, and she knew that his questions were prompted by the kindliest motives.

But in this matter she felt that she was entirely justified in thinking and acting for herself.

"You don't quite understand," she said, with just a shade of impatience. "Jim and I are engaged, and you must leave us to settle matters ourselves. If you press me I shall speak the plain truth, and then you will have a wrong impression of the position. I perfectly understand my own feelings. I am not blinded by them. I shall act as I think best, and you must rely on my own judgment. I quite realize that you want to help me. But neither you nor any one else can do that, uncle. Ah, here is auntie," she exclaimed, with evident relief.

Mrs. Chepstow came in. She was hot from her work in the kitchen, where she was operating, with the aid of her " hired " girl, a large bake of cakes for the poorer villagers. She looked at the clock sharply.

"Why, it's half-past five and no tea," she exclaimed, her round face shining, and her gentle eyes wide open. "Where's Jim? Not here? Why, I am astonished. Betty, what are you thinking of? —and after five years, too."

"Betty hasn't got him in proper harness yet," laughed the parson, but there was a look in his eyes which was not in harmony with his laugh.

"Harness? Don't be absurd, Tom." Then she turned to Betty. "Did you tell him five?"

Tom Chepstow picked up his hat, and before the girl could answer he was at the door.

"I'm going to fetch him," he said, and was gone before Betty's protest reached him.

· "I do wish uncle wouldn't interfere," the girl said, as her aunt laughed at her husband's precipitate exit.

"Interfere, my dear!" she exclaimed. "You can't stop him. He's got a perverted notion that we women are incapable of taking care of ourselves. He goes through life determined to fight our battles. Determined to help us out when we don't need it. He's helped me 'out' all our married life. He spends his life doing it, and I often wish he'd—he'd leave me 'in' sometimes. I've never seen a man who could upset a woman's plans more completely than your uncle, and all with the best intention. One of these days I'll start to help him out, and then we'll see how he likes it," she laughed good-humoredly. "You know, if he finds Jim he's sure to upset the boy, and he'll come back thinking he's done his duty by you. Poor Tom, and he does mean so well."

"I know he does, auntie, and that's why we all love him so. Everybody loves him for it. He never thinks of himself. It's always others, and——"

"Yes, my dear, you're right. But all the same I think he's right just now. Why isn't Jim here? Why didn't he come straight away? Why has he been in Malkern five hours before he comes to see you? Betty, my child, I've not said a word all these years. I've left you to your own affairs because I know your good sense; but, in view of the stories that have reached us about Jim, I feel that the time has come for me to speak. Are you going to verify those stories?"

Mrs. Chepstow established her comfortable form in a basket chair, which audibly protested at the weight it was called upon to bear. She folded her hands in her lap, and, assuming her most judicial air, waited for the girl's answer. Betty was thinking of her meeting with Jim on the bridge.

"I shall hear what he has to say," she said decidedly, after a long pause.

Her aunt stared.

"You're going to let him tell you what he likes?" she cried in astonishment.

"He can tell me what he chooses, or—he need tell me nothing."

Her aunt flushed indignantly.

"You will never be so foolish," she said, exasperated.

"Auntie, if Uncle Tom had been away five years, would you ask him for proof of his life all that time?" Betty demanded with some warmth.

The other stirred uneasily.

"That depends," she said evasively.

"No, no, auntie, it doesn't. You would never question uncle. You are a woman, and just as foolish and stupid about that sort of thing as the rest of us. We must take our men on trust. They are men, and their lives are different from ours. We cannot judge them, or, at any rate, we would rather not. Why does a woman cling to a scoundrelly husband who ill-treats her and makes her life one long round of worry, and even misery? Is it because she simply has to? No. It is because he is her man. He is hers, and she would rather have his unkindness than another man's caresses. Foolish we may be, and I am not sure but that we would rather be foolish—where our men are concerned. Jim has come back. His past five years are his. I am going to take up my little story where it was broken five years ago. The stories I have heard are nothing to me. So, if you don't mind, dear, we will close the subject."

" And—and you love him? " questioned the elder woman.

But the girl had turned to the window. She pointed out down the road in the direction of the village.

" Here is uncle returning," she said, ignoring the question. " He's hurrying. Why—he's actually running ! "

" Running? "

Mrs. Chepstow bustled to the girl's side, and both stood watching the vigorous form of the parson racing up the trail. Just as he came to the veranda they turned from the window and their eyes met. Betty's were full of pained apprehension, while her aunt's were alight with perplexed curiosity. Betty felt that she knew something of the meaning of her uncle's undignified haste. She did not actually interpret it, she knew it meant disaster, but the nature of that disaster never entered into her thought. Something was wrong, she knew instinctively ; and, with the patience of strength, she made no attempt to even guess at it, but simply waited.   Her aunt rushed at the parson as he entered the room and flung aside his soft felt hat.   Betty gazed mutely at the flaming anger she saw in his blue eyes, as his wife questioned him.

" What is it ? " she demanded.   " What has happened ? "

Parson Tom drew a chair up to the table and flung himself into it.

" We'll have tea," he said curtly.

His wife obediently took her seat.

" And Jim ? " she questioned.

The angry blue eyes still flashed.

" We won't wait for him."

Then Betty came to the man's side and laid one small brown hand firmly on his shoulder.

" You—you saw him ? " she demanded.

Her uncle shook her hand off almost roughly.

" Yes—I saw him," he said.

" And why isn't he here ? " the girl persisted without a tremor, without even noticing his rebuff.

" Because he's lying on his bed at the hotel— drunk.   Blind drunk,—confound him."

CHAPTER VII

THE WORK AT THE MILLS

IT was sundown. The evening shadows, long drawn out, were rapidly merging into the purple shades of twilight. The hush of night was stealing upon the valley.

There was one voice alone, one discordant note, to jar upon the peace of Nature's repose. It was the voice of Dave's mills, a voice that was never silent. The village, with all its bustling life, its noisy boarding-houses, its well-filled drinking booths, its roystering lumber-jacks released from their day's toil, was powerless to disturb that repose. But the harsh voice of the driving machinery rose dominant above all other sounds. Repose was impossible, even for Nature, where the restless spirit of Dave's enterprise prevailed.

The vast wooden structures of the mills, acres of them, stood like some devouring growth at the very core of Nature's fair body. It almost seemed like a living organism feeding upon all the best she had to yield. Day and night the saws, like the gleaming fangs of a voracious life, tore, devoured, digested, and the song of its labors droned without ceasing.

Controlling, directing, ordering to the last detail, Dave sat in his unpretentious office. Love of the lumberman's craft ran hot in his veins. He had

been born and bred to it.   He had passed through
its every phase.   He was a sawyer whose name
was historical in the forests of Oregon.   As a cant-
hook man he had few equals.   As foreman he could
extract more work from these simple woodsman
giants than could those he employed in a similar
capacity.

In work he was inevitable.   His men knew that
when he demanded they must yield.   In this direction he displayed no sympathy, no gentleness.   He
knew the disposition of the lumber-jack.   These
woodsmen rate their employer by his driving
power.   They understand and expect to be ruled by
a stern discipline, and if this treatment is not forthcoming, their employer may just as well abandon
his enterprise for all the work they will yield him.

But though this was Dave in his business, it was
the result of his tremendous force of character
rather than the nature of the man.   If he drove, it
was honestly, legitimately.   He paid for the best a
man could give him, and he saw that he got it.
Sickness was sure of ready sympathy, not out-
spoken, but practical.   He was much like the prai-
rie man with his horse.   His beast is cared for far
better than its master cares for himself, but it must
work, and work enthusiastically to the last ounce of
its power.   Fail, and the horse must go.   So it
was with Dave.   The man who failed him would
receive his " time " instantly.   There was no question, no excuse.   And every lumber-jack knew this
and gladly entered his service.

Dave was closeted with his foreman, Joel Dawson, receiving the day's report.

" The tally's eighty thousand," Dawson was saying.

Dave looked up from his books. His keen, humorous eyes surveyed the man's squat figure.

" Not enough," he said.

" She's pressing hard now," came the man's rejoinder, almost defensively.

" She's got to do twenty thousand more," retorted Dave finally.

" Then y'll have to give her more saw room."

" We'll see to it.   Meanwhile shove her.   How are the logs running?   Is Mason keeping the length ? "

" Guess he cayn't do better.   We ain't handled nothin' under eighty foot."

" Good.   They're driving down the river fast ? "

" The boom's full, an' we're workin' 'em good an' plenty."   The man paused.   " 'Bout more saw beds an' rollers," he went on a moment later. " Ther' ain't an inch o' space, boss.   We'll hev to build."

Dave shook his head and faced round from his desk.

" There's no time.   You'll have to take out the gang saws and replace them for log trimming."

Dawson spat into the spittoon.   He eyed the ugly, powerful young features of his boss speculatively while he made a swift mental calculation.

" That'll mebbe give us eight thousand more.

'Tain't enough, I guess," he said emphatically.
" Say, there's that mill up river. Her as belongs
to Jim Truscott. If we had her runnin' I 'lows
we'd handle twenty-five thousand on a day and
night shift. Givin' us fifty all told."

Dave's eyes lit.

" I've thought of that," he said. " That'll put us
up with a small margin. I'll see what can be
done. How are the new boys making ? I've had
a good report from Mason up on No. 1 camp.
He's transferred his older hands to new camps, and
has the new men with him. He's started to cut on
Section 80. His estimate is ten million in the
stump on that cut; all big stuff. He's running a
big saw-gang up there. The roads were easy making and good for travoying, and most of the timber
is within half a mile of the river. We don't need
to worry about the ‘drive.’ He's got the stuff
plenty, and all the ‘hands’ he needs. It's the mill
right here that's worrying."

Dawson took a fresh chew.

" Yes, it's the mill, I guess," he said slowly.
" That an' this yer strike. We're goin' to feel it—
the strike, I mean. The engineers and firemen are
going ‘ out,’ I hear, sure."

" That doesn't hit us," said Dave sharply. But
there was a keen look of inquiry in his eyes.

" Don't it ? " Dawson raised his shaggy eye-
brows.

" Our stuff is merely to be placed on board
here. The government will see to its transport."

The foreman shook his head.

"What o' them firemen an' engineers in the mill? Say, they're mostly union men, an' —— "

"I see." Dave became thoughtful.

"Guess that ain't the only trouble neither," Dawson went on, warming. "Strikes is hell-fire anyways. Ther' ain't no stoppin' 'em when they git good an' goin'. Ther's folk who'd hate work wuss'n pizin when others, of a different craft, are buckin'. I hate strikes, anyway, an' I'll feel a sight easier when the railroaders quits."

"You're alarming yourself without need," Dave said easily, closing his books and rising from his seat. "Guess I'll get to supper. And see you remember I look to you to shove her. Are you posting the ' tally ' ? "

"Sure. They're goin' up every shift."

A few minutes later the foreman took his departure to hand over to Simon Odd, who ran the mills at night. Dave watched him go. Then, instead of going off to his supper, he sat down again.

Dawson's warning was not without its effect on him, in spite of the easy manner in which he had set it aside. If his mills were to be affected by the strike it would be the worst disaster that could befall—short of fire. To find himself with millions of feet coming down the river on the drive and no possibility of getting it cut would mean absolute ruin. Yes, it was a nasty thought. A thought so unpleasant that he promptly set it aside and turned his attention to more pleasant matters.

One of the most pleasant that occurred to him was the condition of things in the village. Malkern had already begun to boom as the first result of his sudden burst of increased work. Outside capital was coming in for town plots, and several fresh buildings were going up. Addlestone Chicks, the dry-goods storekeeper, was extending his premises to accommodate the enormous increase in his trade. Two more saloons were being considered, both to be built by men from Calford, and the railroad had promised two mails a day instead of one.

Dave thought of these things with the satisfaction of a man who is steadily realizing his ambitions. It only needed his success for prosperity to come automatically to the village in the valley. That was it, his success. This thought brought to his mind again the matter of Jim Truscott's mill, and this, again, set him thinking of Jim himself.

He had seen nothing of Jim since his meeting with him on the bridge, and the memory of that meeting was a dark shadow in his recollection. Since that time two days had passed, two days spent in arduous labor, when there had been no time for more than a passing thought for anything else. He had seen no one outside of his mills. He had seen neither Betty nor her uncle; no one who could tell him how matters were going with the prodigal. He felt somehow that he had been neg-lectful, he felt that he had wrongfully allowed him-self to be swamped in the vortex of the whirling waters of his labors. He had purposely shut out every other consideration.

Now his mind turned upon Betty, and he suddenly decided to take half an hour's respite and visit Harley-Smith's saloon. He felt that this would be the best direction in which to seek Jim Truscott. Five years ago it would have been different.

He rose from his seat and stretched his cumbersome body. Young as he was, he felt stiff. His tremendous effort was making itself felt. Picking up his pipe he lit it, and as he dropped the charred end of the match in the spittoon a knock came at the door. It opened in answer to his call, and in the half-light of the evening he recognized the very man whom he had just decided to seek.

It was Jim Truscott who stood in the doorway peering into the darkened room. And at last his searching eyes rested on the enormous figure of the lumberman. Dave was well in the shadow, and what light came in through the window fell full upon the newcomer's face.

In the brief silence he had a good look at him. He saw that now he was clean-shaven, that his hair had been trimmed, that his clothes were good and belonged to the more civilized conditions of city life. He was good-looking beyond a doubt; a face, he thought, to catch a young girl's fancy. There was something romantic in the dark setting of the eyes, the keen aquiline nose, the broad forehead. It was only the lower part of the face that he found fault with. There was that vicious weakness about the mouth and chin, and it set him pondering. There were the marks of dissipation about the eyes too, only now they were a hundredfold more pronounced. Where before the rounded cheeks had once so smoothly sloped away, now there were puffings, with deep, unwholesome furrows which, in a man of his age, had no right to be there.

Jim was the first to speak, and his manner was almost defiant.

" Well ? " he ejaculated.

" Well ? " responded Dave ; and the newly-opened waters suddenly froze over again.

They measured each other, eye to eye. Both had the memory of their meeting two days ago keenly alive in their thought. Finally Jim broke into a laugh that sounded harshly.

" After five years' absence your cordiality is overwhelming," he said.

" I seem to remember meeting you on the bridge two days ago," retorted Dave.

Then he turned to his desk and lit the lamp. The mill siren hooted out its mournful cry. Its roar was deafening, and answered as an excuse for the silence which remained for some moments between the two men. When the last echo had died out Truscott spoke again. Evidently he had availed himself of those seconds to decide on a more conciliatory course.

" That's nerve-racking," he said lightly.

" Yes, if your nerves aren't in the best condi-

tion," replied Dave.   Then he indicated a chair and
both men seated themselves.

Truscott made himself comfortable and lit a cigar.

" Well, Dave," he said pleasantly, " after five years
I return here to find everybody talking of you, of
your work, of the fortune you are making, of the
prosperity of the village—which, by the way, is cred-
ited to your efforts.   You are the man of the moment in the valley; you are it !"

Dave nodded.

" Things are doing."

" Doing, man!   Why, it's the most wonderful
thing.   I leave a little dozy village, and I come
back to a town thrilling with a magnificent prosperity, with money in plenty for everybody, and on
every hand talk of investment, and dreams of fortunes to be made.   I'm glad I came.   I'm glad I
left that benighted country of cold and empty
stomachs and returned to this veritable Tom Tid-
dler's ground.   I too intend to share in the prosperity you have brought about.   Dave, you are a
wonder."

" I thought you'd come to talk of other matters,"
said Dave quietly.

His words had ample effect.   The enthusiasm
dropped from the other like a cloak.   His face lost
its smile, and his eyes became watchful.

" You mean ——"

" Betty," said Dave shortly.

Truscott stirred uneasily.   Dave's directness was
a little disconcerting.   Suddenly the latter leant

forward in his chair, and his steady eyes held his visitor.

"Five years ago, Jim, you went away, and, going, you left Betty to my care—for you. That child has always been in my thoughts, and though I've never had an opportunity to afford her the protection you asked of me, it has not been my fault. She has never once needed it. You went away to make money for her, so that when you came back you could marry her. I remember our meeting two days ago, and it's not my intention to say a thing of it. I have been so busy since then that I have seen nobody who could tell me of either her or you, so I know nothing of how your affairs stand. But if you've anything to say on the matter now I'm prepared to listen. Did you make good up there in the Yukon?"

Dave's tone was the tone Truscott had always known. It was kindly, it was strong with honesty and purpose. He felt easier for it, and his relief sounded in his reply.

"I can't complain," he said, settling himself more comfortably in his chair.

"I'm glad," said Dave simply. "I was doubtful of the experiment, but—well, I'm glad. And ——?"

Suddenly Jim sprang to his feet and began to pace the room. Dave watched him. He was reading him. He was studying the nervous movements, and interpreting them as surely as though their meaning were written large in the plainest lettering. It was the same man he had known five years ago—the same, only with a difference. He beheld the weakness he had realized before, but now, where there had been frank honesty in all his movements and expressions, there was a furtive undercurrent which suggested only too clearly the truth of the stories told about him.

"Dave," he burst out at last, coming to a sudden stand in front of him. "I've come to you about Betty. I've come to you to tell you all the regret I have at that meeting of ours on the bridge, and all I said at the time. I want to tell you that I'm a rotten fool and blackguard. That I haven't been near Betty since I came back. I was to have gone to tea that afternoon, and didn't do so because I got blind drunk instead, and when her uncle came to fetch me I told him to go to hell, and insulted him in a dozen ways. I want to tell you that while I was away I practically forgot Betty, I didn't care for her any longer, that I scarcely even regarded our engagement as serious. I feel I must tell you this. And now it is all changed. I have seen her and I want her. I love her madly, and—and I have spoiled all my chances. She'll never speak to me again. I am a fool and a crook—an utter wrong 'un, but I want her. I must have her!"

The man paused breathlessly. His words carried conviction. His manner was passion-swept. There could be no doubt as to his sincerity, or of the truth of the momentary remorse conveyed in his self-accusation.

Dave's teeth shut tight upon his pipe-stem.

" And you did all that?" he inquired with a tenseness that made his voice painfully harsh.

" Yes, yes, I did. Dave, you can't say any harder things to me than I've said to myself. When I drink there's madness in my blood that drives me where it will."

The other suddenly rose from his seat and towered over him. The look on his rugged face was one of mastery. His personality dominated Truscott at that moment in a manner that made him shrink before his steady, luminous eyes.

" How've you earned your living?" he demanded sharply.

" I'm a gambler," came Jim's uneasy reply, the truth forced from him against his will.

" You're a drunkard and a crook?"

" I'm a fool. I told you."

Dave accepted the admission.

" Then for God's sake get out of this village, and write and release Betty from her engagement. You say you love her. Prove it by releasing her, and be a man."

Dave's voice rang out deep with emotion. At that moment he was thinking of Betty, and not of the man before him. He was not there to judge him, his only thought was of the tragedy threatening the girl.

Truscott had suddenly become calm. and his eyes had again assumed that furtive watchfulness as he looked up into the larger man's face. He shook his head.

"I can't give her up," he said obstinately, after a pause.

Dave sat down again, watching the set, almost savage expression of the other's face. The position was difficult; he was not only dealing with this man, but with a woman whose sense of duty and honor was such that left him little hope of settling the matter as he felt it should be settled. Finally he decided to appeal again to the man's better nature.

"Jim," he said solemnly, "you come here and confess yourself a crook, and, if not a drunkard, at least a man with a bad tendency that way. You say you love Betty, in spite of having forgotten her while you were away. On your conscience I ask you, can you wilfully drag this girl, who has known only the purest, most innocent, and God-fearing life, into the path you admit you have been, are treading? Can you drag her down with you? Can you in your utter selfishness take her from a home where she is surrounded by all that can keep a woman pure and good? I don't believe it. That is not the Jim I used to know. Jim, take it from me, there is only one decent course open to you, one honest one. Leave her alone, and go from here yourself. You have no right to her so long as your life is what it is."

"But my life is going to be that no longer," Truscott broke in with passionate earnestness.

"Dave, help me out in this. For God's sake, do. It will be the making of me. I have money now, and I want to get rid of the old life. I, too, want to be decent. I do. I swear it. Give me this chance to straighten myself. I know your influence with her. You can get her to excuse that lapse. She will listen to you. My God! Dave, you don't know how I love that girl."

While the lumberman listened his heart hardened. He understood the selfishness, the weakness underlying this man's passion. He understood more than that, Betty was no longer the child she was five years ago, but a handsome woman of perfect moulding. And, truth to tell, he felt this sudden reawakening of the man's passion was not worthy of the name of the love he claimed for it, but rather belonged to baser inspiration. But his own feelings prevented his doing what he would like to have done. He felt that he ought to kick the man out of his office, and have him hunted out of the village. But years ago he had given his promise of help, and a promise was never a light thing with him. And besides that, he realized his own love for Betty, and could not help fearing that his judgment was biassed by it. In the end he gave the answer which from the first he knew he must give.

"If you mean that," he said coldly, "I will do what I can for you."

Jim's face lit, and he held out his hand impulsively.

"Thanks, Dave," he cried, his whole face clearing and lighting up as if by magic. "You're a bully friend. Shake!"

But the other ignored the outstretched hand. Somehow he felt he could no longer take it in friendship. Truscott saw the coldness in his eyes, and instantly drew his hand away. He moved toward the door.

"Will you see her to-night?" he asked over his shoulder.

"I can't say. You'll probably hear from her."

At the door the man turned, and Dave suddenly recollected something.

"Oh, by the way," he said, still in his coldest manner, "I'd like to buy that old mill of yours—or lease it. I don't mind which. How much do you want for it?"

Jim flashed a sharp glance at him.

"My old mill?" Then he laughed peculiarly. "What do you want with that?"

The other considered for a moment.

"My mill hasn't sufficient capacity," he said at last. "You see, my contract is urgent. It must be completed before winter shuts down—under an enormous penalty. We are getting a few thousand a day behind on my calculations. Your mill will put me right, with a margin to spare against accidents."

"I see." And the thoughtfulness of Truscott's manner seemed unnecessary. He avoided Dave's eyes. "You're under a penalty, eh? I s'pose the government are a hard crowd to deal with?"

Dave nodded.

" If I fail it means something very like—ruin," he said, almost as though speaking to himself.

Truscott whistled.

" Pretty dangerous, traveling so near the limit," he said.

" Yes. Well?   What about the mill? "

" I must think it over.   I'll let you know."

He turned and left the office without another word, and Dave stared after him, speechless with surprise and disgust.

CHAPTER VIII

Two days later brought Tom Chepstow's church bazaar. Dave had not yet had the opportunity of interceding with Betty and her uncle on behalf of Jim, but to-day he meant to fulfil his obligations as Tom's chief supporter in church affairs, and, at the same time, to do what he could for the man he had promised to help.

The whole morning the valley was flooded with a tremendous summer deluge. It was just as though the heavens had opened and emptied their waters upon the earth. Dave viewed the prospect with no very friendly eye. He knew the summer rains only too well; the possibilities of flood were well grounded, and just now he had no desire to see the river rise higher than it was at present. Still, as yet there was no reason for alarm. This was the first rain, and the glass was rising.

By noon the clouds broke, and the barometer's promise was fulfilled, so that, by the time he had clad himself in his best broadcloth, he left his office under a radiant sky. In spite of the wet under foot it was a delight to be abroad. The air was fresh and sparkling; the dripping trees seemed to be studded with thousands of diamonds as the poising rain-drops glistened in the blazing sun. The valley rang with the music of the birds, and the health-giving scent of the pine woods was wafted upon the gentlest of zephyrs. Dave's soul was in perfect sympathy with the beauties about him. To him there could be no spot on God's earth so fair and beautiful as this valley.

Passing the mill on his way out of the yards he was met by Joel Dawson, whose voice greeted him with a note of satisfaction in it.

" She's goin' full, boss," he said. " We set the last saws in her this mornin' an' she's steaming hard. Ther' ain't nothin' idle. Ther' ain't a ' band' or ' gang ' left in her."

And Dave without praise expressed his satisfaction at the rapidity with which his orders had been carried out. This was his way. Dawson was an excellent foreman, and his respect for his " boss " was largely based on the latter's capacity to extract work out of his men. While praise might have been pleasant to him, it would never have fallen in with his ideas of how the mills should be run. His pride was in the work, and to keep his respect at concert pitch it was necessary that he should feel that his " boss " was rather favoring him by entrusting to him the more important part of the work.

Dave passed out of the yards certain that nothing would be neglected in his absence. If things went wrong Dawson would receive no more consideration than a common lumber-jack, and Dawson had no desire to receive his " time."

The Meeting House stood slightly apart from the

rest of the village. It was a large, staring frame building, void of all pretentiousness and outward devotional sign. The weather-boarding was painted; at least, it had been. But the winter snows had long since robbed it of its original terra-cotta coloring and left its complexion a drab neutral tint. The building stood bare, with no encompassing fence, and its chief distinctive features were a large doorway, a single row of windows set at regular intervals, and a pitched roof.

As Dave drew near he saw a considerable gathering of men and horses about the doorway and tiepost. He was greeted cordially as he came up. These men were unfeignedly glad to see him, not only because he was popular, but in the hopes that he would show more courage than they possessed, and lead the way within to the feminine webs being woven for their enmeshing.

He chatted for some moments, then, as no one seemed inclined to leave the sunshine for the tempting baits so carefully set out inside the building, he turned to Jenkins Mudley —

"Are you fellows scared of going in?" he inquired, with his large laugh.

Jenkins shook his head shamefacedly, while Harley-Smith, loud and vulgar, with a staring diamond pin gleaming in his necktie, answered for him.

"'Tain't that," he said. "His wife's kind o' dep'ty for him. She's in ther' with his dollars."

"And you?" Dave turned on him quickly.

" Me? Oh, I ain't no use for them cirkises. Too much tea an' cake an' kiddies to it for me. Give me a few of the ' jacks ' around an' I kind o' feel it homely."

" Say, they ain't got a table for ' draw ' in there, have they ? " inquired Checks facetiously. " That's what Harley-Smith needs."

Dave smilingly shook his head.

" I don't think there's any gambling about this— unless it's the bran tub. But that is scarcely a gamble. It's a pretty sure thing you get bested over it. Still, there might be a raffle, or an auction. How would that do you, Harley-Smith ? "

The saloon-keeper laughed boisterously. He liked being the object of interest ; he liked being noticed so much by Dave. It tickled his vulgar vanity. But, to his disappointment, the talk was suddenly shifted into another channel by Checks. The dry-goods merchant turned to Dave with very real interest.

" Talking of ' draw,' " he said pointedly, " you know that shanty right opposite me. It's been empty this year an' more. Who was it lived there ? Why, the Sykeses, sure. You know it, it's got a shingle roof, painted red."

" Yes, I know," replied Dave. " It belongs to me. I let Sykes live there because there wasn't another house available at the time. I used to keep it as a storehouse."

" Sure, that's it," exclaimed Checks. " Well, there's some one running a game there at night.

I've seen the boys going in, and it's been lit up. Some guy is running a faro bank, or something of the sort. My wife swears it's young Jim Truscott. She's seen him going in for the last two nights. She says he's always the first one in and the last to leave."

" Psha ! " Jenkins Mudley exclaimed, with fine scorn. " Jim ain't no gambler. I'd bet it's some crook in from Calford. There's lots of that kidney coming around, seeing the place is on the boom. The bees allus gets around wher' the honey's made."

" Grows," suggested Checks amiably.

Harley-Smith laughed loudly.

" Say, bully for you," he cried sarcastically. " Young Jim ain't no gambler? Gee! I've see him take a thousand of the best bills out of the boys at ' craps,' right there in my bar. Gambler ? Well, I'd snigger ! "

And he illustrated his remark loudly and long.

Dave had dropped out of the conversation at the mention of Jim Truscott's name. He felt that he had nothing to say. And he hoped to avoid being again brought into it. But Jenkins had purposely told him. Jenkins was a rigid churchman, and he knew that Dave was also a strong supporter of Parson Tom's. His wife had been very scandalized at the opening of a gambling house directly opposite their store, and he felt it incumbent upon him to fall in with her views. Therefore he turned again to Dave.

" Well, what about it, Dave ? " he demanded.
" What are you going to do ? "

The lumberman looked him straight in the eye
and smiled.

" Do ? Why, what all you fellows seem to be
scared to do. I'm going into this bazaar to do my
duty by the church. I'm going to hand them all
my spare dollars, and if there's any change coming,
I'll take it in dry-goods."

But the lightness of his tone and smile had no
inspiration from his mood. He was angry ; he was
disappointed. So this was the worth of Jim's
promises ! This was the man who, in a perfect
fever of passion, had said that the old life of gambling and debauchery was finished for him. And
yet he had probably left his (Dave's) office and gone
straight to a night of heavy gaming, and, if Checks
were right, running a faro bank. He knew only
too well what that meant. No man who had grad-
uated as a gambler in such a region as the Yukon
was likely to run a faro bank straight.

Then a light seemed to flash through his brain,
and of a sudden he realized something that fired
the blood in his veins and set his pulses hammering
feverishly. For the moment it set his thoughts
chaotic ; he could not realize anything quite clearly.
One feeling thrilled him, one wild hope. Then,
with stern self-repression, he took hold of himself.
This was neither time nor place for such weakness,
he told himself. He knew what it was. For the
moment he had let himself get out of hand. He

had for so long regarded Betty as belonging to Jim;
he had for so long shut her from his own thoughts
and only regarded her from an impersonal point of
view, that it had never occurred to him, until that
instant, that there was a possibility of her engagement to Jim ever falling through.

This was what had so suddenly stirred him.
Now, actuated by his sense of duty and honor, he
thrust these things aside. His loyalty to the girl,
the strength of his great love for her, would not,
even for a moment, permit him to think of himself. Five years ago he had said good-bye to any
hopes and thoughts such as these. On that day he
had struggled with himself and won. He was not
going to destroy the effects of that victory by any
selfish thought now. His love for the girl was
there, nothing could alter that. It would remain
there, deep down in his heart, dormant but living.
But it was something more than a mere human
passion, it was something purer, loftier; something
that crystallized the human clay of his thought into
the purest diamonds of unselfishness.

In the few moments that it took him to pass into
the Meeting House and launch himself upon his
task of furthering the cause of Tom Chepstow's
church, his mind cleared. He could not yet see
the line of action he must take if the gossip of Mr.
Addlestone Checks were true. But one thing was
plain, that gossip must not influence him until its
truth were established. Just as he was seized upon
by at least half a dozen of the women who had

wares to sell, and were bent on morally picking his pockets, he had arrived at his decision.

The hall was ablaze with colored stuffs. There were festoons and banners, and rosettes and evergreen. Every bare corner was somehow concealed. There were drapings of royal blue and staring white, and sufficient bunting to make a suit of flags for a war-ship.

All the seats and benches had been removed, and round the walls had been erected the stalls and booths of the saleswomen. One end of the room was given up to a platform, on which, in the evening, the most select of the local vocalists would perform. Beside this was a bran tub, where one could have a dip for fifty cents and be sure of winning a prize worth at least five. Then there was a fortune-telling booth on the opposite side, presided over by a local beauty, Miss Eva Wade, whose father was a small rancher just outside the valley. This institution was eyed askance by many of the women. They were not sure that fortune-telling could safely be regarded as strictly moral. Parson Tom was responsible for its inception, and his lean shoulders were braced to bear the consequences.

Dave was by no means new to church bazaars. Any one living in a small western village must have considerable experience of such things. They are a form of taxation much in favor, and serve multifarious purposes. They are at once a pleasant social function where young people can safely meet under the matronly eye; they keep all in close

touch with religion; they give the usually idle
something to think of and work for, and the busy
find them an addition to their burdens. They
create a sort of central bureau for the exchange of
scandal, and a ready market for trading useless
articles to people who do not desire to purchase,
but having purchased feel that the moral sacrifice
they have made is at least one step in the right
direction to make up for many backslidings in the
past.

Dave doubtless had long since considered all
this. But he saw and appreciated the purpose underlying it. He knew Tom Chepstow to be a
good man, and though he had little inspiration as a
churchman, he spared no pains in his spiritual
labors, and the larger portion of his very limited
stipend went in unobtrusive charity. No sick bed
ever went uncheered by his presence, and no poor
ever went without warm clothing and wholesome
food in the terrible Canadian winter so long as he
had anything to give. Therefore Dave had come
well provided with money, which he began at once
to spend with hopeless prodigality.

The rest of the men followed in the lumberman's
wake, and soon the bustle and noise waxed furious.
They all bought indiscriminately. Dave started on
Mrs. Checks' "gentlemen's outfitters" stall. His
heart rejoiced when he sighted a pile of handker-
chiefs which the lady had specially made for him,
and which she now thrust at him with an exorbi-
tant price marked upon them. He bought them

all. He bought a number of shirts he could not possibly have worn. He bought underclothing that wouldn't have been a circumstance on his cumbersome figure. He passed on to Louisa Mudley's millinery stall and bought several hats, which he promptly shed upon the various women in his vicinity. He did his duty royally, and bought dozens of things which he promptly gave away. And his attentions in this matter were quite impartial. He did it with the air of some great good-natured schoolboy that set everybody delighted with him, with themselves, with everything; and the bazaar, as a result, went with a royal, prosperous swing. Here, as in his work, his personality carried with it the magic of success.

At last he reached Betty's stall. She was presiding over a hideous collection of cheap bric-à-brac. With her usual unselfishness and desire to promote harmony amongst the workers, and so help the success of the bazaar, she had sacrificed herself on the altar of duty by taking charge of the most unpopular stall. Nobody wanted the goods she had to sell; consequently Dave found her deserted. She smiled up at him a little pathetically as he came over to her.

"Are you coming as a friend or as a customer? Most of the visits I have received have been purely friendly." She laughed, but Dave could see that the natural spirit of rivalry was stirred, and she was a little unhappy at the rush of business going on everywhere but at her stall.

" I come as both," he said, with that air of frank
kindliness so peculiarly his own.

The girl's eyes brightened.

" Then let's get to work on the customer part of
your visit first," she said at once; " the other can
wait. Now here I have a nice plate. You can
hang it in your office on the wall. You see it's
already wired. It might pass for old Worcester if
you don't let in too much light. But there, you
never have your windows washed, do you? Then
I have," she hurried on, turning to other articles,
" this. This is a shell—at least I suppose it is,"
she added naïvely. " And this is a Toby jug; and
this is a pipe-rack; this is for matches; this is for a
whisk brush; and these two vases, they're real fine.
Look at them. Did you ever see such colors?
No, and I don't suppose anybody else ever did."
She laughed, and Dave joined in her laugh.

But her laugh suddenly died out. The man
heard a woman, only a few feet away, mention Jim
Truscott's name, and he knew that Betty had heard
it too. He knew that her smiling chatter, which
had seemed so gay, so irresponsible, had all been
pretense, a pretense which had suddenly been
swept aside at the mere mention of Jim's name.
At that moment he felt he could have taken the
man up in his two strong hands and strangled him.
However, he allowed his feelings no display, but at
once took up the challenge of the saleswoman.

" Say, Betty, there's just one thing in the world
I'm crazy about: it's bits of pots and things such as

you've got on your stall. It seems like fate you should be running this stall. Now just get right to it, and fetch out some tickets—a heap of 'em—and write 'sold' on 'em, and dump 'em on all you like. How much for the lot?"

"What do you mean, Dave?" the girl cried, her eyes wide and questioning.

"How much? I don't want anybody else buying those things," Dave said seriously. "I want 'em all."

Betty's eyes softened almost to tears.

"I can't let you do it, Dave," she said gently. "Not all. Some."

But the man was not to be turned from his purpose.

"I want 'em all," he said doggedly. "Here. Here's two hundred dollars. That'll cover it." He laid four bills of fifty dollars each on the stall. "There," he added, "you can sell 'em over again if any of the boys want to buy."

Betty was not sure which she wanted to do, cry or laugh. However, she finally decided on the latter course. Dave's simple contradiction was quite too much for her.

"You're the most refreshing old simpleton I ever knew," she said. "But I'll take your money—for the church," she added, as though endeavoring to quiet her conscience.

Dave sighed in relief.

"Well, that's that. Now we come to the friendly side of my visit," he said. "I've got a heap to say to you. Jim Truscott's been to me."

He made his statement simply, and waited. But no comment was forthcoming. Betty was stooping over a box, collecting cards to place on the articles on her stall. Presently she looked up, and her look was an invitation for him to go on.

The man's task was not easy. It would have been easy enough had he not spoken with Checks outside, but now it was all different. He had promised his help, but in giving it he had no clear conscience.

He propped himself against the side-post of her stall, and his weight set the structure shaking perilously.

"I've often wondered, Betty," he said, in a rumbling, confidential tone, "if there ever was a man, or for that matter a woman, who really understood human nature. We all think we know a lot about it. We size up a man, and we reckon he's good, bad, or indifferent, and if our estimate happens to prove, we pat ourselves, and hold our heads a shade higher, and feel sorry for those who can't read a man as easy as we can."

Betty nodded while she stuck some "Sold" cards about her stall.

"A locomotive's a great proposition, so long as it's on a set track. It's an all-fired nuisance without. Guess a locomotive can do everything it shouldn't when it gets loose of its track. My word, I'd hate to be around with a loco. up to its fool-tricks, running loose in a city. Seems to me that's how it is with human nature."

Betty's brown eyes were thoughtfully contemplating the man's ugly features.

" I suppose you mean we all need a track to run on ? "

" Why, yes," Dave went on, brightening. " Some of us start out in life with a ready-made track, with ' points ' we can jump if we've a notion. Some of us have a track without ' points,' so there's no excuse for getting off it. Some of us have to lay down our own track, and keep right on it, building it as we go. That's the hardest. We're bound to have some falls. You see there's so much ballasting needed, the ground's so mighty bumpy. I seem to know a deal about that sort of track. I've had to build mine, and I've fallen plenty. Sometimes it's been hard picking myself up, and I've been bruised and sore often. Still, I've got up, and I don't seem no worse for falling."

Betty's eyes were smiling softly.

" But *you* picked yourself up, Dave, didn't you ? " she asked gently.

" Well—not always. You see, I've got a mother. She's helped a whole heap. You see, she's mostly all my world, and I used to hate to hurt her by letting her see me down. She kind of thinks I'm the greatest proposition ever, and it tickles my vanity. I want her to go on thinking it, as it keeps me hard at work building that track. And now, through her, I've been building so long that it comes easier, and thinking of her makes me hang on so tight I don't get falling around now. There's other fellows haven't got a mother, or—you see, I've always had her with me. That's where it comes in. Now, if she'd been away from me five years, when I was very young ; you see——"

Dave broke off clumsily. He was floundering in rough water. He knew what he wanted to say, but words were not too easy to him.

" Poor Jim!" murmured Betty softly.

Dave's eyes were on her in a moment. Her manner was somehow different from what he had expected. There was sympathy and womanly tenderness in her voice ; but he had expected —— Then his thoughts went back to the time when they had spoken of Jim on the bridge. And, without knowing why, his pulses quickened, and a warmth of feeling swept over him.

" Poor Jim!" he said, after a long pause, during which his pulses had steadied and he had become master of his feelings again. " He's fallen a lot, and I'm not sure it's all his fault. He always ran straight when he was here. He was very young to go away to a place like the Yukon. Maybe— maybe you could pick him up ; maybe you could hold him to that track, same as mother did for me ?"

Betty was close beside him. She had moved out of her stall and was now looking up into his earnest face.

" Does he want me to ? " she asked wistfully. " Do *you* think I can help him?"

The man's hands clenched tightly. For a moment he struggled.

" You can," he said at last. " He wants you ; he wants your help. He loves you so, he's nearly crazy."

The girl gazed up at him with eyes whose question the man tried but failed to read. It was some seconds before her lips opened to speak again.

But her words never came. At that moment Addlestone Checks hurried up to them. He drew Dave sharply on one side. His manner was mysterious and important, and his face wore a look of outraged piety.

" Something's got to be done," he said in a stage whisper. " It's the most outrageous thing I've seen in years. Right here—right here in the house where the parson preaches the Word ! It sure is enough to set it shakin' to its foundation. Drunk ! That's what he is—roarin', flamin', fightin' drunk ! You must do something. It's up to you."

" What do you mean ? Who is drunk ? " cried Dave, annoyed at the man's Pharisaical air.

Before he could get a reply there was a commotion at the far end of the bazaar. Voices were raised furiously, and everybody had flocked in that direction. Once Dave thought he heard Chepstow's voice raised in protest. Betty ran to his side directly the tumult began.

" Oh, Dave, what's the matter down there ? I thought I heard Jim's voice ? "

" So you did, Miss Betty," cried Checks, with sanctimonious spleen. " So you did—the drunken ——"

" Shut up, or I'll break your neck!" cried Dave, threatening him furiously.

The dry-goods dealer staggered back just as Betty's hand was gently, but firmly, laid on Dave's upraised arm.

" Don't bother, Dave," she said piteously. " I've seen him. Oh, Jim—Jim!" And she covered her face with her hands.

CHAPTER IX

IT was the day after the bazaar. Betty had just returned home from her school for midday dinner. She was sitting at the open window, waiting while her aunt set the meal. The cool green of the wild-cucumbers covering the veranda tempered the blistering summer heat which oppressed the valley. The girl was looking out upon the village below her, at the woodland slopes opposite, at the distant narrowing of the mighty walls which bounded her world, but she saw none of these things. She saw nothing of the beauty, the gracious foliage, the wonderful sunlight she loved. Her gaze was introspective. She saw only the pictures her thoughts conjured up.

They were not pleasant pictures either, but they were absorbing. She knew that she had arrived at a crisis in her life. The scene she had witnessed at the bazaar was still burning in her brain. The shame stung and revolted her. The horror of it was sickening. Jim's disgrace was complete; yet, in spite of it, she could not help remembering Dave's appeal for him.

He had said that Jim needed her more than ever now, and the thought made her uneasy, and her tender heart urged her in a direction she knew she must not take. It was so easy for her to condemn, she who knew nothing of temptation. And yet her position was so utterly impossible. Jim had been in the village all this time and had not been near her, that is except on this one occasion, when he was drunk. He was evidently afraid to come near her. He was a coward, and she hated cowards.

He had even persuaded Dave to intercede for him. She smiled as she thought of it. But her smile was for Dave, and not at the other's display of cowardice. It was not a smile of amusement either. She only smiled at the absurdity of Dave pleading for one whom he knew to be wholly unworthy. It was the man's large heart, she told herself. And almost in the same breath she found herself resenting his kindly interference, and wishing he would mind his own business. Why should he be always thinking of others? Why should he not think sometimes of himself?

Her dreaming now became of Dave alone, and she found herself reviewing his life as she knew it. Her eyes grew tender, and she basked in the sunlight of a world changed to pleasant thought. His ugliness no longer troubled her—she no longer saw it. She saw only the spirit inside the man, and somehow his roughnesses of voice, manner and appearance seemed a wholly fitting accompaniment to it. Her thoughts of Jim had gone from her entirely. The crisis which she was facing had receded into the shadows. Dave became her dominant thought, and she started when her uncle's voice suddenly broke in upon her reverie.

"Betty," he said, coming up behind her and laying one lean hand upon her rounded shoulder, "I haven't had time to speak to you about it since the bazaar, but now I want to tell you that you can have nothing more to do with young Truscott He is a thorough-paced young scoundrel and ——"

"You need say no more, uncle," the girl broke in bitterly. "You can tell me nothing I do not already know of him."

"Then I trust you will send him about his business at once," added her aunt, who had entered the room bearing the dinner joint on a tray, just in time to hear Betty's reply.

Betty looked at her aunt's round, good-natured face. For once it was cold and angry. From her she looked up at her uncle's, and the decision she saw in his frank eyes left her no alternative but a direct reply.

"I intend to settle everything this afternoon," she said simply.

"In what way?" inquired her uncle sharply.

Betty rose from her seat and crossed the room to her aunt's side. The latter, having set the dinner, was waiting beside her chair ready to sit down as soon as the matter should be settled. Betty placed her arm about her stout waist, and the elder woman's face promptly relaxed. She could never long keep up even a pretense of severity where Betty was concerned.

The girl promptly addressed herself to her uncle with all the frankness of one assured of a sympathetic hearing.

"You have always taught me, uncle dear, that duty must be my first consideration in life," she began steadily. "I have tried to live up to that, and it has possibly made my conscience a little over keen." Her face clouded, but the clouds broke immediately, chased away by a plaintive smile. "When Jim asked me to marry him five years ago I believed I loved him. At one time I'm sure I did, in a silly, girlish fashion. But soon after he went away I realized that a girlish infatuation is not real love. This knowledge I tried to hide even from myself. I would not believe it, and for a long time I almost managed to convince myself. That was until Jim's letters became fewer and colder. With his change I no longer attempted to conceal from myself the real state of my own feelings. But even then my conscience wouldn't let me alone. I had promised to wait for him, and I made up my mind that, come what might, unless he made it impossible I would marry him." She sighed. "Well, you know the rest. He has now made it impossible. What his real feelings are for me," she went on with a pathetic smile, "I have not had an opportunity of gauging. As you know, he has not been near me. I shall now make it my business to see him this afternoon and settle everything. My conscience isn't by any means easy about it, but I intend to give him up."

Her aunt squeezed her arm sympathetically, and her uncle nodded his approval.

"Where are you going to see him?" the latter asked. "You mustn't see him alone." Then he burst out wrathfully, "He's a blackguard, and ——"

"No, no, uncle, don't say that," Betty interrupted him. "Surely he is to be pitied. Remember him as he was. You cannot tell what temptations have come his way."

The parson's face cleared at once. His angry outbursts were always short-lived.

"I'm sorry, Betty," he said. "My dear, you shame me. I'm afraid that my hasty temper is always leading to my undoing as a churchman." The half-humorous smile which accompanied his words passed swiftly. "Where are you going to see him?" he again demanded.

"Down at Dave's office," the girl replied, after a moment's thought.

"Eh?" Her uncle was startled; but Mary Chepstow smiled on her encouragingly.

"Yes, you see," she went on, "Dave had a good deal to do with—our engagement—in a way, and ——"

"I'm glad Dave is going to help you through this business," said her aunt, with a glance which effectually kept her husband silent. "He's a dear fellow, and—let's have our dinner—it's nearly cold."

Aunt Mary was not brilliant, she was not meddlesome, but she had all a woman's intuition. She felt that enough had been said. And for some obscure reason she was glad that Dave was to have a hand in this matter. Nor had her satisfaction anything to do with the man's ability to protect her niece from possible insult.

That afternoon Dave received an unexpected visit. He was alone in his office, clad for hard work, without coat, waistcoat, collar or tie. He had no scruples in these matters. With all an American's love of freedom he abandoned himself to all he undertook with a whole-heartedness which could not tolerate even the restraint of what he considered unnecessary clothing. And just now, in the terrific heat, all these things were superfluous.

Betty looked particularly charming as she hurried across the lumber-yard. She was dressed in a spotless white cotton frock, and, under her large sun-hat, her brown hair shone in the sunlight like burnished copper. Without the least hesitation she approached the office and knocked peremptorily on the door.

The man inside grudgingly answered the summons. His books were occupying all his attention, and his thoughts were filled with columns of figures. But the moment he beheld the white, smiling vision the last of his figures fled precipitately from his mind.

"Why, come right in, little Betty," he cried, hastily setting the only available chair for her. Then he bethought himself of his attire. "Say, you might have let me know. Just half a minute and I'll fix myself up."

But the girl instantly protested. " You'll do just as you are," she exclaimed. " Now you look like a lumberman. And I like you best that way."

Dave grinned and sat down a little self-consciously. But Betty had no idea of letting any conventionalities interfere with the matter she had in hand. She was always direct, always single-minded, when her decision was taken. She gave him no time to speculate as to the object of her visit.

" Dave," she began seriously, " I want you to do me a great favor." Then she smiled. " As usual," she added. " I want you to send for Jim Truscott and bring him here."

Dave was on his feet in an instant and crossed to the door. The next moment his voice roared out to one of his foremen. It was a shout that could have been heard across his own milling floor with every saw shrieking on the top of its work.

He waited, and presently Simon Odd came hurrying across the yard. He spoke to him outside, and then returned to the office.

" He'll be along in a few minutes," he said. " I've sent Odd with the buckboard."

" Are you sure he'll come ? "

Dave smiled confidently.

" I told Odd to bring him."

" I hope he'll come willingly," the girl said, after a thoughtful pause.

" So do I," observed Dave dryly. " Well, little girl ? "

Betty understood the inquiry, and looked him fearlessly in the eyes.

" You sowed your wheat on barren soil, Dave," she said decidedly. " Your appeal for Jim has borne no fruit."

The man shifted his position. It was the only sign he gave. But the fires were stirred into a sudden blaze, and his blood ran fiercely through his veins.

" That's not a heap like you, Betty," was all he said.

" Isn't it?" The girl turned to the window. The dirt on the glass made it difficult for her to see out of it, but she gazed at it steadily.

" I suppose you'll think me a mean, heartless creature," she said slowly. " You'll think little enough of my promises, and still less of—of my loyalty." She paused. Then she raised her head and turned to him again. " I cannot marry Jim. I cannot undertake his reformation. I cannot give up my life to a man whom I now know I never really loved. I know you will not understand. I know, only too well, your own lofty spirit, your absolute unselfishness. I know that had you been in my place you would have fulfilled your promise at any cost. But I can't. I simply can't."

" No."

It was the man's only comment. But his mind was busy. He knew Betty so well that he understood a great deal without asking questions.

" Aunt Mary and uncle know my decision," the

girl went on. " They know I am here, and that I am going to see Jim in your presence. You see, I thought if I sent for him to come to our house he might refuse. He might insult uncle again. I thought, somehow, it would be different with you."

Dave nodded.

" I don't blame your uncle and aunt for making you give him up," he said. " I'd have done it in their place."

" Yet you appealed for him?"

Betty's eyes questioned him.

" Sure, I promised to help him. That was before the bazaar."

Suddenly Betty held out her hands with a little appealing movement. Dave wanted to seize them and crush them in his own, but he did not stir.

" Tell me you don't think badly of me. Tell me you do not think me a heartless, wretched woman. I have thought and thought, and prayed for guidance. And now it seems to me I am a thoroughly wicked girl. But I cannot—I must not marry him."

The man rose abruptly from his seat. He could no longer look into her troubled eyes and keep his own secret. When he spoke it was with his back to her, as he made a pretense of filling his pipe at the tobacco jar on the table. His voice was deep with emotion.

" I thank God you've decided," he said. " You've done right by everybody. And you've shown more courage refusing him than if you'd gone through with your promise, because you've done it against your conscience. No, little Betty," he went on, turning to her again with infinite kindness in his steady eyes, " there's no one can call you heartless, or any other cruel name—and— and they'd better not in my hearing," he finished up clumsily.

A few minutes later the rattle of buckboard wheels sounded outside, and before Betty could reply Dave took the opportunity of going to the door. Jim Truscott was standing outside with the gigantic Simon Odd close behind him, much in the manner of a warder watching his prisoner. The flicker of a smile came and went in the lumberman's eyes at the sight. Then his attention was held by the anger he saw in Jim's dissipated face. He was not a pleasant sight. His eyes were heavy and bloodshot, and the lines about them were accentuated by his general unwashed appearance. Even at that distance, as they stood there facing each other, he caught the reek of stale brandy the man exhaled. His clothes, too, had the appearance of having been flung on hurriedly, and the shirt and collar he wore were plainly filthy. Altogether he was an object for pity, and at the same time it was not possible to feel anything for him but a profound repugnance.

" He was abed," said the giant Odd, the moment Dave appeared. Then with a complacent grin, " But he guessed he'd come right along when I told him you was kind o' busy an' needed him important."

But Jim's angry face flamed.

"Nothing of the sort. This damned ruffian of yours dragged me out, blast him."

"Cut it!" Dave warned him sharply. "There's a lady here to see you. Come right in."

The warning had instant effect. Truscott stepped into the room and stood face to face with Betty. Dave closed the door and stood aside. For a few intense moments no word was spoken. The man stared stupidly into the girl's unsmiling face; then he looked across at Dave. It was Betty who finally broke the silence.

"Well, Jim," she said kindly, "at last we meet." She noted all the signs of dissipation in the young face, which, but a few years ago, had been so fresh and clean and good-looking. Now it was so different, and, to her woman's eyes, there was more than the mere outward signs. There was a spirit looking out of his bloodshot eyes that she did not recognize. It was as though the soul of the man had changed; it had degenerated to a lower grade. There was something unwholesome in his expression, as though some latent brutality had been stirred into life, and had obliterated every vestige of that clean, boyish spirit that had once been his.

"And," she went on, as he remained silent, "you had to be cajoled into coming to see me."

Still the man did not speak. Whether it was shame that held him silent it was impossible to tell. Probably not, for there was a steadily growing light in his eyes that suggested thoughts of anything but

of a moral tone.   He was held by her beauty—he
was held as a man is sometimes held by some ravish-
ing vision that appeals to his lower senses.   He lost
no detail of her perfect woman's figure, the seductive
contours so wonderfully moulded.   His eyes drank
in the sight, and it set his blood afire.

Dave never turned his eyes.   He too was watching.   And he understood, and resented, the storm
that was lashing through the man's veins.

" Have you nothing to say to me after these long
years ? " the girl asked again, forced to break the
desperate silence.   Then the woman in her found
voice, " Oh! Jim, Jim ! the pity of it.   And I
thought you so strong."

Dave clenched his hands at his sides, but made
no other movement.   Then Betty's manner suddenly changed.   All the warmth died out of her
voice, and, mistress of herself again, she went
straight to her object.

" Jim, it was I who sent for you.   I asked Dave to
do this for me."

" A word from you would have been enough,"
the man said, with a sudden fire that lost nothing
of its fierce passion in the hoarse tone in which he
spoke.

" A word from me ? "   There was unconscious
irony in the girl's reply.

" Yes, a word.   I know.   You are thinking of
when your uncle came to me ; you're thinking of
our first meeting on the bridge ; you're thinking of
yesterday.   I was drunk.   I admit it.   But I'm not

always drunk. I tell you a word from you would have been enough."

The girl's eyes reproached him.

" A word from me, after five years' absence? It seems to me you should not have needed a word from me. Jim, had you come to me, whatever your state, poor or rich, it would have made no difference to me. I should have met you as we parted, ready to fulfil my pledge."

" You mean ——"

The man's bloodshot eyes were alight. A tremendous passion was urging him to the limits of his restraining powers. He had almost forgotten where he was. He had quite forgotten Dave. The sight of this woman with her beautiful figure, her sweet face and serious eyes, almost maddened him. He was from the wilds, where he had long since buried his wholesome youthful ideals. The life he had lived had entirely deadened all lofty thought. He only saw with a brain debased to the level of the animal. He desired her. He madly desired her now that he had seen her again, and he realized that his desire was about to be thwarted.

Betty drew back a step. The movement was unconscious. It was the woman's instinct at the sight of something threatening which made her draw away from the passion she saw blazing in his eyes. Dave silently watched the man.

" I mean," said the girl solemnly, " that you have made our pledge impossible. I mean," she, went on, with quiet dignity, " that I cannot marry you now, even if you wish it. No, no," as Jim made a sudden movement to speak, " it is quite useless to discuss the matter further. I insisted on this meeting to settle the matter beyond question. Dave here witnessed our engagement, and I wished him to witness its termination. You will be better free, and so shall I. There could have been no happiness in a marriage between us ——"

" But I won't give you up," the man suddenly broke out. He had passed the narrow limits of his restraint. His face flushed and showed blotched in the sudden scarlet. For a second, after that first fiery outburst, no words came. Then the torrent flowed forth. " Is this what I went away for? Is this what I have slaved for in the wilds of the Yukon? Is this what I am to find now that I have made the money you desired? No, no, you can't get rid of me like that; you don't mean it, you can't mean it. Betty, I want you more than anything on earth," he rushed on, his voice dropping to a persuasive note. " I want you, and without you life is nothing to me. I must have you!" He took a step forward. But it was only a step, for the girl's steady eyes held him, and checked his further advance. And something in her attitude turned his mood to one of fierce protest. " What is it that has come between us? What is it that has changed you ? "

Betty snatched at his pause.

" Such questions come well from you, Jim," she said, with some bitterness. " You know the truth.

You do not need me to tell you." Her tone suddenly let the demon in the man loose. His passion-lit eyes lowered, and a furtive, sinister light shone in them when he lifted them again.

" I know. I understand," he cried. " This is an excuse, and it serves you well." The coldness of his voice was in painful contrast to his recent passion. " The old story, eh? You have found some one else. I never thought much of a woman's promise, anyhow. I wonder who it is." Then with a sudden vehemence. " But you shan't marry him. Do you hear? You shan't while I am ——"

" Quit it!"

Dave's great voice suddenly filled the room and cut the man's threats short.

Jim turned on him in a flash; until that moment he had entirely forgotten the lumberman. He eyed the giant for a second. Then he laughed cynically.

" Oh, I'd forgotten you. Of course," he went on. " I see now. I never thought of it before. I remember, you were on the bridge together when I first ——"

Dave had taken a couple of strides and now stood between the two. His movement silenced the man, while he addressed himself to Betty.

" You're finished with him? " he inquired in a deep, harsh voice.

There was something so compelling about him that Betty simply nodded. Instantly he swung round on the younger man.

" You'll vacate this place—quick," he said deliberately.

The two men eyed each other for some seconds. Truscott's look meant mischief, Dave's was calmly determined. The latter finally stepped aside and crossing to the door held it open.

" I said you'll—vacate," he said sharply.

Truscott turned and glanced at the open door. Then he glanced at Betty, who had drawn farther away. Finally his frigid eyes turned upon Dave's great figure standing at the door. For an instant a wicked smile played round his lips, and he spoke in the same cynical tone.

" I never thought of you in the marriage market, Dave," he said, with a vicious laugh. " I suppose it's only natural. Nobody ever associated you with marriage. Somehow your manner and appearance don't suggest it. I seem to see you handling lumber all your life, not dandling children on your knee. But there, you're a good catch—a mighty good one. And I was fool enough to trust you with my cause. Ye gods ! Well, your weight of money has done it, no doubt. I congratulate you. She has lied to me, and no doubt she will lie ——"

But the man, if he finished his remark at all, must have done so to the stacks of lumber in the yards, and to the accompaniment of the shriek of the saws. There was no fuss. Scarcely any struggle. Dave moved with cat-like swiftness, which in a man of his size was quite miraculous, and in a flash Jim

Truscott was sprawling on the hard red ground on the other side of the doorway.

And when Dave looked round at Betty the girl's face was covered with her hands, and she was weeping. He stood for a second all contrition, and clumsily fumbling for words. He believed she was distressed at his brutal action.

" I'm sorry, little Betty," he blurted out at last. " I'm real sorry. But I just couldn't help it."

CHAPTER X

MALKERN as a village had two moments in the day when it wore the appearance of a thoroughly busy city. At all other times there was little outward sign to tell of the prosperity it really enjoyed. Malkern's really bustling time was at noon, when its workers took an hour and a half recess for the midday meal, and at six o'clock in the evening, when the day and night " shifts " at the mill exchanged places.

There was no eight-hour working day in this lumbering village. The lumber-jacks and all the people associated with it worked to make money, not to earn a mere living. They had not reached that deplorable condition of social pessimism when the worker for a wage believes he is the man who is making millions for an employer, who is prospering only by his, the worker's, capacity to do. They were working each for himself, and regarded the man who could afford them such opportunity as an undisguised blessing. The longer the " time " the higher the wages, and this was their whole scheme of life.

Besides this, there is a certain pride of achievement in the lumber-jack. He is not a mere automaton. He is a man virile, strong, and of a wonderful independence all his own. His spirits are animal, keen of perception, keen for all the joys of life such as he knows. He lives his life, whether in play or work. Whether he be a scaler, a cant-hook man, a teamster, or an axeman, his pride is in his skill, and the rating of his skill is estimated largely by the tally of his day's work, on which depends the proportion of his wages.

It was the midday dinner-hour now, and the mill was debouching its rough tide of workers upon the main street. Harley-Smith's bar was full of men seeking unnecessary " appetizers." Every boarding-house was rapidly filling with hungry men clamoring for the ample, even luxurious meal awaiting them. These men lived well; their work was tremendous, and food of the best, and ample, was needed to keep them fit. The few stores which the village boasted were full of eager purchasers demanding instant service lest the precious time be lost.

Harley-Smith's hotel abutted on the main road, and the tide had to pass its inviting portals on their way to the village. Usually the veranda was empty at this time, for the regular boarders were at dinner, and the bar claimed those who were not yet dining. But on this occasion it possessed a solitary occupant.

He was sitting on a hard windsor chair, tilted back at a dangerous angle, with his feet propped upon the veranda rail in an attitude of ease, if not

of elegance. He was apparently quite uncon-
cerned at anything going on about him. His
broad-brimmed hat was tilted well forward upon
his nose, in a manner that served the dual purpose
of shading his eyes from the dazzling sunlight, and
permitting his gaze to wander whither he pleased
without the observation of the passers-by. To
give a further suggestion of indolent indifference,
he was luxuriously smoking one of Harley-Smith's
best cigars.

But the man's attitude was a pretense. No one
passed the veranda who escaped the vigilance of
his quick eyes. He scanned each face sharply, and
passed on to the next; nor did his watchfulness
relax for one instant. It was clear he was looking
for some one whom he expected would pass that
way, and it was equally evident he had no desire to
advertise the fact.

Suddenly he pushed his hat back from his face,
and, at the same time, his feet dropped to the
boarded floor. This brought his chair on its four
legs with a jolt, and he sat bolt upright. Now he
showed the bloated young face of Jim Truscott.
There was a look in his eyes of something approaching venomous satisfaction. He had seen the
man he was looking for, and promptly beckoned to
him.

Dick Mansell was passing at that moment, and
his small, ferret-like eyes caught the summons.
He hesitated, nor did he come at once in response
to the other's smile of good-fellowship.

"Dick!" Truscott said. Then he added genially, "I was wondering if you'd come along this way."

Mansell nodded indifferently. His face was ill-humored, and his small eyes had little friendliness in them. He nodded, and was about to pass on, but the other stayed him with a gesture.

"Don't go," he said. "I want to speak to you. Come up to my room and have a drink."

He kept his voice low, but he might have saved himself the trouble. The passing crowd were far too intent upon their own concerns to bother with him. The fact was his attitude was the result of nearly forty-eight hours of hard thinking, thinking inspired by a weak character goaded to offense by the rough but justifiable treatment meted out to him in Dave's office. This man's character, at no time robust, was now morally run-down, and its condition was like the weakly body of an un-healthy man. It collected to itself every injurious germ and left him diseased. His brain and nerves were thrilling with resentment, and a desire to get even with the "board." He was furiously deter-mined that Dave should remember with regret the moment he had laid hands upon him, and that he had come between him and the girl he had in-tended to make his own.

Mansell, stepping on to the veranda, paused and looked the other full in the eye.

"Well," he said, after a moment's doubtful con-sideration, "what is it? 'Tain't like you givin' drink away—'specially to me. What monkey tricks is it?"

There was truculence in the sawyer's tone. There was offense in his very attitude.

"Are you coming to my room for that drink?"

Truscott spoke quite coldly, but he knew the curse of the man's thirst. He had reason to.

Mansell laughed without any mirth.

"Guess I may as well drink your brandy. It'll taste the same as any other. Go ahead."

His host at once led the way into the hotel and up the stairs to his room. It was a front room on the first floor, and comparatively luxurious. The moment the door closed behind him Mansell took in the details with some interest.

"A mighty swell apartment—fer you," he observed offensively.

Truscott shrugged as he turned his back to pour out drinks at the table.

"That's my business," he said. "I pay for it, and," he added, glancing meaningly over his shoulder, "I can afford to pay for it—or anything else I choose to have."

Mansell was a fine figure of a man, and beside him the other looked slight, even weedy. But his face and head spoiled him. Both were small and mean, and gave the impression of a low order of intelligence. Yet he was reputed one of the finest sawyers in the valley, and a man, when not on the drink, to be thoroughly trusted. Before he went away to the Yukon with Jim he had been a teeto-

taler for two years, and on that account, and his
unrivaled powers as a sawyer, he had acted as the
other's foreman in his early lumbering enterprise.
Except, however, for those two years his past had
in it far more shadows than light.

He grinned unpleasantly.

" No need to ast how you came by the stuff," he
said.

Truscott was round on him in an instant. His
eyes shone wickedly, but there was a grin about his
lips.

" The same way you tried to come by it too, only
you couldn't keep your damned head clear. You
couldn't let this stuff alone." He handed the man
a glass of neat brandy. " You and your cursed
drink nearly ruined my chances. It wasn't your
fault you didn't. When I ran that game up in
Dawson I was a fool to take you into it. I did it
out of decency, because you had gone up there
with me, and quite against my best judgment
when I saw the way you were drinking. If you'd
kept straight you'd be in the same position as I am.
You wouldn't have returned here more or less broke
and only too ready to set rotten yarns going around
about me."

The sawyer had taken the brandy and swallowed
it. Now he set the glass down on the table with a
vicious bang.

" What yarns ? " he demanded angrily.

" Tchah ! Hardwig's a meddling busybody.
You might have known it would come back to me

sooner or later. But I didn't bring you here to throw these things up in your face. You brought it on yourself. Keep a civil tongue, and if you like to stand in I'll put you into a good thing. You're not working? And you've got no money?"

Truscott's questions came sharply. His plans were clear in his mind. These points he had made sure of already. But he wanted to approach the matter he had in hand in what he considered the best way in dealing with a man like Mansell. He knew the sawyer to have scruples of a kind, that is until they had been carefully undermined by brandy. It was his purpose to undermine them now.

" You seem to know a heap," Mansell observed sarcastically. Then he became a shade more interested. " What's the ' good thing ' ? "

Jim poured some brandy out for himself, at the same time, as though unconsciously, replenishing the other's glass liberally. The sawyer watched him while he waited for a reply, and suddenly a thought occurred to his none too ready brain.

" Drink, eh ? " he laughed mockingly, as though answering a challenge on the subject. " Drink? Say, who's been doing the drink since you got back ? Folks says as your gal has gone right back on you, that ther' wench as you was a-sparkin' 'fore we lit out. An' it's clear along of liquor. They say you're soused most ev'ry might, an' most days too. You should git gassin'—I don't think."

The man's mean face was alight with brutish glee. He felt he had handed the other a pretty retort.

And in his satisfaction he snatched up his glass and drank off its contents at a gulp.   Indifferent to the gibe, Jim smiled his satisfaction as he watched the other drain his glass.

" You've got no work ? " he demanded, as Mansell set it down empty.

" Sure I ain't," the other grinned.   " An'," he added, under the warming influence of the spirit, " I ain't worritin' a heap neither.   My credit's good with the boardin'-house boss.   Y' see," he went on, his pride of craft in his gimlet eyes, " I'm kind o' known here for a boss sawyer.   When they want sawyers there's allus work for Dick Mansell."

" Your credit's good ? " Truscott went on, ignoring the man's boasting.   " Then you have no money ? "

" I allows the market's kind o' low."

Mansell's mood had become one of clumsy jocularity under the influence of the brandy.

" If you can get work so easily, why don't you ? " Truscott demanded, filling the two glasses again as he spoke.

Mansell seated himself on the bed unbidden.

" Wal," he began expansively, " I'm kind o' holi-day-makin', as they say.   Y' see," he went on with a leer, " I worked so a'mighty hard gittin' back from the Yukon, I'm kind o' fatigued.   Savee? Guess I'll git to work later.   Say, one o' them for me ? " he finished up, pointing at the glasses.

Truscott nodded, and Mansell helped himself greedily.

The former fell in with the other's mood. He found him very easy to deal with. It was just a question of sufficient drink.

"Well, I don't believe in work, anyway. That is unless it happens to be my pleasure, too. I worked hard up at Dawson, but it was my pleasure. I made good money, too—a hell of a sight more than you or anybody else ever had any idea of."

"You ran a dandy game," agreed the sawyer.

"With plenty of customers with mighty fat rolls of money."

Mansell nodded.

"I was a fool to quit you," he said regretfully.

"You were. But it isn't too late. If you aren't yearning to work too hard."

Truscott's smile was crafty. And, even with the drink in him, Mansell saw and understood it.

"Monkey tricks?" he said.

"Monkey tricks—if you like."

Mansell looked over at the bottle.

"Hand us another horn of that pizen an' I'll listen," he said.

The other poured out the brandy readily, taking care to be more than liberal. He watched the sawyer drink, and then, drawing a chair forward, he sat down.

"What's that old mill of mine worth?" he asked suddenly.

They exchanged glances silently. Truscott was watching the effect of his question, and the other was trying to fathom the meaning of it.

"I'd say," Mansell replied slowly, giving up the puzzle and waiting for enlightenment—"I'd say, to a man who needs it bad, it's worth anything over fifteen thousand dollars. Fer scrappin', I'd say it warn't worth but fi' thousand."

"I was thinking of a man needing it."

"Fifteen thousand an' over."

Truscott leant forward in his chair and became confidential.

"Dave wants to buy that mill, and I'm going to sell it to him," he said impressively. "I'll take twenty thousand for it, and get as much more as I can. See? Now I don't want that money. I wouldn't care to handle his money. I've got plenty, and the means of making heaps more if I need it."

He paused to let his words sink in. Mansell nodded with his eyes on the brandy bottle. As yet he did not see the man's drift. He did not see where he came in. He waited, and Truscott went on.

"Now what would you be willing to do for that twenty thousand—or more?" he asked smilingly.

The other turned his head with a start, and, for one fleeting second, his beady eyes searched his companion's face. He saw nothing there but quiet good-nature. It was the face of the old Jim Truscott—used to hide the poisoned mind behind it.

"Give me a drink," Mansell demanded roughly. "This needs some thinkin'."

Truscott handed him the bottle, and watched him while he drank nearly half a tumbler of the raw spirit.

" Well ? "

Mansell breathed heavily.

" Seems to me I'd do—a heap," he said at last.

" Would you take a job as sawyer in Dave's mill, and—and act under my orders ? "

" It kind o' depends on the orders." For some reason the lumberman became cautious. The price was high—almost too high for him.

Truscott suddenly rose from his seat, and crossing the room, turned the key in the door. Then he closed the window carefully. He finally glanced round the room, and came back to his seat. Then, leaning forward and lowering his tone, he detailed carefully all that the lumberman would have to do to earn the money. It took some time in the telling, but at last he sat back with a callous laugh.

" That's all it is, Dick, my boy," he cried familiarly. " You will be as safe as houses. Not only that, but I may not need your help at all. I have other plans which are even better, and which may do the job without your help. See ? This is only in case it is necessary. You see I don't want to leave anything to chance. I want to be ready. And I want no after consequences. You understand? You may get the money for doing nothing. On the other hand, what you have to do entails little enough risk. The price is high, simply because I do not want the money, and I want to be sure I can rely on you."

The man's plausibility impressed the none too bright-witted lumberman. Then, too, the brandy had done its work. His last scruple fled, banished by his innate crookedness, set afire by the spirit and the dazzling bait held out to him. It was a case of the clever rascal dominating the less dangerous, but more brutal, type of man. Mansell was as potter's clay in this man's hands. The clay dry would have been impossible to mould, but moistened, the artist in villainy had no difficulty in handling it. And the lubricating process had been liberally supplied.

" I'm on," Mansell said, his small eyes twinkling viciously. " I'm on sure. Twenty thousand! Gee! But I'll need it all, Jim," he added greedily. " I'll need it all, and any more you git. You said it yourself, I was to git the lot. Yes," as though reassuring himself, " I'm on."

Truscott nodded approvingly.

" Good boy," he said pleasantly. " But there's one thing more, Dick. I make it a proviso you don't go on any teetotal racket. I know you. Anyway, I don't believe in the water wagon worth a cent. It don't suit you in work like this. But don't get drunk and act foolish. Keep on the edge. See? Get through this racket right, and you've got a small pile that'll fill your belly up like a distillery—after. You'll get the stuff in a bundle the moment you've done the work."

Mansell reached out for the bottle without invitation, picked it up, and put the neck to his lips. Nor did he put it down till he had drained it. It was the culminating point. The spirit had done its work, and as Truscott watched him he knew

that, body and soul, the man was his.   The lumberman flung the empty bottle on the bed.

"I'll do it, you damned crook," he cried.   "I'll
do it, but not because I like you, or anything to do
with you.   It's the bills I need sure—green, crisp,
crinkly bills.   But I'll need fifty of 'em now.
Hand over, pard," he cried exultingly.   "Hand
over, you imp of hell.   I want fifty now, or I don't
stir a hand.   Hand 'em ——"

Suddenly the man staggered back and fell on the
bed, staring stupidly at the shining silver-plated revolver in the other's hands.

"Hold your noise, you drunken hog," Jim cried
in a biting tone.   "This is the sort of thing I suppose I can expect from a blasted fool like you.
Now understand this, I'm going to give you that
fifty, not because you demand it, but to seal our
compact.   And by the Holy Moses, when you've
handled it, if you attempt to play any game on me,
I'll blow you to hell quicker than any through mail
could carry you there.   Get that, and let it sink into
your fool brain."

CHAPTER XI

THE SUMMER RAINS

TRUSCOTT looked up from his paper and watched the rain as it hissed against the window. It was falling in a deluge, driven by a gale of wind which swept the woodlands as though bent on crushing out the last dignity of the proud forest giants. The sky was leaden, and held out no promise of relenting. It was a dreary prospect, yet to the man watching it was a matter of small moment.

It was nearly midday, and as yet he had not broken his fast. In fact his day was only just beginning. His appearance told plainly the story of his previous night's dissipation. Still, his mood was in no way depressed—he was too well seasoned to the vicious life he had adopted for that. Besides, the prosperity of Malkern brought much grist to his mill, and its quality more than made up for the after effects of his excesses.

He turned to his paper again. It was a day old. A large head-line faced him announcing the spreading of the railway strike. Below it was a column describing how business was already affected, and how, shortly, if a settlement were not soon arrived at, it was feared that the trans-continental traffic could only be kept open with the aid of military engineers. The rest of the paper held no interests for him; he had only read this column, and it seemed to afford him food for much thought. He had read it over twice, and was now reading it for a third time.

At last he threw the paper aside and walked across to the table to pour himself out a drink. The thought of food sickened him. The only thing possible was a whiskey-and-milk, and he mixed the beverage and held it to his lips. But the smell of it sickened him, and he set it down and moved away to the window.

There was little enough to attract him thither, but he preferred the prospect to the sight and smell of whiskey at that hour of the day. After some moments he made another attempt on his liquid breakfast. He knew he must get it down somehow. He turned and looked at it, shuddered, and turned again to the window. And at that instant he recognized the great figure of Dave, clad from head to foot in oilskins, making his way back from the depot to the mill.

The sight fixed his attention, and all the venom in his distorted nature shone in the wicked gleam that sprang into his eyes. His blood was fired with hatred.

" Betty for you ? Never in your life," he muttered at the passing figure. " Never in mine, Dave, my boy. It's you and me for it, and by God I'll never let up on you ! "

All unconscious of the venomous thoughts the sight of him had inspired, Dave strode on through the rain. He was deep in his own concerns, and at that moment they were none too pleasant. The deluge of rain damped his spirits enough, but the mail he had just received had brought him news that depressed him still more. The Engineers' Union had called for a general cessation of work east of Winnipeg, and he was wondering how it was likely to affect him. Should his engineers go out, would it be possible to replace them? And if he could, how would he be able to cope with the trouble likely to ensue? He could certainly fall in with the Union's demands, but—well, he would wait. It was no use anticipating trouble.

But more bad news was awaiting him when he reached his office. Dawson, in his absence, had opened a letter which had arrived by runner from Bob Mason, the foreman of the camps up in the hills.

Dawson was no alarmist. He always looked to Dave for everything when a crisis confronted them. He felt that if not a crisis, something very like it was before them now, and so he calmly handed Mason's letter to his boss, confident in the latter's capacity to deal with the situation.

"This come along by hand," he said easily. "Guess, seein' it's wrote 'important' on it, I opened it."

Dave nodded while he threw off his oilskins. He made no particular haste, and deposited his mail on his desk before he took the letter from his foreman. At last, however, he unfolded the sheet of foolscap on which it was written, and read the ominous contents. It was a long letter dealing with the business of the camps, but the one paragraph which had made the letter important threw all the rest into insignificance. It ran—

" I regret to have to report that an epidemic of mountain fever has broken out in two of our camps —the new No. 8 and No. 1. We have already nearly eighty cases on the sick list, chiefly amongst the new hands from Ottawa who are not yet acclimatized. The summer rains have been exceedingly heavy, which in a large measure accounts for the trouble. I shall be glad if you will send up medical aid, and a supply of drugs, at once. Dysentery is likely to follow, and you know what that means.

" We are necessarily short-handed now, but, by increasing hours and offering inducements, and by engaging any stray hands that filter up to the camps, I hope to keep the work going satisfactorily. I am isolating the sick, of course, but it is most important that you send me the medical aid at once," etc., etc.

Dave was silent for a while after reading the letter, and the gravity of his expression was enhanced by the extreme plainness of his features. His steady eyes were looking out through the open doorway at the mill beyond, as though it were some living creature to whom he was bound by ties of the deepest affection, and for whom he saw the foreshadowing of disaster. At last he turned.

" Damn the rain," he said impatiently. Then he added, " I'll see to it."

Dawson glanced quickly at his chief.

" Nothin' I ken do, boss ? " he inquired casually.

A grim smile played over Dave's rugged features.

" Nothing, I guess," he said, " unless you can fix a nozzle on to heaven's water-main and turn it on to the strikers down east."

The other shook his head seriously.

" I ain't worth a cent in the plumbin' line, boss," he said.

Dawson left the office. The mill claimed him at all times. He never neglected his charge, and rarely allowed himself long absences beyond the range of its strident music. The pressure of work seemed to increase every day. He knew that the strain on his employer was enormous, and somehow he would have been glad if he could have shared this new responsibility.

Dave had just taken his slicker from the wall again when Dawson came back to the door.

" Say, ther's that feller Mansell been around this mornin' lookin' fer a job. I sed he'd best come around to-morrer. I didn't guess I'd take him on till I see you. He's a drunken bum anyway."

Dave nodded.

" He used to be a dandy sawyer," he said, " and we need 'em. Is he drinking now ? "

" I've heard tell. He stank o' whiskey 's mornin'. That's why I passed him on. Yes, he's a dandy sawyer, sure. He was on the ' water wagon' 'fore he went off up north with young Truscott. Mebbe he'll sober up agin—if we put him to work."

Dave clenched the matter in his decided way.

" Put him on the ' time sheet ' to-morrow, and set him on the No. 1 rollers, beside our night office. You can keep a sharp eye on him there. He's a bit of a backslider, but if giving him a job'll pull him up and help him, why, give it him. We've no right to refuse."

He struggled into his slicker again as Dawson went off. He inspected the weather outside with no very friendly eye. It meant so much to him. At the moment the deluge was like a bursting waterspout, and the yards were like a lake dotted with islands of lumber. But he plunged out into it without a moment's hesitation. His work must go on, no matter what came.

He hurried off in the direction of Chepstow's house. It was some time since he had seen his friend, and though the cause of his present visit was so serious, he was glad of the opportunity of making it.

Tom Chepstow saw him coming, and met him on the veranda. He was always a man of cheery spirits, and just now, in spite of the weather, he was well enough satisfied with the world. Matters between Betty and Jim Truscott had been settled just as he could wish, so there was little to bother him.

" I was really considering the advisability of a telephone from here to your office, Dave," he said, with a smiling welcome. " But joking apart, I never seem to see you now. How's things down there ? If report says truly, you're doing a great work."

Dave shook his head.

" The mills are," he said modestly.

Chepstow laughed heartily.

" That's your way of putting it. You and the mills are one. Nobody ever speaks of one without including the other. You'll never marry, my boy. You are wedded to the shriek of your beloved buzz-saws. Here, take off those things and come in. We've got a drop of Mary's sloe gin somewhere."

They went into the parlor, and Dave removed his oilskins. While he hung them to drain on a nail outside, the parson poured him out a wineglass of his wife's renowned sloe gin. He drank it down quickly, not because he cared particularly about it, but out of compliment to his friend's wife. Then he set his glass down, and began to explain his visit.

" This isn't just a friendly visit, Tom," he said. " It's business. Bad business. You've got to help me out."

The parson opened his eyes. It was something quite new to have Dave demanding help.

" Go ahead," he said, his keen eyes lighting with amusement.

Dave drew a bunch of letters from his coat pocket. He glanced over them hastily, and picked out Mason's and handed it to the other. In picking it out he had discovered another letter he had left unopened.

" Read that," he said, while he glanced at the address on the unopened envelope.

The handwriting was strange to him, and while Tom Chepstow was reading Mason's letter he tore the other open. As he read, the gravity of his face slowly relaxed. At last an exclamation from the parson made him look up.

" This is terrible, Dave ! "

" It's a bit fierce," the other agreed. " Have you read it all ? " he inquired.

" Yes."

" Then you've got my meaning in coming to you ? "

" I see. I hadn't thought of it."

Dave smiled into the other's face.

" You're going to do it for me ? It may mean weeks. It may even mean months. You see, it's an epidemic. At the best it might be only a couple of weeks. They're tough, those boys. On the other hand it might mean—anything to me."

Chepstow nodded. He understood well enough what an epidemic of mountain fever in his lumber camps must mean to Dave. He understood the conditions under which he stood with regard to his contract. A catastrophe like that might mean ruin. And ruin for Dave would mean ruin for nearly all connected with Malkern.

" Yes, I'll do it, Dave. Putting all friendship on one side, it is clearly my duty. Certainly. I'll go up there and lend all the aid I possibly can. You must outfit me with drugs and help."

Dave held out his hand, and the two men gripped.

" Thanks, Tom," he said simply, although he experienced a world of relief and gratitude. " I wouldn't insult you with a bribe before you consented, but when you come back there's a thumping check for your charities lying somewhere around my office."

The parson laughed in his whole-hearted fashion, while his friend once more donned his oilskins.

" I'm always open to that sort of bribery, old boy," he said, and was promptly answered by one of Dave's slow smiles.

" That's good," he said. Then he held up his other letter, but he did not offer it to be read.

" Betty told you what happened at my office the other day—I mean, what happened to Jim Truscott ? " The parson's face clouded with swift anger.

" The ras ——"

" Just so. Yes, we had some bother ; but he's just sent me this. A most apologetic letter. He offers to sell me his mill now. I wanted to buy it, you know. He wants twenty thousand dollars cash for it. I shall close the deal at once." He laughed.

" Hard up, I s'pose ? "

Dave shook his head.

" I don't think so. His change of front is curious, though," he went on thoughtfully. "How-

ever, that don't matter. I want the mill, and—I'm
going to buy. So long. I've got to go and look
at that piece of new track I'm getting laid down.
My single line to the depot isn't sufficient. I'll let
you know about starting up to the camps. I've
got a small gang of lumber-jacks coming up from
Ottawa. Maybe I'll get you to go up with them
later. Thanks, Tom."

The two men shook hands again, and Dave departed.

He battled his way through the driving rain to
his railroad construction, and on the road he
thought a good deal of Truscott's neglected letter.
There was something in its tone he could not convince himself about. Why, he asked himself,
should he, so closely following on the events which
had happened in his offiee, deliberately turn round
and display such a Christian-like spirit? Somehow
it didn't seem to suit him. It didn't carry conviction. Then there was the letter; its wording
was too careful. It was so deliberately careful that
it suggested a suppression of real feeling. This
was his impression, and though Dave was usually
an unsuspicious man, he could not shake it off.

He thought of little else but that letter all the
way to his works, and after reviewing the man's
attitude from what, in his own simple honesty, he
considered to be every possible standpoint, he
finally, with a quaint, even quixotic, kindliness
assured himself that there could after all be but one
interpretation to it. The man was penitent at his

painful exhibition before Betty, and his vile accusations against himself. That his moral strength
was not equal to standing the strain of a personal
interview. That his training up at the Yukon,
where he had learned the sordid methods of a
professional gambler, had suggested the selling of
his mill to him as a sort of peace-offering. And
the careful, stilted tone of the letter itself was due
to the difficulty of its composition. Further, he
decided to accept his offer, and do so in a cordial,
friendly spirit, and, when opportunity offered, to
endeavor, by his own moral influence, to drag him
back to the paths of honest citizenship. This was
the decision to which his generous nature prompted
him. But his head protested.

CHAPTER XII

WHEN Dave reached the construction camp the work was in full swing. The men, clad in oilskins, paid little heed to the rain. Ahead was the gang spreading the heavy stone gravel bed, behind it came those laying and trimming ties. Following close upon their heels came others engaged in setting and bolting the rails, while hard in the rear followed a gang leveling, checking guage, and ballasting. It was very rough railroad construction, but the result was sufficient for the requirements. It was rapid, and lacked the careful precision of a " permanent way," but the men were working at high pressure against time.

Dave saw that all was well here. He exchanged a few words with the foreman, and gave his orders. Then he passed on, intending to return to the mill for his buckboard. Crossing the bridge to take a short cut, he encountered Betty driving home from her school in her uncle's buggy. She drew up at once.

" Whither away, Dave ? " she cried. Then she hastily turned the dozy old mare aside, so as to open the wheels to let the man climb in. " Come along; don't stand there in the rain. Isn't it awful? The river'll be flooding to-morrow if it doesn't stop soon. Back to the mills?"

Dave clambered into the buggy and divested himself of his dripping oilskins. The vehicle was a covered one, and comparatively rain-proof, even in such a downpour.

"Well, I guess so," he said. "I'm just going back to get my buckboard. Then I'm going up to get a look at Jim Truscott's old mill. He's sent word this morning to say he'll sell it me."

The girl chirruped at the old mare, but offered no comment. The simple process of driving over a road nothing could have induced the parson's faithful beast to leave seemed to demand all her attention.

"Did he send, or—have you seen him?" she asked him presently. And it was plain that the matter was of unusual interest to her.

"I said he sent. He wrote to me—and mailed the letter."

"Was there anything—else in the letter?"

The girl's tone was cold enough. Dave, watching her, was struck by the decision in her expression. He wanted to hear what she thought of the letter. He was anxious to see its effect on her. He handed it to her, and quietly took the reins out of her hands.

"You can read it," he said. And Betty eagerly unfolded the paper.

The mare plodded on, splashing solemnly and indifferently through the torrential streams flooding the trail, and they were nearly through the village by the time she handed the letter back and resumed the reins.

"Curious. I—I don't think I understand him at all," she said gravely.

"It's an apology," said Dave, anxious for her to continue.

"Yes, I suppose it is." She paused. "But why to you?" Then a whimsical smile spread over her round face. "I thought you two were nearly square. Now, if the apology had come to me——"

"Yes, I hadn't thought of that."

Both sat thinking for some time. They arrived at the point where the trail turned up to Tom Chepstow's house. Betty ignored the turning and kept on.

"Is that mill worth all that money?" she asked suddenly.

Dave shook his head.

"You've come too far," he said, pointing at her uncle's house. And the girl smiled.

"I want to have a look at the mill. Why are you buying it at that price, Dave?"

"Because there's no time to haggle, and—I want it."

Betty nodded. She was looking straight ahead, and the man failed to see the tender light his words had conjured in her eyes. She knew that Dave would never have paid that money to anybody else, no matter how much he wanted the mill. He was doing it for Jim. However unworthy the man was, it made no difference to his large-hearted nature.

The tenderness still lingered in her eyes when she turned to him again.

" Is Jim hard up ? " she inquired.

The frigidity of her tone was wholly at variance with her expression. But it told plainly of her feelings for the subject of her inquiry. Dave shook his head.

" From all I've heard, and from his own talk, I'd guess not."

Betty suddenly became very angry. She wanted to shake somebody, even Dave, since he was the only person near enough to be shaken.

" He says in his letter, ' as the mill is no further use to me,' " she cried indignantly. " Dave, your Christian spirit carries you beyond all bounds. You have no right to give all that money for it. It isn't worth it anyway. You are—and he—he— oh, I've simply no words for him ! "

" But your uncle, with due regard for his cloth, has," Dave put in quickly.

Betty's indignation was gone in an instant, lost in the laugh which responded to his dry tone.

He had no intention of making her laugh, but he was glad she did so. It told him so much. It reassured him of something on which he had needed reassurance. Her parting with Jim, giving up as it did the habit and belief of years, had troubled him. Then in some measure he had felt himself responsible, although he knew perfectly well that no word of his had ever encouraged her on the course she had elected. He was convinced now. Her regard for Jim was utterly dead, had been dead far longer than probably even she realized.

With this conviction a sudden wild hope leapt within him; but, like summer lightning, its very brilliancy left the night seemingly darker. No, it could never be now. Betty liked him, liked him only too well. Her frank friendliness was too out-spoken, and then—ah, yes, he knew himself. Did he ever get the chance of forgetting? Did not his mirror remind him every morning? Did not his hair brushes, even, force it upon him as they loyally struggled to arrange some order in his obstinate wiry hair? Did not every chair, even his very bed, cry out at the awful burden they were called upon to support? Somehow his thoughts made him re-bellious. Why should he be so barred? Why should he be denied the happiness all men are created for? But in a man like Dave such rebel-lion was not likely to find vent in words, or even mood.

In the midst of his thought the drone of his own distant mills came to him through the steady hiss of the rain. The sound held him, and he experi-enced a strange comfort. It was like an answer to his mute appeal. It reminded him that his work lay before him. It was a call to which he was wedded, bound; it claimed his every nerve; it de-manded his every thought like the most exacting mistress; and, for the moment, it gripped him with all the old force.

"Say," he cried, holding up a warning finger, untidy with years of labor, "isn't she booming? Hark at the saws," he went on, his eyes glowing with pride and enthusiasm. "They're singing to beat the band. It's real music."

They listened.

"Hark!" he went on presently, and Betty's eyes watched him with a tender smile in their brown depths. "Hear the rise and fall of it as the breeze carries it. Hear the 'boom' of the 'ninety-footers' as they drop into the shoots. Isn't it great? Isn't it elegant music?"

Betty nodded. Her sympathy was with him if she smiled at his words.

"A lumbering symphony," she said.

Dave's face suddenly fell.

"Ah," he said apologetically, "you weren't brought up on a diet of buzz-saw trimmings."

Betty shook her head.

"No," she said gently, "patent food."

Dave's enthusiasm dropped from him, and his face, unlit by it, had fallen back into its stern set. At the sight of the almost tragic change Betty's heart smote her, and she hastened to make amends, fearful lest he should fail to realize the sympathy she had for him.

"Ah, no, Dave," she cried. "I know. I understand. I, too, love those mills for what they mean to you, to us, to Malkern. They are your world.

They are our world. You have slowly, laboriously built them up. You have made us—Malkern. Your prosperity means happiness and prosperity to hundreds in our beloved valley. You do not love those mills for the fortune they are piling up for you, but for the sake of those others who share in your great profits and whose lives you have been able to gladden. I know you, Dave. And I understand the real music you hear."

The man shook his head, but his voice rang with deep feeling. He knew that he did not deserve all this girl's words conveyed, but, coming from her, it was very sweet.

"Little Betty," he said, " you kind of run away with things. There's a fellow called 'Dave' I think about a heap. I think about him such a heap I'm most always thinking of him. He's got ambition bad—so bad he thinks of precious little else. Then he's most terrible human. You'd marvel if you knew just how human he was. Now you'd think, maybe, he'd not want anything he hasn't got, wouldn't you? You'd think he was happy and content to see everything he undertakes prospering, and other folks happy. Well, he just isn't, and that's a fact. He's mighty thankful for mercies received, but there's a heap of other mercies he grumbles because he hasn't got."

There was so much sincerity in the man's voice that Betty turned and stared at him.

"And aren't you happy, Dave?" she asked, hardly knowing what she said, but, woman-like, fixing on the one point that appealed to her deepest sympathy.

He evaded the direct question.

" I'm as happy as a third child in playtime," he said; and then, before she could fully grasp his meaning, " Ah, here's the mill. Guess we'll pull up right here."

The old mare came to a standstill, and Dave sprang out before Betty could answer him. And as soon as she had alighted he led the horse to a shed out of the rain.

Then together they explored the mill, and their talk at once became purely technical. The man became the practical lumberman, and, note-book in hand, he led the way from room to room and floor to floor, observing every detail of the conditions prevailing. And all the time they talked, Betty displaying such an exhaustive knowledge of the man's craft that at times she quite staggered him. It was a revelation, a source of constant wonder, and it added a zest to the work which made him love every moment spent in carrying it out.

It was over an hour before the inspection was finished, and to Dave it scarcely seemed more than a matter of minutes. Then there was yet the drive home with Betty at his side. As they drove away the culminating point in the man's brief happiness was reached when the girl, with interest such as his own might have been, pointed out the value of his purchase.

" It will take you exactly a week to outfit that

mill, I should say," she said. " Its capacity for big
stuff is so small you shouldn't pay a cent over ten
thousand dollars for it."

Dave smiled. Sometimes Betty's keenness of
perception in his own business made him feel very
small. Several times already that morning she had
put things so incisively before him that he found
himself wondering whether he had considered them
from the right point of view. He was about to answer her, but finally contented himself with a wondering exclamation.

" For Heaven's sake, Betty, where did you learn
it all?"

It was a delighted laugh that answered him.

"Where? Where do you think? Why, from
the one man competent to teach me. You forget
that I came to you for instruction five years ago."

The girl's eyes were dancing with pleasure.
Somehow the desire for this man's praise and approval had unconsciously become part of her whole
outlook. Her simple honesty would not let her
deny it—showed her no reason for denying it.
She sometimes told herself it was just her vanity; it
was the desire of a pupil for a master's praise.
She, as yet, could see no other reason for it, and
would have laughed at the idea that any warmer
feeling could possibly underlie it.

Dave's pleasure in her acknowledgment was very
evident.

" I haven't forgotten, Betty," he said. " But I
never taught you all that. It's your own clever lit-

tle head. You could give Joel Dawson a start and beat him."

"You don't understand," the girl declared quickly. "It was you who gave me the ground-work, and then I thought and thought. You see, I—I wanted to help Jim when he came back."

Dave had no reply to make. The girl's plain statement had damped his enthusiasm. He had forgotten Jim. She had done this for love of the other man.

"I want you to do me a great favor," she went on presently. "I want it very—very much. You think I've learned a lot. Well, I want to learn more. I don't know quite why—I s'pose it's because I'm interested. I want to see the big lumber being trimmed. I want to see your own mill in full work, and have what I don't understand explained to me. Will you do it? Some night. I'd like to see it all in its most inspiring light. Will you, Dave?"

She laid a coaxing hand on his great arm, and looked eagerly into his eyes. At that moment the lumberman would have promised her the world. And he would have striven with every nerve in his body to fulfil his promise.

"Sure," he said simply. "Name your own time."

And for once the girl didn't thank him in her usual frank way. She simply drew her hand away and chirruped at the old mare.

For the rest of the drive home she remained

silent. It was as though Dave's ready, eager promise had suddenly affected her in some disturbing way. Her brown eyes looked straight ahead along the trail, and they were curiously serious.

They reached the man's home. He alighted, and she drove on to her own destination with a feeling of relief not unmixed with regret.

Dave's mother had been long waiting dinner for her boy. She had seen the buggy and guessed who was in it, and as he came up she greeted him with pride and affection shining in her old eyes.

" That was Betty?" she inquired, moving across to the dinner-table, while the man removed his slicker.

" Yes, ma," he said coolly. He had no desire to discuss Betty with any one just then, not even with his mother.

" Driving with her, dear?" she asked, with smiling, searching eyes upon his averted face.

" She gave me a lift," Dave replied, coming over and sitting down at the table.

His mother, instead of helping him to his food, suddenly came round to his side and laid one affectionate hand upon his great shoulder. The contrast in these two had something almost ridiculous in it. He was so huge, and she was so small. Perhaps the only things they possessed in common, outside of their mutual adoration, were the courage and strength which shone in their gray eyes, and the abounding kindliness of heart for all humanity. But whereas these things in the

mother were always second to her love for her boy,
the boy's first thought and care was for the great
work his own hands had created.

"Dave," she said very gently, "when am I
going to have a daughter? I'm getting very, very
old, and I don't want to leave you alone in the
world."

The man propped his elbow on the table and
rested his head on his hand. His eyes were almost
gloomy.

"I don't want to lose you, ma," he said. "It
would break me up ter'ble. Life's mostly lonesome
anyhow." Then he looked keenly up into her
face, and his glance was one of concern. "You—
you aren't ailing any?"

The old woman shook her head, and her eyes
smiled back at him.

"No, boy, I'm not ailing. But I worry some at
times. You see, I like Betty very, very much. In
a different way, I'm almost as fond of her as you
are ——"

Dave started and was about to break in, but his
mother shook her head, and her hand caressed his
cheek with infinite tenderness.

' "Why don't you marry her, now—now that the
other is broken off ——"

But Dave turned to her, and, swept by an almost
fierce emotion, would not be denied.

"Why, ma? Why?" he cried, with all the
pent-up bitterness of years in the depth of his tone.
" Look at me! Look at me! And you ask me

why." He held out his two hands as though to let her see him as he was. " Would any woman think of me—look at me with thoughts of love? She couldn't. What am I? A mountain of muscle, brawn, bone, whatever you will, with a face and figure even a farmer would hate to set up over a corn patch at harvest time." He laughed bitterly. " No—no, ma," he went on, his tone softening, and taking her worn hand tenderly in his. " There are folks made for marriage, and folks that aren't. And when folks that aren't get marrying they're doing a mean thing on the girl. I'm not going to think a mean thing for Betty—let alone do one."

His mother moved away to her seat.

" Well, boy, I'll say no more, but I'm thinking a time'll come when you'll be doing a mean thing by Betty if you don't, and she'll be the one that'll think it ——"

" Ma!"

" The dinner's near cold."

CHAPTER XIII

BETTY DECIDES

Two nights later Dave was waiting in the tally room for his guests to arrive. The place was just a corner partitioned off from the milling floor. It was here the foreman kept account of the day's work—a bare room, small, and hardly worth the name of "office." Yet there was work enough done in it to satisfy the most exacting master.

The master of the mills had taken up a position in the narrow doorway, in full view of the whole floor, and was watching the sawyer on No. 1. It was Mansell. He beheld with delight the wonderful skill with which the man handled the giant logs as they creaked and groaned along over the rollers. He appeared to be sober, too. His deliberate movements, timed to the fraction of a second, were sufficient evidence of this. He felt glad that he had taken him on his time-sheet. Every really skilful sawyer was of inestimable value at the moment, and, after all, this man's failing was one pretty common to all good lumbermen.

Dawson came up, and Dave nodded in the sawyer's direction.

"Working good," he observed with satisfaction.

"Too good to last, if I know anything," grumbled the foreman. "He'll get breakin' out, an then —— I've a mind to set him on a ' buzz-saw.' These big saws won't stand for tricks if he happens to git around with a ' jag ' on."

" You can't put a first-class sawyer on to a ' buzzer,' " said Dave decisively. " It's tantamount to telling him he doesn't know his work. No, keep him where he is. If he ' signs ' in with a souse on, push him out till he's sober. But so long as he's right let him work where he is."

" Guess you're ' boss ' o' this lay-out," grumbled the foreman.

" Just so."

Then, as though the matter had no further concern for him, Dawson changed the subject.

" There's twenty ' jacks ' scheduled by to-night's mail," he said, as though speaking of some dry-goods instead of a human freight.

" They're for the hills to-night. Mr. Chepstow's promised to go up and dose the boys for their fever. I'm putting it to him to-night. He'll take 'em with him. By the way, I'm expecting the parson and Miss Betty along directly. They want to get a look at this." He waved an arm in the direction of the grinding rollers. " They want to see it— busy."

Dawson was less interested in the visitors.

" I see 'em as I come up," he said indifferently. " Looked like they'd been around your office."

Dave turned on him sharply.

" Go down and bring 'em along up. And say— get things ready for sending up to the camps to-

night.   Parson'll have my buckboard and the black
team.   He's got to travel quick.   They can come
right away back when he's got there.   See he's got
plenty of bedding and rations.   Load it down good.
There's a case of medical supplies in my office.
That goes with him.   Then you'll get three
'democrats' from Mulloc's livery barn for the boys.
See they've got plenty of grub too."

When Dave gave sharp orders, Dawson simply
listened and obeyed.   He understood his employer,
and never ventured criticism at such times.   He
hurried away now to give the necessary orders, and
then went on to find the visitors.

Directly he had gone the master of the mills
moved over to the sawyer on No. 1.

"You haven't forgotten your craft, Mansell," he
said pleasantly, his deep voice carrying, clarion-
like, distinctly over the din of the sawing-floor.

"Would you fergit how t' eat, boss?" the man
inquired surlily, measuring an oncoming log keenly
with his eye.   He bore down on a "jolting" lever
and turned the log into a fresh position.   Then he
leant forward and tipped the end of it with chalk.
Hand and eye worked mechanically together.   He
knew to a hairsbreadth just where the trimming blade
should strike the log to get the maximum square
of timber.

Dave shook his head.

"It would take some forgetting," he said, with a
smile.   "You see there's always a stomach to
remind you."

The log was passing, and the man had a moment's breathing space while it traveled to the fangs of the rushing saw. He looked up with a pair of dark, brooding eyes in which shone a peculiarly offensive light.

" Jest so," he vouchsafed. " I learned this when I learned t' eat, an' it's filled my belly that long, fi' year ain't like to set me fergittin'."

He turned to the rollers and watched the log. He saw it hit the teeth of the saw plumb on his chalk mark.

" An awful waste out of a lumberman's life, that five years," Dave went on, when the crucial moment had passed. " That mill would have been doing well now, and—and you were foreman."

He was looking straight into the fellow's mean face. He noted the terrible inroads drink had made upon it, the sunken eyes, the pendulous lip, the lines of dissipation in deep furrows round his mouth. He pitied him from the bottom of his heart, but allowed no softness of expression.

" Say," exclaimed the sawyer, with a vicious snap, " when I'm lumberin' I ain't got time fer rememberin' anything else—which is a heap good. I don't guess it's good for any one buttin' in when the logs are rollin'. Guess that log's comin' right back."

The man's unnecessary insolence was a little staggering. Yet Dave rather liked him for it. The independence of the sawyer's spirit appealed to him. He really had no right to criticize Mansell's past, to stir up an unpleasant memory for him.

He knew his men, and he realized that he had overstepped his rights in the matter. He was simply their employer. It was for him to give orders, and for them to obey. In all else he must take them as man and man. He felt now that there was nothing more for him to say, so while the sawyer clambered over to the return rollers, ready for the second journey of the log, he walked thoughtfully back to his office.

At that moment his visitors appeared, escorted by Dawson. The foreman was piloting them with all the air of a guide and the pride of his association with the mills. Betty was walking beside him, and while taking in the wonderful scene that opened out before her, she was listening to the conversation of the two men.

The foreman had taken upon himself to tell the parson of the orders he had received for the night journey, and the details of the preparations being made for it. The news came to Chepstow unpleasantly, yet he understood that its urgency must be great, or Dave would never have decided upon so sudden a journey. He was a little put out, but quite ready to help his friend.

It was the first Betty had heard of it. She was astonished and resentful. She had heard that there was fever up in the hills, but her uncle had told her nothing of Dave's request to him. Therefore, before greetings had been exchanged, and almost before the door of the tally room had closed upon the departing foreman, she opened a volley of questions upon him.

"What's this about uncle going up to the hills to-night, Dave?" she demanded. "Why has it been kept secret? Why so sudden? Why to-night?"

Her inquiring glance turned from one to the other.

Dave made no hurry to reply. He was watching the play of the strong, eager young face. The girl's directness appealed to him even more than her beauty. To-night she looked very pretty in a black clinging gown which made her look almost fragile. She seemed so slight, so delicate, yet her whole manner had such reserve of virile force. He thought now, as he had often thought before, she possessed a brain much too big and keen for her body, yet withal so essentially womanly as to be something to marvel at.

The girl became impatient.

"Why wasn't I told? For goodness' sake don't stand there staring, Dave."

"There's no secrecy exactly, Betty," the lumberman said, "that is, except from the folks in the village. You see, anything likely to check our work, such as fever up in the camps, is liable to set them worrying and talking. We didn't mean to keep it from you ——"

"Yes, yes," the girl broke in. "But why this hurry? Why to-night?"

And so she forced Dave into a full explanation, which alone would satisfy her. At the end of it she turned to her uncle, who had stood quietly by enjoying the manner in which she dictated her will upon the master of the mills.

"It's an awful shame you've got to go, uncle, especially while you've got all the new church affairs upon your hands. But I quite see Dave's right, and we must get the boys well as quickly as possible. We've got to remember that these mills are not only Dave's. They also belong to Malkern —one might almost say to the people of this valley. It is the ship, and—and we are its freight. So we start at midnight. Does auntie know?"

Instantly two pairs of questioning eyes were turned upon her. That coupling of herself with her uncle in the matter had not escaped them.

"Your Aunt Mary knows I am going some time. But she hasn't heard the latest development, my dear," her uncle said. "But—but you said 'we' just now?"

Dave understood. He knew what was coming. But then he understood Betty as did no one else. He smiled.

"Of course I said 'we,'" Betty exclaimed, with a laugh which only served to cloak the resolve that lay behind it. "You are not going alone. Besides, you can physic people well enough, uncle dear, but you can't nurse them worth—worth a cent. School's all right, and can get on without me for a while. Well?" She smiled quickly from one to the other. "Well, we're ready, aren't we? We can't let this interfere with our view of the mill."

Her uncle shook his head.

" You can't go up there, Betty," he said seriously.
" You can't go about amongst those men. They're
good fellows. They're men. But ——" he looked
over at Dave as though seeking support, a thing he
rarely needed. But he was dealing with Betty
now, and where she was concerned, there were times
when he felt that a little support might be welcome.

Dave promptly added his voice in support of his
friend's protest.

" You can't go, little Betty," he said. " You can't,
little girl," he reiterated, shaking his shaggy head.
" You think you know the lumber-jacks, and I'll
allow you know them a lot. But you don't know
'em up in those camps. They're wild men.
They're just as savage as wolves, and foolish as
babes. They're just great big baby men, and as
irresponsible as half-witted schoolboys. I give
you my word I can't let you go up. I know how
you want to help us out. I know your big heart.
And I know still more what a help you'd be ——"

" And that's just why I'm going," Betty snapped
him up. That one unfortunate remark undid all
the impression his appeal might otherwise have
made. And as the two men realized the finality of
her tone, they understood the hopelessness of turning her from her purpose.

" Uncle dear," she went on, " please say ' yes.'
Because I'm going, and I'd feel happier with your
sanction. Dave," she turned with a smile upon the
lumberman, " you've just got to say ' yes,' or I'll
never—never let you subscribe to any charity or—

or anything I ever get up in Malkern again. Now you two dears, mind, I'm going anyway. I'll just count three, and you both say ' yes ' together."

She counted deliberately, solemnly, but there was a twinkle in her brown eyes.

" One—two—three ! "

And a simultaneous " Yes " came as surely as though neither had any objection to the whole proceeding. And furthermore, both men joined in the girl's laugh when they realized how they had been cajoled. To them she was quite irresistible.

" I don't know whatever your aunt will say," her uncle said lugubriously.

" It's not so much what she'll say as—as what may happen up there," protested Dave, his conscience still pricking him.

But the girl would have no more of it.

" You are two dear old—yes, ' old '—sillies. Now, Dave, the mills ! "

Betty carried all before her with these men who were little better than her slaves. They obeyed her lightest command hardly knowing they obeyed it. Her uncle's authority, whilst fully acknowledged by her, was practically non-existent. Her loyalty to him and her love for both her guardians left no room for the exercise of authority. And Dave— well, he was her adviser in all things, and like most people who have an adviser, Betty went her own sweet way, but in such a manner that made the master of the mills believe that his help and advice were practically indispensable to her.

CHAPTER XIV

THE MILLS

Dave obediently led the way out of the tally room to the great milling floor, and at once they were in the heart of his world.

It was by no means new to Betty; she had seen it all before, but never had the mills been driven at such a pressure as now, and the sensation the knowledge gave her was one which demanded the satisfaction of optical demonstration. She was thrilled with a sense of emergency. The roar of the machinery carried with it a meaning it had never held before. There was a current of excitement in the swift, skilful movements of the sawyers as they handled the mighty logs.

To her stirred imagination there was a suggestion of superhuman agency, of some nether world, in the yellow light of the flares which lit that vast sea of moving rollers. As she gazed out across it at the dim, distant corners she felt as though at any moment the machinery might suddenly become manned by hundreds of hideous gnomes, such as she had read of in the fairy tales. Yet it was all real, real and human, and Dave was the man who controlled, whose brain and eyes watched over every detail, whose wonderful skill and power were carrying that colossal work to the goal of success.

As she looked, she sighed. She envied the man whose genius had made all this possible.

Above the roar Dave's voice reached her.

"This is only part of it," he said; "come below."

And she followed him to the spiral iron staircase which led to the floor below. Her uncle brought up the rear.

At ordinary times the lower part of the mills was given over to the shops for the manufacture of smaller lumber, building stuff, doors and windows, flooring, and tongue and groove. Betty knew this. She knew every shop by heart, just as she knew most of the workmen by sight. But now it was all changed. The partitions had been torn down, and the whole thrown into one floor. It was a replica of the milling floor above.

Here again were the everlasting rollers; here again were the tremendous logs traveling across and across the floor; here again were the roar and shriek of the gleaming saws. The girl's enthusiasm rose. Her eyes wandered from the fascinating spectacle to the giant at her side. She felt a lump rise in her throat; she wanted to laugh, she wanted to cry; but she did neither. Only her eyes shone as she gazed at him; and his plainness seemed to fall from him. She saw the man standing at her side, but the great ungainly Dave had gone, leaving in his place only such a hero as her glowing heart could create.

They stood there watching, watching. None of the three spoke. None of them had any words.

Dave saw and thought. His great unimaginative head had no care for the picture side of it. His eyes were on the sawyers, most of them stripped to the waist in the heat of their labors in the summer night. To him the interest of the scene lay in the precision and regularity with which log followed log over the rollers, and the skill with which they were cut.

Parson Tom, with a little more imagination, built up in his mind the future prosperity of their beloved valley, and thanked the Almighty Providence that It had sent them such a man as Dave. But Betty, in spite of her practical brain, lost sight of all the practical side of the work. As she watched she was living in such a dream as only comes once in a lifetime to any woman. At that moment her crown of glory was set upon Dave's rough head. All she had hoped for, striven for all her life seemed so small at the thought of him. And the delight of those moments became almost painful. She had always looked upon him as " her Dave," her beloved " chum," her adviser, her prop to lean on at all times. But no. No, no ; he was well and truly named. He was no one's Dave. He was just Dave of the Mills.

They moved on to a small doorway, and passing along a protected gallery they worked their way toward the "boom." The place was a vast backwater of the river, enlarged to accommodate millions of feet of logs. It was packed with a mass of tumbled lumber, over which, in the dim light thrown by waste fire, a hundred and more "jacks" could be seen, clambering like a colony of monkeys, pushing, prizing, easing, pulling with their peaveys to get the logs freed, so that the grappling tackle could seize and haul them up out of the water to the milling floors above.

Here again they paused and silently gazed at the stupendous work going on. There was no more room for wonder either in the girl or her uncle. The maximum had been reached. They could only silently stare.

Dave was the first to move. His keen eyes had closely watched the work. He had seen log after log fly up in the grapple of the hydraulic cranes, he had seen them shot into the gaping jaws of the building, he had seen that not an idle hand was down there in the boom, and he was satisfied. Now he wanted to go on.

"There's the ' waste,' " he said casually. " But I guess you've seen that heaps, only it's a bit bigger now, and we've had to build two more ' feeders.' "

Betty answered him, and her tone was unusually subdued.

" Let's see it all, Dave," she said, almost humbly.

All her imperiousness had gone, and in its place was an ecstatic desire to see all and anything that owed its existence to this man.

Dave strode on. He was quite unconscious of the change that had taken place in Betty's thoughts of him. To him these things had become every-day matters of his work. They meant no more to him than the stepping-stones toward success which every one who makes for achievement has to tread.

Their way took them up another iron staircase outside the main building. At the top of it was an iron gallery, which passed round two angles of the mill, and terminated at the three feeders, stretching out from the mills to the great waste fire a hundred yards away. From this gallery there was an inspiring view of the " everlasting " fire. It had been lit when the mill first started its operations years ago, and had been burning steadily ever since; and so it would go on burning as long as the saws inside continued to rip the logs.

The feeders were three shafts, supported on iron trestle work, each carrying an ever-moving, endless bed on which the waste trimmings of the logs were thrown. These were borne upward and outward for a hundred yards till the shafts hung high above the blazing mass. Here the endless band doubled under, and its burden was precipitated below, where it was promptly devoured by the insatiable flames.

For some moments they watched the great timber pass on its way to the fire, and so appalling appeared the waste that Parson Tom protested.

" This seems to me positively wanton," he said. " Why, the stuff you're sending on to that fire is perfect lumber. At the worst, what grand fuel it would make for the villagers."

Dave nodded his great head. He often felt the same about it.

"Makes you sicken some to see it go, doesn't it?" he said regretfully. "It does me. But say, we've got a waste yard full, and the folks in Malkern are welcome to all they can haul away. Even Mary uses it in her stoves, but they can't haul or use it fast enough. If it wasn't for this fire there wouldn't be room for a rat in Malkern inside a year. Guess it's got to be, more's the pity."

There was no more to be said, and the three watched the fire in silent awe. It was a marvelous sight. The dull red-yellow light shone luridly over everything. The mill on the one hand loomed majestically out of the dark background of night. The fire, over forty feet in height, lit the buildings in a curious, uncanny fashion, throwing grotesque and lurid shadows in every direction. Then all around, on the farther sides, spread the distant dark outline of ghostly pine woods, whose native gloom resisted a light, which, by contrast, was so insignificantly artificial. It gave a weird impression that had a strong effect upon Betty's rapt imagination.

Dave again broke the spell. He could not spare too much time, and, as they moved away, Betty sighed.

"It's all very, very wonderful," she said, moving along at his side. "And to think even in winter, no matter what the snowfall, that fire never goes out."

Dave laughed.

"If it rained like it's been raining to-day for six

months," he said, " I don't guess it could raise more than a splutter." Then he turned to Tom Chepstow. " Is there anything else you'd like to see ? You've got three hours to midnight."

But the parson had seen enough; and as he had yet to overhaul the supplies he was to take up to the hill camps, they made their way back to the tally room. At the rollers on which Mansell was working Dave paused with Betty, while her uncle went on.

They watched a great log appear at the opening over the boom. The chains of the hydraulic crane creaked under their burden. Dave pointed at it silhouetted against the light of the waste fire beyond.

" Watch him," he said. " That's Dick Mansell."

The pride in his tone was amply justified. Mansell was at the opening, waiting, peavey in hand. They saw the log dripping and swaying as it was hauled up until its lower end cleared the rollers. On the instant the sawyer leant forward and plunged his hook into the soft pine bark. Then he strained steadily and the log came slowly onward. A whistle, and the crane was eased an inch at a time. The man held his strain, and the end lowered ever further over the rollers until it touched. Two more whistles, and the log was lowered faster until it lay exactly horizontal, and then the rollers carried it in. Once its balance was passed, the sawyer struck the grappling chains loose with his peavey, and, with a rattle, they fell clear, while the prostrate giant lumbered ponderously into the mill.

It was all done so swiftly.

Now Mansell sprang to the foremost end and chalked the log as it traveled. Then, like a cat, he sprang to the rear of it and measured with his eye. Dissatisfied, he ran to its side and prized it into a fresh position, glancing down it, much as a rifleman might glance over his sights. Satisfied at length, he ran on ahead of the moving log to his saws. Throwing over a lever, he quickened the pace of the gleaming blade. On came the log. The yielding wood met the merciless fangs of the saw upon the chalk line, and passed hissing and shrieking on its way as though it had met with no obstruction.

The girl took a deep breath.

"Splendid," she cried. Well as she knew this work, to-night it appealed to her with a new force, a deeper and more personal interest.

"Easy as pie," Dave laughed. Then more seriously, "Yet it's dangerous as—as hell."

Betty nodded. She knew.

"But you don't have many accidents, thank goodness."

Dave shrugged.

"Not many—considering. But you don't often see a sawyer with perfectly sound hands. There's generally something missing."

"I know. Look at Mansell's arm there." Betty pointed at a deep furrow on the man's forearm.

" Yes, Mansell's been through it. I remember
when he got that. Like an Indian holds his first
scalp as a sign of his prowess, or the knights of old
wore golden spurs as an emblem of their knight-
hood, the sawyer minus a finger or so has been literally 'through the mill,' and can claim proficiency in
his calling. But those are not the dangers I was
figgering on."

Betty waited for him to go on.

" Yes," he said solemnly. " It's the breaking
saw. That's the terror of a sawyer's life. And just
now of mine. It's always in the back of my head
like a black shadow. One breaking saw would do
more damage cutting up this big stuff than it would
take a fire to do in an hour. It would be the next
best thing to bursting a charge of dynamite. Take
this saw of Mansell's. A break, a bend out of the
truth, the log slips while it's being cut. Any of
these things. You wouldn't think a ' ninety-footer '
could be thrown far. If any of those things happened, good-bye to anything or anybody with
whom it came into contact. But we needn't to
worry. Let's get in there to your uncle."

CHAPTER XV

In the office they found Parson Tom at work with pencil and note-book. The latter he closed as they came in.

" For goodness' sake shut that door behind you," he laughed. " I've been trying to think of the things I need for my journey to-night, but that uproar makes it well-nigh impossible."

The words brought Betty back to matters of the moment. Everything had been forgotten in the interest of her tour of the mills at Dave's side. Now she realized that time was short, and she too must make her preparations.

Dave closed the door.

" We'd best get down to the barn and fix things there," he said. " Then you can get right back home and arrange matters with Mary. Betty could go on and prepare her."

The girl nodded her approval.

" Yes," she said, " and I can get my own things together."

Both men looked at her.

She answered their challenge at once, but now there was a great change in her manner. She no longer laughed at them. She no longer carried things with a high hand. She intended going up to the camps, but it almost seemed as though she desired their justification to support her decision. Somehow that tour of the mills at Dave's side had lessened her belief in herself.

"Yes," she said, "I know neither of you wants me to go. Perhaps, from your masculine point of view, you are both right. But—but I want to go. I do indeed. This is no mere whim. Uncle, speak up and admit the necessity for nursing. Who on earth is up there to do it? No one."

Then she turned to Dave, and her earnest eyes were full of almost humble entreaty.

"You won't refuse me, Dave?" she said. "I feel I must go. I feel that some one, some strange voice, is calling to me to go. That my presence there is needed. I am only a woman, and in these big schemes of yours it is ridiculous to think that I should play a part. Yet somehow—somehow —— Oh, Dave, won't you let me help, if only in this small way? It will be something for me to look back upon when you have succeeded; something for me to cherish, this thought that I have helped you even in so small a way. You won't refuse me. It is so little to you, and it means so—so much to me."

Her uncle was watching the grave face of the lumberman; and when she finished he waited, smiling, for the effect of her appeal.

It was some moments before Dave answered. Betty's eyes were shining with eager hope, and at last her impatience got the better of her.

" You said ' yes' once to-night," she urged softly.

Her uncle's smile broadened. He was glad the onus of this thing was on the broad shoulders of his friend.

" Betty," said Dave at last, looking squarely into her eyes, " will you promise me to keep to the sick camps, and not go about amongst the ' jacks' who aren't sick without your uncle?"

There was something in the man's eyes which made the girl drop hers suddenly. She colored slightly, perhaps with vexation. She somehow felt awkward. And she had never felt awkward with Dave in her life before. However, she answered him gladly.

" I promise—promise willingly."

" Then I'll not go back on my promise. Go and get ready, little girl," he said gently.

She waited for no more. Her eyes thanked him, and for once, though he never saw it, nor, if he had, would he have understood it, there was a shyness in them such as had never been there before.

As the door closed behind her he turned with a sigh to his old friend.

" Well, Tom," he said, with a dry, half regretful smile, " it strikes me there are a pair of fools in this room."

The parson chuckled delightedly.

" But one is bigger than the other. You wait until Mary sees you. My word!"

Betty hurried out of the mill. She knew the

time was all too short; besides, she did not want to give the men time to change their minds. And then there was still her aunt to appease.

Outside in the yards the thirsty red sand had entirely lapped up the day's. rain. It was almost as dry as though the summer rains were mere showers. The night was brilliantly fine, and though as yet there was no moon, the heavens were diamond-studded, and the milky way spread its ghostly path sheer across the sky. Half running in her eagerness, the girl dodged amongst the stacks of lumber, making her way direct to a point in the fence nearest to her home. To go round to the gates would mean a long, circuitous route that would waste at least ten minutes.

As she sped, the din of the mill rapidly receded, and the shadows thrown by the flare lights of the yards behind her lengthened and died out, merged in the darkness of the night beyond their radiance. At the fence she paused and looked about for the easiest place to climb. It was high, and the lateral rails were wide apart. It was all the same whichever way she looked, so, taking her courage in both hands, and lifting her skirts knee high, she essayed the task. It was no easy matter, but she managed it, coming down on the other side much more heavily than she cared about. Still, in her excited state, she didn't pause to trouble about a trifle like that.

She was strangely happy without fully understanding the reason. This trip to the hills would be a break in the monotony of her daily routine. But somehow it was not that that elated her. She loved her work, and at no time wanted to shirk it. No, it was not that. Yet it was something to do with her going. Something to do with the hill camps; something to do with helping—Dave—ah! Yes, it was that. She knew it now, and the knowledge thrilled her with a feeling she had never before experienced.

Her course took her through a dense clump of pine woods. She was far away from the direct trail, but she knew every inch of the way.

Somehow she felt glad of the cool darkness of those woods. Their depth of shadow swallowed her up and hid her from all the rest of the world, and, for the moment, it was good to be alone. She liked the feeling that no one was near her—not even Dave. She wanted to think it all out. She wanted to understand herself. This delight that had come to her, this joy. Dave had promised to let her help him in his great work. It was too good to be true. How she would work. Yes, she would strain every nerve to nurse the men back to health, so that there should be no check in the work.

Suddenly she paused in her thought. Her heart seemed to stand still, then its thumping almost stifled her. She had realized her true motive. Yes, she knew it now. It was not the poor sick men she was thinking of. She was not thinking of her uncle, who would be slaving for sheer love of

his fellow men.   No, it was of Dave she was thinking.   Dave—her Dave.

Now she knew.   She loved him.   She felt it
here, here, and she pressed both hands over her
heart, which was beating tumultuously and thrilling
with an emotion such as she had never known before.   Never, even in the days when she had believed herself in love with Jim Truscott.   She
wanted to laugh, to cry aloud her happiness to the
dark woods which crowded round her.   She wanted
to tell all the world.   She wanted everything about
her to know of it, to share in it.   Oh, how good
God was to her.   She knew that she loved Dave.
Loved him with a passion that swept every thought
of herself from her fevered brain.   She wanted to
be his slave; his—his all.

Suddenly her passion-swept thoughts turned
hideously cold.   What of Dave?   Did he?—could
he?   No, he looked upon her as his little " chum "
and nothing more.   How could it be otherwise?
Had he not witnessed her betrothal to Jim
Truscott?   Had he not been at her side when she
renounced him?   Had he not always looked after
her as an elder brother?   Had he ——

She came to a dead standstill in the heart of the
woods, gripped by a fear that had nothing to do
with her thoughts.   It was the harsh sound of a
voice.   And it was just ahead of her.   It rang
ominously in her ears at such an hour, and in such
a place.   She listened.   Who could be in those
woods at that hour of the night?   Who beside her-

self? The voice was so distinct that she felt it must be very, very near. Then she remembered how the woods echo, particularly at night, and a shiver of fear swept over her at the thought that perhaps the sound of her own footsteps had reached the ears of the owner of the voice. She had no desire to encounter any drunken lumber-jacks in such a place. Her heart beat faster, as she cast about in her mind for the best thing to do.

The voice she had first heard now gave place to another, which she instantly recognized. The recognition shocked her violently. There could be no mistaking the second voice. It was Jim Truscott's. Hardly knowing what she did, she stepped behind a tree and waited.

"I can't get the other thing working yet," she heard Truscott say in a tone of annoyance. "It's a job that takes longer than I figured on. Now, see here, you've got to get busy right away. We must get the brakes on him right now. My job will come on later, and be the final check. That's why I wanted you to-night."

Then came the other voice, and, to the listening girl, its harsh note had in it a surly discontent that almost amounted to open rebellion.

"Say, that ain't how you said, Jim. We fixed it so I hadn't got to do a thing till you'd played your 'hand.' Play it, an' if you fail clear out, then it's right up to me, an' I'll stick to the deal."

Enlightenment was coming to Betty. This was some gambling plot. She knew Jim's record.

Some poor wretch was to be robbed. The other man was of course a confederate. But Jim was talking again. Now his voice was commanding, even threatening.

" This is no damned child's play ; we're going to have no quibbling. You want that money, Mansell, and you've got to earn it. It's the spirit of the bargain I want, not the letter. Maybe you're weakening. Maybe you're scared. Damn it, man ! it's the simplest thing—do as I say and—the money's yours."

At the mention of the man's name Betty was filled with wonder. She had seen Mansell at work in the mill. The night shift was not relieved until six o'clock in the morning. How then came he there ? What was he doing in company with Jim ?

But now the sawyer's voice was raised in downright anger, and the girl's alarm leapt again.

" I said I'd stick to the deal," he cried. Then he added doggedly, " And a deal's a deal."

Jim's reply followed in a much lower key, and she had to strain to hear.

" I'm not going to be fooled by you," he said. " You'll do this job when I say. When I say, mind ——"

But at this point his voice dropped so low that the rest was lost. And though Betty strained to catch the words, only the drone of the voices reached her. Presently even that ceased. Then she heard the sound of footsteps receding in different directions, and she knew the men had parted. When the silence of the woods had swallowed up the last sound she set off at a run for home.

She thought a great deal about that mysterious encounter on her way. It was mysterious, she decided. She wondered what she should do about it. These men were plotting to cheat and rob some of Dave's lumber-jacks. Wasn't it her duty to try and stop them? She was horrified at the thought of the depths to which Jim had sunk. It was all so paltry, so—so mean.

Then the strangeness of the place they had selected for their meeting struck her. Why those woods, so remote from the village? A moment's thought solved the matter to her own satisfaction. No doubt Mansell had made some excuse to leave the mill for a few minutes, and in order not to prolong his absence too much, Jim had come out from the village to meet him. Yes, that was reasonable.

Finally she decided to tell Dave and her uncle. Dave would find a way of stopping them. Trust him for that. He could always deal with such things better—yes, even better than her uncle, she admitted to herself in her new-born pride in him.

A few minutes later the twinkling lights through the trees showed her her destination. Another few minutes and she was explaining to her aunt that she was off to the hill camps nursing. As had been expected, her news was badly received.

"It's bad enough that your uncle's got to go in the midst of his pressing duties," Mrs. Tom exclaimed with heat. " What about the affairs of the new church? What about the sick folk right here? What about old Mrs. Styles? She's likely to die any minute. Who's to bury her with him away? And what about Sarah Dingley? She's haunted— delusions—and there's no one can pacify her but him. And now they must needs take you. It isn't right. You up there amongst all those rough men. It's not decent. It's ——"

" I know, auntie," Betty broke in. " It's all you say. But—but think of those poor helpless sick men up there, with no comfort. They've just got to lie about and either get well, or—or die. No one to care for them. No one to write a last letter to their friends for them. No one to see they get proper food, and ——"

" Stuff and nonsense!" her aunt exclaimed. " Now you, Betty, listen to me. Go, if go you must. I'll have nothing to do with it. It's not with my consent you'll go. And some one is go- ing to hear what I think about it, even if he does run the Malkern Mills. If—if Dave wasn't so big, and such a dear good fellow, I'd like—yes, I'd like to box his ears. Be off with you and see to your packing, miss, and don't forget your thickest flannels. Those mountains are terribly cold at nights, even in summer." Then, as the girl ran off to her room, she exploded in a final burst of anger. " Well there, they're all fools, and I've no patience with any of 'em."

It did not take long for Betty to get her few

things together and pitch them into a grip. The barest necessities were all she required, and her practical mind guided her instinctively. Her task was quite completed when, ten minutes later, she heard the rattle of buckboard wheels and her uncle's cheery voice down-stairs in the parlor.

Then she hurried across to her aunt's room. She knew her uncle so well. He wouldn't bother to pack anything for himself. She dragged a large kit bag from under the bed, and, ransacking the bureau, selected what she considered the most necessary things for his comfort and flung them into it. It was all done with the greatest possible haste, and by the time she had everything ready, her uncle joined her and carried the grips down-stairs. In the meantime Mary Chepstow, all her anger passed, was busily loading the little table with an ample supper. She might disapprove her niece's going, she might resent the sudden call on her husband, but she would see them both amply fed before starting, and that the buckboard was well provisioned for the road.

For the most part supper was eaten in silence. These people were so much in the habit of doing for others, so many calls were made upon them, that such an occasion as this presented little in the way of emergency. It was their life to help others, their delight, and their creed. And Mary's protest meant no more than words, she only hesitated at the thought of Betty's going amongst these rough lumber-jacks. But even this, on reflection, was not so terrible as she at first thought. Betty was an unusual girl, and she expected the unusual from her. So she put her simple trust in the Almighty, and did all she knew to help them.

It was not until the meal was nearly over that Chepstow imparted a piece of news he had gleaned on his way from the mill. He suddenly looked up from his plate, and his eyes sought his niece's face. She was lost in a happy contemplation of the events of that night at the mill. All her thoughts, all her soul was, at that moment, centred upon Dave. Now her uncle's voice startled her into a self-conscious blush.

"Who d'you think I met on my way up here?" he inquired, searching her face.

Betty answered him awkwardly. "I—I don't know," she said.

Her uncle reached for the salad, and helped himself deliberately before he enlightened her further.

"Jim Truscott," he said at last, without looking up.

"Jim Truscott?" exclaimed Aunt Mary, her round eyes wondering. Then she voiced a thought which had long since passed from her niece's mind. "What was he doing out here at this hour of the night?"

The parson shrugged.

"It seems he was waiting for me. He didn't call here, I s'pose?"

Mary shook her head. Betty was waiting to hear more.

"I feel sorry for him," he went on. "I'm inclined to think we've judged him harshly. I'm sure we have. It only goes to show how poor and weak our efforts are to understand and help our fellows. He is very, very repentant. Poor fellow, I have never seen any one so down on his luck. He doesn't excuse himself. In fact, he blames himself even more than we have done."

"Poor fellow," murmured Aunt Mary.

Betty remained silent, and her uncle went on.

"He's off down east to make a fresh start. He was waiting to tell me so. He also wanted to tell me how sorry he was for his behavior to us, to you, Betty, and he trusted you would find it possible to forgive him, and think better of him when he was gone. I never saw a fellow so cut up. It was quite pitiful."

"When's he going?" Betty suddenly asked, and there was a hardness in her voice which startled her uncle.

"That doesn't sound like forgiveness," he said. "Don't you think, my dear, if he's trying to do better you might——"

Betty smiled into the earnest face.

"Yes, uncle, I forgive him everything, freely, gladly—if he is going to start afresh."

"Doubt?"

But Betty still had that conversation in the woods in her mind.

"I mustn't judge him. His own future actions are all that matter. The past is gone, and can be wiped out. I would give a lot to see him—right himself."

" That is the spirit, dear," Aunt Mary put in. " Your uncle is quite right: we must forgive him."

Betty nodded; but remained silent. She was half inclined to tell them all she had heard, but it occurred to her that perhaps she had interpreted it all wrong—and yet—anyway, if he were sincere, if he really meant all he had said to her uncle she must not, had no right to do, or say, anything that could prejudice him. So she kept silent, and her uncle went on.

" He's off to-morrow on the east-bound mail. That's why he was waiting to see me to-night. He told me he had heard I was going up into the hills, and waited to catch me before I went. Said he couldn't go away without seeing me first. I told him I was going physicking, that the camps were down with fever, and the spread of it might seriously interfere with Dave's work. He was very interested, poor chap, and hoped all would come right. He spoke of Dave in the most cordial terms, and wished he could do something to help. Of course, that's impossible. But I pointed out that the whole future of Malkern, us all, depended on the work going through. Dave would be simply ruined if it didn't. There's a tremendous lot of good in that boy. I always knew it. Once he gets away from this gambling, and cuts out the whiskey, he'll get right again. I suggested his turning teetotaler, and he assured me he'd made up his mind to it. Well, Betty my dear, time's up."

Chepstow rose from the table and filled his pipe. Betty followed him, and put on her wraps. Aunt Mary stood by to help to the last.

It was less than an hour from the time of Betty's return home that the final farewells were spoken and the buckboard started back for the mill. Aunt Mary watched them go. She saw them vanish into the night, and slowly turned back across the veranda into the house. They were her all, her loved ones. They had gone for perhaps only a few weeks, but their going made her feel very lonely. She gave a deep sigh as she began to clear the remains of the supper away. Then, slowly, two unbidden tears welled up into her round, soft eyes and rolled heavily down her plump cheeks. Instantly she pulled herself together, and dashed her hand across her eyes. And once more the steady courage which was the key-note of her life asserted itself. She could not afford to give way to any such weakness.

CHAPTER XVI

NIGHT closed in leaden-hued. The threat of storm had early brought the day to a close, so that the sunset was lost in the massing clouds banking on the western horizon.

Summer was well advanced, and already the luxurious foliage of the valley was affected by the blistering heat. The emerald of the trees and the grass had gained a maturer hue, and only the darker pines resisted the searching sunlight. The valley was full ripe, and kindly nature was about to temper her efforts and permit a breathing space. The weather-wise understood this.

Dave was standing at his office door watching the approach of the electric storm, preparing to launch its thunders upon the valley. Its progress afforded him no sort of satisfaction. Everybody but himself wanted rain. It had already done him too much harm.

He was thinking of the letter he had just received from Bob Mason up in the hills. Its contents were so satisfactory, and this coming rain looked like undoing the good his staunch friends in the mountain camps had so laboriously achieved.

While Mason reported that the fever still had the upper hand, its course had been checked; the epidemic had been grappled with and held within bounds. That was sufficiently satisfactory, seeing Chepstow had only been up there ten days. Then, too, Mason had had cause to congratulate himself on another matter. A number of recruits for his work had filtered through to his camps from Heaven and themselves alone knew where. This was quite good. These men were not the best of lumbermen, but under the "camp boss" they would help to keep the work progressing, which, in the circumstances, was all that could be asked.

A few minutes later Dave departed into the mills. Since the mill up the river had been converted and set to work, and Simon Odd had been given temporary charge of it, he shared with Dawson the work of overseeing.

As he mounted to the principal milling floor the great syren shrieked out its summons to the night shift, and sent the call echoing and reëchoing down the valley. There was no cessation of work. The "relief" stood ready, and the work was passed on from hand to hand.

Dave saw his foreman standing close by No. 1, and he recognized the relief as Mansell. Dawson was watching the man closely, and judging by the frown on his face, it was plain that something was amiss. He moved over to him and beckoned him into the office.

"What's wrong?" he demanded, as soon as the door was closed.

Dawson was never the man to choose his words

when he had a grievance. That was one of the reasons his employer liked him. He was so rough, and so straightforward. He had a grievance now.

" I ain't no sort o' use for these schoolhouse ways," he said, with the added force of an oath.

Dave waited for his next attempt.

" That skunk Mansell. He's got back to-night. He ain't been on the time-sheet for nigh to a week."

" You didn't tell me? Still, he's back."

Dave smiled into the other's angry face, and his manner promptly drew an explosion from the hot-headed foreman.

" Yes, he's back. But he wouldn't be if I was boss. That's the sort o' Sunday-school racket I ain't no use for. He's back, because you say he's to work right along. Sort of to help him. Yes, he's back. He's been fightin'-drunk fer six nights, and I'd hate to say he's dead sober now."

" Yet you signed him on. Why? "

" Oh, as to that, he's sober, I guess. But the drink's in him. I tell you, boss, he's rotten— plumb rotten—when the drink's in him. I know him. Say ——"

But Dave had had enough.

" You say he's sober—well, let it go at that. The man can do his work. That's the important thing to us. Just now we can't bother with his morals. Still, you'd best keep an eye on him."

He turned to his books, and Dawson busied him-self with the checkers' sheets. For some time both men worked without exchanging a word, and the only interruption was the regular coming of the tally boys, who brought the check slips of the lumber measurements.

Through the thin partitions the roar of machinery was incessant, and at frequent intervals the hoarse shouts of the " checkers " reached them. But this disturbed them not at all. It was what they were used to, what they liked to hear, for it told of the work going forward without hitch of any sort.

At last the master of the mills looked up from a mass of figures. He had been making careful calculations.

" We're short, Dawson," he said briefly.

" Short by half a million feet," the foreman returned, without even looking round.

" How's Odd doing up the river ? "

" Good. The machinery's newer, I guess."

" Yes. But we can't help that. We've no time for installing new machinery here. Besides, I can't spare the capital."

Dawson looked round.

" 'Tain't that," he said. " We're short of the right stuff in the boom. Lestways, we was yesterday. A hundred and fifty logs. We're doing better to-day. Though not good enough. It's that dogone fever, I guess."

" What's in the reserve ? "

" Fifteen hundred logs now. I've drew on them mighty heavy. We've used up that number twice over a'ready. I'm scairt to draw further. You see, it's a heap better turning out short than using up that. If we're short on the cut only us knows it. If we finish up our reserve, and have to shut down some o' the saws, other folks'll know it, and we ain't lookin' for that trouble."

Dave closed his book with a slam. All his recent satisfaction was gone in the discovery of the shortage. He had not suspected it.

"I must send up to Mason. It's—it's hell!"

"It's wuss!"

Dave swung round on his loyal assistant.

"Use every log in the reserve. Every one, mind. We've got to gamble. If Mason keeps us short we're done anyway. Maybe the fever will let up, and things 'll work out all right."

Dave flung his book aside and stood up. His heavy face was more deeply lined than it had been at the beginning of summer. He looked to be nearer fifty than thirty. The tremendous work and anxiety were telling.

"Get out to the shoots," he went on, in a sharp tone of command he rarely used. "I'll see to the tally. Keep 'em right at it. Squeeze the saws, and get the last foot out of 'em. Use the reserve till it's done. We're up against it."

Dawson understood. He gave his chief one keen glance, nodded and departed. He knew, no one better, the tremendous burden on the man's gigantic shoulders.

Dave watched him go. Then he turned back to

the desk. He was not the man to weaken at the vagaries of ill fortune. Such difficulties as at the moment confronted him only stiffened his determination. He would not take a beating. He was ready to battle to the death. He quietly, yet earnestly, cursed the fever to himself, and opened and reread Mason's letter. One paragraph held his attention, and he read it twice over.

" If I'm short on the cut you must not mind too much. I can easily make it up when things straighten out. These hands I'm taking on are mostly 'green.' I can only thank my stars I'm able to find them up here. I can't think where they come from. However, they can work, which is the great thing, and though they need considerable discipline—they're a rebellious lot—I mean to make them work."

It was a great thought to the master of the mills that he had such men as Bob Mason in his service. He glowed with satisfaction at the thought, and it largely compensated him for the difficulties besetting him. He put the letter away, and looked over the desk for a memorandum pad. Failing to find what he required, he crossed over to a large cupboard at the far corner of the room. It was roomy, roughly built, to store books and stationery in. The top shelf alone was in use, except that Dawson's winter overcoat hung in the lower part. It was on the top shelf that Dave expected to find the pad he wanted.

As he reached the cupboard a terrific crash of

thunder shook the building. It was right over-head, and pealed out with nerve-racking force and abruptness. It was the first attack of the threatened storm. The peal died out and all became still again, except for the shriek of the saws beyond the partition walls. He waited listening, and then a strange sound reached him. So used was he to the din of the milling floor that any unusual sound or note never failed to draw and hold his attention. A change of tone in the song of the saws might mean so much. Now this curious sound puzzled him. It was faint, so faint that only his practiced ears could have detected it, yet, to him, it was ominously plain. Suddenly it ceased, but it left him dissatisfied.

He was about to resume his search when again he started; and the look he turned upon the door had unmistakable anxiety in it. There it was again, faint, but so painfully distinct. He drew back, half inclined to quit his search, but still he waited, wondering. The noise was as though a farrier's rasp was being lightly passed over a piece of well-oiled steel. At last he made up his mind. He must ascertain its meaning, and he moved to leave the cupboard. Suddenly a terrific grinding noise shrieked harshly above the din of the saws. It cul-minated in a monstrous thud. Instinctively he sprang back, and was standing half-inside the cup-board when a deafening crash shook the mills to their foundations. There was a fearful rending and smashing of timber. Something struck the walls of the office. It crashed through, and a smashing blow struck the cupboard door and hurled him against the inner wall. He thrust out his arms for protection. The door was fast. He was a prisoner.

Now pandemonium reigned. Crash on crash followed in rapid succession. It was as though the office had become the centre of attack for an overwhelming combination of forces. The walls and floor shivered under the terrific onslaught. The very building seemed to totter as though an earthquake were in progress. But at last the end came with a thunder upon the cupboard door, the panels were ripped like tinder, and something vast launched itself through the wrecked woodwork. It struck the imprisoned man in the chest, and in a moment he was pinned to the wall, gasping under ribs bending to the crushing weight which felt to be wringing the very life out of him.

A deadly quiet fell as suddenly as the turmoil had arisen, and his quick ears told him that the saws were still, and all work had ceased in the mill. But the pause was momentary. A second later a great shouting arose. Men's voices, loud and hoarse, reached him, and the rushing of heavy feet was significant of the disaster.

And he was helpless, a prisoner.

He tried to move. His agony was appalling. His ribs felt to be on the verge of cracking under the enormous weight that held him. He raised his arms, but the pain of the effort made him gasp and drop them. Yet he knew he must escape from his prison. He knew that he was needed outside.

The shouting grew. It took a definite tone, and became a cry that none could mistake. Dave needed no repetition of it to convince him of the dread truth. The fire spectre loomed before his eyes, and horror nigh drove him to frenzy.

In his mind was conjured a picture—a ghastly picture, such as all his life he had dreaded and shut out of his thoughts. His brain suddenly seemed to grow too big for his head. It grew hot, and his temples hammered. A surge of blood rose with a rush through his great veins. His muscles strung tense, and his hands clenched upon the imprisoning beam. He no longer felt any pain from the crushing weight. He was incapable of feeling anything. It was a moment when mind and body were charged with a maddening force that no other time could command. With his elbows planted against the wall behind him, with his lungs filled with a deep whistling breath, he thrust at the beam with every ounce of his enormous strength put forth.

He knew all his imprisonment meant. Not to himself alone. Not to those shouting men outside. It was the mills. Hark! Fire! Fire! The cry was on every hand. The mills—his mills—were afire !

He struggled as never before in his life had he struggled. He struggled till the sweat poured from his temples, till his hands lacerated, till the veins of his neck stood out like straining ropes, till it seemed as though his lungs must burst. He was spurred by a blind fury, but the beam remained immovable.

Hark! The maddening cry filled the air. Fire! Fire! Fire! It was everywhere driving him, urging him, appealing. It rang in his brain with an exquisite torture. It gleamed at him in flaming letters out of the darkness. His mill!

Suddenly a cry broke from him as he realized the futility of his effort. It was literally wrung from him in the agony of his soul; nor was he aware that he had spoken.

" God, give me strength!"

And as the cry went up he hurled himself upon the beam with the fury of a madman.

Was it in answer to his prayer? The beam gave. It moved. It was so little, so slight; but it moved. And now, with every fibre braced, he attacked it in one final effort. It gave again. It jolted, it lifted, its rough end tearing the flesh of his chest under his clothing. It tottered for a moment. He struggled on, his bulging eyes and agonized gasping telling plainly of the strain. Inch by inch it gave before him. His muscles felt to be wrenching from the containing tissues, his breathing was spasmodic and whistling, his teeth were grinding together. It gave further, further. Suddenly, with a crash, it fell, the door was wrenched from its hinges, and he was free!

He dashed out into the wreck of his office. All was in absolute darkness. He stumbled his way over the débris which covered the floor, and finally reached the shattered remains of the doorway.

Now he was no longer in darkness. The milling

floor was all too brilliantly lit by the leaping flames down at the " shoot" end of the No. 1 rollers. He waited for nothing, but ran toward the fire. Beyond, dimly outlined in the lurid glow, he could see the men. He saw Dawson and others struggling up the shoot with nozzle and hose, and he put his hands to his mouth and bellowed encouragement.

" Five hundred dollars if you get her under ! " he cried.

If any spur were needed, that voice was sufficient. It was the voice of the master the lumber-jacks knew.

Dawson on the lead struggled up, and as he came Dave shouted again.

" Now, boy ! Sling it hard ! And pass the word to pump like hell ! "

He reached out over the shoot. Dawson threw the nozzle. And as Dave caught it a stream of water belched from the spout.

None knew better than he the narrowness of the margin between saving and losing the mills. Another minute and all would have been lost. The whole structure was built of resinous pine, than which there is nothing more inflammable. The fire had got an alarming hold even in those few minutes, and for nearly an hour victory and disaster hung in the balance. Nor did Dave relinquish his post while any doubt remained. It was not until the flames were fully under control that he left the lumber-jacks to complete the work.

He was weary—more weary than he knew. It seemed to him that in that brief hour he had gone through a lifetime of struggle, both mental and physical. He was sore in body and soul. This disaster had come at the worst possible time, and, as a result, he saw in it something like a week's delay. The thought was maddening, and his ill humor found vent in the shortness of his manner when Dawson attempted to draw him aside.

" Out with it, man," he exclaimed peevishly.

Dawson hesitated. He noticed for the first time the torn condition of his chief's clothes, and the blood stains on the breast of his shirt. Then he blurted out his thankfulness in a tone that made Dave regret his impatience.

" I'm a'mighty thankful you're safe, boss," he said fervently. Then, after a pause, " But you—you got the racket? You're wise to it?"

Dave shrugged. Reaction had set in. Nothing seemed to matter, the cause or anything. The mill was safe. He cared for nothing else.

" Something broke, I s'pose," he said almost indifferently.

" Sure. Suthin' bust. It bust on purpose. Get it?"

The foreman's face lit furiously as he made his announcement.

Dave turned on him. All his indifference vanished in a twinkling.

" Eh? Not—not an accident?"

In an access of loyal rage Dawson seized him by

the arm in a nervous clutch, and tried to drag him forward.

" Come on," he cried. " Let's find him. It's Mansell ! "

With a sudden movement Dave flung him off, and the force he used nearly threw the foreman off his feet. His eyes were burning like two live coals.

" Come on ! " he cried harshly, and Dawson was left to follow as he pleased.

CHAPTER XVII

THE LAST OF THE SAWYER

DAVE's lead took the foreman in the direction of the wrecked office. Now, in calmer moments, the full extent of the damage became apparent. The first three sets of rollers were hopelessly wrecked, and the saws were twisted and their settings broken and contorted out of all recognition. Then the fire had practically destroyed the whole of the adjacent northwest corner of the mill. The office was a mere skeleton, a shattered shell, and the walls and flooring adjoining had been torn and battered into a complete ruin. In the midst of all this, half a dozen heavy logs, in various stages of trimming, lay scattered about where the machinery happened to have thrown them.

It was a sickening sight to the master of the mills, but in his present mood he put the feeling from him, lost in a furious desire to discover the author of the dastardly outrage.

He paused for a moment as one great log lying across half a dozen of the roller beds barred his way. He glanced swiftly over the wreckage. Then he turned to the man following him.

" Any of the boys cut up? " he inquired.

" Some o' them is pretty mean damaged," Dawson replied. " But it ain't too bad, I guess. I 'lows it was sheer luck. But ther's Mansell. We ain't located him."

Mansell was uppermost in his mind. He could think of nothing, and no one, else. He wanted to get his hands about the fellow's throat. In his rage he felt that the only thing to give him satisfaction at the moment would be to squeeze the fellow's life slowly out of him. Dawson was a savage when roused, nor did he make pretense of being otherwise. If he came across the sawyer—well, perhaps it was a good thing that Dave was with him—that is, a good thing for Mansell.

Dave scrambled over the log and the two men hurried on to the saw that had been Mansell's. Neither spoke until this was reached. Then Dave turned.

" Say, go you right on over by the crane and rake around there. Maybe he jumped the boom and got out that way. I'll be along directly."

It was a mere excuse. He wanted to investigate alone. The foreman obeyed, although reluctantly.

The moment he was gone, Dave jumped up on the rollers to examine the machinery that had held the saw. The light of the dying fire was insufficient, and he was forced to procure a lantern. His first anger had passed now, and he was thoroughly alert. His practiced eye lost no detail that could afford the least possible clue to the cause of the smash. Dawson had said it was Mansell, and that it was no accident. But then he knew well enough that Dawson had a bad enough opinion of the sawyer,

and since the smash had apparently originated on
No. 1, he had probably been only too glad to jump
to the conclusion. For himself, he was personally
determined to avoid any prejudice.

He quickly discovered that the saw in question
had been broken off short. The settings were desperately twisted, and he knew that the force capable of doing this could have only been supplied by
the gigantic log that had been trimming at the
moment. Therefore the indication must come from
the saw itself. He searched carefully, and found
much of the broken blade. The upper portions
were broken clean. There was neither dinge nor
bend in them. But the lower portions were less
clean. One piece particularly looked as though a
sharp instrument had been at work upon it. Then
the memory of that faint rasping sound, which had
been the first thing to attract his attention before
the smash, came back to him. He grew hot with
rising anger, and stuffed the piece of saw-blade inside his shirt.

"The cur!" he muttered. "Why? Why?
Guess Dawson was right, after all. The liquor *was*
in him. But why should he try to smash us?"

He jumped down to the alleyway, intending to
join his foreman, when a fresh thought occurred to
him. He looked over at the remains of the office,
then he glanced up and down at the broken rollers
of No. 1. And his lips shut tight.

"I was in there," he said to himself, with his
eyes on the wrecked office, "and—he knew it."

At that moment Dawson's excited voice interrupted him. " Say, boss, come right along here. Guess I've got him."

Dave joined him hurriedly. He found the foreman bending over a baulk of timber, one that had evidently been hurled there in the smash. It was lying across the sill of the opening over the boom, projecting a long way out. Beneath it, just where it rested on the sill, but saved from its full weight by the cant at which it was resting, a human figure was stretched out face downward.

Dawson was examining the man's face when Dave reached him, and started to explain hurriedly.

" I didn't rightly rec'nize him," he said. " Y' see he's got out of his workin' kit. Might ha' bin goin' to the Meetin'. He was sure lightin' out of here for keeps."

To Dave the prostrate figure suggested all that the foreman said. The man had calculated that smash—manufactured it. No more evidence was needed. He had got himself ready for a bolt for safety, preferring the boom as offering the best means of escape and the least chance of detection. Once outside there would be no difficulty in getting away. As Dawson said, his clothes suggested a hurried journey. They were the thick frieze the lumber-jack wears in winter, and would be ample protection for summer nights out in the open. Yes, it had been carefully thought out. But the reason of this attack on himself puzzled him, and he repeatedly asked himself " Why ? "

There could not be much question as to the man's condition. If he were not yet dead, he must be very near it, for the small of his back was directly under the angle of the beam and crushed against the sill. Dave stood up from his examination.

" Get one of the boys, quick," he said. " Start him out at once for Doc Symons, over at High River. It's only fifteen miles. He'll be along before morning anyhow. I'll carry—this down to the office. Don't say a word around the mill. We've just had an—accident. See? And say, Dawson, you're looking for a raise, and you're going to get it, that is if this mill's in full work this day week. We're short of logs—well, this'll serve as an excuse for saws being idle. ' It's an ill wind,' eh? Meantime, get what saws you can going. Now cut along."

The foreman's gratitude shone in his eyes. Had Dave given him the least encouragement he would undoubtedly have made him what he considered an elegant speech of thanks, but his employer turned from him at once and set about releasing the imprisoned man. As soon as he had prized the beam clear he gathered him up in his arms and bore him down the spiral staircase to the floor below. Then he hurried on to his office with his burden.

And as he went he wondered. The sawyer might dislike Dawson. But he had no cause for grudge against him, Dave. Then why had he waited until he was alone in the tally room? The whole thing looked so like a direct attack upon himself, rather than on the mills, that he was more than ever puzzled. He went back over the time since he had employed Mansell, and he could not remember a single incident that could serve him as an excuse for such an attack. It might have been simply the madness of drink, and yet it seemed too carefully planned. Yes, that was another thing. Mansell had been on the drink for a week, " fighting-drunk," Dawson had said. In the circumstances it was not reasonable for him to plan the thing so carefully. Then a sudden thought occurred to him. Were there others in it? Was Mansell only the tool?

He was suddenly startled by a distinct sound from the injured man. It was the sawyer's voice, harsh but inarticulate, and it brought with it a suggestion that he might yet learn the truth. He increased his pace and reached the office a few moments later.

Here he prepared a pile of fur rugs upon the floor and laid the sawyer upon it. Then he waited for some minutes, but, as nothing approaching consciousness resulted, he finally left him, intending to return again when the doctor arrived. There was so much to be done in the mill that he could delay his return to it no longer.

It was nearly four hours later when he went back to his office. He had seen the work of salvage in order, and at last had a moment to spare to attend to himself. He needed it. He was utterly weary, and his lacerated chest was giving him exquisite pain.

He found Mansell precisely as he left him. Apparently there had been no movement of any sort. He bent over him and felt his heart. It was beating faintly. He lifted the lids of his closed eyes, and the eyeballs moved as the light fell upon them.

He turned away and began to strip himself of his upper garments. There was a gash in his chest fully six inches long, from which the blood was steadily, though sluggishly, flowing. His clothes were saturated and caked with it. He bathed the wound with the drinking water in the bucket, and tearing his shirt into strips made himself a temporary bandage. This done, he turned to his chair to sit down, when, glancing over at the sick man, he was startled to find his eyes open and staring in his direction.

He at once went over to him.

" Feeling better, Mansell? " he inquired.

The man gave no sign of recognition. His eyes simply stared at him. For a moment he thought he was dead, but a faint though steady breathing reassured him. Suddenly an idea occurred to him, and he went to a cupboard and produced a bottle of brandy. Pouring some out into a tin cup, with some difficulty he persuaded it into Mansell's mouth. Then he waited. The staring eyes began to move, and there was a decided fluttering of the eyelids. A moment later the lips moved, and an indistinct but definite sound came from them.

" How are you now ? " Dave asked.

There was another long pause, during which the man's eyes closed again. Then they reopened, and he deliberately turned his head away.

" You—didn't—get—hurt ? " he asked, in faint, spasmodic gasps.

" No." Dave leaned over him. " Have some more brandy ? "

The man turned his head back again. He didn't answer, but the look in his eyes was sufficient. This time Dave poured out more, and there was no difficulty in administering it.

" Well ? " he suggested, as the color slowly crept over the man's face.

" Good—goo ——"

The sound died away, and the eyes closed again. But only to reopen quickly.

" He—said—you'd—get—killed," he gasped.

" He—who ? "

" Jim."

The sawyer's eyelids drooped again. Without a moment's hesitation Dave plied him with more of the spirit.

" You mean Truscott ? " he asked sharply. He was startled, but he gave no sign. He realized that at any time the man might refuse to say more. Then he added : " He's got it in for me."

The sick man remained perfectly still for some seconds. His brain seemed to move slowly. When he did speak, his voice had grown fainter.

" Yes."

Dave's face was hard and cold as he looked down at him. He was just about to formulate another question, when the door opened and Dr. Symons hurried in. He was a brisk man, and took the situation in at a glance.

"A smash?" he inquired. Then, his eyes on the bottle at Dave's side: "What's that—brandy?"

"Brandy." The lumberman passed it across to him. "Yes, a smash-up. This poor chap's badly damaged, I'm afraid. Found him with a heavy beam lying across the small of his back. You were the nearest doctor, so I sent for you. Eh? oh, yes," as the doctor pointed at the blood on his clothes. "When you've finished with him you can put a stitch in me—some of the boys too. I'll leave you to it, Doc, they'll need me in the mill. I gave him brandy, and it roused him to consciousness."

"Right. You might get back in half an hour."

Dr. Symons moved over to the sick man, and Dave put on his coat and left the office.

When he returned the doctor met him with a grave face.

"What's the night like?" he asked. "I've got to ride back."

He went to the door, and Dave followed him out.

"His back is broken," he said, when they were out of ear-shot. "It's just a question of hours."

"How many?"

"Can't say with any certainty. It's badly

smashed, and no doubt other things besides. Paralysis of the ——"

" Has he said anything ? Has he shown any inclination to talk ? "

" No. That is, he looked around the room a good deal as though looking for some one. Maybe you."

" Can nothing be done for the poor chap ? ",

" Nothing. Better get him a parson. I'll come over to-morrow to see him, if he's alive. Anyway I'll be needed to sign a certificate. I must get back to home by daylight. I've got fever patients. Now just come inside, and I'll fix you up. Then I'll go and see to the boys. After that, home."

" You're sure nothing ——"

" Plumb sure! Sure as I am you're going to have a mighty bad chest if you don't come inside and let me stop that oozing blood I see coming through your clothes."

Without further protest Dave followed the doctor into the office, and submitted to the operation.

" That's a rotten bad place," he assured him, in his brisk way. " You'll have to lie up. You ought to be dead beat from loss of blood. Gad, man, you must go home, or I won't answer ——"

But Dave broke in testily.

" Right ho, Doc, you go and see to the boys. Send your bill in to me for the lot."

As soon as he had gone, Dave sat thoughtfully gazing at the doomed sawyer. Presently he glanced round at the brandy bottle. The doctor had positively said the poor fellow was doomed. He rose from his seat and poured out a stiff drink. Then he knelt down, and supporting the man's head, held it to his lips. He drank it eagerly. Dave knew it had been his one pleasure in life. Then he went back to his chair.

" Feeling comfortable ? " he inquired gently.

" Yes, boss," came the man's answer promptly. Then, " Wot did the Doc say ? "

" Guess you're handing in your checks," Dave replied, after a moment's deliberation.

The sawyer's eyes were on the brandy bottle.

" How long ? " he asked presently.

" Maybe hours. He couldn't say."

" 'E's wrong, boss. 'Tain't hours. I'm mighty cold, an'—it's creepin' up quick."

Dave looked at his watch. It was already past two o'clock.

" He said he'd come and see you in the morning."

" I'll be stiff by then," the dying man persisted, with his eyes still on the bottle. " Say, boss," he went on, " that stuff's a heap warming—an' I'm cold."

Dave poured him out more brandy. Then he took off his own coat and laid it over the man's legs. His fur coat and another fur robe were in the cupboard, and these he added. And the man's thanks came awkwardly.

" I can't send for a parson," Dave said regretfully, after a few moments' silence. " I'd like to, but Parson Tom's away up in the hills. It's only right——."

" He's gone up to the hills?" the sick man interrupted him, as though struck by a sudden thought.

" Yes. It's fever."

Mansell lay staring straight up at the roof. And as the other watched him he felt that some sort of struggle was going on in his slowly moving mind. Twice his lips moved as though about to speak, but for a long time no sound came from them. The lumberman felt extreme pity for him. He had forgotten that this man had so nearly ruined him, so nearly caused his death. He only saw before him a dimly flickering life, a life every moment threatening to die out. He knew how warped had been that life, how worthless from a purely human point of view, but he felt that it was as precious in the sight of One as that of the veriest saint. He racked his thoughts for some way to comfort those last dread moments.

Presently the dying man's head turned slightly toward him.

" I'm goin', boss," he said with a gasp. " It's gettin' up—the cold."

" Will you have—brandy?"

The lighting of the man's eyes made a verbal answer unnecessary. Dave gave him nearly half a tumbler, and his ebbing life flickered up again like a dying candle flame.

" The Doc said you wus hurt bad, boss. I heard him. I'm sorry—real miser'ble sorry—now."

" Now ? "

" Yep—y' see I'm—goin'."

" Ah."

" I'm kind o' glad ther' ain't no passon around. Guess ther's a heap I wouldn't 'a' said to him."

The dying man's eyes closed for a moment. Dave didn't want to break in on his train of thought, so he kept silent.

" Y' see," Mansell went on again almost at once, " he kind o' drove me to it. That an' the drink. He give me the drink too. Jim's cur'us mean by you."

" But Jim's gone east days ago."

" No, he ain't. He's lyin' low. He ain't east now."

" You're sure ? " Dave's astonishment crept into his tone.

Mansell made a movement which implied his certainty.

" He was to give me a heap o' money. The money you give fer his mill. He wants you smashed. He wants the mill smashed. An' I did it. Say, I bust that saw o' mine, an' she was a beaut'," he added, with pride and regret. " I got a rasp on to it. But it's all come back on me. Guess I'll be goin' to hell fer that job—that an' others. Say, boss ——"

He broke off, looking at the brandy bottle. Dave made no pretense at demur. The man was rapidly dying, and he felt that the spirit gave him a certain ease of mind. The ethics of his action did not

trouble him. If he could give a dying man comfort, he would.

"There's no hell for those who are real sorry,"
he said, when the fellow had finished his drink.
"The good God is so thankful for a man's real sorrow for doing wrong that He forgives him righ
out. He forgives a sight easier than men do
You've nothing to worry over, lad. You're sorry
—that's the real thing."

"Sure, boss?"

"Dead sure."

"Say, boss, I'd 'a' hate to done you up. But ther'
was the money, an'—I wanted it bad."

"Sure you did. You see we all want a heap the
good God don't reckon good for us ——"

The man's eyes suddenly closed while Dave was
speaking. Then they opened again, and this time
they were staring wildly.

"I'm—goin'," he gasped.

Dave was on his knees in a second, supporting
his head. He poured some brandy into the gasping mouth, and for a brief moment the man rallied.
Then his breathing suddenly became violent.

"I'm—done!" he gasped in a final effort, and a
moment later the supporting hand felt the lead-like
weight of the lolling head. The man was dead.

The lumberman reverently laid the head back
upon the rugs, and for some minutes remained
where he was kneeling. His rough, plain face was
buried in his hands. Then he rose to his feet and
stood looking down upon the lifeless form. A

great pity welled up in his heart. Poor Mansell was beyond the reach of a hard fate, beyond the reach of earthly temptation and the hard knocks of men. And he felt it were better so. He covered the body carefully over with the fur robe, and sat down at his desk.

He sat there for some minutes listening to the sounds of the workers at the mills. He was weary —so weary. But at last he could resist the call no longer, and he went out to join in the labor that was his very life.

CHAPTER XVIII

FACE TO FACE

FOR the few remaining hours of night Dave took no leisure. He pressed forward the work of repairing the damage, with a zest that set Joel Dawson herding his men on to almost superhuman feats. There was no rest taken, no rest asked. And it said something for the devotion of these lumberjacks to their employer that no " grouse " or murmur was heard.

The rest which the doctor had ordered Dave to take did not come until long after his breakfast hour, and then only it came through sheer physical inability to return to his work. His breakfast was brought to the office, and he made a weak pretense of eating. Then, as he rose from his seat, for the first time in his life he nearly fainted. He saved himself, however, by promptly sitting down again, and in a few seconds his head fell forward on his chest and he was sound asleep, lost in the dreamless slumber of exhaustion.

Two hours later Dawson put his head in through the office doorway. He saw the sleeping man and retreated at once. He understood. For himself, he had not yet come to the end of his tether. Besides, Simon Odd would relieve him presently. Then, too, there were others upon whom he could depend for help.

It was noon when a quiet tap came at the office door. Dave's old mother peeped in. She had heard of the smash and was fearful for her boy. Seeing him asleep she tiptoed across the room to him. She had met the postmaster on her way, and brought the mail with her. Now she deposited it on his desk and stood looking down at the great recumbent figure with eyes of the deepest love and anxiety. All signs of his lacerated chest were concealed, and she was spared what would have been to her a heartbreaking sight. Her gentle heart only took in the unutterably weary attitude of the sleeper. That was sufficient to set her shaking her gray head and sighing heavily. The work, she told herself sadly, was killing him. Nor did she know at the moment how near to the truth she was.

For a moment she bent over him, and her aged lips lightly touched his mass of wiry hair. To the world he might be unsightly, he might be ungainly, he might be—well, all he believed himself to be ; to her he possessed every beauty, every virtue a doting mother can bestow upon her offspring.

She passed out of the office as silently as she came, and the man's stertorous breathing rose and fell steadily, the only sound in that room of death.

Two hours later he awoke with a start. A serving girl blundered into the room with a basket of food. His mother had sent over his dinner.

The girl's apologies were profuse.

" I jest didn't know, Mr. Dave. I'm sure sorry. Your ma sent me over with these things, an' she said as I was to set 'em right out for you. Y' see she didn't just say you was sleepin', she ——"

"All right, Maggie," Dave said kindly. Then he looked at his watch, and to his horror found it was two o'clock. He had slept the entire morning through.

He swiftly rose from his seat and stretched himself. He was stiff and sore, and that stretch reminded him painfully of his wounded chest. Then his eyes fell upon the ominous pile of furs in the corner. Ah, there was that to see to.

He watched the girl set out his dinner and remembered he was hungry. And the moment she left the room he fell upon the food with avidity. Yes, he felt better—much better, and he was glad. He could return to his work, and see that everything possible was done, and then there was—that other matter.

He had just finished his food when Dr. Symons came in with an apology on his lips.

"A bit late," he exclaimed. "Sorry I couldn't make it before. Ah," his quick eyes fell upon the pile of furs. "Dead?" he inquired.

Dave nodded.

"Sure," the other rattled on. "Had to be. Knew it. Well, there are more good sawyers to be had. Let's look at your chest."

Dave submitted, and then the doctor, at the lumberman's request, went off with a rush to see about the arrangements for the sawyer's burial.

He had hardly left the place, and Dave was just

thinking of going across to the mill again, when there was another call. He was standing at the window. He wanted to return at once to his work, but for some, to him, unaccountable reason he was a prey to a curious reluctance; it was a form of inertia he had never before experienced, and it half annoyed him, yet was irresistibly fascinating. He stood there more or less dreamily, watching the buzzing flies as they hurled themselves against the dirty glass panes. He idly tried to count them. He was not in the least interested, but at that moment, as a result of his wound and his weariness, his brain felt that it needed the rest of such trivialities.

It was while occupied in this way that he saw Jim Truscott approaching, and the sight startled him into a mental activity that just then his best interests in the mills failed to stir him to.

Then Mansell had told the truth. Jim had not gone east as he had assured Tom Chepstow it was his intention to do. Why was he coming to him now? A grim thought passed through his mind. Was it the fascination which the scene of a crime always has for the criminal? He sat down at his desk, and, when his visitor's knock came, appeared to be busy with his mail.

Truscott came in. Dave did not look up, but the tail of his eye warned him of a peculiarly furtive manner in his visitor.

" Half a minute," he said, in a preoccupied tone. " Just sit down."

The other silently obeyed, while Dave tore open
a telegram at haphazard, and immediately became
really absorbed in its contents.

It was a wire from his agent in Winnipeg, and
announced that the railroad strike had been settled,
and the news would be public property in twenty-
four hours. It further told him that he hoped in
future he would have no further hitch to report in
the transportation of the Malkern timber, and that
now he could cope with practically any quantity
Dave might ship down. The news was very satisfactory, except for the reminder it gave him of the
disquieting knowledge that his mills were temporarily wrecked, and he could not produce the quan-
tities the agent hoped to ship. At least he could
not produce them for some days, and—yes, there
was that shortage from the hills to cope with, too.

This brought him to the recollection that the
author of half his trouble was in the office, and
awaiting his pleasure. He turned at once to his
visitor, and surveyed him closely from head to foot.

Truscott was sitting with his back to the pile of
rugs concealing the dead sawyer. Presently their
eyes met, and in the space of that glance the lumberman's thought flowed swiftly. Nor, when he
spoke, did his tone suggest either anger or resentment, merely a cool inquiry.

" You—changed your mind? " he said.

" What about? " Truscott was on the defensive
at once.

" You didn't go east, then ? "

The other's gaze shifted at once, and his manner suggested annoyance with himself for his display.

"Oh, yes. I went as far as Winnipeg. Guess I got hung up by the strike, so—so I came back again. Who told you?"

"Tom Chepstow."

Truscott nodded. It was some moments before either spoke again. There was an awkwardness between them which seemed to increase every second. Truscott was thinking of their last meeting, and—something else. Dave was estimating the purpose of this visit. He understood that the man had a purpose, and probably a very definite one.

Suddenly the lumberman rose from his seat as though about to terminate the interview, and his movement promptly had the effect he desired. Truscott detained him at once.

"You had a bad smash, last night. That's why I came over."

Dave smiled. It was just the glimmer of a smile, and frigid as a polar sunbeam. As he made no answer, the other was forced to go on.

"I'm sorry, Dave," he continued, with a wonderful display of sincerity. Then he hesitated, but finally plunged into a labored apology. "I dare say Parson Tom has told you something of what I said to him the night he went away. He went up to clear out the fever for you, didn't he? He's a good chap. I hoped he'd tell you anyway. I just—hadn't the face to come to you myself after what had happened between us.   Look here, Dave, you've treated me 'white' since then—I mean about that mill of mine.   You see—well, I can't just forget old days and old friendships.   They're on my conscience bad.   I want to straighten up. I want to tell you how sorry I am for what I've done and said in the past.   You'd have done right if you'd broken my neck for me.   I went east as I said, and all these things hung on my conscience like—like cobwebs, and I'm determined to clear 'em away.   Dave, I want to shake hands before I go for good.   I want you to try and forget.   The strike's over now, and I'm going away to-day. I——''

He broke off.   It seemed as though he had suddenly realized the frigidity of Dave's silence and the hollow ring of his own professions.   It is doubtful if he were shamed into silence.   It was simply that there was no encouragement to go on, and, in spite of his effrontery, he was left confused.

" You're going to-day ? "   Dave's calmness gave no indication of his feelings.   Nor did he offer to shake hands.

Truscott nodded.   Then —

" The smash—was it a very bad one ? "

" Pretty bad."

" It—it won't interfere with your work—I hope ? "

" Some."   ╲

Dave's eyes were fixed steadily upon his visitor, who let his gaze wander.   There was something painfully disconcerting in the lumberman's cold regard, and in the brevity of his replies.

" Doc Symons told me about it," the other went on presently. " He was fetched here in the night. He said you were hurt. But you seem all right."

Dave made it very hard for him. There were thoughts in the back of his head, questions that must be answered. For an instant a doubt swept over him, and his restless eyes came to a standstill on the rugged face of the master of the mills. But he saw nothing there to reassure him, or to give him cause for alarm. It was the same as he had always known it, only perhaps the honest gray eyes lacked their kindly twinkle.

" Yes, I'm all right. Doc talks a heap."

" Did he lie ? "

Dave shrugged.

" It depends what he calls hurt. Some of the boys were hurt."

" Ah. He didn't mention them."

Again the conversation languished.

" I didn't hear how the smash happened," Truscott went on presently.

Dave's eyes suddenly became steely.

" It was Mansell's saw. Something broke. Then we got afire. I just got out—a miracle. I was in the tally room."

The lumberman's brevity had in it the clip of snapping teeth. If Truscott noticed it, it suited him to ignore it. He went on quickly. His interest was rising and sweeping him on.

" On Mansell's saw!" he said. " When I heard you'd got him working I wondered. He's bad for drink. Was he drunk ? "

Dave's frigidity was no less for the smile that accompanied his next words.

" Maybe he'd been drinking."

But Truscott was not listening. He was thinking ahead, and his next question came with almost painful sharpness.

" Did he get—smashed ? "

" A bit."

" Ah. Was he able to account for the—accident ? "

The man was leaning forward in his anxiety, and his question was literally hurled at the other. There was a look, too, in his bleared eyes which was a mixture of devilishness and fear. All these things Dave saw. But he displayed no feeling of any sort.

"Accidents don't need explaining," he said slowly. " But I didn't say this was an accident. Here, get your eye on that."

He drew a piece of saw-blade from his pocket. It was the piece he had picked up in the mill.

" Guess it's the bit where it's ' collared' by the driving arm."

Truscott examined the steel closely.

" Well ? "

" It's—just smashed ? " Truscott replied questioningly.

Dave shook his head.

" You can see where it's been filed."

Truscott reëxamined it and nodded.

" I see now. God ! "

The exclamation was involuntary. It came at the sudden realization of how well his work had been carried out, and what that work meant. Dave, watching, grasped something of its meaning. There was that within him which guided him surely in the mental workings of his fellow man. He was looking into the very heart of this man who had so desperately tried to injure him. And what he saw, though he was angered, stirred him to a strange pity.

" It's pretty mean when you think of it," he said slowly. " Makes you think some, doesn't it ? Makes you wonder what folks are made of. If you hated, could you have done it ? Could you have deliberately set out to ruin a fellow—to take his life ? The man that did this thing figured on just that."

" Did he say so ? "

Truscott's face had paled, and a haunting fear looked out of his eyes. It was the thought of discovery that troubled him.

Dave ignored the interruption, and went on with his half-stern, half-pitying regard fixed upon the other.

" Had things gone right with him, and had the fire got a fair hold, nothing could have saved us." He shook his head. " That's a mean hate for a man I've never harmed. For a man I've always

helped. You couldn't hate like that, Truscott?
You couldn't turn on the man that had so helped
you? It's a mean spirit; so mean that I can't hate
him for it. I'm sorry—that's all."

" He must be a devil."

The fear had gone out of Truscott's eyes. All
his cool assurance had returned. Dave was blam-
ing the sawyer, and he was satisfied.

The lumberman shrugged his great shoulders.

" Maybe he is. I don't know. Maybe he's only
a poor weak foolish fellow whose wits are all
mussed up with brandy, and so he just doesn't
know what he's doing."

" The man who filed that steel knew what he was
doing," cried Truscott.

" Don't blame him," replied Dave—his deep
voice full and resonant like an organ note.

But Truscott had achieved his object, and he felt
like expanding. Dave knew nothing. Suspected
nothing. Mansell had played the game for him—
or perhaps ——

" I tell you it was a diabolical piece of villainy
on the part of a cur who ——"

" Don't raise your voice, lad," said Dave, with a
sudden solemnity that promptly silenced the other.
" Reach round behind you and lift that fur robe."

He had risen from his seat and stood pointing
one knotty finger at the corner where the dead
man was lying. His great figure was full of
dignity, his manner had a command in it that was
irresistible to the weaker man.

Truscott turned, not knowing what to expect. For a second a shudder passed over him. It spent itself as he beheld nothing but the pile of furs. But he made no attempt to reach the robe until Dave's voice, sternly commanding, urged him again.

" Lift it," he cried.

And the other obeyed even against his will. He reached out, while a great unaccountable fear took hold of him and shook him. His hand touched the robe. He paused. Then his fingers closed upon its furry edge. He lifted it, and lifting it, beheld the face of the dead sawyer. Strangely enough, the glazed eyes were open, and the head was turned, so that they looked straight into the eyes of the living.

The hand that held the robe shook. The nerveless fingers relinquished their hold, and it fell back to its place and shut out the sight. But it was some moments before the man recovered himself. When he did so he rose from his chair and moved as far from the dead man as possible. This brought him near the door, and Dave followed him up.

" He's dead ! "

Truscott whispered the words half unconsciously, and the tone of his voice was almost unrecognizable. It sounded like inquiry, yet he had no need to ask the question.

" Yes, he's dead—poor fellow," said Dave solemnly.

Then, after a long pause, the other dragged his

courage together. He looked up into the face above him.

" Did—did he say why he did it—or was he ——"

It was a stumbling question, which Dave did not let him complete.

" Yes, he told me al' —the whole story of it. That's the door, lad. You won't need to shake hands—now."

CHAPTER XIX

IN THE MOUNTAINS

I⊤ was Sunday evening. Inside a capacious " dugout " a small group of two men and a girl sat round the stove which had just been lit.

In the mountains, even though the heat of August was still at its height, sundown was the signal for the lighting of fires. Dave's lumber camps were high up in the hills, tapping, as they did, the upper forest belts, where grew the vast primordial timbers. In the extreme heat of summer the air was bracing, crisp, and suggested the process of breathing diamonds, but with the setting of the sun a cold shiver from the ancient glaciers above whistled down through the trees and bit into the bones.

The daylight still lingered outside, and the cotton-covered windows of the dugout let in just sufficient of it to leave the remoter corners of the hut bathed in rapidly growing shadow. There was a good deal of comfort in the room, though no luxury. The mud cemented walls were whitewashed and adorned with illustrations from the *Police Gazette*, and other kindred papers. For the most part the furniture was of " home " manufacture. The chairs, and they were all armchairs of sorts, were mere frames with seats of strung rawhide. The table was of the roughest but most solid make, strong enough to be used as a chopping-block, and large enough for an extra bed to be made down upon it. There was a large cupboard serving the dual purpose of larder and pantry, and, in addition to the square cook-stove, the room was heated by a giant wood stove. The only really orthodox piece of furniture was the small writing-desk.

For a dugout it was capacious, and, unlike the usual dugout, it possessed three inner rooms backing into the hill against which it was built. One of these was a storeroom for dynamite and other camp equipment, one was a bedroom, and the other was an armory. The necessity for the latter might be questioned, but Bob Mason, the camp "boss," the sole authority over a great number of lumber-jacks, more than a hundred and fifty miles from the faintest semblance of civilization, was content that it should be there.

The three faces were serious enough as they gazed down in silence at the glowing, red-hot patch in the iron roof of the stove, and watched it spread, wider and wider, under the forced draught of the open damper. They had been silent for some moments, and before that one of them had practically monopolized the talk. It was Betty who had done most of the talking. Bronzed with the mountain air and sun, her cheeks flushed with interest and excitement, her sweet brown eyes aglow, she had finished recounting to her uncle and Bob Mason a significant incident that had occurred to her that afternoon on her way from the sick camp to the dugout.

Walking through a patch of forest which cut the sick quarters off from the main, No. 1, camp, she had encountered two lumber-jacks, whom she had no recollection of having seen before.

" They weren't like lumber-jacks," she explained, " except for their clothes. You can't mistake a lumber-jack's manner and speech, particularly when he is talking to a girl. He's so self-conscious and —and shy. Well, these men were neither. Their speech was the same as ours might be, and their faces, well, they were good-looking fellows, and might never have been out of a city. I never saw anybody look so out of place, as they did, in their clothes. There was no beating about the bush with them. They simply greeted me politely, asked me if I was Miss Somers, and, when I told them I was, calmly warned me to leave the hills without delay—not later than to-morrow night. I asked them for an explanation, but they only laughed, not rudely, and repeated their warning, adding that you, uncle, had better go too, or they would not be answerable for the consequences. I reminded them of the sick folk, but they only laughed at that too. One of them cynically reminded me they were all 'jacks' and were of no sort of consequence whatever, in fact, if a few of them happened to die off no one would care. He made me angry, and I told them we should certainly care. He promptly retorted, very sharply, that they had not come there to hold any sort of debate on the matter, but to give me warning. He said that his reason in doing so was simply that I was a girl, and that you, uncle, were a much-respected parson, and they had no desire that any harm should come to either of us. That was all. After that they turned away and went off into the forest, taking an opposite direction to the camp."

Mason was the first to break the silence that followed the girl's story.

" It's serious," he said, speaking with his chin in his hands and his elbows resting on his parted knees.

" The warning ? " inquired Chepstow, with a quick glance at the other's thoughtful face.

Mason nodded.

" I've been watching this thing for weeks past," he said, " and the worst of it is I can't make up my mind as to the meaning of it. There's something afoot, but —— Do you know I've sent six letters down the river to Dave, and none of them have been answered ? My monthly budget of orders is a week overdue. That's not like Dave. How long have you been up here ? Seven weeks, ain't it ? I've only had three letters from Dave in that time."

The foreman flung himself back in his chair with a look of perplexity on his broad, open face.

" What can be afoot ? " asked Chepstow, after a pause. " The men are working well."

" They're working as well as 'scabs' generally do," Mason complained. " And thirty per cent. are 'scabs,' now. They're all slackers. They're none of them lumber-jacks. They haven't the spirit of a 'jack.' I have to drive 'em from morning till night. Oh, by the way, parson, that reminds me, I've got a note for you. It's from the sutler. I know what's in it, that is, I can guess." He drew it from his pocket, handed it across to him. "It's to tell you you can't have the store for service to-night. The boys want it. They're going to have a singsong there, or something of the sort."

The churchman's eyes lit.

"But he promised me. I've made arrangements. The place is fixed up for it. They can have it afterward, but ——"

"Hadn't you better read the note, uncle?" Betty said gently. She detected the rising storm in his vehemence.

He turned at once to the note. It was short, and its tone, though apologetic, was decided beyond all question.

"You can't have the store to-night. I'm sorry, but the boys insist on having it themselves. You will understand I am quite powerless when you remember they are my customers."

Tom Chepstow read the message from Jules Lieberstein twice over. Then he passed it across to Mason. Only the brightness of his eyes told of his feelings. He was annoyed, and his fighting spirit was stirring.

"Well, what are you going to do?" Mason inquired, as he passed the paper on to Betty in response to her silent request.

"Do? Do?" Chepstow cried, his keen eyes shining angrily. " Why, I'll hold service there, of course. Jules can't give a thing, and, at the last minute, take it away like that. I've had the room prepared and everything. I shall go and see him. I——"

" The trouble—whatever it is—is in that note, too," Betty interrupted, returning him the paper with the deliberate intention of checking his outburst.

Mason gave her a quick glance of approval. Though he did not approve of women in a lumber camp, Betty's quiet capacity, her gentle womanliness, with her great strength of character and keenness of perception underlying it, pleased him immensely. He admired her, and curiously enough frequently found himself discussing affairs of the camp with her as though she were there for the purpose of sharing the burden of his responsibilities. In the ordinary course this would not have happened, but she had come at a moment when his difficulties were many and trying. And at such a time her ready understanding had become decided moral support which was none the less welcome for the fact that he failed to realize it.

" You're right," he nodded. " There's something doing. What's that?"

All three glanced at the door. And there was a look of uneasiness in each which they could not have explained. Mason hurried across the room with Chepstow at his heels.

Outside, night was closing in rapidly. A gray, misty twilight held the mountain world in a gloomy shroud. The vast hills, and the dark woodland belts, loomed hazily through the mist. But the deathly stillness was broken by the rattle of wheels and the beating of hoofs upon the hard trail. The vehicle, whatever it was, had passed the dugout, and the sounds of it were already dying away in the direction of the distant camp.

" There's a fog coming down," observed Mason, as they returned to the stove.

" That was a buckboard," remarked the parson.

" And it was traveling fast and light," added Betty.

And each remark indicated the point of view of the speaker.

Mason thought less of the vehicle than he did of the fog. Any uneasiness he felt was for his work rather than the trouble he felt to be brewing. A heavy fog was always a deterrent, and, at this time of year, fogs were not unfrequent in the hills. Chepstow was bent on the identity of the arrival, while Betty sought the object of it.

Mason did not return to his seat. He stood by the stove for a moment thinking. Then he moved across to his pea-jacket hanging on the wall and put it on, at the same time slipping a revolver into his pocket. Then he pulled a cloth cap well down over his eyes.

" I'll get a good look around the camp," he said quietly.

" Going to investigate ? " Chepstow inquired.

" Yes. There have been too many arrivals lately —one way and another. I'm sick of 'em."

Betty looked up into his face with round smiling eyes.

" You need a revolver—to make investigations ? " she asked lightly.

The lumberman looked her squarely in the eyes for a moment, and there he read something of the thought which had prompted her question. He smiled back at her as he replied.

" It's a handy thing to have about you when dealing with the scum of the earth. Lumbermen on this continent are not the beau ideal of gentle- folk, but when you are dealing with the class of loafer such as I have been forced to engage lately, well, the real lumber-jack becomes an angel of gentleness by contrast. A gun doesn't take up much room in your pocket, and it gives an added feeling of security. You see, if there's any sort of trouble brewing the man in authority is not likely to have a healthy time. By the way, parson, I'd suggest you give up this service to-night. Of course it's up to you, I don't want to interfere. You see, if the boys want that store, and you've got it—why ——"

He broke off with a suggestive shake of the head. Betty watched her uncle's face.

She saw him suddenly bend down and fling the

damper wider open, and in response the stove roared fiercely. He sat with his keen eyes fixed on the glowing aperture, watching the rapidly brightening light that shone through. The suggestion of fiery rage suited his mood at the moment.

But his anger was not of long duration. His was an impetuous disposition generally controlled in the end by a kindly, Christian spirit, and, a few moments later, when he spoke, there was the mildness of resignation in his words.

"Maybe you're right, Mason," he said calmly. "You understand these boys up here better than I do. Besides, I don't want to cause you any unnecessary trouble, and I see by your manner you're expecting something serious." Then he added regretfully : "But I should have liked to hold that service. And I would have done it, in spite of our Hebrew friend's sordid excuse. However —— By the way, can I be of any service to you?" He pointed at the lumberman's bulging pocket. "If it's necessary to carry that, two are always better than one."

Betty sighed contentedly. She was glad that her uncle had been advised to give up the service. Her woman's quick wit had taken alarm for him, and— well, she regarded her simple-minded uncle as her care, she felt she was responsible to her aunt for him. It was the strong maternal instinct in her which made her yearn to protect and care for those whom she loved. Now she waited anxiously for the foreman's reply. To her astonishment it came with an alacrity and ready acceptance which further stirred her alarm.

"Thanks," he said. "As you say two —— Here, slip this other gun into your coat pocket." And he reached the fellow revolver to his own from its holster upon the wall. "Now let's get on."

He moved toward the door. Chepstow was in the act of following when Betty's voice stopped him.

"What time will you get back?" she inquired. "How shall I know that——"

She broke off. Her brown eyes were fixed questioningly upon the lumberman's face.

"We'll be around in an hour," said Mason confidently. "Meanwhile, Miss Betty, after we're gone, just set those bars across the door. And don't let anybody in till you hear either mine or your uncle's voice."

The girl understood him, she always understood without asking a lot of questions. She was outwardly quite calm, without the faintest trace of the alarm she really felt. She had no fear for herself. At that moment she was thinking of her uncle.

After the men had gone she closed the heavy log door but did not bar it as she had been advised; then, returning to the stove, she sat down and took up some sewing, prepared to await their return with absolute faith and confidence in the lumberman's assurance.

She stitched on in the silence, and soon her thoughts drifted back to the man who had so strangely become the lodestone of her life. The trouble suggested by Mason must be his trouble. She wondered what could possibly happen on top of the fever, which she and her uncle had been fighting for the past weeks, that could further jeopardize his contract. She could see only one thing, and her quickness of perception in all matters relating to the world she knew drove her straight to the reality. She knew it was a general strike Mason feared. She knew it by the warning she had received, by the foreman's manner when he prepared to leave the hut.

She was troubled. In imagination she saw the great edifice Dave had so ardently labored upon toppling about his ears. In her picture she saw him great, calm, resolute, standing amidst the wreck, with eyes looking out straight ahead full of that great fighting strength which was his, his heart sore and bruised but his lips silent, his great cour- age and purpose groping for the shattered founda- tions, that the rebuilding might not be delayed an instant. It was her delight and pride to think of him thus, whilst, with every heart-beat, a nervous dread for him shook her whole body. She tried to think wherein she could help this man who was more to her than her own life. She bitterly hated her own womanhood as she thought of those two men bearing arms at that instant in his interests. Why could not she? But she knew that privilege was denied her. She threw her sewing aside as though the effeminacy of it sickened her, and rose from her seat and paced the room. " Oh, Dave, Dave, why can't I help you?" It was the cry that rang through her troubled brain with every moment that the little metal clock on the desk ticked away, while she waited for the men-folk's return.

CHAPTER XX

THE CHURCH MILITANT

OUTSIDE the hut Mason led the way. The mist had deepened into a white fog which seemed to deaden all sound, so quiet was everything, so silent the grim woods all around. It had settled so heavily that it was almost impossible to see anything beyond the edge of the trail. There was just a hazy shadow, like a sudden depth of mist, to mark the woodland borders; beyond this all was gray and desolate.

The dugout was built at the trail-side, a trail which had originally been made for travoying logs, but had now become the main trail linking up the camp with the eastern world. The camp itself— No. 1, the main camp—was further in the woods to the west, a distance of nearly a mile and a half by trail, but not more than half a mile through the woods. It was this short cut the two men took now. They talked as they went, but in hushed tones. It was as though the gray of the fog, and the knowledge of their mission weighed heavily, inspiring them with a profound feeling of caution.

"You've not had any real trouble before?" Chepstow asked. "I mean trouble such as would serve you with a key to what is going on now?"

"Oh, we've had occasional 'rackets,'" said Mason

easily. " But nothing serious—nothing to guide us in this. No, we've got to find this out. You see there's no earthly reason for trouble that I know. The boys are paid jolly well, a sight better than I would pay them if this was my outfit. The hours are exacting, I admit. This huge contract has caused that. It's affected us in most every way, but Dave is no niggard, and the inducement has been made more than proportionate, so there's no kick coming on that head. Where before axemen's work was merely a full eight hours, it now takes 'em something like nine and ten, and work like the devil to get through even in that time. But their wages are simply out of sight. Do you know, there are men in this camp drawing from four to five dollars a day clear of food and shelter? Why, the income of some of them is positively princely."

" What is it you think is on foot? " Chepstow demanded, as he buttoned his coat close about his neck to keep out the saturating mist. Then, as his companion didn't answer at once, he added half to himself, " It's no wonder there's fever with these mists around."

Bob Mason paid no heed to the last remark. The fever had lost interest for him in the storm-clouds he now saw ahead. Hitherto he had not put his thoughts on the matter into concrete form. He had not given actual expression to his fears. There had been so little to guide him. Besides, he had had no sound reason to fear anything, that is no definite reason. It was his work to feel and understand the pulse of the men under him, and it largely depended on the accuracy of his reading whether or not the work under his charge ran smoothly. He had felt for some time that something was wrong, and Betty's story had confirmed his feeling. He was some moments before he answered, but when he did it was with calm decision.

" Organized strike," he said at last.

Tom Chepstow was startled. The words " organized strike" had an unpleasant sound. He suddenly realized the isolation of these hill camps, the lawless nature of the lumber-jacks. He felt that a strike up here in the mountains would be a very different thing from a strike in the heart of civilization, and that was bad enough. The fact that the tone of Mason's pronouncement had suggested no alarm made him curious to hear his views upon the position.

" The reason ?" he demanded.

The lumberman shrugged.

" Haven't a notion."

They tramped on in silence for some time, the sound of their footsteps muffled in the fog. The gray was deepening, and, with oncoming night, their surroundings were rapidly becoming more and more obscure. Presently the path opened out into the wide clearing occupied by No. 1 camp. Here shadowy lights were visible in the fog, but beyond that nothing could be seen. Mason paused and glanced carefully about him.

" This fog is useful," he said, with a short laugh.

"As we don't want to advertise our presence we'll take to the woods opposite, and work our way round to the far side of the camp."

"Why the far side?"

"The store is that way. And—yes, I think the store is our best plan. Jules Lieberstein is a time-serving ruffian, and will doubtless lend himself to any wildcat scheme of his customers. Besides, this singsong of the boys sounds suggestive to me."

"I see." Chepstow was quick to grasp the other's reasoning. The singsong had suggested nothing to him before.

Now they turned from the open and hastened across to the wood-belt. As they entered its gloomy aisles, the fog merged into a pitchy blackness that demanded all the lumberman's woodcraft to negotiate. The parson hung close to his heels, and frequently had to assure himself of his immediate presence by reaching out and touching him. A quarter of an hour's tramp brought them to a halt.

"We must get out of this now," whispered Mason. "We are about opposite the store. I've no doubt that buckboard will be somewhere around. I've a great fancy to see it."

They moved on, this time with greater caution than before. Leaving the forest they found the fog had become denser. The glow of the camp lights was no longer visible, just a blank gray wall obscured everything. However, this was no deterrent to Mason. He moved along with extreme caution, stepping as lightly and quietly as possible. He wished to avoid observation, and though the fog helped him in this it equally afforded the possibility of his inadvertently running into some one. Once this nearly happened. His straining ears caught the faint sound of footsteps approaching, and he checked his companion only just in the nick of time to let two heavy-footed lumber-jacks cross their course directly in front of them. They were talking quite unguardedly as they went, and seemed absorbed in the subject of their conversation.

" Y're a fool, a measly-headed fool, Tyke," one of them was saying, with a heat that held the two men listening. " Y'ain't got nuthin' to lose. We ain't got no kick comin' from us ; I'll allow that, sure. But if by kickin' we ken drain a few more dollars out of him I say kick, an' kick good an' hard. Them as is fixin' this racket knows, they'll do the fancy work. We'll jest set around an'—an' take the boodle as it comes."

The man laughed harshly. The shrewdness of his argument pleased him mightily.

" But what's it for, though ? " asked the other, the man addressed as " Tyke." " Is it a raise in wages ? "

" Say, ain't you smart ? " retorted the first speaker. " Sure, it's wages. A raise. What else does folks strike for ? "

" But——"

" Cut it. You ain't no sort o' savee. You ain't got nuthin' but to set around ——"

The voice died away in the distance, and Mason turned to his companion.

"Not much doubt about that. The man objecting is 'Tyke' Bacon, one of our oldest hands. A thoroughly reliable axeman of the real sort. The other fellow's voice I didn't recognize. I'd say he's likely one of the scallywags I've picked up lately. This trouble seems to have been brewing ever since I was forced to pick up chance loafers who floated into camp."

Chepstow had no comment to make, yet the matter was fraught with the keenest interest for him. Mason's coolness did not deceive him, and, even with his limited experience of the men of these camps, the thing was more than significant. Caution became more than ever necessary now as they neared their destination, and in a few moments a ruddy glow of light on the screen of fog told them they had reached the sutler's store. They came to a halt in rear of the building, and it was difficult to estimate their exact position. However, the sound of a powerful, clarion-like voice reached them through the thickness of the log walls, and the lumberman at once proceeded to grope his way along in the hope of finding a window or some opening through which it would be possible to distinguish the words of the speaker. At last his desire was fulfilled. A small break in the heavy wall of lateral logs proved to be a cotton-covered pivot-window. It was closed, but the light shone through it, and the speaker's words were plainly audible. Chepstow closed up behind him, and both men craned forward listening.

Some one was addressing what was apparently a meeting of lumber-jacks. The words and voice were not without refinement, and, obviously, were not belonging to a lumberman. Moreover, it struck the listeners that this man, whoever he be, was not addressing a meeting for the first time. In fact Mason had no difficulty in placing him in the calling to which he actually belonged. He was discoursing with all the delectable speciousness of a regular strike organizer. He was one of those products of trade unionism who are always ready to create dissatisfaction where labour's contentment is most nourishing to capital—that is, at a price. He is not necessarily a part of trade unionism, but exists because trade unionism has created a market for his wares, and made him possible.

Just now he was lending all his powers of eloquence and argument to the threadbare quackery of his kind; the iniquity of the possession of wealth acquired by the sweat of a thousand moderately honest brows. It was the old, old dish garnished and hashed up afresh, whose poisonous odors he was wafting into the nostrils of his ignorant audience.

He was dealing with men as ignorant and hard as the timber it was their life to cut, and he painted the picture in all the crude, lurid colors most effective to their dull senses. The blessings of liberal employment, of ample wages, the kindly efforts

made to add to their happiness and improve their
lives were ignored, even rigorously shut out of his
argument, or so twisted as to appear definite sins
against the legions of labor. For such is the
method of those who live upon the hard-earned
wages of the unthinking worker.

For some minutes the two men listened to the
burden of the man's unctuous periods, but at last
an exclamation of disgust broke from the lumberman.

" Makes you sick!" he whispered in his companion's ear. " And they'll believe it all. Here!"
He drew a penknife from his pocket and passed the
blade gently through the cotton of the window.
The aperture was small, he dared not make it bigger
for fear of detection, but, by pressing one eye close
up against it, it was sufficient for him to obtain a
full view of the room.

The place was packed with lumber-jacks, all with
their keenest attention upon the speaker, who was
addressing them from the reading-desk Tom Chepstow had set up for the purposes of his Sunday
evening service. The desecration drew a smothered
curse from the lumberman. He was not a religious
man, but that an agitator such as this should stand
at the parson's desk was too much for him. He
scrutinized the fellow closely, nor did he recognize
him. He was a stranger to the camp, and his
round fat face set his blood surging. Besides this
man there were three others sitting behind him on
the table the parson had set there for the purposes

of administering Holy Communion, and the sight maddened him still more. Two of these he recognized as laborers he had recently taken on his "time sheet," but the other was a stranger to him.

At last he drew back and made way for his companion.

"Get a good look, parson," he said. Then he added with an angry laugh, "I've thought most of what you'll feel like saying. I'd—I'd like to riddle the hide of that son-of-a-dog's-wife. We did well to get around. We're in for a heap bad time, I guess."

Chepstow took his place. Mason heard him mutter something under his breath, and knew at once that the use of his reading-desk and Communion table had struck home.

But the sacrilege was promptly swept from the parson's mind. The speaker was forgotten, the matter of the coming strike, even, was almost forgotten. He had recognized the third man on the table, the man who was a stranger to Mason, and he swung round on the lumberman.

"What's Jim Truscott doing there?" he demanded in a sharp whisper.

"Who? Jim Truscott?"

For a second a puzzled expression set Mason frowning. Then his face cleared. "Say, isn't that the fellow who ran that mill—he's a friend of—Dave's?"

But the other had turned back to the window. And, at that moment, Mason's attention was also caught by the sudden turn the agitator's talk had taken.

" Now, my friends," he was saying, " this is the point I would impress on you. Hitherto we have cut off all communication of a damaging nature to ourselves with the tyrant at Malkern, but the time has come when even more stringent measures must be taken. We wish to conduct our negotiations with the mill-owner himself, direct. We must put before him our proposals. We want no go-betweens. As things stand we cannot reach him, and the reason is the authority of his representative up here. Such obstacles as he can put in our way will be damaging to our cause, and we will not tolerate them. He must be promptly set aside, and, by an absolute stoppage of work, we can force the man from Malkern to come here so that we can talk to him, and insist upon our demands. We must talk to him as from worker to fellow worker. He must be forced to listen to reason. Experience has long since taught me that such is the only way to deal with affairs of this sort. Now, what we propose," and the man turned with a bow to the three men behind him, thus including them with himself, " is that without violence we take possession of these camps and strike all work, and, securing the person of Mr. Mason, and any others likely to interfere with us, we hold them safe until all our plans are fully put through. During the period necessary for the cessation of work, each man will draw an allowance equal to two-thirds of his wages, and he will receive a guarantee of employment when the strike is ended. The sutler, Mr. Lieberstein here, will be the treasurer of the strike funds, and pay each man his daily wage. There is but one thing more I have to say. We intend to take the necessary precautions against interference to-night. The cessation of work will date from this hour. And in the meantime we will put to the vote——"

Chepstow, his keen eyes blazing, turned and faced the lumberman.

"The scoundrels!" he said, with more force than discretion. "Did you hear? It means——"

The lumberman chuckled, but held up a warning hand.

"They're going to take me prisoner," he said. Then he added grimly, "There's going to be a warm time to-night."

But the churchman was not listening. Again his thought had reverted to the presence of Jim Truscott at that meeting.

"What on earth is young Truscott doing in there?" he asked. "He went away east the night I set out for these hills. What's he got to do with that—that rascally agitator? Why—he must be one of the—leaders of this thing. It's—it's most puzzling!"

Chepstow's puzzlement did not communicate itself to Mason. The camp "boss" was less interested in the identity of these people than in the strike itself. It was his work to see that so much lumber was sent down the river every day. That was his responsibility. Dave looked to him. And he was face to face with a situation which threatened the complete annihilation of all his employer's schemes. A strike effectually carried out might be prolonged indefinitely, and then —

" Look here, parson," he said coolly, " I want you to stay right here for a minute or so. They aren't likely to be finished for a while inside there. I want to ' prospect.' I want to find that buckboard. That damned agitator—'scuse the language —must have come up in it, so I guess it's near handy. The fog's good and thick, so there's not a heap of chance of anybody locating us, still——" he paused and glanced into the churchman's alert eyes. " Have a look to your gun," he went on with a quiet smile, " and—well, you are a parson, but if anybody comes along and attempts to molest you I'd use it if I were in your place."

Chepstow made no reply, but there was something in his look that satisfied the other.

Mason hurried away and the parson, left alone, leant against the wall, prepared to wait for his return. In spite of the plot he had listened to, the presence of Jim Truscott in that room occupied most of his thoughts. It was most perplexing. He tried every channel of supposition and argument, but none gave him any satisfactory explanation. One thing alone impressed its importance on his mind. That was the necessity of conveying a warning to Dave. But he remembered they—

these conspirators—had cut communications. Mason and probably he were to be made prisoners.

His ire roused. He blazed into a sudden fury. These rascals were to make them prisoners. Almost unconsciously he drew his gun from his pocket and turned to the window. As he did so the sound of approaching footsteps set him alert and defensive. He swung his back to the wall again, and, gun in hand, stood ready. The next moment he hurriedly returned the weapon to his pocket, but not before Mason had seen the attitude and the fighting expression of his face, and it set him smiling.

"I've found the buckboard," he said in a whisper. Then he paused and looked straight into the churchman's eyes. "We're up against it," he went on. "Maybe you as well as myself. You can't tell where these fellows'll draw the line. And there's Miss Betty to think of, too. Are you ready to buck? Are you game? You're a parson, I know, and these things ——"

"Get to it, boy," Chepstow interrupted him sharply. "I am of necessity a man of peace, but there are things that become a man's duty. And it seems to me to hit hard will better serve God and man just now than to preach peace. What's your plan?"

Mason smiled. He knew he had read the parson aright. He knew he had in him a staunch and loyal support. He liked, too, the phrase by which he excused his weakness for combat.

" Well, I mean to do this sponge-faced crawler down, or break my neck in the attempt. I don't intend to be made a prisoner by any damned strikers. This thing means ruin to Dave, and it's up to me to help him out. I'm going to get word through to him. I understand now how our letters have been intercepted, and no doubt his have been stopped too. I'm going to have a flutter in this game. It's a big one, and makes me feel good. What say? Are you game?"

" For anything!" exclaimed the parson with eyes sparkling.

" Well, there's not a heap of time to waste in talk. I'll just get you to slip back to the dugout. Gather some food and truck into a sack, and a couple of guns cr so, and some ammunition. Then get Miss Betty and slip out. Hike on down the trail a hundred yards or so and wait for me. Can you make it?"

Chepstow nodded.

" And you?" he asked.

" I'm going to get possession of that buckboard, and—come right along. The scheme's rotten, I know. But it's the best I can think of at the moment. It's our only chance of warning Dave. There's not a second to spare now, so cut along. You've got to prepare for a two days' journey."

" Anything else?"

" Nothing. Miss Betty's good grit — in case —— ?"

Chepstow nodded.

"Game all through. How long can you give me?"

"Maybe a half hour."

"Good. I can make it in that."

"Right. S'long."

"S'long."

CHAPTER XXI

Tom Chepstow set out for the dugout. Churchman as he was his blood was stirred to fighting
heat, his lean, hard muscles were tingling with a
nervous desire for action. Nor did he attempt to
check his feelings, or compose them into a condition compatible with his holy calling. Possibly,
when the time had passed for action, and the mantle of peace and good-will toward all men had once
more fallen upon him, he would bitterly regret his
outbreak, but, for the moment, he was a man, human, passionate, unreasoning, thrilling with the joy
of life, and the delight of a moral truancy from all
his accepted principles. No schoolboy could have
broken the bonds of discipline with a greater joy,
and his own subconscious knowledge of wrong-
doing was no mar to his pleasure.

The fog was thick, but it did not cause him great
inconvenience. He took to the woods for his
course, and, keeping close to the edge which encircled the camp clearing, he had little difficulty in
striking the path to the dugout. This achieved he
had but to follow it carefully. The one possibility
that caused him any anxiety was lest he should
overshoot the hut in the fog.

But he need have had no fear of this. Dense as

the fog was, the lights of the dugout were plainly visible when he came to it. Betty, with careful forethought, had set the oil lamps in the two windows. She quite understood the difficulties of that forest land, and she had no desire for the men-folk to spend the night roaming the wilderness.

The parson found her calmly alert. She did not fly at him with a rush of questions. She was far more composed than he, yet there was a sparkling brilliancy in her brown eyes which told of feelings strongly controlled; her eyelids were well parted, and there was a shade of quickening in the dilation of her nostrils as she breathed. She looked up into his face as he turned after closing the door, and his tongue answered the mute challenge.

"There's to be a great game to-night," he said, rubbing the palms of his hands together. The tone, the action, both served to point the state of his mind.

Knowing him as she did Betty needed no words to tell her that the " game " was to be no sort of play.

" It's a 'strike,' " he went on. " A strike, and a bad one. They intend to make a prisoner of Mason, and, maybe, of us. We've got to outwit them. Now, help me get some things together, and I'll tell you while we get ready. We've got to quit to-night."

He picked up a gunny sack while he was speaking and gave it to Betty to hold open. Then he immediately began to deplete the lumberman's larder of any eatables that could be easily carried.

Ever since the men had left her this strike had been in Betty's mind, so his announcement in no way startled her.

"What of Dave?" she asked composedly. "Has he any—idea of it?"

"That's just it. We've got to let him know. He's quite in the dark. Communications cut. Mason must get away at once to let him know. He intends to 'jump' their buckboard and team—I mean these strikers' buckboard." He laughed. He felt ready to laugh at most things. It was not that he did not care. His desire was inspired by the thought that he was to play a part in the "game."

"The one that came in to-night?" Betty asked, taking up a fresh sack to receive some pots and blankets.

"Yes."

"And we are to bolt with him?" she went on in a peculiar manner.

Her uncle paused in the act of putting firearms and ammunition into the sack. Her tone checked his enthusiasm. Then he laughed.

"We're not 'bolting,' Betty, we're escaping so that Dave may get the news. His fortune depends on our success. Remember our communications are cut."

But his arguments fell upon deaf ears. Betty smiled and shook her brown head.

" We're bolting, uncle. Listen. There's no need for us to go. In fact, we can't go. Think for a moment. Things depend on the speed with which Dave learns of the trouble. We should make two more in the buckboard of which the horses are already tired. Mason, by himself, will travel light. Besides, a girl is a deterrent when it comes to—fighting. No, wait." She held up a warning finger as he was about to interrupt. " Then there are the sick here. We cannot leave them. They—are our duty. Besides, Dave's interests would be ill served if we left the fever to continue its ravages unchecked."

In her last remark Betty displayed her woman's practical instinct. Perhaps she was not fully aware of her real motive. Perhaps she conscientiously believed that it was their duty that claimed her. Nevertheless her thought was for the man she loved, and it guided her every word and action; it inspired her. The threat of imprisonment up here did not frighten her, did not even enter into her considerations at all. Dave—her every nerve vibrated with desire to help him, to save him.

Chepstow suddenly reached out and laid a hand on her shoulder. His enthusiasm had passed, and, for the moment, the churchman in him was uppermost again.

" You're right, Betty," he said with decision. " We stay here."

The girl's eyes thanked him, but her words were full of practical thought.

" Will Mason come here? Because, if so, we'll get these things outside ready."

" No. We've got to carry them down the trail and meet him there. There may be a rush. There may be a scuffle. We don't know. I half think you'd better stay here while I go and meet him."

Betty shook her head.

" I'm going to help," she exclaimed, with a flash of battle in her eyes.

" Then come on." Her uncle shouldered the heavier of the two sacks, and was about to tuck the other under his arm, but Betty took it from him, and lifted it to her shoulder in a twinkling.

" Halves," she cried, as she moved toward the door.

The man laughed light-heartedly and blew out the lights. Then, as he reached the girl's side, a distant report caused him to stop short.

" What's that? " he demanded.

" A pistol shot," cried Betty. " Come along! "

They ran out of the hut and down the trail, and, in a moment, were swallowed up in the fog.

*   *   *   *   *   *

Bob Mason intended to give Chepstow a fair start. He knew, if he were to be successful, his task would occupy far less time than the other's. And a vital point in his scheme lay in meeting his two friends at the appointed spot.

He was fully alive to the rank audacity of his plan. It was desperate, and the chances were heavily against him. But he was not a man to shrink from an undertaking on such a score. He had to warn Dave, and this was the only means that suggested itself. If he were not a genius of invention, he was at least full of courage and determination.

On his previous reconnoitre he had located the buckboard at the tying-posts in front of the store. Quite why it had been left there he could not understand, unless the strike-leader intended leaving camp that night. However, the point of interest lay in the fact of the vehicle and horses being there ready for his use if he could only safely possess himself of them, so speculation as to the reason of its being there was only of secondary interest.

When he made his first move Tom Chepstow had been gone some ten minutes. He groped his way carefully along the wall until the front angle of the building was reached, and here he paused to ascertain the position of things. The meeting was still in progress inside, and, as yet, there seemed to be no sign of its breaking up. The steady hum of voices that reached him told him this.

About twenty yards directly in front of him was the buckboard; while to the right, perhaps half that distance away, was the open door of the store, and adjacent to it a large glass window. Both were lit up, and the glow from the oil lamps shone dully on the fog bank. He was half inclined to reconnoitre these latter to ascertain if any one were about, but finally decided to go straight for his goal and chance everything. With this intention he moved straight out from the building and vanished in the fog.

He walked quickly. Fortune favored him until he was within a few yards of the tying-post, when suddenly the clanging of an iron-handled bucket being set roughly upon the ground brought him to a dead standstill. Some one was tending the horses— probably watering them. Evidently they were being got ready for a journey. Almost unconsciously his hand went to the pocket in which he carried his revolver.

At that moment a roar of applause came from the store, and he knew the meeting was drawing to a close. Then came a prolonged cheering, followed by the raucous singing of " He's a jolly good fellow." It *was* the end.

He could delay no longer. Taking his bearings as well as the fog would permit, he struck out for the tail end of the buckboard. He intended reaching the " near-side " of the horses, where he felt that the reins would be looped up upon the harness, and as the best means of avoiding the man with the bucket.

In this he had little difficulty, and when he reached the vehicle he bent low, and, passing clear of the wheels, drew up toward the horses' heads. By this time the man with the bucket was moving away, and he breathed more freely.

But his relief was short-lived. The men were already pouring out of the store, and the fog-laden air was filled with the muffled tones of many voices.

To add to his discomfiture he further became aware of footsteps approaching.   He   could   delay   no longer.   He   dared   not   wait   to   let   them   pass. Then, they might be the owners of the buckboard. His movements became charged with almost electrical activity.

He reached out and assured himself that the bits were   in   the   horses'   mouths.   Then   he   groped for the   reins;   as he   expected,   they   were   looped in the harness.   Possessing   himself   of   them,   he   reached for the collar-chain securing the horses to the posts. He   pressed   the   swivel   open,   and,   releasing   it, lowered   the   chain   noiselessly.   And   a   moment later two men loomed up out of the fog on the " off- · side."   They were talking, and he listened.

" It's   bad   med'cine   you   leaving   to-night," he heard the voice of the strike-leader say in a grumbling tone.

" I   can't   help   that," came   the   response.   It was a voice he did not recognize.

" Well, we've   got   to   secure   this   man   Mason to-night.   You can't trust these fellows a heap.   Give 'em time, and some one will blow the game.   Then he'll be off like a rabbit."

" Well, it's   up   to   you   to   get   him," the strange voice retorted sharply.   " I'm   paying   you   heavily. You've   undertaken   the   job.   Besides, there's   that cursed parson and his niece up here.   I daren't take a   chance   of   their   seeing   me.   I   oughtn't   to   have come   up   here   at   all.   If   Lieberstein   hadn't   been such a grasping pig of a Jew there would have been no need for my coming. You've just got to put everything through on your own, Walford. I'm off."

Mason waited for no more. The buckboard belonged to the stranger, and he was about to use it. He laughed inwardly, and his spirits rose. Everything was ready. He dropped back to the full extent of the reins as stealthily and as swiftly as possible. This cleared him of the buckboard and hid him from the view of the men. Then with a rein in each hand he slapped them as sharply as he could on the quarters of the cold and restless horses. They jumped at the neck-yoke, and with a " yank " he swung them clear of the tying-posts. He shouted at them and slapped the reins again, and the only too willing beasts plunged into a gallop.

He heard an exclamation from one of the men as the buckboard shot past them, and the other made a futile grab for the off-side rein. For himself he seized the rail of the carryall with one hand and gave a wild leap. He dropped into the vehicle safely but with some force, and his legs were left hanging over the back.

But he had not cleared the danger yet. He was in the act of drawing in his legs when they were seized in an arm embrace, and the whole weight of a man hung upon him in an effort to drag him off the vehicle. There was no time to consider. He felt himself sliding over the rail, which only checked his progress for an instant. But that instant gave him a winning chance. He drew his revolver, and leveling it, aimed point-blank at where he thought the man's shoulder must be. There was a loud report, and the grip on his legs relaxed. The man dropped to the ground, and he was left to scramble to his feet and climb over into the driving-seat.

A blind, wild drive was that race from the store. He drove like a fury in the fog, trusting to the instinct of the horses and the luck of the reckless to guide him into the comparative safety of the eastward trail.

As the horses flew over the ground the cries of the strikers filled the air. They seemed to come from every direction, even ahead. The noise, the rattle of the speeding wheels, fired his excitement. The fog—the dense gray pall that hung over the whole camp—was his salvation, and he shouted back defiance.

It was a useless and dangerous thing to do, and he realized his folly at once. A great cry instantly went up from the strikers. He was recognized, and his name was shouted in execration. He only laughed. There was joy in the feel of the reins, in the pulling of the mettlesome horses. They were running strong and well within themselves.

It was only a matter of seconds from the time of his start to the moment when he felt the vehicle bump heavily over a series of ruts. He promptly threw his weight on the near-side rein, and the horses swung round. It was the trail he was looking for. And as the horses settled down to it he breathed more freely. It was only after this point had been gained and passed that he realized the extent of his previous risk. He knew that the entrance to the trail on its far side was lined by log shanties, and he had been driving straight for them.

In the midst of his freshly-acquired ease of mind came a sudden and unpleasant recollection. He remembered the path through the woods to the dugout; it was shorter than the trail he was on by nearly a mile. While he had over a mile and a half to go, those in pursuit, if they took to the path, had barely half.

He listened. But he knew beforehand that his fears were only too well founded. Yes, he could hear them. The voices of the pursuers sounded away to the left. They were abreast of him. They had taken to the woods. He snatched the whip from its socket and laid it heavily across the horses' backs, and the animals stretched out into a race. The buckboard jumped, it rattled and shrieked. The pace was terrific. But he was ready to take every chance now, so long as he could gain sufficient time to take up those he knew to be waiting for him ahead.

In another few minutes he would know the worst—or the best. Again and again he urged his horses. But already they were straining at the top of their speed. They galloped as though the spirit of the race had entered their willing souls. They could do no more than they were doing; it was only cruelty to flog them. If their present speed was insufficient then he could not hope to outstrip the strikers. If he only could hear their voices dropping behind.

The minutes slipped by. The fog worried him. He was watching for the dugout, and he feared lest he should pass it unseen. Nor could he estimate the distance he had come. Hark! the shouts of the pursuers were drawing nearer, and—they were still abreast of him! He must be close on the dugout. He peered into the fog, and suddenly a dark shadow at the trail-side loomed up. There was no mistaking it. It was the hut; and it was in darkness. His friends must be on ahead. How far! that was the question. On that depended everything.

What was that? The hammering of heavy feet on the hard trail sounded directly behind him. He had gained nothing. Then he thought of that halt that yet remained in front of him, and something like panic seized him. He slashed viciously at his horses.

He felt like a man obsessed with the thought of trailing bloodhounds. He must keep on, on. There must be no pause, no rest, or the ravening pack would fall on him and rend him. Yet he knew that halt must come. He was gaining rapidly enough now. Without that halt they could never come up with him. But—his ears were straining for Chepstow's summons. Every second it was withheld was something gained. He possessed a frantic hope that some guiding spirit might have induced the churchman to take up a position very much further on than he had suggested.

" Hallo ! "

The call had come. Chepstow was at the edge of the trail. Mason's hopes dropped to zero. He abandoned himself to the inevitable, flung his weight on the reins, and brought his horses to a stand with a jolt.

" Where's Miss Betty ? " he demanded. But his ears caught the sound of the men behind him, and he hurried on without waiting for a reply. " Quick, parson ! The bags ! fling 'em in, and jump for it ! They're close behind ! "

" Betty's gone back," cried Chepstow, flinging the sacks into the carryall. " I'm going back too. You go on alone. We've got the sick to see to. Tell Dave we're all right. So long ! Drive on ! Good luck ! Eh ? "

A horrified cry from Mason had caused the final ejaculation.

He was pointing at the off-side horse standing out at right angles to the pole.

" For God's sake, fix that trace," he cried. " Quick, man ! It's unhooked ! Gee ! What infern ——"

Chepstow sprang to secure the loosened trace. He, too, could hear the pursuers close behind. He fumbled the iron links in his anxiety, and it took some moments to adjust.

" Right," he cried at last, after what seemed an

interminable time. Mason whipped up his horses, and they sprang to their traces. But as they did so there was a sudden rush from behind, and a figure leapt on to the carryall. The buckboard rocked and the driver, in the act of shouting at his horses, felt himself seized by the throat from behind.

Fortunately the churchman saw it all. His blood rushed to his brain. As the buckboard was sweeping past him he caught the iron rail and leapt. In an instant he was on his feet and had closed with Mason's assailant. He, too, went for the throat, with all the ferocity of a bulldog. The mantle of the church was cast to the winds. He was panting with the lust for fight, and he crushed his fingers deep into the man's windpipe. They dropped together on the sacks.

Mason, released, dared not turn. He plied his whip furiously. He had the legs of his pursuers and he meant to add to his distance. He heard the struggle going on behind him. He heard the gasp of a choking man. And, listening, he reveled in it as men of his stamp will revel in such things.

" Choke him, parson ! Choke the swine ! " he hurled viciously over his shoulder.

He got no answer. The struggle went on in silence, and presently Mason began to fear for the result. He slackened his horses down and glanced back. Tom Chepstow's working features looked up into his.

" I've got him," he said : then of a sudden he

looked anxiously down at the man he was kneeling on. " He's—he's unconscious. I hope —— You'd better pull up."

" I wish you'd choke the life out of him," cried Mason furiously.

" I did my best, I'm afraid," the parson replied ruefully. " You'd better pull up."

But the lumberman kept on.

" Half a minute. Get these matches, and have a look at him. I'll slow down."

The churchman seized the matches, and, in his anxiety at what he had done, struck several before he got one burning long enough to see the unconscious man's face. Finally he succeeded, and an ejaculation of surprise broke from him.

" Heavens ! It's Jim Truscott !" he cried.

He pressed his hand over the man's heart.

" Thank God ! he's alive," he added.

Mason drew up sharply. A sudden change had come over his whole manner. He sprang to the ground.

" Here, help me secure him," he said almost fiercely. " I'll take him down to Dave."

They lashed their prisoner by his hands and feet. Then Mason seized the churchman excitedly by the arm.

" Get back, parson !" he cried. " Get back to the dugout quick as hell'll let you ! There's Miss Betty ! "

" God ! I'd forgotten ! And there's those— strikers ! "

CHAPTER XXII

FEAR drove Chepstow headlong for the dugout. Mason's words, his tone and manner, had served to excite him to a pitch closely bordering upon absolute terror. What of Betty? Over and over again he asked himself what might not happen to her, left alone at the mercy of these savages? What if, baulked of their prey, they turned to loot and wreck his hut? ·It was more than possible. To his fear-stricken imagination it was inevitable. His gorge rose and he sickened at the thought, and he raced through the fog to the girl's help.

The self-torture he suffered in those weary minutes was exquisite. He railed at his own criminal folly in letting her leave his side. He reviled Mason and his wild schemes. Dave and his interests were banished from his mind. The well-being of Malkern, of the mills, of anybody in the world but the helpless girl, mattered not at all to him. It was Betty—of Betty alone he thought.

An innocent girl in the hands of such ruthless brutes as these strikers—what could she do? It was a maddening thought. He prayed to Heaven as he went, that he might be in time, and his prayers rang with a fervor such as they never possessed in his vocation as a churchman. And this mood alternated with another, which was its direct antithesis. The vicious thoughts of a man roused to battle ran through his brain in a fiery torrent. His whole outlook upon life underwent a change. All the kindly impulses of his heart, all the teachings of his church, all his best Christian beliefs, fell from him, and left him the naked, passionate man. Churchman, good Christian he undoubtedly was, but, before all things, he was a man; and just now a man in fighting mood.

It probably took him less than twenty minutes to make the return journey, yet it seemed to him hours—he certainly endured hours of mental anguish. But at last it ended with almost ludicrous abruptness. In the obscurity of the fog he was brought to a halt by impact with the walls of the dugout.

He recovered himself and stood for a moment listening. There was no sound of any one within, nor was there any sign of the strikers. He moved round to the door; a beam of light shone beneath it. He breathed more freely. Then, to his dismay, at his first touch, the door swung open. His fears leapt again, he dreaded what that open door might disclose. Then, in the midst of his fears, a cry of relief and joy broke from him.

" Thank God, you're safe !" he exclaimed, as he rushed into the room.

Betty looked up from the work in her lap. She was seated beside the box-stove sewing. Her calm-

ness was in flat contrast to her uncle's excited state.
She smiled gently, and her soft eyes had in them a
questioning humor that had a steadying effect upon
the man.

" Safe ? Why, dear, of course I'm safe," she
said. " But—I was a little anxious about you.
You were so long getting back. Did Bob Mason
get safely away? "

Chepstow laughed.

" Yes, oh yes.   *He* got away safely."

" He ? "

The work lay in Betty's lap, and her fingers had
become idle.

" Yes.   But we captured one of the strikers."

The parson suddenly turned to the door and
barred it securely.   Then, as he went on, he crossed
to the windows, and began to barricade them.

" Yes, we had a busy time.   They were hard on
his heels when he pulled up for me.   We nailed the
foremost.   He jumped on the buckboard and almost strangled Mason.   I jumped on it too, and—
and almost strangled him."

He laughed harshly.   His blood was still up.
Betty bent over her work and her expressive face
was hidden.

" Who was he ?   I mean your prisoner.   Did you
recognize him, or was he a new hand? "

Chepstow's laugh abruptly died out.   He had
suddenly remembered who his prisoner was ; and
he tried to ignore the question.

" Oh, yes, we recognized him.   But," he went on

hurriedly, " we must get some supper. I think we are in for a busy time."

But Betty was not so easily put off. Besides, her curiosity was roused by her uncle's evident desire to avoid the subject.

" Who was he ? " she demanded again.

There was no escape, and the man knew it. Betty could be very persistent.

" Eh ? Oh, I'm afraid it was Jim—Jim Truscott," he said reluctantly.

Betty rose from her chair without a word. She stirred the fire in the cook-stove, and began to pre- pare a supper of bacon and potatoes and tea, while her uncle went on with his task of securing the win- dows. It was the latter who finally broke the silence.

" Has any one—has anybody been here ? " he asked awkwardly.

Betty did not look up from her work.

" Two men paid me a visit," she said easily. " One asked for you. He seemed angry. I—I told him you had gone over to the sick camp—that you were coming back to supper. He laughed— fiercely. He said ıf you didn't come back I'd find myself up against it. Then he hurried off—and I was glad."

" And the other ? "

Chepstow's work was finished. He had crossed over and was standing beside the cook-stove. His question came with an undercurrent of fierceness that Betty was unused to, but she smiled up into his face.

"The other? I think he had been drinking. He was one of those two I met in the woods. He asked me why I hadn't taken his warning. I told him I was considering it. He leered at me and said it was too late, and assured me I must take the consequences. Then he—tried to kiss me. It was rather funny."

"Funny? Great Heavens! And you ——"

Betty's smile broadened as she pointed to a heavy revolver lying in the chair she had just vacated.

"I didn't have any trouble. I told him there were five barrels in that, all loaded, and each barrel said he'd better get out."

"Did—did he go?"

Chepstow could scarcely control his fury. But Betty answered him in a quiet determined manner.

"Not until I had emptied one of them," she said. Then with a rueful smile she added, "But it went very wide of its mark."

Her uncle tried to laugh, but the result was little better than a furious snort.

"Why did you leave the door open?" he inquired a moment later.

"Well, you were out. You might have returned in—in a hurry and —— But sit down, uncle dear, food's ready."

The man sat down and Betty stood by to supply him with all he needed. Then he noticed she had only prepared food for one.

"Why, child, what about you?" he demanded kindly.

"I've had some biscuits and tea, before you came in. I'm not hungry. Now don't bother about it, dear. Yes, I am quite well." She shook her head and smiled at him as he attempted to interrupt her, but the smile was a mere cloak to her real feelings. She had eaten before he came in, as she said. But if she hadn't she could have eaten nothing now. Her mind was swept with a hot tide of anxious thought. She had a thousand and one questions unanswered, and she knew it would be useless putting any one of them to her kindly, impetuous uncle. He was to her the gentlest of guardians, but quite impossible as a confidant for her woman's fears, her woman's passionate desire to help the man she loved. He was staunch and brave, and in what might lay before them she could have no better companion, no better champion, but where the subtleties of her woman's feelings were concerned there could be no confidence in him.

She watched him eat in silence, and, presently, when he looked up at her, her soft brown eyes were lit by an almost maternal regard for him. He had no understanding of that look, and Betty knew it, otherwise it would not have been there.

"I can't understand it all," he said. "Jim is a worse—a worse rascal than I thought. I believe he's not only in this strike, but one of the organizers. Why? That's what I can't make out. Is it mischief—wanton mischief? Is it jealousy of Dave's success? It's a puzzle I can't solve anyhow. After all his protestations to me the thing's inconceivable. It's enough to destroy all one's belief in human nature."

" Or strengthen it."

" Eh ? "

" It is only natural for people to err," Betty said seriously. " And having erred it is human nature, whatever our motives, however good our intentions, to find that the mire into which we have fallen sucks hard. It is more often than not the floundering to save ourselves that drives us deeper into it. Poor Jim. He needs our pity and help, just as we so often need help."

Her uncle stared into the grave young face. His astonishment kept him silent for a moment. He pushed impatiently away from the table. But it was not until Betty had moved back to her chair at the stove that he found words to express himself. He was angry, quite angry with her. It was not that he was really unchristian, but when he thought of all that this strike meant, he felt that sympathy for the man who was possibly the cause of it was entirely out of place.

" Truscott needs none of your pity, Betty," he said sharply. " If pity be needed it is surely for those whom one man's mischief will harm. Do you know what this strike means, child? Before it reaches the outside of these camps it will turn a tide of vice loose upon the men themselves. They will drink, gamble. They will quarrel and fight. And when such men fight it more often than not results in some terrible tragedy. Then, like some

malignant cuttlefish, this strike will grope its crushing feelers out from here, its lair, seeking prey on
which to fix its sucking tentacles.   They will reach
Malkern, and work will be paralyzed.   That means
ruin to more than half the villagers who depend
upon their weekly wage.   It goes further than that.
The mills will shut down.   And if the mills shut,
good-bye to all trade in Malkern.   It means ruin
for everybody.   It means the wrecking of all
Dave's hopes—hopes which have for their object
the welfare of the people of our valley.   It is a
piece of rascality that nothing can justify.   Jim
Truscott does not need our pity.   It is the penitentiary he needs.   Betty, I'm—I'm ——"

But Betty looked up with passionate, glowing
eyes from the work she had resumed.

"Do you think I don't know what it means, uncle?" she demanded, with a depth of feeling that
silenced him instantly.   "Do you think because I
pity poor Jim that I do not understand the enor-
mity of his wickedness in this matter?   Have I
spent the best part of my life in our valley carrying
on the work that has fallen to my share—work that
has been my joy and happiness to do—without understanding the cruelty which this strike means to
our people, those who are powerless to help themselves against it?   Do you think I don't understand what it means to Dave?   Oh, uncle, if you
but knew," she went on reproachfully.   "I know it
means practically the end of all things for Dave if
his contract fails.   I know that he is all out for the

result. That his resources are even now taxed to their uttermost limit, and that only the smooth running of the work can save him from a disaster that will involve us all. If I had a man's strength there is nothing I would not do to serve him. If my two hands, if my brain could assist him in the smallest degree, he would not need to ask for them. They are his—his!" she cried, with a passion that thrilled the listening man. " You are angry with me because I feel sorry for an erring man. I *am* sorry for him. Yet should evil come to our valley —to Dave—through his work, no wildcat would show him less mercy than I. Oh, why am I not a man with two strong hands?" she cried despair-ingly. " Why am I condemned to be a useless burden to those I love? Oh, Dave, Dave," she cried with a sudden self-abandonment, so passion-ate, so overwhelming that it alarmed her uncle, " why can't I help you? Why can't I stand beside you and share in your battles with these two hands?" She held out her arms, in a gesture of ap-peal. Then they dropped to her side. In a mo-ment she turned almost fiercely upon her uncle, swept on by a tide of feeling long pent up behind the barrier of her woman's reserve, but now no longer possible of restraint. " I love him! I love him! I know! You are ashamed for me! I can see it in your face! You think me unwomanly! You think I have outraged the conventions which hem our sex in! And what if I have? I don't care! I care for nothing and no one but him!

He is the world to me—the whole, wide world. I love him so I would give my life for him. Oh, uncle, I love him, and I am powerless to help him."

She sank into her chair, and buried her face in her hands. Blame, displeasure, contempt, nothing mattered. The woman was stirred, let loose; the calm strength which was so great a part of her character, had been swept aside by her passion, which saw only the hopelessness with which this strike confronted the man she loved.

Chepstow watched her for some moments. He was no longer alarmed. His heart ached for her, and he wanted to comfort her. But it was not easy for him. At last he moved close to her side, and laid a hand upon her bowed head. The action was full of a tender, even reverential sympathy. And it was that, more than his words, which helped to comfort the woman's stricken heart.

"You're a good child, Betty," he said awkwardly. "And—and I'm glad you love him. Dave will win out. Don't you fear. It is the difficulties he has had to face that have made him the man he is. Remember Mason has got away, and—— What's that?"

Something crashed against the door and dropped to the ground outside. Though the exclamation had broken from the man he needed no answer. It was a stone. A stone hurled with vicious force.

Betty sat up. Her face had suddenly returned to its usual calm. She looked up into her uncle's eyes, and saw that the light of battle had been rekindled there. Her own eyes brightened. She, too, realized that battle was imminent. They were two against hundreds. Her spirit warmed. Her recent hopelessness passed and she sprang to her feet.

" The cowards !" she cried.

The man only laughed.

CHAPTER XXIII

BETTY and her uncle spent the next few hours in preparing for eventualities. They explored the storeroom and armory, and in the latter they found ample provision for a stout defense. There were firearms in plenty, and such a supply of ammunition as should be sufficient to withstand a siege. The store of dynamite gave them some anxiety. It was dangerous where it was, in case of open warfare, but it would be still more dangerous in the hands of the strikers. Eventually they concealed it well under a pile´of other stores in the hopes, in case of accident, it might remain undiscovered.

During their preparations several more stones crashed against the walls and the door of the building. They were hurled at longish intervals, and seemed to be the work of one person. Then, finally no more were thrown, and futile as the attack had been, its cessation brought a certain relief and ease of mind. To the man it suggested the work of some drunken lumber-jack—perhaps the man who had been so forcibly rebuffed by Betty earlier in the evening.

It was one o'clock when Chepstow took a final look round his barricades. Betty was sitting at the table with a fine array of firearms spread out before her. She had just finished loading the last one when her uncle came to her side. She looked up at him with quiet amusement in her eyes.

" I was wondering," she said, with just a suspicion of satire in her manner, " whether we are in a state of siege, or—panic?"

But her uncle's sense of humor was lacking at the moment. He saw only the gravity of his responsibility.

" You'd best get to bed," he said a little severely. " I shall sit up. You must get all the rest you can. We do not know what may be in store for us."

Betty promptly fell in with his mood.

" But the sick?" she said. " We must visit them to-morrow. We cannot let them suffer."

" No. We must wait and see what to-morrow brings forth. In the meantime ——"

He broke off, listening. Betty too had suddenly turned her eyes upon the barred door. There was a long pause, during which the murmur of many voices reached them, and the faint but distinct sound of tramping feet. The man's eyes grew anxious, his lean face was set and hard. It was easy enough to read his thoughts. He was weighing the possibilities of collision with these strikers, and calculating the chances in his favor. Betty seemed less disturbed. Her eyes were steady and interested rather than alarmed.

" There's a crowd of them," said her uncle in a hushed voice.

The girl listened for something which perhaps
her uncle had forgotten. Sober, she did not expect much trouble from these people. If they had
been drinking it would be different.

The voices grew louder. The shuffling, clumping
footsteps grew louder. They drew near. They
were within a few yards of the building. Finally
they stopped just outside the door. Instantly there
was a loud hammering upon it, and a harsh demand for admittance.

Neither stirred.

" Open the door ! " roared the voice, and the cry
was taken up by others until it grew into a perfect
babel of shouting and cursing.

Betty moved to her uncle's side and laid a hand
upon his arm. She looked up into his face and
saw the storm-clouds of his anger gathering there.

" We shall have to open it, uncle," she said.
" That's—that's Tim Canfield's voice."

He looked down into her eager young face. He
saw no fear there. He feared, but not for himself:
it was of her he was thinking. He wanted to open
the door. He wanted to vent his anger in scathing
defiance, but he was thinking of the girl in his
charge. He was her sole protection. He knew,
only too well, what " strike " meant to these men.
It meant the turning of their savage passions loose
upon brains all too untutored to afford them a semblance of control. Then there was the drink, and
drink meant —

The clamor at the door was becoming terrific.

He stirred, and, walking swiftly across the room, put his mouth to the jamb.

" What do you want?" he shouted angrily. " What right have you to come here disturbing us at such an hour?"

Instantly the noise dropped. Then he heard Tim's voice repeating his words to the crowd, and they were greeted with a laugh that had in it a note of rebellion.

The laugh died out as the spokesman turned again to the door.

" Open this gorl-durned door, or we'll bust it in!" he shouted. And a chorus of " Break it in!" was taken up by the crowd.

The parson's anger leapt. His keen nerves were on edge in a moment. Even Betty's gentle eyes kindled. He turned to her, his eyes blazing.

" Hand me a couple of guns!" he cried, in a voice that reached the men outside. " Get hold of a couple yourself! If there's to be trouble we'll take a hand!" Then he turned to the door, and his voice was thrilling with " fight." " I'll open the door to no one till I know what you want!" he shouted furiously. " Beat the door in! I warn you those who step inside will get it good and plenty! Beat away!"

His words had instant effect. For several seconds there was not a sound on the other side of the door. Then some one muttered something, and instantly the crowd took up a fierce cry, urging their leaders on.

But the men in front were not to be rushed into a reckless assault, and a fierce altercation ensued. Finally silence was restored, and Tim Canfield spoke again, but there was a conciliatory note in his voice this time.

" You ken open it, passon," he said. " We're talkin' fair. We ain't nuthin' up agin you. We're astin' you to help us out some. Ef you open that door, me an' Mike Duggan'll step in, an' no one else. We'll tell you what's doin'. Ther' don't need be no shootin' to this racket."

The churchman considered. The position was awkward. His anger was melting, but he knew that, for the moment, he had the whip hand. However, he also knew if he didn't open the door, ultimately force would certainly be used. These were not the men to be scared easily. But Betty was in his thoughts, and finally it was Betty who decided for him.

" Open it," she whispered. " It's our best course. I don't think they mean any harm—yet."

The man reluctantly obeyed, but only after some moments' hesitation. He withdrew the bars, and as the girl moved away beyond the stove, and sat down to her sewing, he stepped aside, covering the doorway with his two revolvers.

" Only two of you!" he cried, as the door swung open.

The two men came in and, turning quickly, shut the rest of the crowd out and rebarred the door.

Then they confronted the churchman's two guns.

There was something tremendously compelling in Chepstow's attitude and the light of battle that shone in his eyes. He meant business, and they knew it. Their respect for him rose, and they watched him warily until presently he lowered the guns to his side.

He eyed them severely. They were men he knew, men who were real lumber-jacks, matured in the long service of Dave's mills, men who should have known better. They were powerfully built and grizzled, with faces and eyes as hard as their tremendous muscles. He knew the type well. It was the type he had always admired, and a type, once they were on the wrong path, he knew could be very, very dangerous.

" Well, boys," he demanded, in a more moderate tone, yet holding them with the severity of his expression. " What's all this bother about? What do you mean by this intolerable—bulldozing?"

The men suddenly discovered Betty at the far side of the stove. Her attitude was one of preoccupation in her sewing. It was pretense, but it looked natural. They abruptly pulled off their caps, and for the moment, seemed half abashed. But it was only for the moment. The next, Canfield turned on the churchman coldly.

" You're actin' kind o' foolish, passon," he said. " It ain't no use talkin' gun-play when ther' ain't no need whatever. It's like to make things ridic'lous awkward, an' set the boys sore. We come along here peaceful to talk you fair ——"

" So you bring an army," broke in Chepstow, impatiently, " after holding a meeting at the store, and considering the advisability of making prisoners of my niece and me."

" Who said?" demanded Tim fiercely.

" I did," retorted Chepstow militantly.

The promptness of his retort silenced the lumberman. He grinned, and leered round at his companion.

" Well?" The parson's voice was getting sharper.

" Well, it's like this, passon. Ther' ain't goin' to be no prisoner-makin' if you'll act reas'nable. Ther' ain't nuthin' up to you nor the leddy but wot's good an' clean. You've see to our boys who's sick, an' just done right by us—we can't say the same fer others. We just want you to come right along down to the camp. Ther's a feller bin shot by that all-fired skunk Mason, an' I guess he's jest busy bleedin' plumb to death. Will you come?"

" Who is it?"

The shortness of Chepstow's tone was uncompromising.

The lumber-jack stirred uneasily. He glanced round at his companion. The churchman saw the look and understood.

" Come on, Mike Duggan, out with it. I'm not going to be played with," he said. " Your mate doesn't seem easy about it. I suppose it's one of the ringleaders of your strike, and you want me to patch him up so he can go on with his dirty work. Well? I'm waiting."

Duggan's eyes flashed.

" Easy, passon," he said sharply. " The feller's name is Walford. You ain't like to know him fer sure. He's kind o' runnin' things fer us. He's hit in the shoulder bad."

" Ah, it's that fellow who was speaking at your meeting. So he's got his medicine. Good. Well, you want me to fix him up?"

The lumber-jacks nodded.

" That's it," said Duggan cheerfully.

Chepstow considered for a moment. Then he glanced over at Betty. Their eyes met, and his had a smile of encouragement in them. He turned back at once to the waiting men.

" I'll help you, but on one or two conditions. I demand my own conditions absolutely. They're easy, but I won't change them or moderate them by a single detail.'   '

" Get to it, passon," said Canfield, as he paused. " Make 'em easy, an' ther' won't be no kick comin'."

" You must bring the fellow here, and leave him with us until he is sufficiently recovered. Any of you can come and see him, if he's not too sick. Then you must give me a guarantee that my niece and I can visit the sick camp to tend the boys up there without any sort of molestation. You understand? You must guarantee this. You must guarantee that we are in no way interfered with,

and if at any time we are out of this hut, no one
will enter it without our permission.   We are here
for peace.   We are here to help your sick comrades.   Your affairs with your employers have nothing to do with us.   Is it a deal?"

"Why sure, passon," replied Duggan.   And Tim
nodded his approval.

"It's folks like you makes things easy fer us,"
added the latter, with hearty good-will.   "Guess
we'll shake on it."

He held out his hand, and Chepstow promptly
gripped it.   He also shook the other by the hand.

"Now, boys," he said genially, "how about those
others outside?   How will you guarantee them?"

"We'll fix that quick.   Say, Mike, just open that
door."   Canfield turned again to Chepstow, while
Mike obeyed orders.   "I'll give 'em a few words,"
he went on, "an' we'll send right off for Walford.
He's mighty bad, passon.   He's ——"

The door was open by this time, and the two
men hurried out.   Chepstow secured it behind
them, and stood listening for what was to happen.
He heard Canfield haranguing the crowd, and his
words seemed to have the desired effect, for presently the whole lot began to move off, and in two
minutes the last sound of voices and receding footsteps had died out.   Betty drew a sigh of relief.

"Uncle," she said, smiling affectionately across at
him as he left the door and came toward the stove,
"you are a genius of diplomacy."

The man laughed self-consciously.

" Well, we have gained a point," he said doubt-fully.

Betty let her eyes fall upon her sewing again.

" Yes, we have gained a point. I wonder how long that point will hold good, when—when the drink begins to flow."

" That's what I'm wondering."

And their question was answered in less than twenty-four hours.

Half an hour later the wounded strike-leader was brought to the hut. He was in a semi-conscious state, and a swift examination showed him to be in a pretty bad way. The bullet had ploughed its way through the shoulder, smashing both the col-lar-bone and the shoulder-blade. Then, though no vital spot had been touched, the loss of blood had been terrific. He had been left lying at the store ever since he was shot by Mason, with just a rough bandage of his own shirt, which had been quite powerless to stop the flow of blood.

It took Chepstow nearly two hours to dress the wound and set the bones, and by that time the man's weakness had plunged him into absolute un-consciousness. Still, this was due solely to loss of blood, and with careful nursing there was no real reason why he should not make a satisfactory re-covery.

The rest of the night was spent at the sick man's bedside. Betty and her uncle shared the vigil in reliefs, and, weary work as it was, they never hesitated. A life was at stake, and though the man was the cause of all the trouble, or instrumental in it, they were yet ready to spare no effort on his behalf. With the parson it was sheer love of his duty toward all men that gave him inspiration. With Betty there may have been a less Christian spirit in her motives. All this man's efforts had been directed against the man she loved, and she hated him for it; but a life was at stake, and a life, to her, was a very sacred thing.

The next day was spent between care for the sick at the fever camp and the wounded man in their own quarters, and the guarantee of the strikers was literally carried out. There were one or two visits to their sick leader, but no interference or molestation occurred. Then at sundown came the first warning of storm.

Betty was returning to the dugout. She was tired and sick at heart with her labors. For both it had been a strenuous day, but it had found her strength out a good deal more than it had her uncle's. Ahead of her she knew there yet lay a long night of nursing the wounded man.

It was a gorgeous evening. The fog had quite passed away. A splendid sunset lit the glittering peaks towering about her with a cloak of iridescent fire. The snow caps shone with a ruddy glow, while the ancient glaciers suggested molten streams pouring from the heart of them to the darkling wood-belts below. The girl paused and for a moment the wonder of the scene lifted her out of her weariness. But it was only momentary. The whole picture was so transient. It changed and varied with kaleidoscopic suddenness, and vanished altogether in less than five minutes. Again the mountains assumed the gray cold of their unlit beauties. The sun had gone, and day merged into night with almost staggering abruptness. She turned with a sigh to resume her journey.

It was then that her attention was drawn elsewhere. In the direction of the lumber camp, in the very heart of it, it seemed, a heavy smoke was rising and drifting westward on the light evening breeze. It was not the haze of smoke from campfires just lit, but a cloud augmented by great belches from below. And in the growing dusk she fancied there was even a ruddy reflection lighting it. She stared wlth wide-open, wondering eyes.

Suddenly a great shaft of flame shot up into its midst, and, as it lit the scene, she heard the shouting of men mingling with the crash of falling timber. She stood spellbound, a strange terror gripping her heart. It was fear of the unknown. There was a fire—burning what? She turned and ran for the dugout.

Bursting into the hut, she poured out her tidings to her uncle, who was preparing supper. The man listening to her hasty words understood the terror that beset her. Fire in those forest regions might well strike terror into the heart. He held a great check upon himself.

" Sit down, child," he said gently, at the conclusion of her story. "Sit down and have some food. Afterward, while you see to Walford, I'll cut through the woods and see what's doing."

He accomplished his object. Betty calmed at once, and obediently sat down to the food he set before her. She even forced herself to eat, and presently realized she was hungry. The churchman said nothing until they had finished eating. Then he lit his pipe.

"It's drink, I expect," he said, as though he had been striving to solve the matter during supper. "Likely they're burning the camp. We know what they are."

Betty took a deep breath.

"And if they're doing that here, what about the outlying camps?"

She knew that such an event would mean absolute ruin to Dave, and again her terror rose. This time it was for Dave, and the feeling sickened her.

Her uncle put on his hat. He had no answer for her. He understood what was in her mind.

"Don't leave this place, Betty," he said calmly. "Redress Walford's wound the way I showed you. Keep this door barred, and don't let any one in. I'll be back soon."

He was gone. And the manner of his going suggested anything but the calmness with which he spoke.

Once outside, the terror he had refused to display in Betty's presence lent wings to his feet. Night

had closed in by the time he took to the woods.
Now the air was full of the burning reek, and he
tried to calculate the possibilities. He snuffed at
the air to test the smell, fearful lest it should be the
forest that was burning. He could not tell. He
was too inexperienced in woodcraft to judge ac-
curately. In their sober senses these lumber-jacks
dreaded fire as much as a sailor dreads it at sea,
then there could be little doubt as to the cause of it
now. The inevitable had happened. Drink was
flowing, scorching out the none too acute senses of
these savages. Where would their orgy lead them?
Was there any limit that could hold them? He
thought not. If he were inexperienced in the
woodsman's craft, he knew these woodsmen, and he
shuddered at the pictures his thoughts painted.

As he drew nearer the camp the smoke got into
his lungs. The fire must be a big one. A sudden
thought came to him, and with it his fears receded.
He wondered why it had not occurred to him before. Of course. His eyes brightened almost to a
smile. If what he suspected had happened, perhaps it was the hand of Providence working in
Dave's interest. Working in Dave's, and——
Perhaps it was the cleansing fires of the Almighty
sent to wipe out the evil inspired by the erring
mind of man.

He reached the fringe of woods which surrounded the clearing of the camp, and in another
few seconds he stood in the open.

" Thank God," he exclaimed. Then, in a moment, the horror of a pitying Christian mind shone in his eyes. His lips were tight shut, and his hands clenched at his sides. Every muscle strung tense with the force of his emotions.

In the centre of the clearing the sutler's store was a blazing pile. But it was literally in the centre, with such a distance between it and the surrounding woods as to reduce the danger of setting fire to them to a minimum. It was this, and the fact that it was the store where the spirits were kept, that had inspired his heartfelt exclamation. But his horror was for that which he saw besides.

The running figures of the strikers about the fire were the figures of men mad with drink. Their shoutings, their laughter, their antics told him this. But they were not so drunk but what they had sacked the store before setting it ablaze. Ah, he understood now, and he wondered what had happened to the Jew trader.

He drew nearer. He felt safe in doing so. These demented savages were so fully occupied that they were scarcely likely to observe him. And if they did, he doubted if he were running much personal risk. They had no particular animosity for him.

And as he came near, the sights he beheld sickened him. There were several fights in progress. Not individual battles, but drunken brawls in groups; mauling, savaging masses of men whose instinct, when roused, it is to hurt, hurt anyhow, and if possible to kill. These men fought as beasts fight, tearing each other with teeth and hands, gouging, hacking, clawing. It was a merciless display of brute savagery inspired by a bestial instinct, stirred to fever pitch by the filthy spirit served in a lumber camp.

At another point, well away from the burning building, the merchandise was piled, tossed together in the reckless fashion only to be expected in men so inspired. Around this were the more sober, helping themselves greedily, snatching at clothing, at blankets, at the tools of their craft. Some were loaded with tin boxes of fancy biscuits and canned meats, others had possessed themselves of the cheap jewelry such as traders love to dazzle the eyes of their simple customers with. Each took as his stomach guided him, but with a gluttony for things which can be had for nothing always to be found in people of unbridled passions. It was a sight little less revolting than the other, for it spoke of another form of unchecked savagery.

Not far from this, shown in strong relief by the lurid fires, was gathered a shouting, turbulent crowd round a pile of barrels and cases. Three barrels were standing on end, apart from the rest, and their heads had been removed, and round these struggled a maddened crew with tin pannikins. They were dipping the fiery spirit out of the casks, and draining each draught as hurriedly as the scorching stuff could pass down their throats, so as to secure as much as possible before it was all gone. The watching man shuddered. Truly a more terrible display was inconceivable. The men were not human in their orgy. They were wild beasts. What, he asked himself, what would be the result when the liquor had saturated the brains of every one of them? It was too terrible to contemplate.

The roar of the blazing building, the babel of shouting, the darkly lurid light shining amidst the shadows of surrounding woods, the starlit heavens above, the stillness of mountain gloom and solitude; these things created a picture so awful of contemplation as to be unforgettable. Every detail drove into the watching man's heart as though graven there with chisel and hammer. It was a hellish picture, lit with hellish light, and set in the midst of gloom profound. The men might have been demons silhouetted against the ruddy fire; their doings, their antics, had in them so little that was human. It was awful, and at last, in despair, the man on the outskirts of the clearing turned and fled. Anything rather than this degrading sight; he could bear it no longer. He sickened, yet his heart yearned for them. There was nothing he could do to help them or check them. He could only pray for their demented souls, and—see to the safeguarding of Betty.

Betty heard her uncle's voice calling, and flung down the bars of the door. She looked into his ghastly face as he hurried in. She asked no question, and watched him as with nervous hands he closed and secured the door behind him. Her eyes followed his movements as he crossed to the stove and flung himself into a chair. She saw his head droop forward, and his hands cover his eyes in a gesture of despair. Still she waited, her breath coming more quickly as the moments passed.

She moved a step toward him, and slowly he raised a drawn haggard face, and his horrified eyes looked into hers.

" You must not leave this hut on any pretense, Betty," he said slowly. Then he raised his eyes to the roof. " God have pity on them! They are mad! Mad with drink, and ready for any debauchery. I could kill the men," he went on, shaking his two clenched fists in the air, " who have driven them ——"

" Hush, uncle!" the girl broke in, laying a restraining hand upon his upraised arms. " One of them lies over there, and—and he is wounded. We must do what we can to help."

CHAPTER XXIV

IN THE DEAD OF NIGHT

IT was sundown in the Red Sand Valley. The hush of evening had settled upon Malkern, and its calm was only broken by the droning machinery of the mills. The sky was lit by that chilly, yellow afterglow of sunset which, eastward, merges into the gray and purple of twilight. Already the long-drawn shadows had expanded into the dusk so rapidly obscuring the remoter distance. Straight and solemn rose spires of smoke from hidden chimneys, lolling in the still air, as though loath to leave the scented atmosphere of the valley below. It was the moment of delicious calm when Nature is preparing to seek repose.

Two women were standing at the door of Dave's house, and the patch of garden surrounding them, so simple, so plain, was a perfect setting for their elderly, plainly clad figures. Dave's mother, very old, but full of quiet energy, was listening to the gentle complaint of Mrs. Chepstow. She was listening, but her gaze was fixed on the distant mills, an attitude which had practically become her settled habit. The mill, to her, was the end of the earth; there was nothing beyond.

" I am dreadfully worried," Mrs. Tom was saying,

the anxious wrinkles of her forehead lifting her brows perplexedly. "It's more than six weeks since I heard from Tom and Betty. It's not like him, he's so regular with letters usually. It was madness letting Betty go up there. I can't think what we were doing. If anything has happened to them I shall never forgive myself. I think I shall go down and talk to Dave about it. He may know something. He's sure to know if they are well."

The other slowly withdrew her gaze from the mills. It was as though the effort required to do so were a great one, and one she reluctantly undertook. The pivot of her life was her boy. A pivot upon which it revolved without flagging or interruption. She had watched him grow to a magnificent man-hood, and with all a pure woman's love and wonderful instinct she had watched and tended him as she might some great oak tree raised from the frailest sapling. Then, when his struggles came, she had shared them with him with a supreme loyalty, helping him with a quiet, strong sympathy which found expression in little touches which probably even he never realized. All his successes and disasters had been hers; all his joys, all his sorrows. And now, in her old age, she clung to this love with the pathetic tenacity of one who realizes that the final parting is not far distant.

Her furrowed face lit with a wonderful smile.

"I cannot say for sure," she said. "There are times when Dave will not admit me to the thoughts which disturb him. At such times I know that things are not running smoothly. There are other times when he talks quite freely of his hopes, his fears. Then I know that all is well. When he complains I know he is questioning his own judgment, and distrusts himself. And when he laughs at things I know that the trouble is a sore one, and I prepare for disaster. All his moods have meaning for me. Just now I am reading from his silence, and it tells me that much is wrong, and I am wondering. But I do not think it concerns Betty—and, consequently, not your husband; if anything were wrong with her I think I should know." She smiled with all the wisdom of old age.

Mrs. Tom's anxiety was slightly allayed, but her curiosity was proportionately roused.

" Why would you know—about Betty ? " she asked.

The older woman's eyes were again turned in the direction of the mill.

" Why—why ? " She smiled and turned to the churchman's wife. " It would produce a fresh mood in my boy, one I'm not familiar with." Then she became suddenly grave. " I think I should dread that mood more than any other. You see, deep down in his heart there are passionate depths that no one has yet stirred. Were they let loose I fear to think how they might drive him. Dave's head only rules just as far as his heart chooses."

" But Betty ? " demanded Mrs. Tom. " How is she ——"

" Betty?" interrupted the other, humorously eye-ing the eager face. "The one great passion of Dave's life is Betty. I know. And he thinks it is hopeless. I am betraying no confidence. Dave hugs his secret to himself, but he can't hide it from me. I'm glad he loves her. You don't know how glad. You see, I am in love with her myself, and—and I am getting very old."

" And—does Betty know?"

Dave's mother shook her head and smiled.

" Betty loves him, but neither understands the other's feelings. But that is nothing. Love be-longs to Heaven, and Heaven will straighten this out. Listen!"

The old woman's eyes turned abruptly in the direction of the mill. There was a curious, anxious look in them, and a perplexed frown drew her brows together. One hand was raised to hold the other woman's attention. It was as though some-thing vital had shocked her, as though some sud-den spasm of physical pain had seized her. Her face slowly grew gray.

Three people passing along the trail in front of the house had also stopped. Their eyes were also turned in the direction of the mill. Further along a child at play had suddenly paused in its game to turn toward the mill. There were others, too, all over the village who gave up their pursuits to lis-ten.

" The mills have stopped work!" cried Mrs. Tom breathlessly.

But Dave's mother had no response for her. She had even forgotten the other's presence at her side.

The drone of the machinery was silent.

Dawson was interviewing his employer in the latter's office. Both men looked desperately worried. Dave's eyes were lit with a brooding light. It was as though a cloud of storm had settled upon his rugged features. Dawson had desperation in every line of his hard face.

" Have you sent up the river ? " demanded Dave, eyeing his head man as though he alone were responsible for the trouble which was upon them.

" I've sent, boss. We've had jams on the river before, an' I guessed it was that. I didn't worrit any for four-an'-twenty hours. It's different now. Ther' ain't bin a log come down for nigh thirty-six hours."

" How many men did you send up ? "

" Six. Two teams, an' all the gear needed for breakin' the jam."

" Yes. You're sure it is a jam ? "

" Ther' ain't nothin' else, boss. Leastways, I can't see nothin' else."

" No. And the boom ? You've worked out the ' reserve ' ? "

" Clean right out. Ther' ain't a log in it fit to cut."

Dave sat down at his desk. He idled clumsily for some moments with the pen in his fingers. His eyes were staring blankly out of the grimy window.

The din of the saws rose and fell, and the music for once struck bitterly into his soul. It jarred his nerves, and he stirred restlessly. What was this new trouble that had come upon him? No logs! No logs! Why? He could not understand. A jam? Dawson said it must be a jam on the river. He was a practical lumberman, and to him it was the only explanation. He had sent up men to find out and free it. But why should there be a jam? The river was wide and swift, and the logs were never sent down in such crowds as to make a thing of that nature possible at this time of year. Later, yes, when the water was low and the stream slack, but now, after the recent rains, it was still a torrent. No logs! The thought was always his nightmare, and now—it was a reality.

"It must be a jam, I s'pose," said Dave presently, but his tone carried no conviction.

"What else can it be, boss?" asked the foreman anxiously.

His employer's manner, his tone of uncertainty, worried Dawson. He had never seen Dave like this before.

"That's so."

Then a look of eager interest came into his eyes. He pointed at the window.

"Here's Odd," he said. "And he's in a hurry."

Dawson threw open the door, and Simon Odd lumbered hurriedly into the room. He seemed to fill up the place with his vast proportions. His face was anxious and doubtful.

" I've had to shut down at the other mill, boss,"
he explained abruptly. " Ther' ain't no logs.
Ther've been none for——"

" Thirty-six hours," broke in Dave, with an impatient nod. " I know."

" You know, boss ? "

" Yes."

The master of the mills turned again to the
window, and the two men watched him in silence.
What would he do? This man to whom they
looked in difficulty; this man who had never yet
failed in resource, in courage, to meet and overcome every obstacle, every emergency that harassed
a lumberman's life.

Suddenly he turned to them again. In his eyes
there was a peculiar, angry light.

" Well? " he demanded, in a fierce way that was
utterly foreign to him. " Well? " he reiterated,
" what are you standing there for? Get you out,
both of you. Shut this mill down, too!"

Simon Odd moved to the door, but Dawson remained where he was. It almost seemed as if he
had not understood. The mill was to be shut down
for the first time within his knowledge. What did
it mean? In all his years of association with Dave
he had seen such wonders of lumbering done by
him that he looked upon him as almost infallible.
And now—now he was tacitly acknowledging defeat without making a single effort. The realization, the shock of it, held him still. He made no
move to obey the roughly-spoken command.

Suddenly Dave turned on him. His face was flushed.

"Get out!" he roared. "Shut down the mill!"

It was the cry of a man driven to a momentary frenzy. For the time despair—black, terrible despair—drove the lumberman. He felt he wanted to hit out and hurt some one.

Dawson silently followed Odd to the door, and in five minutes the saws were still.

Dave sat on at his desk waiting. The moment the shriek of the machinery ceased he sprang to his feet and began pacing the floor in nervous, hurried strides. What that cessation meant to him only those may know who have suddenly seen their life's ambitions, their hopes, crushed out at one single blow. Let the saws continue their song, let the droning machinery but keep its dead level of tone, and failure in any other form, however disastrous, could not hurt in such degree as the sudden silencing of his lumberman's world.

For some minutes he was like a madman. He could not think, his nerves shivered from his feet to the crown of his great ugly head. His hands were clenched as he strode, until the nails of his fingers cut the flesh of the palms into which they were crushed. For some minutes he saw nothing but the black ruin that rose like a wall before him and shut out every thought from his mind. The cessation of machinery was like a pall suddenly burying his whole strength and manhood beneath its paralyzing weight.

But gradually the awful tension eased. It could not hold and its victim remain sane. So narrow was his focus during those first passionate moments that he could not see beyond his own personal loss. But with the passing minutes his view widened, and into the picture grew those things which had always been the inspiration of his ambitions. He flung himself heavily into his chair, and his eyes stared through the dirty window at the silent mill beyond. And for an hour he sat thus, thinking, thinking. His nervous tension had passed, his mind became clear, and though the nature of his thoughts lashed his heart, and a hundred times drove him to the verge of that first passion of despair again, there was an impersonal note in them which allowed the use of his usually clear reasoning, and so helped him to rise above himself once more.

His castles had been set a-tumbling, and he saw in their fall the crushing of Malkern, the village which was almost as a child to him. And with the crushing of the village must come disaster to all his friends. For one weak moment he felt that this responsibility should not be his—it was not fair to fix it on him. What had he done to deserve so hard a treatment? He thought of Tom Chepstow, loyal, kindly, always caring and thinking for those who needed his help. He thought of the traders of the village who hoped and prayed for his success, that meant prosperity for themselves and happiness for their wives and children. And these things began to rekindle the fighting flame within him; the flame which hitherto had always burned so fiercely. He could not let them go under.

Then with a rush a picture rose before his mind, flooding it, shutting out all those others, every thought of self or anybody else. It was Betty, with her gentle face, her soft brown hair and tender smiling eyes. Their steady courageous light shone deep down into his heart, and seemed to smite him for his weakness. His pulses began to throb, the weakened tide of his blood was sent coursing through his veins and mounted, mounted steadily to his brain. God! He must not go under. Even now the loyal child was up in the hills fighting his battles for him with ——

He broke off, and sprang to his feet. A terrible fear had suddenly leapt at his heart and clutched him. Betty was up there in the hills. He had not heard from the hill camps for weeks. And now the supply of logs had ceased. What had happened? What was happening up there?

The lethargy of despair lifted like a cloud. He was alert, thrilling with all the virility of his manhood set pulsing through his veins. Once more he was the man Dawson had failed to recognize when he ordered the mills to be closed down. Once more he was the man whose personal force had lifted him to his position as the master of Malkern mills. He was the Dave whom all the people of the village knew, ready to fight to the last ounce of his power, to the last drop of his blood.

" They shan't beat us!" he muttered, as he strode out into the yard. Nor could he have said of whom he was speaking, if anybody at all.

It was nearly midnight. Again Dawson and Simon Odd were in their employer's office. But this time a very different note prevailed. Dawson's hard face was full of keen interest. His eyes were eager. He was listening to the great man he had always known. Simon Odd, burly and unassuming, was waiting his turn when his chief had finished with his principal foreman.

" I've thought this thing out, Dawson," Dave said pleasantly, in a tone calculated to inspire the other with confidence, and in a manner suggesting that the affair of the logs had not seriously alarmed him, " and evolved a fresh plan of action. No doubt, as you say, the thing's simply a jam on the river. If this is so, it will be freed in a short time, and we can go ahead. On the other hand, there may be some other reason for the trouble. I can't think of any explanation myself, but that is neither here nor there. Now I intend going up the river to-night. Maybe I shall go on to the camps. I shall be entirely guided by circumstances. Anyway I shall likely be away some days. Whatever is wrong, I intend to see it straight. In the meantime you will stand ready to begin work the moment the logs come down. And when they come down I intend they shall come down at a pace that shall make up for all the time we have lost. That's all I have for you. I simply say, be ready. Good-night."

The man went out with a grin of satisfaction on his weather-beaten face. This was the Dave he knew, and he was glad.

Simon Odd 'received his orders. He too must be ready. He must have his men ready. His mill must be asked to do more than ever before when the time came, and on his results would depend a comfortable bonus the size of which quite dazzled the simple giant.

With his departure Dave began his own preparations. There was much to see to in leaving everything straight for his foremen. Dawson was more than willing. This new responsibility appealed to him as no other confidence his employer could have reposed in him. They spent some time together, and finally Dave returned to his office.

During the evening inquirers from the village flooded the place. But no official information on the subject of the cessation of work was forthcoming, nor would Dave see any of them. They were driven to be content with gleanings of news from the mill hands, and these, with the simple lumberman's understanding of such things, explained that there was a jam on the river which might take a day, or even two days, to free. In this way a panic in the village was averted.

Dave required provisions from home. But he could not spare the time to return there for them. He intended to set out on his journey at midnight.

Besides, he had no wish to alarm his old mother. And somehow he was afraid she would drag the whole truth of his fears out of him. So he sent a note by one of the men setting out his requirements.

His answer came promptly. The man returned with the kit bag only, and word that his mother was bringing the food down herself, and he smiled at the futility of his attempt to put her off.

Ten minutes later she entered his office with her burden of provisions. Her face was calmly smiling. There was no trace of anxiety in it. So carefully was the latter suppressed that the effort it entailed became apparent to the man.

" You shouldn't have bothered, ma," he protested. " I sent the man up specially to bring those things down."

His mother's eyes had a shrewd look in them.

" I know," she said. " There's a ham and some bacon, biscuit, and a fresh roast of beef here. Then I've put in a good supply of groceries."

" Thanks, dear," he said gently. " You always take care of my inner man. But I wish you hadn't bothered this way."

" It's no sort of trouble," she said, raising her eyes to his. Then she let them drop again. " Food don't need a lumberman's rough handling."

The smile on Dave's face was good to see. He nodded.

" I'd better tell you," he said. " You know, we've—stopped ? "

His eyes lingered fondly on the aged figure.
This woman was very precious to him.

" Yes, I know." There was the very slightest
flash of anxiety in the old eyes. Then it was gone.

" I'm going up the river to find things out."

" That's what I understood. Betty is up there—
too."

The quiet assurance of his mother's remark
brought a fresh light into the man's eyes, and the
blood surged to his cheeks.

" Yes, ma. That's it—chiefly."

" I thought so. And—I'm glad. You'll bring
her back with you ? "

" Yes, ma."

" Good-bye, boy." His simple assurance satisfied her. Her faith in him was the faith of a
mother.

The man bent down and kissed the withered, upturned face.

She went out, and Dave turned to the things she
had brought him. She had thought of everything.
And the food—he smiled. She was his mother,
and the food had the amplitude such as is characteristic of a mother when providing for a beloved son.

He must visit the barn to see about his horses.
He went to the door. Opening it, he paused.
Standing there he became aware of the sound of
approaching wheels. The absence of any noise
from the mills had made the night intensely silent,
so that the rattle of wheels upon the hard sand

trail, though distant, sounded acutely on the night air. He stood listening, with one great hand grasping the door casing. Yes, they were wheels. And now, too, he could hear the sharp pattering of horses' hoofs. The sound was uneven, yet regular, and he recognized the gait. They were approaching at a gallop. Nearer they came, and of a sudden he understood they were practically racing for the mill.

He left the doorway and moved out into the yard. He thought it might be the team which Dawson had sent out returning, and perhaps bringing good news of the jam on the river. He walked toward the yard gates and stood listening intently. The night was dark, but clear and still, and as he listened he fancied in the rattle of the vehicle he recognized the peculiar creak of a buckboard.

Nearer and nearer it came, louder and louder the clatter of hoofs and the rattle of wheels. The gallop seemed labored, like the clumsy gait of weary horses, and the waiting man straining could plainly hear a voice urging them on.

Suddenly he thought of the gates, and promptly opened them. He hardly knew why he did so. It must have been the effect of the pace at which the horses were being driven. It must have been that the speed inspired him with an idea of emergency. Now he stood out in the road, and stooping, glanced along it till the faint light of the horizon revealed a dark object on the trail. He drew back and slowly returned to the office.

The man's voice urging his horses on required no effort to hear now. It was hoarse with shouting, and the slashing of his whip told the waiting man of the pace at which he had traveled. The vehicle entered the yard gates. The urging voice became silent, the weary horses clattered up to the office door and came to a standstill.

From the doorway Dave surveyed the outfit. He did not recognize it, but something about the man climbing out of the vehicle was familiar.

" That you, Mason? " he asked sharply.

" Yes—and another. Will you bear a hand to get him out ? "

Dave went to his assistance, wondering. Mason was busy undoing some ropes. Dave's wonder increased. As he came up he saw that the ropes held a man captive in the carryall.

" Who is it? " he inquired.

" Jim Truscott—whoever he may be," responded Mason with a laugh, as he freed the last rope.

" Ah! Well, come right in—and bring him along too."

But Mason remembered the animals that had served him so well.

" What about the ' plugs' ? " He was holding his captive, who stood silent at his side.

" You go inside. I'll see to them."

Dave watched Mason conduct his prisoner into the office, then he sprang into the buckboard and drove it across to the barn.

CHAPTER XXV

In a few minutes Dave returned from the barn. He had chosen to attend to the horses himself, for his own reasons preferring not to rouse the man who looked after his horses.

His thoughts were busy while he was thus occupied. As yet he had no idea of what had actually occurred in the camps, but Mason's presence at such a time, the identity of his prisoner, the horses' condition of exhaustion; these things warned him of the gravity of the situation, and something of the possibilities. By the time he reëntered the office he was prepared for anything his " camp-boss " might have to tell him.

He noted the faces of the two men carefully. In Mason he saw the weariness of a long nervous strain. His broad face was drawn, his eyes were sunken and deeply shadowed. From head to foot he was powdered with the red dust of the trail. Dave was accustomed to being well served, but he felt that this man had been serving him to something very near the limits of his endurance. Jim Truscott's face afforded him the keenest interest. It was healthier looking than he had seen it since his first return to Malkern. The bloated puffiness,

the hall-mark of his persistent debauches, had almost entirely gone.   The health produced by open-
air and spare feeding showed in the tan of his skin.
His eyes were clear, and though he, too, looked
worn out, there was less of exhaustion about him
than his captor.   On the other hand there was none
of Mason's fearless honesty in his expression.
There was a truculent defiance in his eyes, a furious
scowl in the drawn brows.   There was a nervous-
ness in the loose, weak mouth.   His wrists were
lashed securely together by a rope which had been
applied with scant mercy.   Dave's eyes took all
these things in, and he pointed to the latter as he
addressed himself to his overseer.

" Better loose that," he said, in that even voice
which gave away so little of his real feelings.
" Guess you're both pretty near done in," he went
on, as Mason unfastened the knots.   " Got down
here in a hurry ? "

" Yes ; got any whiskey ? "

Mason had finished removing the prisoner's
bonds when he spoke.

" Brandy."

" That'll do."

The overseer laughed as men will laugh when
they are least inclined to.   Dave poured out long
drinks and handed them to the two men.   Mason
drank his down at a gulp, but Truscott pushed his
aside without a word.

" There's a deal to tell," said the overseer, as he
set his glass down.

" There's some hours to daylight," Dave replied.
" Go right ahead, and take your own time."

The other let his tired eyes rest on his prisoner
for some moments and remained silent. He was
considering how best to tell his story. Suddenly
he looked up.

" The camp's on ' strike,' " he said.

" Ah!" And it was Dave's eyes that fell upon
Jim Truscott now.

There was a world of significance in that ejaculation and the expression that leapt to the lumberman's eyes. It was a desperate blow the overseer
had dealt him; but it was a blow that did not crush.
It carried with it a complete explanation. And
that explanation was of something he understood
and had power to deal with.

" And—this?" Dave nodded in Jim's direction.

" Is one of the leaders."

" Ah!"

Again came Dave's meaning ejaculation. Then
he settled himself in his chair and prepared to listen.

" Get going," he said; but he felt that he required
little more explanation.

Mason began his story by inquiries about his own
letters to his employer, and learned that none of
them had been received during the last few weeks,
and he gave a similar reply to Dave's inquiries as
to the fate of his letters to the camp. Then he
went on to the particulars of the strike movement,
from the first appearance of unrest to the final moment when it became an accomplished fact. He

told him how the chance " hands " he had been
forced to take on had been the disturbing element,
and these, he was now convinced, had for some
reason been inspired. He told of that visit on the
Sunday night to the sutler's store, he told of his
narrow escape, and of his shooting down one of the
men, and the fortunate capture, made with the
timely assistance of Tom Chepstow, of his prisoner.
Dave listened attentively, but his eyes were always
on Truscott, and at the finish of the long story his
commendation was less hearty than one might have
expected.

" You've made good, Mason, an' I'm obliged,"
he said, after a prolonged silence. " Say," he went
on, glancing at his watch, " there's just four and a
half hours to the time we start back for the camp.
Go over to Dawson's shack and get a shake-down.
Get what sleep you can. I'll call you in time.
Meanwhile I'll see to this fellow," he added, indi-
cating the prisoner. " We'll have a heap of time
for talk on the way to the camps."

The overseer's eyes lit.

" Are you going up to the camps ? " he inquired
eagerly.

" Yes, surely. We'll have to straighten this out."
Then a sudden thought flashed through his mind.
" There's the parson and ——— ! "

Mason nodded.

" Yes. They've got my shack. There's plenty
of arms and ammunition. I left parson to hurry
back to ———"

" He wasn't with her when you left?"

There was a sudden, fierce light in Dave's eyes. Mason shook his head, and something of the other's apprehension was in his voice as he replied —

" He was going back there."

Dave's eyes were fiercely riveted upon Truscott's face.

" We'll start earlier. Get an hour's sleep."

There was no misunderstanding his employer's tone. In fact, for the first time since he had left the camp Mason realized the full danger of those two he had left behind him. But he knew he had done the only possible thing in the circumstances, and besides, his presence there would have added to their danger. Still, as he left the office to seek the brief rest for which he was longing, he was not without a qualm of conscience which his honest judgment told him he was not entitled to.

Dave closed the door carefully behind him. Then he came back to his chair, and for some moments surveyed his prisoner in silence. Truscott stirred uneasily under the cold regard. Then he looked up, and all his bitter hatred for his one-time friend shone in the defiant stare he gave him.

" I've tried to understand, but I can't," Dave said at last, as though his words were the result of long speculation. " It is so far beyond me that —— This is your doing, all your doing. It's nothing to do with those—those 'scabs.' You, and you alone have brought about this strike. First you pay a man to wreck my mills—you even try to kill me.

Now you do this. You have thought it all out with devilish cunning. There is nothing that could ruin me so surely as this strike. You mean to wreck me; nor do you care who goes down in the crash. You have already slain one man in your villainy. For that you stand branded a—murderer. God alone knows what death and destruction this strike in the hills may bring about. And all of it is aimed at me. Why? In God's name, why?"

Dave's manner was that of cold argument. He displayed none of the passion that really stirred him. He longed to take this man in his two great hands, and crush the mean life out of him. But nothing of such feeling was allowed to show itself. He began to fill his pipe. He did not want to smoke, but it gave his hands something to do, and just then his hands demanded something to do.

His words elicited no reply. Truscott's eyes were upon the hands fumbling at the bowl of the pipe. He was not really observing them. He was wrapped in his own thoughts, and his eyes simply fixed themselves on the only moving thing in the room. Dave put his pipe in his mouth and refolded his pouch. Presently he went on speaking, and his tone became warmer, and his words more rapid.

" There was a time when you were a man, a decent, honest, happy man; a youngster with all the world before you. At that time I did all in my power to help you. You remember? You ran that mill. It was a matter of hanging on and waiting till fortune turned your way for success and

prosperity to come. Then one day you came to
me ; you and she. It was decided that you should
go away—to seek your fortune elsewhere. We
shook hands. Do you remember? You left her
in my care. All this seems like yesterday. I
promised you then that always, in the name of
friendship, you could command me. Your trust I
carried out to the letter, and all I promised I was
ready to fulfil. Need I remind you of what has
happened since? Need I draw a picture of the
drunkard, gambler who returned to Malkern, of the
insults you have put upon her, everybody? Of her
patience and loyalty? Of the manner in which
you finally made it impossible for her to marry
you? It is not necessary. You know it all—if you
are a sane man, which I am beginning to doubt.
And now—now why are you doing all this? I
intend to know. I mean to drag it out of you
before you leave this room !"

He had risen from his seat and stood before his
captive with one hand outstretched in his direction,
grasping his pipe by the bowl. His calmness had
gone, a passion of angry protest surged through his
veins. He was no longer the cool, clear-headed
master of the mills, but a man swept by a fury of
resentment at the injustice, the wanton, devilish,
mischievous injustice of one whom he had always
befriended. Friendship was gone and in its place
there burned the human desire for retaliation.

Truscott's introspective stare changed to a wicked
laugh. It was forced, and had for its object the

intention of goading the other. Dave calmed
immediately. He understood that laugh in time,
and so it failed in its purpose and died out. In its
place the man's face darkened. It was he who fell
a victim to his own intention. All his hatred for
his one-time friend rose within him suddenly, and
swept him on its burning tide.

"You stand there preaching! You!" he cried
with a ferocity so sudden that it became appalling.
"You dare to preach to me of honesty, of friendship, of promises fulfilled? You? God, it makes
me boil to hear you! If ever there was a traitor to
friendship in this world it is you. I came back to
marry Betty. Why else should I come back?
And I find—what? She is changed. You have
seen to that. For a time she kept up the pretense
of our engagement. Then she seized upon the first
excuse to break it. Why? For you! Oh, your
trust was well fulfilled. You lost no time in my
absence. Who was it I found her with on my
return? You! Who was present to give her
courage and support when she refused to marry
me? You! Do you think I haven't seen the way
it has all been worked? You have secured her
uncle's and aunt's support. You! You have
taken her from me! You! And you preach
friendship and honesty to me. God, but you're a
liar and a thief!"

For a moment the lumberman's fury leapt and in
another he would have crushed the man's life out
of him, but, in a flash, his whole mood changed.

The accusations were so absurd even from his own point of view. Could it be? For a moment he believed that the loss of Betty had unhinged Truscott's mind. But the thought passed, and he grew as calm now as a moment before he had been furious, and an icy sternness chilled him through and through. There was no longer a vestige of pity in him for his accuser. He sat down and lit his pipe, his heavy face set with the iron that had entered his soul.

" You have lied to yourself until you have come to believe it," he said sternly. " You have lied because it is your nature to lie, because you have not an honest thought in your mind. I'll not answer your accusations, because they are so hopelessly absurd; but I'll tell you what I intend to do."

" You won't answer them because you cannot deny them ! " Truscott broke in furiously. " They are true, and you know it. You have stolen her from me. You ! Oh, God, I hate you ! "

His voice rose to a strident shout and Dave raised a warning hand.

" Keep quiet ! " he commanded coldly. " I have listened to you, and now you shall listen to me."

The fire in the other's eyes still shone luridly, but he became silent under the coldly compelling manner, while, like a savage beast, he crouched in his chair ready to break out into passionate protest at the least chance.

"I don't know yet how far things have gone in the way you wish them to go up there in the hills, but you have found the way to accomplish your end in ruining me. If the strike continues I tell you frankly you will have done what you set out to do. My resources are taxed now to the limit. That will rejoice you."

Truscott grinned savagely as he sprang in with his retort.

"The strike is thoroughly established, and there are those up there who'll see it through. Yes, yes, my friend, it is my doing; all my doing, and it cannot fail me now. The money I took from you for the mill I laid out well. I laid out more than that—practically all I had in the world. Oh, I spared nothing; I had no intention of failing. I would give even my life to ruin you!"

"Don't be too sure you may not yet have to pay that price," Dave said grimly.

"Willingly."

Truscott's whole manner carried conviction. Dave read in the sudden clipping of his teeth, the deadly light of his eyes, the clenching of his hands that he meant it.

"I'll ruin you even if I die for it, but I'll see you ruined first," cried Truscott.

"You have miscalculated one thing, Truscott," Dave said slowly. "You have forgotten that you are in my power and a captive. However, we'll let that go for the moment. I promise you you shall never live to see me suffer in the way you hope.

You shall not even be aware of it. I care nothing for the ruin you hope for, so far as I am personally concerned, but I do care for other reasons. In dragging me down you will drag Malkern down, too. You will ruin many others. You will even involve Betty in the crash, for she, like the rest of us, is bound up in Malkern. And in this you will hurt me—hurt me as in your wildest dreams you never expected to do." Then he leant forward in his seat, and a subtle, deliberate intensity, more deadly for the very frigidity of his tone was in his whole attitude. His hands were outstretched toward his captive, his fingers were extended and bent at the joints like talons ready to clutch and rend their prey. " Now, I tell you this," he went on, " as surely as harm comes to Betty up in that camp, through any doings of yours, as surely as ruin through your agency descends upon this valley, as Almighty God is my Judge I will tear the life out of you with my own two hands."

For a moment Truscott's eyes supported the frigid glare of Dave's. For a moment he had it in his mind to fling defiance at him. Then his eyes shifted and he looked away, and defiance died out of his mind. The stronger nature shook the weaker, and an involuntary shudder of apprehension slowly crept over him. Dave stirred to the pitch of threatening deliberate slaughter had been beyond his imagination. Now that he saw it the sight was not pleasant.

Suddenly the lumberman sprang to his feet.

"We'll start right away," he said, in his usual voice.

"We?" The monosyllabic question sprang from Truscott's lips in a sudden access of fear.

"Yes. We. Mason, you, and me."

CHAPTER XXVI

TO THE LUMBER CAMP

THE gray morning mist rolled slowly up the hill-sides from the bosom of the warming valley below. Great billows mounted, swelling in volume till, overweighted, they toppled, surging like the breaking rollers of a wind-swept ocean. Here and there the rosy sunlight brushed the swirling sea with a tenderness of color no painter's brush could ever hope to produce. A precocious sunbeam shot athwart the leaden prospect. It bored its way through the churning fog searching the depths of some benighted wood-lined hollow, as though to rouse its slumbering world.

Dense spruce and hemlock forests grew out of the mists. The spires of gigantic pines rose, piercing the gray as though gasping for the warming radiance above. A perching eagle, newly roused from its slumbers, shrieked its morning song till the rebounding cries, echoing from a thousand directions, suggested the reveille of the entire feathered world. The mournful whistle of a solitary marmot swelled the song from many new directions, and the raucous chorus had for its accompaniment the thundering chords of hidden waters, seething and boiling in the mighty cañons below.

The long-drawn, sibilant hush of night was gone;

the leaden mountain dawn had passed; day, glorious in its waking splendor, had routed the grim shadows from the mystic depths of cañon, from the leaden-hued forest-laden valleys. The sunlight was upon the dazzling mountain-tops, groping, searching the very heart of the Rocky Mountains.

Dave's buckboard, no more conspicuous than some wandering ant in the vast mountain world, crawled from the depths of a wide valley and slowly mounted the shoulders of a forest-clad ridge. It vanished into the twilight of giant woods, only to be seen again, some hours later, at a greater altitude, climbing, climbing the great slopes, or descending to gaping hollows, but always attaining the higher lands.

But his speed was by no means a crawl in reality, only did it appear so by reason of the vastness of the world about him. His horses were traveling as fresh, mettlesome beasts can travel when urged by such a man as Dave, with his nerves strung to a terrific tension by the emergency of his journey. The willing beasts raced down the hills over the uneven trail with all the sure-footed carelessness of the prairie-bred broncho. They took the inclines with scarcely perceptible slackening of their gait. And only the sharp hills served them for breathing space.

Dave occupied the driving-seat while Mason sat guard over Jim Truscott in the carryall behind. Those two days on the trail had been unusually silent, even for men such as they were, and even

346 THE TRAIL OF THE AXE

taking into consideration the object of their journey.
Truscott and Mason were almost " dead beat" with
all that had gone before, and Dave—he was wrapped
in his own thoughts.

His thoughts carried him far away from his com-
panions into a world where love and strife were
curiously blended. Every thread of such thought
sent him blundering into mires of trouble, the
possibilities of which set his nerves jangling with
apprehension. But their contemplation only stiffened his stern resolve to fight the coming battle
with a courage and resource such as never yet had
he brought to bear in his bid for success. He
knew that before him lay the culminating battle of
his long and ardent sieging of Fortune's stronghold. He knew that now, at last, he was face to
face with the great test of his fitness. He knew
that this battle had always been bound to come
before the goal of his success was reached;
although, perhaps, its method and its cause may
have taken a thousand other forms. It is not in
the nature of things that a man may march un-
tested straight to the golden pastures of his
ambitions. He must fight every foot of his way,
and the final battle must ever be the sternest, the
cruelest. God help the man if he has not the
fitness, for Fate and Fortune are remorseless foes.

But besides his native courage, Dave was stirred
to even greater efforts by man's strongest motive,
be his cause for good or evil. Love was the main-
spring of his inspiration. He had desired success

with a passionate longing all his life, and his success was not all selfishness. But now, before all things, he saw the sweetly gentle face of Betty Somers gazing with a heartful appeal, beckoning him, calling him to help her. Every moment of that long journey the vision remained with him; every moment he felt might be the moment of dire tragedy for her. He dared not trust himself to consider the nature of that tragedy, or he must have turned and rended the man who was its cause. Only he blessed each moment that passed, bringing him nearer to her side. He loved her as he loved nothing and no one else on earth, and somehow there had crept into his mind the thought of a possibility he had never yet dared to consider. It was a vague ray of hope that the impossibility of his love was not so great as he had always be-heved.

How it had stolen in upon him he hardly knew. Perhaps it was his mother's persistent references to Betty. Perhaps it was the result of his talk with the man who had brought her to the straits she was now placed in. Perhaps it was one of these things, or both, coupled with the memory of trifling incidents in the past, which had seemed to mean nothing at the time of their happening.

Whatever it was, his love for the girl swept through him now in a way that drove him head-long to her rescue. His own affairs of the mills, the fate of his friends in Malkern, of the village itself; all these things were driven into the background of his thoughts. Betty needed him. The thought set his brain whirling with a wild thrilling happiness, mazed, every alternate moment, with a horrible fear that drove him to the depths of despair.

It was high noon when smoke ahead warned him that the journey was nearly over. The buckboard was on the ridge shouldering a wide valley, and below it was the rushing torrent of the Red Sand River. From his position Dave had a full view of the dull green forest world rolling away, east and west, in vast, undulating waves as far as the eye could reach. Only to the south, beyond the valley, was there a break in the dense, verdant carpet. And here it was he beheld the telltale smoke of the lumber camp.

"That's the camp," he said, looking straight ahead, watching the slowly rising haze with longing eyes. "Guess we haven't to cross the river. Good."

Mason was looking out over his shoulder.

"No," he said after a moment's pause, while he tried to read the signs he beheld. "We don't cross the river. Keep to the trail. It takes us right past my shack."

"Where Parson Tom and ——— ?"

"Yes, where they're living."

In another quarter of a mile they would be descending the hollow of a small valley diverging from the valley of the Red Sand River. As they drew near the decline, Dave spoke again.

"Can you make anything out, Mason?" he asked. "Seems to me that smoke is thick for—for stovepipes. There's two lots; one of 'em nearer this way."

Mason stared out for some moments, shielding his eyes from the dazzling sun.

"I can't be sure," he said at last. "The nearest smoke should be my shack."

A grave anxiety crept into Dave's eyes.

"It isn't thick there," he said, as though trying to reassure himself. "That's your stovepipe?"

"Maybe."

Mason's reply expressed doubt.

Suddenly Dave leant over and his whip fell sharply across the horses' backs. They sprang at their neck-yoke and raced down into the final dip.

CHAPTER XXVII

In the dugout Tom Chepstow was standing with his ear pressed against the door-jamb. He was listening, straining with every nerve alert to glean the least indication of what was going on outside. His face was pale and drawn, and his eyes shone with anxiety. He was gripped by a fear he had never known before, a fear that might well come to the bravest. Personal, physical danger he understood, it was almost pleasant to him, something that gave life a new interest. But this—this was different, this was horrible.

Betty was standing just behind him. She was leaning forward craning intently. Her hands were clenched at her sides, and a similar dread was looking out of her soft eyes. Her face was pale with a marble coldness, her rich red lips were compressed to a fine line, her whole body was tense with the fear that lay behind her straining eyes. There was desperation in the poise of her body, the desperation of a brave woman who sees the last hope vanishing, swallowed up in a tide of disaster she is powerless to stem.

For nearly a week these two had been penned up in the hut. But for the last thirty-six hours their stronghold had actually been in a state of siege. From the time of her uncle's realization of the conditions obtaining outside Betty had not ventured without the building, while the man himself had been forced to use the utmost caution in moving abroad. It had been absolutely necessary for him to make several expeditions, otherwise he, too, would have remained in their fortress. They required water and fire-wood, and these things had to be procured. Then, too, there were the sick.

But on the third day the climax was reached. Returning from one of his expeditions Chepstow encountered a drunken gang of lumber-jacks. Under the influence of their recent orgy their spirit-soaked brains had conceived the pretty idea of " ilin' the passon's works "; in other words, forcing drink upon him, and making him as drunk as themselves. In their present condition the joke appealed to them, and it was not without a violent struggle that their intended victim escaped.

He was carrying fire-wood at the time, and it served him well as a weapon of defense. In a few brief moments he had left one man stunned upon the ground and another with a horribly broken face, and was himself racing for the dugout. He easily outstripped his drunken pursuers, but he was quickly to learn how high a price he must pay for the temporary victory. He had brought a veritable hornets' nest about his ears.

The mischief began. The attack upon himself had only been a drunken practical joke. The subsequent happenings were in deadly earnest. The

mob came in a blaze of savage fury. Their
first thought was for vengeance upon him. In all
probability, up to that time, Betty's presence in the
hut had been forgotten, but now, as they came to
the dugout, they remembered. In their present
condition it was but a short step from a desire to
revenge themselves upon him, to the suggestion of
how it could be accomplished through the girl.
They remembered her pretty face, her delicious
woman's figure, and instantly they became ravening brutes, fired with a mad desire to possess themselves of her.

They were no longer strikers, they were not
even men. The spirit taken from the burning store
had done its work. A howling pack of demons had
been turned loose upon the camp, ready for any
fiendish prank, ready for slaughter, ready for anything. These untutored creatures knew no better,
they were powerless to help themselves, their passions alone guided them at all times, and now all
that was most evil in them was frothing to the surface. Sober, they were as tame as caged wolves
kept under by the bludgeon of a stern discipline.
Drunk, they were madmen, driven by the un-
tamed passions of the brute creation. They were
animals without the restraining instincts of the animal, they lusted for the exercise of their great muscles, and the vital forces which swept through their
veins in a passionate torrent.

Their first effort was a demand for the surrender
of those in the hut, and they were coldly refused.

They attempted a parley, and received no encouragement. Now they were determined upon capture, with loudly shouted threats of dire consequences for the defenders' obstinacy.

It was close upon noon of the second day of the siege. The hut was barricaded at every point. Door and windows were blocked up with every available piece of furniture that could be spared, and the repeating-rifles were loaded ready, and both uncle and niece were armed with revolvers. They were defending more than life and liberty, and they knew it. They were defending all that is most sacred in a woman's life. It was a ghastly thought, a desperate thought, but a thought that roused in them both a conviction that any defense brain could conceive was justified. If necessary not even life itself should stand in the way of their defense.

The yellow lamplight, threw gloomy shadows about the barricaded room. Its depressing light added to the sinister aspect of their extremity. The silence was ominous, it was fraught with a portend of disaster; disaster worse than death. How could they hope to withstand the attack of the men outside? They were waiting, waiting for what was to happen. Every conceivable method had been adopted by the besiegers to dislodge their intended victims. They had tried to tear the roof off, but the heavy logs were well dovetailed, and the process would have taken too long, and exposed those attempting it to the fire of the rifles in the capable hands of the defenders. Chepstow had illustrated his determination promptly by a half dozen shots fired at the first moving of one of the logs. Then had come an assault on the door, but, here again, the ready play of the rifle from one of the windows had driven these besiegers hurriedly to cover. Some man, more blinded with drink than the rest of his comrades, had suggested fire. But his suggestion was promptly vetoed. Had it been the parson only they would probably have had no scruples, but Betty was there, and they wanted Betty.

For some time there had been no further assault.

" I wish I knew how many there were," Chepstow said, in a low voice.

" Would that do any good ? "

The man moved his shoulders in something like a despairing shrug.

" Would anything do any good ? "

" Nothing I can think of," Betty murmured bitterly.

" I thought if there were say only a dozen I might open this door. We have the repeating-rifles."

The man's eyes as he spoke glittered with a fierce light. Betty saw it, and somehow it made her shiver.

It brought home to her their extremity even more poignantly than all that had gone before. When a brave churchman's thoughts concentrated in such a direction she felt that their hopes were small indeed.

She shook her head.

" No, uncle dear. We must wait for that until they force an entrance." She was cool enough in her desperation, cooler far than he.

" Yes," he nodded reluctantly, " perhaps you're right, but the suspense is—killing. Hark! Listen, they are coming at us again. I wonder what it is to be this time."

The harsh voices of the drunken mob could be plainly heard. They were coming nearer. Brutal laughter assailed the straining ears inside, and set their nerves tingling afresh. Then came a hush. It lasted some seconds. Then a single laugh just outside the door broke upon the silence.

" Try again," a voice said. " Say, here's some more. 'Struth you're a heap of G—— d—— foolishness."

Another voice broke in angrily.

" God strike you !" it snarled, " do it your b—— self."

" Right ho !"

Then there came a shuffling of feet, and, a moment later, a scraping and scratching at the foot of the door. Chepstow glanced down at it, and Betty's eyes were irresistibly drawn in the same direction.

" What are they doing now ? "

It was the voice of the wounded strike-leader on his bunk at the far end of the room. He was staring over at the door, his expression one of even greater fear than that of the defenders themselves. He felt that, in spite of the part he had played in bringing the strike about, his position was no better than these others. If anything happened to them all help for him was gone. Besides, he, too, understood that these men outside were no longer strikers, but wolves, whiskey-soaked savages beyond the control of any strike-leader.

He received no reply. The scraping went on. Something was being thrust into the gaping crack which stood an inch wide beneath the door. Suddenly the noise ceased, followed by a long pause. Then, in the strong draught under the door, a puff of oil smoke belched into the room, and its nauseous reek set Chepstow coughing. His cough brought an answering peal of brutal laughter from beyond the door, and some one shouted to his comrades —

" Bully fer you, bo'! Draw 'em! Draw 'em like badgers. Smoke 'em out like gophers."

The pungent smoke belched into the room, and the man darted from the door.

" Quick!" he cried. " Wet rags! A blanket!"

Betty sprang to his assistance. The room was rapidly filling with smoke, which stung their eyes and set them choking. A blanket was snatched off the wounded strike-leader, but the process of saturating it was slow. They had only one barrel of water, and dared not waste it by plunging the blanket into it. So they were forced to resort to the use of a dipper. At last it was ready and the man crushed it down at the foot of the door, and stamped it tight with his foot.

But it had taken too much time to set in place. The room was dense with a fog of smoke that set eyes streaming and throats gasping. In reckless despair the man sprang at one of the windows and began to tear down the carefully-built barricade.

But now the cunning of the besiegers was displayed. As the last of the barricade was removed Chepstow discovered that the cotton covering of the window was smouldering. He tore it out to let in the fresh air, but only to release a pile of smouldering oil rags, which had been placed on the thickness of the wall, and set it tumbling into the room. The window was barricaded on the outside!

The smoke became unbearable now, and the two prisoners set to work to trample the smouldering rags out. It was while they were thus occupied that a fresh disaster occurred. There was a terrific clatter at the stove, and a cloud of smoke and soot practically put the place in darkness. Nor did it need the sound of scrambling feet on the roof to tell those below what had happened. The strikers, by removing the topmost joint of the pipe, where it protruded through the roof, had been able, by the aid of a long stick, to dislodge the rest of the pipe and send it crashing to the floor. It was a master-stroke of diabolical cunning, for now, added to the smoke and soot, the sulphurous fumes of the blazing stove rendered the conditions of the room beyond further endurance.

Half blinded and gasping Chepstow sprang at the table and seized a rifle. Betty had dropped into a chair choking. The strike-leader lay moaning, trying to shut out the smoke with his one remaining blanket.

" Come on, Betty," shouted the man, in a frenzy of rage. " You've got your revolver. I'm going to open the door, and may God Almighty have mercy on the soul of the man who tries to stop us ! "

CHAPTER XXVIII

DAVE—THE MAN

DAVE's buckboard swept up the slope of the last valley. It reached the dead level of the old travoy trail, which passed in front of Mason's dugout on its way to the lumber camp. He was looking ahead for signs which he feared to discover; he wanted the reason of the smoke he had seen from afar off. But now a perfect screen of towering pine forest lined the way, and all that lay beyond was hidden from his anxious eyes.

He flogged his horses faster. The perfect mountain calm was unbroken; even the speeding horses and the rattle of his buckboard were powerless to disturb that stupendous quiet. It was a mere circumstance in a world too vast to take color from a detail so insignificant. It was that wondrous peace, that thrilling silence that aggravated his fears. His apprehension grew with each passing moment, and, though he made no display, his clutch upon the reins, the sharpness with which he plied his whip, the very immobility of his face, all told their tale of feelings strung to a high pitch.

Mason was standing directly behind him in the carryall. He steadied himself with a grip upon the back of the driving-seat. Beside him the wretched Truscott was sitting on the jolting slats of the body of the vehicle, mercilessly thrown about by the bumping over the broken trail. Mason, too, was staring out ahead.

"Seems quiet enough," he murmured, half to himself.

Dave caught at his words.

"That's how it seems," he said, in a tone of doubt.

"It's less than half a mile now," Mason went on a moment later. "We're coming to the big bend."

Dave nodded. His whip fell across his horses' quarters. "Best get ready," he said significantly. Then he laughed mirthlessly and tried to excuse himself. "I don't guess there'll be a heap of trouble, though."

"No."

Mason's reply carried no conviction. Both men were in doubt. Neither knew what to expect. Neither knew in what way to prepare for the meeting that was now so near.

Now the trail began to swing out to the right. It was the beginning of the big bend. The walls of forest about them receded slightly, opening out where logs had been felled beside the trail in years past. The middle of the curve was a small clearing. Then, further on, as it inclined again to the left, it narrowed down to the bare breadth of the trail.

"Just beyond this——"

Mason broke off. His words were cut short by a loud shout just ahead of them. It was a shout of triumph and gleeful enjoyment. Dave's whip fell again, and the horses laid on to their traces. From that moment to the moment when the horses were almost flung upon their haunches by the sudden jolt with which Dave pulled them up was a matter of seconds only. He was out of the buckboard, too, having flung the reins to Mason, and was standing facing a small group of a dozen men whom it was almost impossible to recognize as lumber-jacks. In truth, there were only three of them who were, the others were some of those Mason had been forced to engage in his extremity.

At the sight of Dave's enormous figure a cry broke from the crowd. Then they looked at the buckboard with its panting horses, and Mason standing in the carryall, one hand on the reins and one resting on the revolver on his hip. Their cry died out. But as it did so another broke from their midst. It was Betty's voice, and her uncle's. There was a scuffle and a rush. Gripping the girl by the arm Tom Chepstow burst from their midst and ran to Dave's side, dragging Betty with him.

" Thank God!" he cried.

But there was no answering joy from Dave. He scarcely even seemed to see them. A livid, frozen rage glared out of his eyes. His face was terrible to behold. He moved forward. His gait was cat-like, his head was thrust forward, it was almost as if he tiptoed and was about to spring upon the mob. As he came within a yard of the foremost of the men he halted, and one great arm shot out with its fist clenching.

"Back!" he roared; "back to your camp, every man of you! Back, you cowardly hounds!"

There were twelve of them; fierce, savage, half-drunken men. They cared for no one, they feared no one. They were ready to follow whithersoever their passions led them. There was not a man among them that would not fight with the last breath in his body. Yet they hesitated at the sound of that voice. They almost shrank before that passion-lit face. The man's enormous stature was not without awe for them. And in that moment of hesitation the battle was won for Dave. Chepstow's repeating-rifle was at his shoulder, and Mason's revolver had been whipped out of its holster and was held covering them.

Suddenly there was a movement in the crowd, somewhere behind. If Dave saw it he gave no sign. But Mason saw it, and, sharply incisive, his voice rang out —

"The first man that moves this way I'll shoot him like a dog!"

Instantly every eye among the strikers was turned upon the two men with their ready weapons, and to a man they understood that the game was up.

"Get out! Get out—quick!" Dave's great voice split the air with another deep roar. And the retreat began on the instant with those in the rear. Some one started to run, and in a moment the rest had joined in a rush for the camp, vanishing into the forest like a pack of timber wolves, flinging back fierce, vengeful glances over their shoulders at those who had so easily routed them.

No one stirred till the last man had disappeared. Then Dave turned.

"Quick!" he cried, in an utterly changed voice, "get into the buckboard!"

But Betty turned to him in a half-hysterical condition.

"Oh, Dave, Dave!" she cried helplessly.

But Dave was just now a man whom none of them had ever seen before. He had words for no one—not even for Betty. He suddenly caught her in his arms and lifted her bodily into the buckboard. He scrambled in after her, while Chepstow jumped up behind. In a moment, it seemed, they were racing headlong for the camp.

* · * ⸰ ⸰

The camp was in a ruinous condition. The destructive demon in men temporarily demented was abroad and his ruthless hand had fallen heavily. The whole atmosphere suggested the red tide of anarchy. The charred remains of the sutler's store was the centre of a net of ruin spread out in every direction, and from this radiated the wreckage of at least a dozen shanties, which had, like the store, been burned to the ground.

In the circumstances it would be impossible to guess at the reasons for such destruction : maybe it was the result of carelessness, maybe a mischievous delight in sweeping away that which reminded these men of their obligations to their employer, maybe it was merely a consequence of the settlement of their own drunken feuds. Whatever the cause, the hideous effect of the strike was apparent in every direction.

In the centre of the clearing was a great gathering of the lumbermen. Their seared faces expressed every variety of mental attitude, from fierce jocularity down to the blackest hatred of interference from those whose authority had become anathema to them.

They were gathered at the call of those who had fled from the dugout, spurred to a defense of what they believed to be their rights by a hurried, garbled account of the summary treatment just meted out to them. They were ready for more than the mere assertion of their demands. They were ready to enforce them, they were ready for any mischief which the circumstances prompted.

It was a deadly array. Many were sober, many were sobering, many were still drunk. The latter were those whose cunning had prompted them, at the outset of the strike, to secrete a sufficient supply of liquor from their fellows. And the majority of these were not the real lumber-jacks, those great simple children of the forest, but the riffraff that had drifted into the camp, or had been sent thither by those who promoted the strike. The real lumber-jacks were more or less incapable of such foresight and cunning. They were slow-thinking creatures of vast muscle, only swift and keen as the axes they used when engaged in the work which was theirs.

Through the rank animal growth of their bodies their minds had remained too stunted to display the low cunning of the scallywags whose unscrupulous wits alone must supply their idle bodies with a livelihood. But simple as babes, simple and silly as sheep, and as dependent upon their shepherd, as these men were, they were at all times dangerous, the more dangerous for their very simplicity. Just now, with their unthinking brains sick with the poison of labor's impossible argument, and the execrable liquor of the camp, they were a hundred times more deadly.

Men had come in for the orgy from all the outlying camps. They had been carefully shepherded by those whose business it was to make the strike successful. Discontent had been preached into every ear, and the seed had fallen upon fruitful, virgin soil. Thus it was that a great concourse had foregathered now.

There was an atmosphere of restrained excitement abroad among them. For them the news of Dave's arrival had tremendous possibilities. A babel of harsh voices debated the situation in loud tones, each man forcing home his argument with a mighty power of lung, a never-failing method of supporting doubtful argument. The general attitude was threatening, yet it hardly seemed to be unanimous. There was too much argument. There seemed to be an undercurrent of uncertainty with no single, capable voice to check or guide it.

As the moments sped the crowd became more and more threatening, but whether against the master of the mills, or whether the result of hot blood and hot words, it would have been difficult to say. Then, just as the climax seemed to be approaching, a magical change swept over the throng. It was wrought by the sudden appearance of Dave's buckboard, which seemed to leap upon the scene from the depth of the forest. And as it came into view a hoarse, fierce shout went up. Then, in a moment, an expectant hush fell.

Dave's eyes were fixed upon the crowd before him. He gave no sign. His face, like a mask, was cold, hard, unyielding. No word was spoken by those in the buckboard. Every one, with nerves straining and pulses throbbing, was waiting for what was to happen ; every one except the prisoner, Truscott.

The master of the mills read the meaning of what he beheld with the sureness of a man bred to the calling of these men. He knew. And knowing, he had little blame for them. How could it be otherwise with these unthinking souls ? The blame must lie elsewhere. But his sympathy left his determination unaltered. He knew, no one better, that here the iron heel alone could prevail, and for the time his heel was shod for the purpose.

He drew near. Some one shouted a furious epithet at him, and the cry was taken up by others.

The horses shied. He swung them back with a heavy hand, and forced them to face the crowd, his whip falling viciously at the same time. But, for a moment, his face relaxed its cold expression. His quick ears had detected a lack of unanimity in the execration. Suddenly he pulled the horses up. He passed the reins to Mason and leaped to the ground.

It was a stirring moment. The mob advanced, but the movement seemed almost reluctant. It was not the rush of blind fury one might have expected, but rather as though it were due to pressure from behind by those under cover of their comrades in front.

Dave moved on to meet them, and those in the buckboard remained deathly still. Mason was the first to move. He had just become aware that Dave had left his revolver on the seat of the vehicle. Instantly he lifted the reins and walked the horses closer to the crowd.

" He's unarmed," he said, in explanation to the parson.

Chepstow nodded. He moved his repeating-rifle to a handier position. Betty looked up.

" He left that gun purposely," she said. " I saw him."

Her face was ghastly pale, but a light shone in her eyes which nobody could have failed to interpret. Mason saw it and no longer hesitated.

" Will you take these reins?" he said. " And— give me your revolver."

The girl understood and obeyed in silence.

" I think there'll be trouble," Mason went on a moment later, as he saw Dave halt within a few yards of the front rank of the strikers.

He watched the men close about his chief in a semicircle, but the buckboard in rear always held open a road for retreat. Now the crowd pressed up from behind. The semicircle became dense. Those in the buckboard saw that many of the men were carrying the tools of their calling, prominent among them being the deadly peavey, than which, in case of trouble, no weapon could be more dangerous at close quarters.

As he halted Dave surveyed the sea of rough, hard faces glowering upon him. He heard the mutterings. He saw the great bared arms and the knotty hands grasping the hafts of their tools. He saw all this and understood, but the sight in no way disturbed him. His great body was erect, his cold eyes unwavering. It was the unconscious pose of a man who feels the power to control within him.

" Well ? " he inquired, with an easy drawl.

Instantly there was silence everywhere. It was the critical moment. It was the moment when, before all things, he must convince these lawless creatures of his power, his reserve of commanding force.

" Well?" he demanded again. "Where's your leader? Where's the gopher running this layout? I've come right along to talk to you boys to see if we can't straighten this trouble out. Where's your leader, the man who was hired to make you think I wasn't treating you right; where is he? Speak up, boys, I can't rightly hear all you're saying. I want to parley with your leaders."

Mason listening to the great voice of the lumber-man chuckled inaudibly. He realized something of Dave's method, and the shrewdness of it.

The mutterings had begun afresh. Some of the front rank men drew nearer. Dave did not move. He wanted an answer. He wanted an indication of their actual mood. Somebody laughed in the crowd. It was promptly shouted down. It was the indication the master of the mills sought. They wanted to hear what he had to say. He allowed the ghost of a smile to play round the corners of his stern mouth for a moment. But his attitude remained uncompromising. His back stiffened, his great shoulders squared, he stood out a giant amongst those giants of the forest.

" Where's your man?" he cried, in a voice that could be heard by everybody. " Is he backing down? That's not like a lumber-jack. P'r'aps he's not a lumber-jack. P'r'aps he's got no clear argu-ment I can't answer. P'r'aps he hasn't got the grit to get out in the open and talk straight as man to man. Well, let it go at that. Guess you'd best set one of you up as spokesman. I've got all the time you need to listen."

" Your blasted skunk of a foreman shot him down!" cried a voice in the crowd, and it was sup-ported by ominous murmurs from the rest.

"By God, and Mason was right!" cried Dave, in a voice so fierce that it promptly silenced the murmurs. His dilating eyes rested on several familiar faces. The faces of men who had worked for him for years, men whose hair was graying in the service of the woods. He also flashed his lightning glance upon faces unfamiliar, strangers to his craft. "By God, he was right!" he repeated, as though to force the violence of his opinion upon them. "I could have done it myself. And why? Because he has come here and told you you are badly treated. He's told you the tale that the profits of this work of yours belong to you. He's told you I am an oppressor, who lives by the sweat of your labors. He tells you this because he is paid to tell you. Because he is paid by those who wish to ruin my mills, and put me out of business, and so rob you all of the living I have made it possible for you to earn. You refuse to work at his bidding; what is the result? My mill is closed down. I am ruined. These forests are my right to cut. There is no more cutting to be done. You starve. Yes, you starve like wolves in winter. You'll say you can get work elsewhere. Go and get it, and you'll starve till you get it at half the wage I pay you. I am telling you what is right. I am talking to you with the knowledge of my own ruin staring me in the face. You have been told you can squeeze me, you can squeeze a fraction more of pay out of me. But you can't, not one cent, any man of you; and if you go to work again to keep our ship afloat you'll have to work harder than ever before—for the same pay. Now pass up your spokesman, and I'll talk to him. I can't bellow for all the world to hear."

It was a daring beginning, so daring that those in the buckboard gasped in amazement. But Dave knew his men, or, at least, he knew the real lumber-jack. Straight, biting talk must serve him, or nothing would.

Now followed a buzz of excited talk. There were those among the crowd who from the beginning had had doubts, and to these Dave's words appealed. He had voiced something of what they had hazily thought. Others there were who were furious at his biting words. Others again, and these were not real lumber-jacks, who were for turning upon him the savage brutality of their drink-soaked brains.

An altercation arose. It was the dispute of factions suddenly inflamed. It was somewhere in rear of the crowd. Those in front turned to learn the cause. Dave watched and listened. He understood. It was the result of his demand for a spokesman. Opinions were divided, and a dozen different men were urged forward. He knew he must check the dispute. Suddenly his voice rang out above the din.

"It's no use snarling about it like a lot of coyotes," he roared. "Pass them all through, and I'll listen to 'em all. Now, boys, pass 'em through peaceably."

One of the men in front of him supported him.

"Aye, aye," he shouted. "That's fair, boys, bring 'em along. The boss'll talk 'em straight."

The man beside him hit him sharply in the ribs, and the broad-shouldered "jack" swung round.

"Ther' ain't no 'boss' to this layout, Peter," objected the man who had dealt the blow. "Yonder feller ain't no better'n us."

The man scowled threateningly as he spoke. He was an enormous brute with a sallow, ill-tempered face, and black hair. Dave heard the words and his eyes surveyed him closely. He saw at a glance there was nothing of the lumberman about him. He set him down at once as a French Canadian bully, probably one of the men instrumental in the strike.

However, his attention was now drawn to the commotion caused by six of the lumbermen being pushed to the front as spokesmen. They joined the front rank, and stood sheepishly waiting for their employer. Custom and habit were strong upon them, and a certain awe of the master of the mills affected them.

"Now we'll get doing," Dave said, noting with satisfaction that four of the six were old hands who had worked beside him in his early days. "Well, boys, let's have it. What's your trouble? Give us the whole story."

But as spokesmen these fellows were not brilliant. They hesitated, and, finally, with something approaching a shamefaced grin, one of them spoke up.

"It's—it's jest wages, boss."

"Leave it at ' wages,' Bob!" shouted a voice at the back of the crowd.

"Yes," snarled the sallow-faced giant near by. "We're jest man to man. Ther' ain't no ' bosses ' around."

"Hah!" Dave breathed the ejaculation. Then he turned his eyes, steely hard, upon the last speaker, and his words came in an unmistakable tone. "It seems there are men here who aren't satisfied with their spokesmen. Maybe they'll speak out good and plenty, instead of interrupting."

His challenge seemed to appeal to the original spokesman, for he laughed roughly.

"Say, boss," he cried, "he don't cut no ice, anyways. He's jest a bum roadmaker. He ain't bin in camp more'n six weeks. We don't pay no 'tention to him. Y'see, boss," he went on, emphasizing the last word purposely, "it's jest wages. We're workin' a sight longer hours than is right, an' we ain't gettin' nuthin' extry 'cep' the rise you give us three months back. Wal, we're wantin' more. That's how."

He finished up his clumsy speech with evident relief, and mopped his forehead with his ham-like hand.

"And since when, Bob Nicholson, have you come to this conclusion?" demanded Dave, with evident kindliness.

His tone produced instant effect upon the man. He became easier at once, and his manner changed to one of distinct friendliness.

" Wal, boss, I can't rightly say jest when, fer sure. Guess it must ha' bin when that orator-feller got around ——"

" Shut up!" roared some one in the crowd, and the demand was followed up by distinct cursing in several directions. The sallow-faced roadmaker seized his opportunity.

" It's wages we want an' wages we're goin' to git!" he shouted so that the crowd could hear. " You're sweatin' us. That's wot you're doin', sweatin' us, to make your pile a sight bigger. We're honest men up here ; we ain't skunks what wants wot isn't our lawful rights. Ef you're yearnin' fer extry work you got to pay fer it. Wot say, boys ? "

" Aye! That's it. Extry wages," cried a number of voices in the background. But again the chorus was not unanimous. There were those, too, in the front whose scowling faces, turned on the speaker, showed their resentment at this interference by a man they did not recognize as a lumber-jack.

Dave seized his opportunity.

" You're wanting extra wages for overtime," he cried, in a voice that carried like a steam siren. " Well, why didn't you ask for them ? Why did you go out on strike first, and then ask ? Why ? I'll tell you why. I'll tell you why you chose this damned gopher racket instead of acting like the honest men you boast yourselves to be. I can tell you why you wanted to lock up your camp-boss, and so prevent your wishes reaching me. I can tell you why you had men on the road between here and Malkern to stop letters going through. I can tell you why you honest men set fire to the store here, and stole all the liquor and goods in it. I can tell you why you did these things. Because you've just listened like silly sheep to the skunks who've come along since the fever broke out. Because you've listened to the men who've set out to ruin us both, you and me. Because you've listened to these scallywags, who aren't lumbermen, who've come among you. They're not 'jacks' and they don't understand the work, but they've been draw-ing the same wages as you, and they're trying to rob you of your living, they're trying to take your jobs from you and leave you nothing. That's why you've done these things, you boys who've worked with me for years and years, and had all you needed. Are you going to let 'em rob you? They *are* robbing you, for, I swear before God, my mills are closed down, and they'll remain closed, and every one of you can get out and look for new work unless you turn to at once."

A murmur again arose as he finished speaking, but this time there was a note of alarm in it, a note of anger that was not against their employer. Faces looked puzzled, and ended by frowning into the faces of neighbors. Dave understood the effect he had made. He was waiting for a bigger effect. He was fighting for something that was dearer to him than life, and all his courage and resource were out to the limit. He glanced at the sallow-faced giant. Their eyes met, and in his was a fierce challenge. He drew the fellow as easily as any expert swordsman. The man had been shrewd enough to detect the change in his comrades, and he promptly hurled himself into the fray to try and recover the lost ground. He stepped forward, towering over his fellows. He meant mischief.

"See, mates," he shouted, trying to put a jeer in his angry voice, "look at 'im! He's come here to call us a pack o' skunks an' gophers. Him wot's makin' thousands o' dollars a day out of us. He's come here to kick us like a lot o' lousy curs. His own man shot up our leader, him as was trying to fit things right fer us. I tell you it was murder— bloody murder! We're dirt to him. He can kick us—shoot us up. We're dogs—lousy yeller dogs —we are. You'll listen to his slobbery talk an' you'll go to work—and he'll cut your wages lower, so he can make thousan's more out o' you." Then he suddenly swung round on Dave with a fierce oath. "God blast you, it's wages we want—d'ye hear—wages! An' we're goin' to have 'em! You ain't goin' to grind us no longer, mister! You're goin' to sign a 'greement fer a rise o' wages of a quarter all round. That's wot you're goin' to do!"

Dave was watching, watching. His opportunity was coming.

"I came to talk to honest 'jacks,'" he said icily, "not to blacklegs. I'll trouble you to get right back into the crowd, and hide your ugly head, and keep your foul tongue quiet. The boys have got their spokesmen."

His voice was sharp, but the man failed to apprehend the danger that lay behind it. He was a bigger man than Dave, and, maybe, he thought to cow him. Perhaps he didn't realize that the master of the mills was now fighting for his existence.

There was an instant's pause, and Dave took a step toward him.

"Get back!" he roared.

His furious demand precipitated things, as he intended it should. Like lightning the giant whipped out a gun.

"I'll show you!" he cried.

There was a sharp report. But before he could pull the trigger a second time Dave's right fist shot out, and a smashing blow on the chin felled him to the ground like a pole-axed ox.

As the man fell Dave turned again to the strikers, and no one noticed that his left arm was hanging helpless at his side.

CHAPTER XXIX

THE END OF THE STRIKE

WHEN the master of the mills faced the men again he hardly knew what to expect. He could not be sure how they would view his action, or what attitude they would adopt. He had considered well before provoking the sallow-faced giant, he had measured him up carefully; the thing had been premeditated. He knew the influence of physical force upon these men. The question was, had he used it at the right moment? He thought he had; he understood lumbermen, but there were more than lumbermen here, and he knew that it was this element of outsiders with whom he was really contending.

The fallen man's pistol was on the ground at his feet. He put a foot upon it; then, glancing swiftly at the faces before him, he became aware of a silence, utter, complete, reigning everywhere. There was astonishment, even something of awe in many of the faces; in others doubt mingled with a scowling displeasure. The thing had happened so suddenly. The firing of the shot had startled them unpleasantly, and they were still looking for the result of it. On this point they had no satisfaction. Only Dave knew—he had reason to. The arm hanging limply at his side, and the throb of pain at his shoulder left him in no doubt. But he had no intention of imparting his knowledge to any one else yet. He had not finished the fight which must justify his existence as the owner of the mills.

The effect of his encounter was not an unpleasant one on the majority of the men. The use of a fist in the face of a gun was stupendous, even to them. Many of them reveled in the outsider's downfall, and contemplated the grit of their employer with satisfaction. But there were others not so easily swayed. Amongst these were the man's own comrades, men who, like himself, were not real lumbermen, but agitators who had received payment to agitate. Besides these there were those unstable creatures, always to be found in such a community, who had no very definite opinions of their own, but looked for the lead of the majority, ready to side with those who offered the strongest support.

All this was very evident in that moment of silence, but the moment passed so quickly that it was impossible to say how far Dave's action had really served him. Suddenly a murmur started. In a few seconds it had risen to a shout. It started with the fallen giant's friends. There was a rush in the crowd, an ominous swaying, as of a struggle going on in its midst. Some one put up a vicious cry that lifted clear above the general din.

" Lynch him ! Lynch him !"

The cry was taken up by the rest of the makeshifts and some of the doubters. Then came the sudden but inevitable awakening of the slow, fierce brains of the real men of the woods. The awakening brought with it not so much a desire to champion their employer, as a resentment that these men they regarded as scallywags should attempt to take initiative in their concerns; it was the rousing of the latent hatred which ever exists in the heart of the legitimate tradesman for the interloper. It caught them in a whirlwind of passion. Their blood rose. All other considerations were forgotten, it mattered nothing the object of that mutiny, all thought of wages, all thought of wrongs between themselves and their employer were banished from their minds. They hated nothing so badly as these men with whom they had worked in apparent harmony.

It was at this psychological moment that the final fillip was given. It came from a direction that none of the crowd realized. It came from one who knew the woodsman down to his very core, who had watched every passing mood of the crowd during the whole scene with the intentness of one who only waits his opportunity. It was Bob Mason in the buckboard.

"Down with the blacklegs! Down with the dirty 'scabs'!" he shouted.

In a moment the battle was raging. There was a wild rush of men, and their steel implements were raised aloft. "Down with the 'scabs'!" The cry echoed and reëchoed in every direction, taken up by every true lumberman. A tumult of shouting and cursing roared everywhere. The crowd broke.

It spread out. Groups of struggling combatants were dotted about till the sight suggested nothing so much as a massacre. It was a fight of brutal savagery that would stop short only at actual slaughter. It was the safety-valve for the accumulated spleen of a week's hard drinking. It was the only way to steady the shaken, drink-soaked nerves, and restore the dull brains to the dead level of a desire to return to work and order.

Fortunately it was a short-lived battle too. The lumber-jacks were the masters from the outset. They were better men, they were harder, they had more sheer "grit." Then, too, they were in the majority. The "scabs" began to seek refuge in flight, but not before they had received a chastisement that would remain a sore memory for many days to come. Those who went down in the fight got the iron-shod boots of their adversaries in their ribs, till, in desperation, they scrambled to their feet and took their punishment like men. But the victory was too easy for the lumber-jacks' rage to last. Like the wayward, big-hearted children of nature they were, their fury passed as quickly as it had stirred. The terror-stricken flight of those upon whom their rage had turned inspired in them a sort of fiendish amusement, and in this was perhaps the saving of a terrible tragedy. As it was, a few broken limbs, a liberal tally of wounds and bruises were the harvest of that battle. That, and the final clearing out of the element of discontent. It was victory for the master of the mills.

In less than ten minutes the victors were straggling back from their pursuit of a routed foe. Dave had not moved.   He was still standing beside the fallen giant, who was now recovering consciousness from the knock-out blow he had received. They came up in small bands, laughing and recounting episodes of the fight.   They were in the saving mood for their employer.   All thoughts of a further strike had passed out of their simple heads.   They came back to Dave, like sheep, who, after a wild stampede, have suddenly refound their shepherd, and to him they looked for guidance. And Dave was there for the purpose.   He called their attention and addressed them.

" Now, boys," he said cheerfully, " you've got nicely rid of that scum, and I'm going to talk to you.   We understand each other.   We've worked too long together for it to be otherwise.   But we don't understand those others who're not lumbermen. Say, maybe you can't all hear me; my voice isn't getting stronger, so I'll just call up that buckboard and stand on it, and talk from there."

Amidst a murmur of approval the buckboard was drawn up, and not without tremendous pain Dave scrambled up into the driving-seat.   Then it was seen by both lumbermen and those in the buckboard that he had left a considerable pool of blood where he had been standing.

Betty, with horror in her eyes, turned to him.

" What is it? " she began.   But he checked her with a look, and turned at once to the men.

" I'm first going to tell you about this strike, boys," he said. " After that we'll get to business, and I guess it won't be my fault if we don't figger things out right. Here, do you see this fellow sitting here? Maybe some of you'll recognize him?" He pointed at Jim Truscott sitting in the carryall. His expression was surly, defiant. But somehow he avoided the faces in front of him. " I'm going to tell you about him. This is the man who organized the strike. He found the money and the men to do the dirty work. He did it because he hates me and wants to ruin me. He came to you with plausible tales of oppression and so forth. He cared nothing for you, but he hated me. I tell you frankly he did this thing because he knew I was pushed to the last point to make good my contract with the government, because he knew that to delay the output of logs from this camp meant that I should go to smash. In doing this he meant to carry you down with me. That's how much he cares for your interests." A growl of anger punctuated his speech. But he silenced them with a gesture and proceeded. His voice was getting weaker, and a deadly pallor was stealing over his face. Chepstow, watching him, was filled with anxiety. Betty's brown eyes clung to his face with an expression of love, horror and pity in them that spoke far louder than any words. Mason was simply calculating in his mind how long Dave could keep up his present attitude.

" Do you get my meaning, boys?" he went on.

"It's this, if we don't get this work through before winter I'm broke—broke to my last dollar. And you'll be out of a billet—every mother's son of you—with the winter staring you in the face."

He paused and took a deep breath. Betty even thought she saw him sway. The men kept an intense silence.

"Well?" he went on a moment later, pulling himself together with an evident effort. "I'm just here to talk straight business, and that's what you're going to listen to. First, I'll tell you this fellow's going to get his right medicine through me in the proper manner. Then, second and last, I want to give you a plain understanding of things between ourselves. There's going to be no rise in wages. I just can't do it. That's all. But I'm going to give each man in my camp a big bonus, a nice fat wad of money with which to paint any particular town he favors red, when the work's done. That's to be extra, above his wages. And the whole lot of you shall work for me next season on a guarantee. But from now to the late fall you're going to work, boys, you're going to work as if the devil himself was driving you. We've got time to make up, and shortage besides, and you've got to make it up. I don't want any slackers. Men who have any doubts can get right out. You've got to work as you never worked in your lives before. Now, boys, give us your word. Is it work or ———"

Dave got no further. A shout—hearty, enthusiastic—went up from the crowd. It meant work, and he was satisfied.

The next few minutes were passed in a scene of the wildest excitement. The men closed round the buckboard, and struggled with each other to grip the big man's hand. And Dave, faint and weary as he was, knew them too well to reject their friendly overtures. Besides, they were, as he said, like himself, men of the woods, and he was full of a great sympathy and friendliness for them. At last, however, he turned to Chepstow.

"Drive back to the dugout, Tom," he said. "Things are getting misty. I think—I'm—done."

CHAPTER XXX

IN THE DUGOUT

THREE arduous and anxious days followed the ending of the strike, and each of the occupants of Mason's dugout felt the strain of them in his or her own particular way. Next to the strike itself, Dave's wound was the most serious consideration. He was the leader, the rudder of his ship; his was the controlling brain; and he was a most exasperating patient. His wound was bad enough, though not dangerous. It would be weeks before the use of his left arm was restored to him; but he had a way of forgetting this, of forgetting that he had lost a great quantity of blood, until weakness prostrated him and roused him to a peevish perversity.

Betty was his self-appointed nurse. Tom Chepstow might examine his wound and consider his condition, but it was Betty who dressed his wound, Betty who prepared his food and ministered to his lightest needs. From the moment of his return to the dugout she took charge of him. She consulted no one, she asked for no help. For the time, at least, he was her possession, he was hers to lavish all the fulness of her great love upon, a love that had something almost maternal in its wonderful protective instinct.

Mason was busy with the work of reorganization.

His was the practical hand and head while Dave was on his sick-bed. From daylight to long after dark he took no rest. Dave's counsel guided him to an extent, but much had to be done without any consultation with the master of the mills. Provisioning the camp was a problem not easily solved. It was simple enough to order up food from Malkern, but there would be at least a week's delay before its arrival. Finally, he surmounted this difficulty, through the return of Lieberstein, who had fled to the woods with his cash-box and a supply of provisions, at the first sign of trouble. Now he had returned to save what he could from the wreck. The Jew needed assistance to recover his looted property—what remained of it. The overseer gave him that assistance, and at the same time arranged that all provisions so recovered should be redistributed (at a price) as rations to the men. Thus the delay in the arrival of supplies from Malkern was tided over. But though he availed himself of this means of getting over his difficulty he was fully determined to rid the camp, at the earliest opportunity, of so treacherous a rascal as Lieberstein.

In two days the work of restoration was in full swing. The burned store and shanties were run up with all a lumberman's rapidity and disregard for finish. Time was the thing that mattered. And so wonderfully did Mason drive and cajole his men, that on the third day the gangs once more marched out into the woods. Once again the forests echoed with the hiss of saw, the ringing clang of smiting axe, the crash of falling trees, the harsh voices of the woodsmen, and the hundred and one sounds of bustling activity which belong to a lumber camp in full work.

That day was a pleasant one for the occupants of the dugout. It was a wonderful work Mason had done. They all knew and appreciated his devotion to his wounded employer, and though none spoke of it, whenever he appeared in their midst their appreciation of him showed in their manner. Betty was very gentle and kindly. She saw that he wanted for nothing in the way of the comforts which the dugout could povide.

Tom Chepstow was far too busy with his sick to give attention to anything else. His hands were very full, and his was a task that showed so little result. Dave, for the most part, saw everything that was going on about him, and had a full estimate of all that was being done in his interests by the devoted little band, and, absurdly enough, the effect upon him was to stir him to greater irritability.

It was evening, and the slanting sunlight shone in through one of the windows. It was a narrow beam of light, but its effect was sufficiently cheering. No dugout is a haven of brightness, and just now this one needed all that could help to lift the shadow of sickness and disaster that pervaded it.

Betty was preparing supper, and Dave, lying on his stretcher, his vast bulk only half concealed by the blanket thrown over him, was watching the girl with eyes that fed hungrily upon the swift, graceful movements of her pretty figure, the play of expression upon her sweet, sun-tanned face, the intentness, the whole-hearted concentration in her steady, serious eyes as she went about her work.

Now and again she glanced over at his rough bed, but he seemed to be asleep every time she turned in his direction. The result was an additional care in her work. She made no noise lest she should waken him. Presently she stooped and pushed a log into the fire-box of the cook-stove. The cinders fell with a clatter, and she glanced round apprehensively. Her movement was so sudden that Dave's wide-open eyes had no time to shut. In a moment she was all contrition at her clumsiness.

" I'm so sorry, Dave," she exclaimed. " I did so hope you'd sleep on till supper. It's half an hour yet."

" I haven't been sleeping at all."

" Why, I ——".

He smiled and shook his head, and his smile delighted the girl. It was the first she had seen in him since his arrival in the camp. His impatience at being kept to his bed was perhaps dying out. She had always heard that the most active and impatient always became reconciled to bed in the end.

" Yes, I did it on purpose," Dave said, still smiling. " You see I wanted to think. You'd have talked if I hadn't. I ——"

" Oh, Dave !"

Betty's reproach had something very like resentment in it. She turned abruptly to the boiler of
stew and tasted its contents, while the man chuckled
softly.

But she turned round on him again almost immediately.

" Why are you laughing?" she demanded
quickly.

But he did not seem inclined to enlighten her.

" Half an hour to supper?" he said musingly.
" Tom'll be in directly—and Mason."

Betty was still looking at him with her cooking
spoon poised as it had been when she tasted the
stew.

" Yes," she said, " they'll be in directly. I've
only just got to make the tea." She dropped the
spoon upon the table and replaced the lid of the
boiler. Then she came over to his bedside. " What
did you mean saying I should have talked?" she
asked, only now there was a smiling response to
the smile still lurking in the gray depths of the
man's eyes. Dave drew a long sigh of resignation.

" Well, y' see, Betty, if I'd laid here with my eyes
open, staring about the room, at you, at the roof, at
the window for a whole heap of time, you'd have
said to yourself, ' Dave's suffering sure. He can't
sleep. He's miserable, unhappy.' You'd have
said all those things, and with all your kind little
heart, you'd have set to work to cheer me up—same
as you'd no doubt have done for that strike-leader
fellow you shipped over to the sick camp to make

room for me. Well, I just didn't want that kind of cheering. I was thinking—thinking mighty hard—figgering how best to make a broken-winged—er—owl fly without waiting for the wing to mend. Y' see, thinking's mostly all I can do just now, and I need to do such a mighty heap to keep me from getting mad and breaking things. Y' see every hour, as I lie here, I kind of seem to be storing up steam like a locomotive, and sometimes I feel— feel as if I was going to bust. Being sick makes me hate things." His smiling protest was yet perfectly serious. The girl understood. A moment later he went on. "Half an hour to supper?" he said, as though suddenly reaching a decision that had cost him much thought. "Well, just sit right down on this stretcher, and I'm going to talk you tired. I'm sick, so you can't refuse."

The man's eyes still smiled, but the seriousness of his manner had increased. Nor was Betty slow to observe it. She gladly seated herself on the edge of the stretcher, and without the least embarrassment, without the least self-consciousness, her soft eyes rested on the rugged face of her patient. She was glad that he wanted to talk—and to her, and she promptly took him up in his own tone.

"Well, I've got to listen, I s'pose," she said, with a bright smile. "As you say, you're sick. You might have added that I am your nurse."

"Yes, I s'pose you are. It seems funny me needing a nurse. I s'pose I do need one?"

Betty nodded; her eyes were bright with an

emotion that the man's words had all unconsciously
stirred. This man, so strong for himself, so strong
to help others—this man, on whom all who came
into contact with him leaned as upon some staunch,
unfailing support—this man, so invincible, so masterful, so eager in the battle where the odds were
against him, needed a nurse! A great pity, a great
sympathy, went out to him. Then a feeling of joy
and gratitude at the thought that she was his nurse
succeeded it. She—she alone had the right to wait
upon him. But her face expressed none of these
feelings when she replied. She nodded gravely.

" Yes, you need a nurse, you poor old Dave.
Just for once you're going to give others a chance
of being to you what you have always been to
them. It breaks my heart to see you on a sick-
bed; but, Dave, you can never know the joy, the
happiness it gives me to be—your nurse. All my
life it has been the other way. All my life you
have been my wise counselor, my ever-ready loyal
friend; now, in ever so small a degree, you have to
lean on me. Don't be perverse, Dave. Let me
help you all I can. Don't begrudge me so small a
happiness. But you said you were going to talk
me tired, and I'm doing it all." She laughed lightly,
but it was a laugh to hide her real feelings.

The man's uninjured arm reached out, and his
great hand rested heavily on one of hers. The
pressure of his fingers, intended to be gentle, was
crushing. His action meant so much. No words
could have thanked her more truly than that hand

pressure. Betty's face grew warm with delight; and she turned her eyes toward the stove as though to see that all was well with her cooking.

" They're cutting to-day? " Dave's eyes were turned upon the window. The sunlight was dying out now, and the gray dusk was stealing upon the room. Betty understood the longing in the man's heart.

" Yes, they're cutting."

He stirred uneasily.

" My shoulder is mending fast," he said a moment later. And the girl saw his drift.

She shook her head.

" It's mending, but it won't be well—for weeks," she said.

" It's got to be," he said, with tense emphasis, after a long pause. His voice was low, but thrilling with the purpose of a mind that would not bend to the weakness of his body.

" You must be patient, Dave dear," the girl said, with the persuasiveness of a mother for her child.

For a moment the man's brows drew together in a frown and his lips compressed.

" Betty, Betty, I can't be patient," he suddenly burst out. " I know I'm all wrong; but I can't be patient. You know what all this means. I'm not going to attempt to tell you. You understand it all. I cannot lie here a day longer. Even now I seem to hear the saws and axes at work. I seem to see the men moving through the forests. I seem to hear Mason's orders in the dead calm of the woods. With the first logs that are travoyed to the river I must leave here and get back to Malkern. There is work to be done, and from now on it will be man's work. It will be more than a fight against time. It will be a battle against almost incalculable odds, a battle in which all is against us. Betty, you are my nurse, and as you hope to see me through with this broken shoulder, so you must not attempt to alter my decision. I know you. You want to see me fit and well. Before all things you desire that. You will understand me when I say that, before all things, I must see the work through. My bodily comfort must not be considered; and as my friend, as my nurse, you must not hinder me. I must leave here to-night."

The man had lifted himself to a half-sitting posture in his excitement, and the girl watched him with anxious eyes. Now she reached out, and one hand gently pressed him back to his pillow. As he had said, she understood; and when she spoke, her words were the words he wished to hear. They soothed him at once.

" Yes, Dave. If you must return, it shall be as you say."

He caught her hand and held it, crushing its small round flesh in the hollow of his great palm. It was his gratitude, his gratitude for her understanding and sympathy. His eyes met hers. And in that moment something else stirred in him. The pressure tightened upon her unresisting hand. The blood mounted to her head. It seemed to in-

toxicate her. It was a moment of such ecstasy as
she had dreamed of in a vague sort of way—a moment when the pure woman spirit in her was ex-
alted to such a throne of spiritual light as is beyond
the dream of human imagination.

In the man, too, was a change. There was
something looking out of his eyes which seemed to
have banished his last thought of that lifelong desire for the success of his labors, something which
left him no room for anything else, something
which had for its inception all the human passionate desire of his tremendous soul. His gray eyes
glowed with a living fire; they deepened; a flush
of hot blood surged over his rugged features, lighting them out of their plainness. His temples
throbbed visibly, and the vast sinews shivered with
the fire that swept through his body.

In a daze Betty understood the change. Her
heart leaped out to him, yielding all her love, all that
was hers to give. It cried aloud her joy in the
passion of those moments, but her lips were silent.
She had gazed into heaven for one brief instant,
then her eyes dropped before a vision she dared no
longer to look upon.

" Betty!"

The man had lifted to his elbow again. A torrent of passionate words rushed to his lips. But
they remained unspoken. His heavy tongue was
incapable of giving them expression. He halted.
That one feverish exclamation was all that came,
for his tongue clave in his mouth. But in that one

word was the avowal of such a love as rarely falls to the lot of woman. It was the man's whole being that spoke.

Betty's hand twisted from his grasp. She sprang to her feet and turned to the door.

"It's Bob Mason," she said, in a voice that was almost an awed whisper, as she rushed to the cook-stove.

The camp-boss strode heavily into the room. There was a light in his eyes that usually would have gladdened the master of the mills. Now, however, Dave's thoughts were far from the matters of the camp.

"We've travoyed a hundred to the river bank!" the lumberman exclaimed in a tone of triumph "The work's begun!"

It was Betty who answered him. Hers was the ready sympathy, the heart to understand for others equally with herself. She turned with a smile of welcome, of pride in his pride.

"Bob, you're a gem!" she cried, holding out a hand of kindliness to him.

And Dave's tardy words followed immediately with characteristic sincerity.

"Thanks, Bob," he said, in his deep tones.

"It's all right, boss, they're working by flare to-night, an' they're going on till ten o'clock."

Dave nodded. His thoughts had once more turned into the smooth channel of his affairs. Betty was serving out supper.

A few moments later, weary and depressed, the

parson came in for his supper. His report was much the same as usual. Progress—all his patients were progressing, but it was slow work, for the recent battle had added to the number of his patients.

There was very little talk until supper was over. Then it began as Mason was preparing to depart again to his work. Dave spoke of his decision without any preamble.

"Say, folks, I'm going back to Malkern tonight," he said, with a smiling glance of humor at his friends in anticipation of the storm of protest he knew his announcement would bring upon himself.

Mason was on his feet in an instant.

"You can't do it, boss!" he exclaimed. "You——"

"No you don't, Dave, old friend," broke in Chepstow, with a shake of his head. "You'll stay right here till I say 'go.'"

Dave's smile broadened, and his eyes sought Betty's.

"Well, Betty?" he demanded.

But Betty understood.

"I have nothing to say," she replied quietly.

Dave promptly turned again to the parson. His smile had gone again.

"I've got to go, Tom," he said. "My work's done here, but it hasn't begun yet in Malkern. Do you get my meaning? Until the cutting began up here I was not needed down there. Now it is different. There is no one in Malkern to head

things. Dawson and Odd are good men, but they
are only my—foremen. It is imperative that I go,
and—to-night."

" But look here, boss, it can't be done," cried
Mason, with a sort of hopeless earnestness. " You
aren't fit to move yet. The journey down—you'd
never stand it. Besides ——"

" Yes, besides, who's to take you down? How
are you going ?" Chepstow broke in sharply. He
meant to clinch the matter once for all.

Dave's manner returned to the peevishness of his
invalid state.

" There's the buckboard," he said sharply.

" Can you drive it?" demanded the parson with
equal sharpness. " I can't take you down. I can't
leave the sick. Mason is needed here. Well?"

" Don't worry. I'm driving myself," Dave said
soberly.

Chepstow sprang to his feet and waved his pipe
in the air in his angry impatience.

" You're mad! You drive? Hang it, man, you
couldn't drive a team of fleas. Get up! Get up
from that stretcher now, and see how much driving
you could do. See here, Dave, I absolutely forbid
you to attempt any such thing."

Dave raised himself upon his elbow. His steady
eyes had something of an angry smile in them.

" See here, Tom," he said, imitating the other's
manner. " You can talk till you're black in the
face. I'm going down to-night. Mason's going to
hook the buckboard up for me and fetch Truscott

along. I'll have to take him down too. It's no use in your kicking, Tom," he went on, as the parson opened his lips for further protest, "I'm going." He turned again to Mason. "I'll need the buckboard and team in an hour. Guess you'll see to it, boy. An' say, just set food for the two of us in it, and half a sack of oats for the horses ——"

"One moment, Bob," interrupted Betty. She had been merely an interested listener to the discussion, sitting at the far end of the supper table. Now she came over to Dave's bedside. "You'd best put in food for three." Then she looked down at Dave, smiling reassurance. From him she turned to her uncle with a laughing glance. "Trust you men to argue and wrangle over things that can be settled without the least difficulty. Dave here must get down to Malkern. I understand the importance of his presence there. Very well, he must go. Therefore it's only a question how he can get there with the least possible danger to himself. It's plain Bob can't go down. He must see the work through here. You, uncle, must also stay. It is your duty to the sick. We cannot send any of the men. They are all needed. Well, I'm going to drive him down. We'll make him comfortable in the carryall, and Truscott can share the driving-seat with me—carefully secured to prevent him getting away. There you are. I will be responsible for Dave's welfare. You need not be anxious."

She turned with such a look of confident affection upon the sick man, that, for the moment, no one had a word of protest to offer. It was Dave who spoke first. He took her hand in his and nodded his great head at her.

"Thanks, little Betty," he said. "I shall be perfectly safe in your charge."

And his words were ample reward to the woman who loved him. It was his acknowledgment of his dependence upon her.

After that there was discussion, argument, protest for nearly half an hour. But Dave and Betty held to their decision, and, at last, Tom Chepstow gave way to them. Then it was that Mason went off to make preparations. The parson went to assist him, and Betty and Dave were once more alone.

Betty let her uncle go and then lit the lamp. For some moments no word was spoken between the sick man and his nurse. The girl cleared the supper things and put a kettle on the stove. Then, while watching for it to boil, she was about to pack up her few belongings for the journey. But she changed her mind. Instead she came back to the table and faced the stretcher on which the sick man was lying.

"Dave," she said, in a low voice, "will you promise me something?"

Dave turned his face toward her.

"Anything," he said, in all seriousness.

The girl waited. She was gauging the meaning

of his reply. In anybody else that answer could not have been taken seriously. In him it might be different.

" It's a big thing," she said doubtfully.

" It don't matter, little girl, I just mean it."

She came slowly over to his side.

" Do you remember, I once got you to teach me the business of the mill? I wanted to learn then so I could help some one. I want to help some one now. But it's a different 'some one' this time. Do you understand? I—I haven't forgotten a single thing I learned from you. Will you let me help you? You cannot do all now. Not until your arm is better." She dropped upon her knees at his bedside. " Dave, don't refuse me. You shall just give your orders to me. I will see they are carried out. We—you and I together—will run your mills to the success that I know is going to be yours. Don't say no, Dave—dear."

The man had turned to her. He was looking into the depths of the fearless brown eyes before him. He had no intention of refusing her, but he was looking, looking deep down into the beautiful, woman's heart that was beating within her bosom.

" I'll not refuse you, Betty. I only thank God Almighty for such a little friend."

CHAPTER XXXI

THE silence of the night was unbroken. The valley of the Red Sand River was wrapped in a peace such as it had never known since Dave had first brought into it the restless activity of his American spirit. But it was a depressing peace to the dwellers in the valley, for it portended disaster. No word had reached them of the prospects at the mill, only a vague rumor had spread of the doings at the lumber camp. Dave knew the value of silence in such matters, and he had taken care to enforce silence on all who were in a position to enlighten the minds which thirsted for such information.

The people of Malkern were waiting, waiting for something definite on the part of the master of the mills. On him depended their future movements. The mill was silent, even though the work of repairing had been completed. But, as yet, they had not lost faith in the man who had piloted them through all the shoals of early struggles to the haven of comparative prosperity. However, the calm, the unwonted silence of the valley depressed and worried them. They longed for the drone, however monotonous, of the mill. They loved it, for it meant that their wheels of life were well oiled, and that they were driving pleasantly along their set track to the terminal of success.

Yet while the village slept all was intense activity at the mills. The men had been gathered together again, late that night, and the army of workers was once more complete. The sawyers were at their saws, oiling and fitting, and generally making ready for work. The engineers were at their engines, the firemen at their furnaces, the lumber-jacks were at the shoots, and in the yards. The boom was manned by men who sat around smoking, peavey in hand, ready to handle the mightiest "ninety-footers" that the mountain forests could send them. The checkers were at their posts, and the tally boys were "shooting craps" at the foot of the shoots. The mill, like a resting giant lying prone upon his back, was bursting with a latent strength and activity that only needed the controlling will to set in motion, to drive it to an effort such as Malkern had never seen before, such as, perhaps, Malkern would never see again. And inside Dave's office, that Will lay watching and waiting.

It was a curious scene inside the office. The place had been largely converted since the master of the mills had returned. It was half sick room, half office, and the feminine touch about the place was quite incongruous in the office of such a man as Dave. But then just now Dave's control was only of the mill outside. In this room he yielded to another authority. He was in the hands of

womenfolk; that is, his body was. He had no
word to say in the arrangement of the room, and
he was only permitted to think his control outside.

It was eleven o'clock, and his mother was preparing to take her departure. Since his return
from the camp she was her son's almost constant
attendant. Betty's chief concern was for the mill
outside, and the careful execution of the man's
orders to his foremen. She took a share of the
nursing, but only in moments of leisure, and these
were very few. Now she had just returned from
a final inspection and consultation with Dawson.
And the glow of satisfaction on her face was good
to see.

" Now, mother dear," she said, after having made
her report to Dave, " you've got to be off home,
and to bed. You've had a long, hard day, and I'm
going to relieve you. Dave is all right, and," she
added with a smile, " maybe he'll be better still before morning. We expect the logs down by daylight, and then—I guess their arrival in the boom
will do more to mend his poor broken shoulder
than all our quacks and nostrums. So be off with
you. I shall be here all night. I don't intend to
rest till the first log enters the boom."

The old woman rose wearily from her rocking-
chair at her boy's bedside. Her worn face was
tired. At her age the strain of nursing was very
heavy. But whatever weakness there was in her
body, her spirit was as strong as the younger
woman's. Her boy was sick, and nothing else

could compare with a disaster of that nature. But now she was ready to go, for so it had been arranged between them earlier.

She crossed to Betty's side, and, placing her hands upon the girl's shoulders, kissed her tenderly on both cheeks.

"God bless and keep you, dearie," she said, with deep emotion. "I'd like to tell you all I feel, but I can't. You're our guardian angel—Dave's and mine. Good-night."

"Good-night, mother dear," said the girl, her eyes brightening with a suspicion of tears. Then, with an assumption of lightness which helped to disguise her real feelings, "Now don't you stay awake. Go right off to sleep, and—in the morning you shall hear—the mills!"

The old woman nodded and smiled. Next to her boy she loved this motherless girl best in the world. She gathered up her few belongings and went to the bedside. Bending over the sick man she kissed his rugged face tenderly. For a moment one great arm held her in its tremendous embrace, then she toddled out of the room.

Betty took her rocking-chair. She sat back and rocked herself in silence for some moments. Her eyes wandered over the curious little room, noting the details of it as though hugging to herself the memory of the smallest trifle that concerned this wonderful time that was hers.

There was Dave's desk before the window. It was hers now. There were the vast tomes that recorded his output of lumber. She had spent hours over them calculating figures for the man beside her. There were the flowers his mother had brought, and which she had found time to arrange so that he could see and enjoy them. There were the bandages it was her duty to adjust. There were the remains of the food of which they had both partaken.

It was all real, yet so strange. So strange to her who had spent her life surrounded by all those duties so essentially feminine, so closely allied to her uncle's spiritual calling. She felt that she had moved out into a new world, a world in which there was room for her to expand, in which she could bring into play all those faculties which she had always known herself to possess, but which had so long lain dormant that she had almost come to regard her belief in their existence as a mere dream, a mere vanity.

It was a wonderful thing this, that had happened to her, and the happiness of it was so overwhelming that it almost made her afraid. Yet the fact remained. She was working for him, she was working with her muscles and brain extended. She sighed, and, placing her hands behind her head, stretched luxuriously. It was good to feel the muscles straining, it was good to contemplate the progress of things in his interests, it was good to love, and to feel that that love was something more practical than the mere sentimentality of awakened passion.

Her wandering attention was recalled by a movement of her patient. She glanced round at him, and his face was turned toward her. Her smiling eyes responded to his steady, contemplative gaze.

" Well?" he said, in a grave, subdued voice, " it ought to be getting near now?"

The girl nodded.

" I don't see how we can tell exactly, but—unless anything goes wrong the first logs should get through before daylight. It's good to think of, Dave." Her eyes sparkled with delight at the prospect.

The man eyed her for a few silent moments, and his eyes deepened to a passionate warmth.

" You're a great little woman, Betty," he said at last. " When I think of all you have done for me —well, I just feel that my life can never be long enough to repay you in. Throughout this business you have been my second self, with all the freshness and enthusiasm of a mind and heart thrilling with youthful strength. I can never forget the journey down from the camp. When I think of the awful physical strain you must have gone through, driving day and night, with a prisoner beside you, and a useless hulk of a man lying behind, I marvel. When I think that you had to do everything, feed us, camp for us, see to the horses for us, it all seems like some fantastic dream. How did you do it? How did I come to let you? It makes me smile to think that I, in my manly superiority, simply lolled about with a revolver handy to en-

force our prisoner's obedience to your orders.   Ah,
little Betty, I can only thank Almighty God that I
have been blest with such a little—friend."

The girl laid the tips of her fingers over his
mouth.

" You mustn't say these things," she said, in a
thrilling voice. " We—you and I—are just here
together to work out your—your plans.   God has
been very, very good to me that He has given me
the power, in however small a degree, to help you.
Now let us put these things from our minds for a
time and be—be practical.   Talking of our prisoner,
what are you going to do with—poor Jim?"

It was some moments before Dave answered her.
It was not that he had no answer to her question,
but her words had sent his mind wandering off
among long past days.   He was thinking of the
young lad he had so ardently tried to befriend.
He was thinking of the " poor Jim" of then and
now.   He was recalling that day when those two
had come to him with their secret, with their
youthful hope of the future, and of all that day had
meant to him.   They had planned, he had planned,
and now it was all so—different.   His inclination
was to show this man leniency, but his inclination
had no power to alter his resolve.

When he spoke there was no resentment in his
tone against the man who had so cruelly tried to
ruin him, only a quiet decision.

" I want you to tell Simon Odd to bring him
here," he said.   Then he smiled.   " I intend him to

spend the night with me. That is, until the first
log comes down the river."

" What are you going to do? "

The man's smile increased in tenderness.

" Don't worry your little head about that, Betty,"
he said. " There are things which must be said between us. Things which only men can say to men.
I promise you he will be free to go when the mill
starts work—but not until then." His eyes grew
stern. " I owe you so much, Betty," he went on,
" that I must be frank with you. So much depends
upon our starting work again that I cannot let him
go until that happens."

" And if—just supposing—that does not happen
—I mean, supposing, through his agency, the mill
remains idle? "

" I cannot answer you. I have only one thing to
add." Dave had raised himself upon his elbow,
and his face was hard and set. " No man may
bring ruin upon a community to satisfy his own
mean desires, his revenge, however that revenge
may be justified. If we fail, if Malkern is to be
made to suffer through that man—God help him!"

The girl was facing him now. Her two hands
were outstretched appealingly.

" But, Dave, should you judge him? Have you
the right? Surely there is but one judge, and His
alone is the right to condemn weak, erring human
nature. Surely it is not for you—us."

Dave dropped back upon his pillow. There was
no relenting in his eyes.

" His **own** work shall judge him," he said in **a** hard voice. " What I may do is between him and me."

Betty looked at **him** long and earnestly. Then she rose from her chair.

"So be it, Dave. I ask you but one thing. Deal with him as your heart prompts you, and not as your head dictates. I will send him to you, and will come back again—when the mill is at work."

Their eyes met in one long ardent gaze. The man nodded, and the smile in his eyes was **very, very** tender.

" Yes, Betty. Don't leave me too long—I can't do without you now."

The girl's eyes dropped before the light she beheld in his.

" I don't want you **to**—do without me," she murmured. And **she** hurried **out** of the room.

CHAPTER XXXII

TWO MEN—AND A WOMAN

It took some time for Betty to carry out Dave's wishes. Simon Odd, who was Jim Truscott's jailer while the mills were idle, and who had him secreted away where curious eyes were not likely to discover him, was closely occupied with the preparations at the other mill. She had to dispatch a messenger to him, and the messenger having found Simon, it was necessary for the latter to procure his prisoner and hand him over to Dave himself. All this took a long time, nearly an hour and a half, which made it two o'clock in the morning before Truscott reached the office under his escort.

Odd presented him with scant ceremony. He knocked on the door, was admitted, and stood close behind his charge's shoulder.

"Here he is, boss," said the man with rough freedom. "Will I stand by in case he gits gay?"

But Dave had his own ideas. He needed no help from anybody in dealing with this man.

"No," he said at once. "You can get back to your mill. I relieve you of all further responsibility of your—charge. But you can pass me some things to prop my pillow up before you go."

The giant foreman did as he was bid. Being just a plain lumberman, with no great nicety of fancy he selected three of the ledgers for the purpose. Having propped his employer into a sitting posture, he took his departure in silence.

Dave waited until the door closed behind him. His cold eyes were on the man who had so nearly ruined him, who, indirectly, had nearly cost him his life. ' As the door closed he drew his right hand from under the blankets, and in it was a revolver. He laid the weapon on the blanket, and his fingers rested on the butt.

Jim Truscott watched his movements, but his gaze was more mechanical than one of active interest. What his thoughts were at the moment it would have been hard to say, except that they were neither easy nor pleasant, if one judged from the lowering expression of his weak face. The active hatred which he had recently displayed in Dave's presence seemed to be lacking now. It almost seemed as though the rough handling he had been treated to, the failure of his schemes for Dave's ruin, had dulled the edge of his vicious antagonism. It was as though he were indifferent to the object of the meeting, to its outcome. He did not even seem to appreciate the significance of the presence of that gun under Dave's fingers.

His attitude was that of a man beaten in the fight where all the odds had seemed in his favor. His mind was gazing back upon the scene of his disaster as though trying to discover the joint in the armor of his attack which had rendered him vulnerable and brought about his defeat.

Dave understood something of this.   His understanding was more the result of his knowledge of a
character he had studied long ago, before the vicious
life the man had since lived had clouded the in-
genuous impulses of a naturally weak but happy
nature.   He did not fathom the man's thoughts, he
did not even guess at them.   He only knew the
character, and the rest was like reading from an
open book.   In his heart he was more sorry for
him than he would have dared to admit, but his
mind was thinking of all the suffering the mischief
of this one man had caused, might yet cause.   Betty
had displayed a wonderful wisdom when she bade
him let his heart govern his judgment in dealing
with this man.

" You'd best sit down—Jim," Dave said.   Already
his heart was defying his head.   That use of a familiar first name betrayed him.   " It may be a long
sitting.   You're going to stay right here with me
until the mill starts up work.   I don't know how
long that'll be."

Truscott made no answer.   He showed he had
heard and understood by glancing round for a chair.
In this quest his eyes rested for a moment on the
closed door.   They passed on to the chair at the
desk.   Then they returned to the door again.   Dave
saw the glance and spoke sharply.

" You'd best sit, boy.   That door is closed—to
you.   And I'm here to keep it closed—to you."

Still the man made no reply.   He turned slowly
toward the chair at the desk and sat down.   His

whole attitude expressed weariness. It was the dejected weariness of a brain overcome by hopelessness.

Watching him, Dave's mind reverted to Betty in association with him. He wondered at the nature of this man's regard for her, a regard which was his excuse for the villainies he had planned and carried out against him, and the mills. His thoughts went back to the day of their boy and girl engagement, as he called it now. He remembered the eager, impulsive lover, weak, selfish, but full of passion and youthful protestations. He thought of his decision to go away, and the manner of it. He remembered it was Betty who finally decided for them both. And her decision was against his more selfish desires, but one that opened out for him the opportunity of showing himself to be the man she thought him. Yes, this man had been too young, too weak, too self-indulgent. There lay the trouble of his life. His love for Betty, if it could be called by so pure a name, had been a mere self-indulgence, a passionate desire of the moment that swept every other consideration out of its path. There was not that underlying strength needed for its support. Was he wholly to blame? Dave thought not.

Then there was that going to the Yukon. He had protested at the boy's decision. He had known from the first that his character had not the strength to face the pitiless breath of that land of snowy desolation. How could one so weak pit himself against the cruel forces of nature such as are to be

found in that land? It was impossible. The inevitable had resulted. He had fallen to the temptations of the easier paths of vice in Dawson, and,
lost in that whirl, Betty was forgotten. His passion
died down, satiated in the filthy dives of Dawson.
Then had come .his return to Malkern. Stinking
with the contamination of his vices, he had returned
caring for nothing but himself. He had once more
encountered Betty. The pure fresh beauty of the
girl had promptly set his vitiated soul on fire. But
now there was no love, not even a love such as had
been his before, but only a mad desire, a desire as
uncontrolled as the wind-swept rollers of a raging
sea. It was the culminating evil of a manhood debased by a long period of loose, vicious living.
She must be his at any cost, and opposition only
fired his desire the more, and drove him to any
length to attain his end. The pity of it! A spirit,
a bright buoyant spirit lost in the mad whirl of a
nature it had not been given him the power to control. His heart was full of a sorrowful regret. His
heart bled for the man, while his mind condemned
his ruthless actions.

He lay watching in a silence that made the room
seem heavy and oppressive. As yet he had no
words for the man who had come so nearly to ruining him. He had not brought him there to preach
to him, to blame him, to twit him with the failure
of his evil plans, the failure he had made of a life
that had promised so much. He held him there
that he might settle his reckoning with him, once

and for all, in a manner which should shut him out of his life forever. He intended to perform an action the contemplation of which increased the sorrow he felt an hundredfold, but one which he was fully determined upon as being the only course, in justice to Betty, to Malkern, to himself, possible.

The moments ticked heavily away. Truscott made no move. He gave not the slightest sign of desiring to speak. His eyes scarcely heeded his surroundings. It was almost as if he had no care for what this man who held him in his power intended to do. It almost seemed as though the weight of his failure had crushed the spirit within him, as though a dreary lassitude had settled itself upon him, and he had no longer a thought for the future.

Once during that long silence he lifted his large bloodshot eyes, and his gaze encountered the other's steady regard. They dropped almost at once, but in that fleeting glance Dave read the smouldering fire of hate which still burned deep down in his heart. The sight of it had no effect. The man's face alone interested him. It looked years older, it bore a tracery of lines about the eyes and mouth, which, at his age, it had no right to possess. His hair, too, was already graying amongst the curls that had always been one of his chief physical attractions. It was thinning, too, a premature thinning at the temples, which also had nothing to do with his age.

Later, again, the man's eyes turned upon the door with a calculating gaze. They came back to the bed where Dave was lying. The movement was unmistakable. Dave's fingers tightened on the butt of his revolver, and his great head was moved in a negative shake, and the ominous shining muzzle of his revolver said plainly, " Don't ! " Truscott seemed to understand, for he made no movement, nor did he again glance at the door.

It was a strange scene. It was almost appalling in its significant silence. What feelings were passing, what thoughts, no one could tell from the faces of the two men. That each was living through a small world of recollection, mostly bitter, perhaps regretful, there could be no doubt, yet neither gave any sign. They were both waiting. In the mind of one it was a waiting for what he could not even guess at, in the other it was for something for which he longed yet feared might not come.

The hands of the clock moved on, but neither heeded them. Time meant nothing to them now. An hour passed. An hour and a half. Two hours of dreadful silence. That vigil seemed endless, and its silence appalling.

Then suddenly a sound reached the waiting ears. It was a fierce hissing, like an escape of steam. It grew louder, and into the hiss came a hoarse tone, like a harsh voice trying to bellow through the rushing steam. It grew louder and louder. The voice rose to a long-drawn " hoot," which must have been heard far down the wide spread of the Red Sand Valley. It struck deep into Dave's heart, and loosed in it such a joy as rarely comes to the heart of man. It was the steam siren of the mill belching out its message to a sleeping village. The master of the mills had triumphed over every ob-stacle. The mill had once more started work.

Dave waited until the last echo of that welcome voice had died out. Then, as his ears drank in the welcome song of his saws, plunging their jagged fangs into the newly-arrived logs, he was content.

He turned to the man in the chair.

" Did you hear that, Jim? D'you know what it means?" he asked, in a voice softened by the emo-tion of the moment.

Truscott's eyes lifted. But he made no answer. The light in them was ugly. He knew.

" It means that you are free to go," Dave went on. " It means that my contract will be success-fully completed within the time limit. It means that you will leave this village at once and never return, or the penitentiary awaits you for the wreck-ing of my mills."

Truscott rose from his seat. The hate in his heart was stirring. It was rising to his head. The fury of his eyes was appalling. Dave saw it. He shifted his gun and gripped it tightly.

" Wait a bit, lad," he said coldly. " It means more than all that to you. A good deal more. Can you guess it? It means that I—and not you—am going to marry Betty Somers."

" God!"

The man was hit as Dave had meant him to be hit. He started, and his clenched hand went up as though about to strike.   The devil in his eyes was appalling.

"Now go l   Quick!"

The word leaped from the lumberman's lips, and his gun went up threateningly.   For a moment it seemed as though Truscott was about to spring upon him, regardless of the weapon's shining muzzle.   But he did not move.   A gun in Dave's hand was no idle threat, and he knew it.   Besides he had not the moral strength of the other.

He moved to the door and opened it.   Then for one fleeting second he looked back.   It may have been to reassure himself that the gun was still there, it may have been a last expression of his hate. Another moment and he was gone.   Dave replaced his gun beneath the blankets and sighed.

Betty sprang into the room.

"Hello, door open?" she demanded, glancing about her suspiciously.   Then her sparkling eyes came back to the injured man.

"Do you hear, Dave?" she cried, in an ecstasy of excitement.   "Did you hear the siren!   I pulled and held the valve cord!   Did you hear it!   Thank God!"

Dave's happy smile was sufficient for the girl. Had he heard it?   His heart was still ringing with its echoes.

"Betty, come here," he commanded.   "Help me up."

"Why——"

" Help me up, dear," the man begged. " I must get up. I must get to the door. Don't you understand, child—I must see."

" But you can't go out, Dave ! "

" I know. I know. Only to the door. But—I must see."

The girl came over to his bedside. She lifted him with a great effort. He sat up. Then he swung his feet off the bed.

" Now, little girl, help me."

It felt good to him to enforce his will upon Betty in this way. And the girl obeyed him with all her strength, with all her heart stirred at his evident weakness.

He stood leaning on her shakily.

" Now, little Betty," he said, breathing heavily, " take me to the door."

He placed his sound arm round her shoulders. He even leaned more heavily upon her than was necessary. It was good to lean on her. He liked to feel her soft round shoulders under his arm. Then, too, he could look down upon the masses of warm brown hair which crowned her head. To him his weakness was nothing in the joy of that moment, in the joy of his contact with her.

They moved slowly toward the door ; he made the pace slower than necessary. To him they were delicious moments. To Betty—she did not know what she felt as her arm encircled his great waist, and all her woman's strength and love was extended to him.

At the door they paused. They stared out into the yards. The great mills loomed up in the ruddy flare light. It was a dark, shadowy scene in that inadequate light. The steady shriek of the saws filled the air. The grinding of machinery droned forth, broken by the pulsing throb of great shafts and moving beams. Men were hurrying to and fro, dim figures full of life and intent upon the labors so long suspended. They could see the trimmed logs sliding down the shoots, they could hear the grind of the rollers, they could hear the shoutings of " checkers"; and beyond they could see the glowing reflection of the waste fire.

It was a sight that thrilled them both. It was a sight that filled their hearts with thanks to God. Each knew that it meant—Success.

Dave turned from the sight, and his eyes looked down upon the slight figure at his side. Betty looked up into his face. Her eyes were misty with tears of joy. Suddenly she dropped her eyes and looked again at the scene before them. Her heart was beating wildly. Her arm supporting the man at her side was shaking, nor was it with weariness of her task. She felt that it could never tire of that. Dave's deep voice, so gentle, yet so full of the depth and strength of his nature, was speaking.

" It's good, Betty. It's good. We've won out— you and I."

Her lips moved to protest at the part she had played, but he silenced her.

" Yes, you and I," he said softly. " It's all ours

—yours and mine. You'll share it with me?" The girl's supporting arm moved convulsively. "No, no," he went on quickly. "Don't take your arm away. I need—I need its support. Betty—little Betty—I need more than that. I need your support always. Say, dear, you'll give it me. You won't leave me alone now? Betty—Betty, I love you—so—so almighty badly."

The girl moved her head as though to avoid his kisses upon her hair. Somehow her face was lifted in doing so, and they fell at once upon her lips instead.

AT MODERATE PRICES

Ask your dealer for a complete list of
A. L. Burt Company's Popular Copyright Fiction.

AT MODERATE PRICES

Ask your dealer for a complete list of
A. L. Burt Company's Popular Copyright Fiction.

Circle, The. By Katherine Cecil Thurston (author of "The
  querader," "The Gambler.")
Colonial Free Lance, A. By Chauncey C. Hotchkiss.
Conquest of Canaan, The. By Booth Tarkington.
Conspirators, The. By Robert W. Chambers.
Cynthia of the Minute. By Louis Joseph Vance.
Dan Merrithew. By Lawrence Perry.
Day of the Dog, The. By George Barr McCutcheon.
Depot Master, The. By Joseph C. Lincoln.
Derelicts. By William J. Locke.
Diamond Master, The. By Jacques Futrelle.
Diamonds Cut Paste. By Agnes and Egerton Castle.
Divine Fire, The. By May Sinclair.
Dixie Hart. By Will N. Harben.
Dr. David. By Marjorie Benton Cooke.
Early Bird, The. By George Randolph Chester.
Eleventh Hour, The. By David Potter.
Elizabeth in Rugen. (By the author of "Elizabeth and Her Ger
  Garden.")
Elusive Isabel. By Jacques Futrelle.
Elusive Pimpernel, The. By Baroness Orczy.
Enchanted Hat, The. By Harold McGrath.
Excuse Me. By Rupert Hughes.
54-40 or Fight. By Emerson Hough.
Fighting Chance, The. By Robert W. Chambers.
Flamsted Quarries. By Mary E. Waller.
Flying Mercury, The. By Eleanor M. Ingram.
For a Maiden Brave. By Chauncey C. Hotchkiss.
Four Million, The. By O. Henry.
Four Pool's Mystery, The. By Jean Webster.
Fruitful Vine, The. By Robert Hichens.
Ganton & Co. By Arthur J. Eddy.
Gentleman of France, A. By Stanley Weyman.
Gentleman, The. By Alfred Ollivant.
Get-Rick-Quick-Wallingford. By George Randolph Chester.
Gilbert Neal. By Will N. Harben.
Girl and the Bill, The. By Bannister Merwin.
Girl from His Town, The. By Marie Van Vorst.
Girl Who Won, The. By Beth Ellis.
Glory of Clementina, The. By William J. Locke.
Glory of the Conquered, The. By Susan Glaspell.
God's Good Man. By Marie Corelli.
Going Some. By Rex Beach.
Golden Web, The. By Anthony Partridge.
Green Patch, The. By Bettina von Hutten.
Happy Island (sequel to "Uncle William). By Jennette Lee.
Hearts and the Highway. By Cyrus Townsend Brady.
Held for Orders. By Frank H. Spearman.
Hidden Water. By Dane Coolidge.
Highway of Fate. The. By Rosa N. Carey.
Homesteaders, The. By Kate and Virgil D. Boyles.
Honor of the Big Snows, The. By James Oliver Curwood.
Hopalong Cassidy. By Clarence E. Mulford.
Household of Peter, The. By Rosa N. Carey.
House of Mystery, The. By Will Irwin.
House of the Lost Court, The. By C. N. Williamson.
House of the Whispering Pines, The. By Anna Katherine Gr

AT MODERATE PRICES

Ask your dealer for a complete list of
A. L. Burt Company's Popular Copyright Fiction.

House on Cherry Street, The. By Amelia E. Barr.
How Leslie Loved. By Anne Warner.
Husbands of Edith, The. By George Barr McCutcheon.
Idols. By William J. Locke.
Illustrious Prince, The. By E. Phillips Oppenheim.
Imprudence of Prue, The. By Sophie Fisher.
Inez. (Illustrated Edition.) By Augusta J. Evans.
Infelice. By Augusta Evans Wilson.
Initials Only. By Anna Katharine Green.
In Defiance of the King. By Chauncey C. Hotchkiss.
Indifference of Juliet, The. By Grace S. Richmond.
In the Service of the Princess. By Henry C. Rowland.
Iron Woman, The. By Margaret Deland.
Ishmael. (Illustrated.) By Mrs. Southworth.
Island of Regeneration, The. By Cyrus Townsend Brady.
Jack Spurlock, Prodigal. By Horace Lorimer.
Jane Cable. By George Barr McCutcheon .
Jeanne of the Marshes. By E. Phillips Oppenheim.
Jude the Obscure. By Thomas Hardy.
Keith of the Border. By Randall Parrish.
Key to the Unknown, The. By Rosa N. Carey.
Kingdom of Earth, The. By Anthony Partridge.
King Spruce. By Holman Day.
Ladder of Swords, A. By Gilbert Parker.
Lady Betty Across the Water. By C. N. and A. M. Williamso
Lady Merton, Colonist. By Mrs. Humphrey Ward.
Lady of Big Shanty, The. By Berkeley F. Smith.
Langford of the Three Bars. By Kate and Virgil D. Boyles.
Land of Long Ago, The. By Eliza Calvert Hall.
Lane That Had No Turning, The. By Gilbert Parker.
Last Trail, The. By Zane Grey.
Last Voyage of the Donna Isabel, The. By Randall Parrish.
Leavenworth Case, The. By Anna Katharine Green.
Lin McLean. By Owen Wister.
Little Brown Jug at Kildare, The. By Meredith Nicholson.
Loaded Dice. By Ellery H. Clarke.
Lord Loveland Discovers America. By C. N. and A. M. William
Lorimer of the Northwest. By Harold Bindloss.
Lorraine. By Robert W. Chambers.
Lost Ambassador, The. By E. Phillips Oppenheim.
Love Under Fire. By Randall Parrish.
Loves of Miss Anne, The. By S. R. Crockett.
Macaria. (Illustrated Edition.) By Augusta J. Evans.
Mademoiselle Celeste. By Adele Ferguson Knight.
Maid at Arms, The. By Robert W. Chambers.
Maid of Old New York, A. By Amelia E. Barr.
Maid of the Whispering Hills, The. By Vingie Roe.
Maids of Paradise, The. By Robert W. Chambers.
Making of Bobby Burnit, The. By George Randolph Chester.
Mam' Linda. By Will N. Harben.
Man Outside, The. By Wyndham Martyn.
Man in the Brown Derby, The. By Wells Hastings.
Marriage a la Mode. By Mrs. Humphrey Ward.
Marriage of Theodora, The. By Molly Elliott Seawell.
Marriage Under the Terror, A. By Patricia Wentworth.
Master Mummer, The. By E. Phillips Oppenheim.
Masters of the Wheatlands. By Harold Bindloss.

AT MODERATE PRICES

Ask your dealer for a complete list of
A. L. Burt Company's Popular Copyright Fiction.

AT MODERATE PRICES

Reconstructed Marriage, A. By Amelia Barr.
Redemption of Kenneth Galt, The. By Will N. Harben.
Red House on Rowan Street. By Roman Doubleday.
Red Mouse, The. By William Hamilton Osborne.
Red Pepper Burns. By Grace S. Richmond.
Refugees, The. By A. Conan Doyle.
Rejuvenation of Aunt Mary, The. By Anne Warner.
Road to Providence, The. By Maria Thompson Daviess.
Romance of a Plain Man, The. By Ellen Glasgow.
Rose in the Ring, The. By George Barr McCutcheon.
Rose of Old Harpeth, The. By Maria Thompson Daviess.
Rose of the World. By Agnes and Egerton Castle.
Round the Corner in Gay Street. By Grace S. Richmond.
Routledge Rides Alone. By Will Livingston Comfort.
Running Fight, The. By Wm. Hamilton Osborne.
Seats of the Mighty, The. By Gilbert Parker.
Septimus. By William J. Locke.
Set in Silver. By C. N. and A. M. Williamson.
Self-Raised. (Illustrated.) By Mrs. Southworth.
Shepherd of the Hills, The. By Harold Bell Wright.
Sheriff of Dyke Hole, The. By Ridgwell Cullum.
Sidney Carteret, Rancher. By Harold Bindloss.
Simon the Jester. By William J. Locke.
Silver Blade, The. By Charles E. Walk.
Silver Horde, The. By Rex Beach.
Sir Nigel. By A. Conan Doyle.
Sir Richard Calmady. By Lucas Malet.
Skyman, The. By Henry Ketchell Webster.
Slim Princess, The. By George Ade.
Speckled Bird, A. By Augusta Evans Wilson.
Spirit in Prison, A. By Robert Hichens.
Spirit of the Border, The. By Zane Grey.
Spirit Trail, The. By Kate and Virgil D. Boyles.
Spoilers, The. By Rex Beach.
Stanton Wins. By Eleanor M. Ingram.
St. Elmo. (Illustrated Edition.) By Augusta J. Evans.
Stolen Singer, The. By Martha Bellinger.
Stooping Lady, The. By Maurice Hewlett.
Story of the Outlaw, The. By Emerson Hough.
Strawberry Acres. By Grace S. Richmond.
Strawberry Handkerchief, The. By Amelia E. Barr.
Sunnyside of the Hill, The. By Rosa N. Carey.
Sunset Trail, The. By Alfred Henry Lewis.

AT MODERATE PRICES

Ask your dealer for a complete list of
A. L. Burt Company's Popular Copyright Fiction.

Susan Clegg and Her Friend Mrs. Lathrop. By Anne Warner
Sword of the Old Frontier, A. By Randall Parrish.
Tales of Sherlock Holmes. By A. Conan Doyle.
Tennessee Shad, The. By Owen Johnson.
Tess of the D'Urbervilles. By Thomas Hardy.
Texican, The. By Dane Coolidge.
That Printer of Udell's. By Harold Bell Wright.
Three Brothers, The. By Eden Phillpotts.
Throwback, The. By Alfred Henry Lewis.
Thurston of Orchard Valley. By Harold Bindloss.
Title Market, The. By Emi'y Post.
Torn Sails. A Tale of a Welsh Village. By Allen Raine.
Trail of the Axe, The. By Ridgwell Cullum.
Treasure of Heaven, The. By Marie Corelli.
Two-Gun Man, The. By Charles Alden Seltzer.
Two Vanrevels, The. By Booth Tarkington.
Uncle William. By Jennette Lee.
Up from Slavery. By Booker T. Washington.
Vanity Box, The. By C. N. Williamson.
Vashti. By Augusta Evans Wilson.
Varmint, The. By Owen Johnson.
Vigilante Girl, A. By Jerome Hart.
Village of Vagabonds, A. By F. Berkeley Smith.
Visioning, The. By Susan Glaspell.
Voice of the People, The. By Ellen Glasgow.
Wanted—A Chaperon. By Paul Leicester Ford.
Wanted: A Matchmaker. By Paul Leicester Ford.
Watchers of the Plains, The. Ridgwell Cullum.
Wayfarers, The. By Mary Stewart Cutting.
Way of a Man, The. By Emerson Hough.
Weavers, The. By Gilbert Parker.
When Wilderness Was King. By Randall Parrish.
Where the Trail Divides. By Will Lillibridge.
White Sister, The. By Marion Crawford.
Window at the White Cat, The. By Mary Roberts Rhinehart.
Winning of Barbara Worth, The. By Harold Bell Wright.
With Juliet in England. By Grace S. Richmond.
Woman Haters, The. By Joseph C. Lincoln.
Woman in Question, The. By John Reed Scott.
Woman in the Alcove, The. By Anna Katharine Green.
Yellow Circle, The. By Charles E. Walk.
Yellow Letter, The. By William Johnston.
Younger Set, The. By Robert W. Chambers.

Lightning Source UK Ltd.
Milton Keynes UK
UKHW011621160119
335572UK00012B/1013/P